THE TREASURE OF CAPRIC

THE KING OF THE CAVES - BOOK ONE

BRANDON M. WILBORN

Beacon Creative Publishing LLC

MERIDIAN, IDAHO

Beacon Creative Publishing LLC
1740 E Fairview Ave #82
Meridian, ID 83642

Publisher's Note: This is a work of fiction. Names, characters, places, and incidents are a product of the author's imagination. Locales and public names are sometimes used for atmospheric purposes. Any resemblance to actual people, living or dead, or to businesses, companies, events, institutions, or locales is completely coincidental. All uses of The Holy Bible are paraphrases with modification prepared from the author's own translation.

Book Layout © 2017 BookDesignTemplates.com
Cover art & design by Darko Tomic **paganus.weebly.com**
Map by Veronika Wunderer **www.veronika-wunderer.com**

The Treasure of Capric/ Brandon M Wilborn. -- 1st ed.
ISBN 978-1-7337922-0-2 Paperback
ISBN 978-1-7337922-1-9 eBook

To my mother, Michele, who sparked my love of stories by
reading to me when I was a kid.

And to my wife, Sharon, who walks with me through it all.

And for the One who invited me on this journey. May He
become greater, while I become less.

Contents

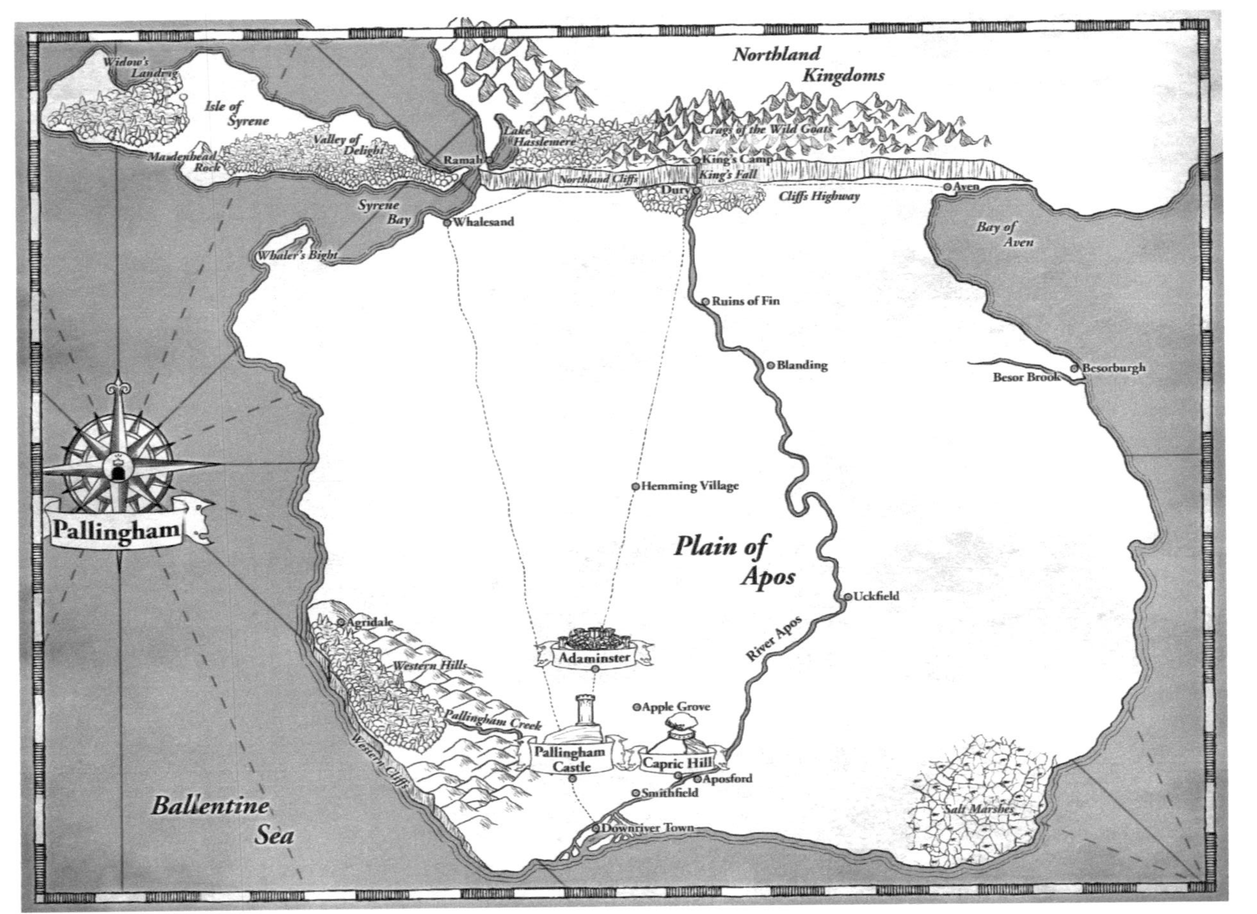

Widow's Landing
Isle of Syrene
Northland Kingdoms
Crags of the Wild Goat
Lake Hasslemere
Valley of Delight
Maidenhead Rock
Ramale
King's Camp
Northland Cliffs
King's Fall
Dury
Cliffs Highway
Aven
Bay of Aven
Syrene Bay
Whalesand
Whaler's Bight
Ruins of Fin
Blanding
Besor Brook
Besorburgh
Pallingham
Hemming Village
Plain of Apos
Uckfield
River Apos
Agridale
Adaminster
Western Hills
Apple Grove
Pallingham Creek
Pallingham Castle
Capric Hill
Aposford
Western Cliffs
Smithfield
Ballentine Sea
Downriver Town
Salt Marshes

Prologue

Capric hill sprouted from the flat Plain of Apos like the kernel of a young mountain. When people first established a small town in the gentle crook of the nearby river, the hill had been the favorite spot of shepherds. Their sheep preferred the tender shrubs and long grasses at its top to the spongy clumps of moss-like grass that grew on the plain below. The shrubs gave the shepherds shade, and the hill's height made it easy to spot predators. But the shepherds and their flocks had long ago given way to the Capric Monks, and the shrubs and grasses had disappeared beneath their fortified compound. For three centuries, the hill had housed the monks, and deep within, it held the secret treasure they protected.

Prophecy told them that the peace and prosperity of the entire nation surrounding the plain depended upon their protection of the treasure. They clung to that belief even after the kingdom fell and the river that gave the land life dried up.

Then a gloom settled over the land of Pallingham, and the Caprics could no longer see far across the plain from the top of their hill. Generations passed without seeing sun or sky, and the monks continued in their devotion. But each class of recruits was more ignorant of the order's purpose, and they were harder to relieve of their doubts.

With each year of increasing drought and dwindling crops, the monks showed their dedication by strengthening the fortifications. The timber wall at the base of the hill was slowly replaced by an earthen rampart with a stone parapet running across the top. The compound erected as a promise of hope was hidden from view. From outside, only the top branches of the Great Oak planted by the Caprics in their first year peeked above the wall as they swayed in the breeze.

PART ONE

CHAPTER ONE

The Capric Monks

Every morning, Kurian Abramson joined his troop for pre-dawn studies in the damp stone cell of their classroom at the foot of Capric hill. Their dean, Noeman Goodman, lectured and quizzed them about the history of their order and the Rule that governed their lives, and then prayed for almost as long as he lectured.

"And for the health of our abbot, we ask your blessing," Dean Goodman said in his most pious tone.

After ten years of the dean's monotonous voice, Kurian could barely focus on distinguishing one word from another. So, he found other ways to keep his mind occupied. He opened one eye and peeked around the room as the dean droned on in prayer. The other boys kept their eyes closed. After much discipline, Kurian had learned to be still and silent during the dean's supplications. He had learned to ignore the desperate need to itch at his coarse robes. He had taught himself how to yawn without opening his mouth or making a sound. But Kurian could still not resist the temptation to open his eyes during prayer and see the unguarded faces of those around him. He glanced at the dean, who had not noticed him this time.

Feeling confident, Kurian opened his other eye, his head still bowed, and looked at each of the boys in turn. Nine other novitiates stood in a circle with their dean. Kurian and Rhys Brock were the eldest, both seventeen. Rhys had grown this year. He already stood a head taller than all of them. Tobin Hart was almost two years younger and was Kurian's best friend. His hay colored hair always fell straight over his face during prayer. It swayed slightly with every move of his head. The rest of their troop was younger still, most at thirteen or fourteen, with Simon being the youngest at only eleven. Simon clenched his eyes so tightly that it made him look like an old man. Kurian almost laughed.

He glanced toward the window and instantly felt the sting of the dean's instruction rod on his thigh. The stifled laugh escaped as a grunt of pain. The other boys flinched at the snap of the rod on his flesh, but did not look up.

"We ask your grace upon this day, to keep us from *foolish distraction*," Noeman continued his prayer. "Let it be." They all looked up with the ritual words, waiting for the dean's direction.

"Mr. Abramson," he said, glaring at Kurian.

"Yes, Dean Goodman?" Kurian stood at attention, his face blank.

"Your continued lack of concentration disturbs me," said Noeman. "I wonder, sometimes, if your father was a field mouse." Rhys and Tobin sniggered from across the circle. The dean frowned at them and continued. "Since extra shifts in the kitchen and corporal punishment have obviously been insufficient to teach you discipline, I will have to conjure up a more severe task for you. And for their outburst, Mr. Brock and Mr. Hart will join you. I want to see the three of you after your exercises."

"Yes, Dean," they said together. The younger boys stood still, hoping to avoid any further distribution of punishment.

"Off to the yard, now. All of you." Noeman waved his hand toward the door to dismiss his students.

Kurian sighed and pulled back his dark curls as he walked through the door. Rhys punched him on the arm before heading up the hill to the practice ring. Kurian followed slowly. The sky was becoming lighter in the east, and already it felt like a long day. The constant gloom of the clouds did not help his mood. Even from the height of Capric, the continuous haze that hovered over the entire region made it difficult to see anything much further than a few miles away, and when standing on the plain it was difficult to see more than a mile.

The old stories said you could once see Smithfield, ten miles to the southwest, from the top of Capric. But he didn't believe them when even Aposford, just over the dry riverbed east of the hill, would often fade from the sight of his caramel colored eyes.

This morning, however, the view of Kurian's childhood home was almost clear. A few dim lights burned in the village. His thoughts vacillated between missing it and wishing it would vanish forever in the mist. Occasionally, he had a turn carrying one of the brothers' bags to town for a mercy visit. It seemed there were no happier reasons to go to Aposford; only illness, death, or starvation brought the monks for a visit. No weddings had happened in Kurian's memory, but then, there were no young people in Aposford—just half-starving old farmers living by a dry river. His father was never in the square during his visits, and he had long ago stopped missing him.

His father had brought him here at the youngest possible age to avoid the fate of so many children in Aposford. Kurian knew he believed it would save him from suffering and give him the only chance for an education, but father had been wrong if he thought this was a better life.

Noeman had made it his personal goal to punish Kurian from the moment he arrived at the Capric Order on his seventh birthday—daily, if possible, and for the smallest infractions of the Rule. This was not the life father had promised when he left him at the gate. These were not the mighty warrior-priests of God from father's tales. None of them went on the adventures in their history books. Few of them went as far as the village for mercy visits. All that happened at Capric was study and training. Study the Rule, study the histories, study the Law set down so long ago. Kurian knew all of it almost by heart after ten years of lectures. It was the training that still challenged him, that kept changing as his body and strength grew. Training was what made the Caprics different from other orders, and to him, gave them greater purpose. Study prepared them to be priests to a town that would likely be empty and dead before Kurian was middle aged; training transformed them into guardians of the most valuable treasure in the ten cities of Pallingham, possibly the entire world.

Kurian reached the top of the hill, removed his robes, folded them to protect the delicate red and white tassels in the hem, and lined up with his troop. Behind them stood the younger troop of novitiates who studied under Dean Tailor. Together, they couldn't fill half of the large practice ring as they stood, shivering in their singlets. Around them, the ordained monks were beginning their own exercises in small groups, most of them under the ancient oak tree at the north end of the hilltop. The oldest of them walked the perimeter of the field, except Sage Marten, the abbot, who watched from a chair in his doorway while his personal attendant tucked a blanket around his legs. Morning exercises were a requirement for all who were able.

Michael Humphrey, the novitiate trainer faced them. The younger brothers called him the Blacksmith—first he heated you up until you were ready to explode, then he beat you into the shape he wanted. He seemed to like the nickname.

"Tell me, little ingots," he said, "what shall we forge you into today?"

"Warriors of Capric, sir," they all shouted.

"And how do Caprics fight?"

"Attack no man. Defend all good. Take no life if it be in your power, but protect the Treasure of Capric to the death." It was a summary of the Rule's guidance on fighting that the Blacksmith had created to remind the boys of their common purpose.

"Good. Today we train with staves." He began to pace before the line of boys. "Staves have been the favored weapon at this compound for over three hundred years. When you have earned it, your staff is your identity outside these walls. People will recognize and welcome you because you carry a Capric staff. They wrongly believe it is our only weapon, because we have built a stout reputation upon it. Few would tussle with a Capric and his staff." He paused, standing back at the center of their line.

"Rhys. Kurian," the Blacksmith pointed. They both stepped forward. "As the oldest, you both had some experience with this weapon years ago. Why don't you spar first to show the little ones how dangerous a little knowledge can be?" Michael tossed a staff to each of them while the rest of the boys retreated to the edge of the practice ring.

Kurian moved to the center of the circle and faced Rhys. They each held their staves vertically with hands together in the center, saluting their opponent, and waiting for the Blacksmith to begin the match. Rhys was over a head taller than Kurian, and easily weighed two stone more. Thick dark hair pushed out of Rhys' singlet at the neckline. More hair spread over his strong, square chin. *When had Rhys beaten him to manhood?* His extra strength was suddenly a concern.

They had sparred often before, and Kurian knew his speed and strategy usually countered Rhys' greater strength. However, their previous matches had always been bare-fisted bouts, or wrestling with wooden daggers. His thoughts lingered for a moment on the time Rhys broke his once straight nose and he cringed at the idea of Rhys swinging an ash pole at his head.

Michael called for the match to begin. Rhys jerked the staff off the ground, caught the end in both hands, and swung the full length of it at Kurian's left shoulder. Kurian had expected Rhys to take the offensive, but the move came so quickly, he had no time to get into a proper guard. He lifted his staff and ducked clumsily. The blow hit his staff just above his hands and he knocked himself on the head.

Rhys was already in a full backswing, and there was no time to block. Kurian dove wildly and rolled behind his opponent. Rhys twisted his body around, continuing his swing and missing Kurian's back by inches. He felt the rod whistle between his shoulder blades. Before he could turn around, Rhys took a step forward and raised his weapon to bring it down on the back of Kurian's skull.

Kurian rolled onto his back and jabbed the butt of his staff into Rhys' gut, forcing him to double over and stumble back. Finally, Kurian had space to stand up and maneuver. He got to his feet and faced Rhys in a low guard, one hand on the butt, and the other about a third way up the staff for control.

Rhys caught his breath and looked up. His face was red, and he trembled with rage. This was the fighting style Kurian knew and expected from his friend—wild anger, without strategy or thought. The only option now was to win, or submit to a beating until the Blacksmith tore Rhys away.

Rhys screamed and charged. Kurian dropped his stance, and when Rhys made a blind swing, he sidestepped and thrust the staff between Rhys' knees. Rhys toppled face first into the sand, but his staff connected with Kurian's outstretched arm. Kurian clutched his arm while Rhys rolled on the ground. The Blacksmith stepped into the ring before Rhys stood up, ending the match.

"Brilliantly clumsy, gentlemen," he said. "Boys, did you notice how dangerous they were? Kurian was fortunate he didn't crack his own skull, while Mr. Brock the Ox enjoyed a breakfast of sand." He turned to the combatants, "You may have some water and rest for a few moments."

Kurian and Rhys shook hands and walked to different water buckets. He knew from experience that Rhys would be in a foul mood the rest of the day after losing. Better to let him steam alone.

"A fine show," said a stranger sitting on the bench next to the water bucket. Visitors rarely came to the order, and they usually wore the robes of another monastery, not the common tunic of this man.

"I'm fortunate it wasn't bloodier," said Kurian, rubbing the side of his head, and checking his nose out of habit.

"Yes," said the stranger, "I imagine your large friend could injure even your instructor with a temper like that."

"Only if he caught the Blacksm—I mean, Master Humphrey in his sleep. Rhys could never get near enough to touch him." Kurian laughed to think of him trying.

The stranger looked across the field at Rhys with steely eyes. "A heart filled with anger is like a raging fire," he said quietly. "Your master may try to tame it in his hearth, but if a single spark strays to the thatch, it can consume a city overnight."

Kurian stared at the man. He was not as simple as he looked. His age was hard to tell; he could be almost as old as Noeman, yet he had the vibrancy of the young men ordained only a few years before. Who was this stranger? The simple clothing was obviously borrowed, for no farmer or craftsman spoke the way he did. Perhaps he was a spy, looking for a weakness in the compound's defense. Or it could be a test for his training, a seemingly simple man to try his knowledge when he was most distracted by the thrill of the fight and the pain in his arm and head.

"What brings you to Capric?" asked Kurian.

"Perhaps the same thing that brought you, young novitiate. I have roamed the ten cities, and now I find myself here."

"I doubt we have the same purpose then, since I have never been further than the tiny village you see across the riverbed."

"The distance makes no matter. Though you were brought here by another, and I wandered here on my own, you still seek something, as I do."

Kurian was surprised for a moment, but he hid it on his face by showing his suspicion. "Do you know me?"

"I know how recruits arrive at such a place." The stranger smiled at Kurian, but his eyes looked like they held a secret. "Tell me about your order."

"We were founded by two servants of King Frederick, one hundred twenty years before the kings at Fin fell. The river was still flowing then, and they say the sky was clear, and as blue as the mountain iris. King Frederick had recovered a great treasure and was returning to Fin. They were camped on this hill when the largest force of Ballentines ever seen attacked. Ward

Finlay, head of the king's personal guard was preparing defenses when Sage Bennett, the king's priest, saw a vision. In it, the chest that carried the treasure sprouted roots and grew into a great tree. While it grew, one of the branches picked up the king and raised him high above the plain where he was safe from any foe and could see all the land that would hold the ten cities.

"Frederick commanded that the treasure not be moved from the spot where it lay, and that it be protected even before his life. Ward Finlay led a few thousand men against an army of fifty thousand. Miracles followed whenever Sage Bennett opened his mouth, and when the Ballentines were finally scattered, King Frederick understood the vision from God: the treasure must remain on the hill for him to have victory and secure his rule. Sage Bennett confirmed this with a prophecy: the kingdom would plunge into an age of pestilence and war, should the treasure be removed from this hill and dishonored by the people.

"Upon hearing this, King Frederick charged both his men to spend their lives protecting the treasure and serving the people of his kingdom. Five hundred of the most faithful soldiers stayed with them to form this order and build the compound you now see. They also planted the great oak there, in the place where the vision occurred. Our leaders have always taken both the names and positions of our founders; Sage to guide us in wisdom, Ward to lead us in battle."

"You tell the story from your histories well," said the stranger. "I would like to know about the order now."

"Our mission has not changed. We are still priests and warriors, as in our founding," said Kurian.

"And how would you judge your order's performance of that mission?" The secretive look was clear on the stranger's face.

"There are mercy visits to the village almost monthly," Kurian said, hearing the defensiveness in his own voice. "We pray for the people, give them bread, provide healing where we can. Visitors like yourself are welcomed and offered food, shelter, and counsel at no cost. We take nothing from any man and accept only the gifts they freely offer to God. Our food we grow, so that we are not a burden to others. Finally, we train daily to protect the treasure entrusted to us. It is our most important task."

"Have you seen this treasure?"

"No, no," Kurian stammered. "I'm not even ordained. Nobody sees it except Sage Marten, who accounts for everything in this compound. And to ensure that nobody snatches a peek, Ward Farrow's sword guards the only entrance to the treasury."

"A large trust. You would die for this treasure you have never seen?" The man crossed his arms and leaned back on the bench.

"I swore my oath to this order before God." Kurian stood over him, fists clenched. "Both men were elected for their fidelity and bravery."

"Does that still the searching feeling in your heart?" the stranger whispered.

Kurian's face burned. He didn't care whether this was a test. "Forgive me, but I have forgotten myself. The rules of our order forbid novitiates from speaking of these things to guests without permission from the abbot," he said, then turned around and rejoined his troop in the practice ring. He'd stretched any reading of the Rule with his excuse, but he would not have his loyalty questioned, regardless of his challenges with Noeman. It didn't matter whether he fully believed the stories, as long as he performed his duties to the people and would give his life to protect the treasure. He had still sworn his oath to God and to the brothers. When he looked again, the man was gone from the bench, but he was not anywhere on the field. No simple farmer could disappear so quickly. Training continued with simple drills he could perform without much attention, allowing his body to follow the motions while his mind worked to figure out who this stranger was, and whether he should mention the encounter to the dean.

"Why so serious?" Tobin asked as they walked to the dining hall for breakfast. His blue eyes peeked through the sweaty blonde strings clinging to his forehead. "Thinking about Rhys almost knocking your head off?"

"He'd have to stop swinging like a mad donkey for that to happen," Kurian said loud enough for Rhys to hear. "Maybe if he slowed down to aim."

"That'd be no fun," Rhys returned. He flexed the arm carrying his robe and shook his fist. "What's the use in training at half my strength? It'd be like Tobin only finishing half of a test."

"He'd still score twice your better," Kurian said, laughing. Tobin blushed and looked away from Rhys before smiling. Though they were friends, Rhys still intimidated him.

"Comparing my brain to his is like matching little Simon against the Blacksmith in the ring," Rhys conceded. They all laughed, but cut themselves short when they saw Noeman waiting at the door.

"Gentlemen," Noeman said, smiling at them. "You look to be in good spirits for men awaiting punishment." None of them answered, but they all bowed their heads. "I have decided to attempt a new strategy regarding your discipline. I would have you perform two tasks for me in Aposford." The boys looked up in shock.

"Alone, Dean?" asked Tobin.

"Alone, Mr. Hart," said Noeman. "Mr. Abramson and Mr. Brock are only months from the age when they *could* qualify for ordination. I was, in fact, ordained only a few months older than you are, Mr. Hart, on special allowance from the former Sage, God be with him." Kurian bowed his head before rolling his eyes. He was so tired of the old braggart, claiming his own perfection at whatever task challenged his students. "But to the point," Noeman continued, "I doubt they will qualify soon. My instruction seems to have done nothing to tame their contumacy, and I believe they will learn nothing unless they are tested and proved inadequate in their own minds. Tobin, I send you with them to be their good sense on my errand."

"But sir," Tobin objected. He looked more nervous than usual. "I haven't been outside the gate in almost a year, and the last time..."

"Fear not, you've grown much since then, Mr. Hart." Tobin did not appear comforted by the dean's words. "Now, to my tasks. I require parchment."

"Your punishment is to send us to town with your money?" Rhys asked, clearly holding back laughter.

"Ha. When the Apos flows again!" Noeman glared at Rhys. Kurian had never heard him use the exclamation so popular in town. "I would sooner trust a pack of dogs to guard my supper. Interrupt me again and you will see how harsh punishment can be. The tanner supplies me parchment in trade and has a bundle prepared for me. It will be simple enough for you to retrieve it and show yourselves competent errand boys. The second task will test your potential as priests."

Tobin perked up at this news. "What do you require, Dean?"

"Service is the task. You must each find one person in the village who needs assistance and complete whatever task they ask of you. You are not to perform any service reserved for ordained monks, although if anyone requests prayer, you may relay the details to me. I demand a full report of your benevolences at tomorrow's morning gathering, and I will inquire about you the next time I travel to town. Leave immediately after your breakfast, and do not return until dark, assuming you have done something noteworthy by then."

The air was warmer as the boys walked toward Aposford, warm enough that the brief walk made them sweat, which made their robes itch more than usual. They ignored the road and walked across the plain through low, springy turf that offered the only color in sight. Gray clouds covered the sky, as always, dimming the rest of the world into shades of slate and preventing them from easily telling how long they had been walking or how long remained to complete their task. With the clouds obscuring the sun, simple dark and light were the only markers of time in Pallingham, dusk and dawn the only hint that one was giving way to the other. Cutting across the grassy plain and the sparse farmlands would save them some time in travel, giving them more time to find and complete their unusual penance before dark.

Kurian remembered his frustration when he left the morning lesson. Now he thought it may have been a stronger feeling, a sense of dread about the day. Novitiates had never left the gates of the compound alone, as far as any of them knew, and it was amazing that Sage Marten had approved Noeman's errand. Normally, the next monk headed to the village took everyone's shopping lists, and older boys would go along to carry packages or attend to the monk while he performed whatever rites of mercy the villagers needed. Sending three novices alone was unprecedented. Perhaps their old teacher was losing his mind. However, his final warning seemed to indicate that he knew the risk. He had threatened to send them away as *gyrovagues* if he heard of any misconduct. Even Rhys had shown a respectful fear toward that prospect. They had all seen that nightmare at least once——failed monks, slaves to their desires, cast off from their sworn order and banned from joining any other. Their only prospect was wandering between monasteries and living on what poor charity they could find. Clothed in rags and covered with lice, most went mad within a year. Noeman knew the power of such a threat and would not make it lightly.

"What should our first priestly task be?" Tobin asked cheerfully.

"It's no priestly anything," Rhys grunted. "You're slave for a day, that's all."

"It's service, even if it's not as a priest," Tobin said.

"I say we find the simplest thing we can," said Rhys. "Carry some old woman's market basket home, then duck off into the fields for a nap. Get this sackcloth robe off for a while. It feels like roaches are climbing all over me."

Tobin looked appalled. "You'd do anything to shirk your responsibilities. I think we should look for something important to do, so we can make a good report tomorrow. Maybe the town elders could find a task that Noeman would approve." Tobin stumbled, stopping him from making a full speech. Rhys nudged him, and Tobin flailed to keep his balance.

"The whole town is elders," Rhys said.

"You're both right," said Kurian. "We must return with a good report, but we don't want to run around the entire village all day."

"What's your idea, then?" Rhys said.

"We help the most people we can with the least effort. If we stand at the well, people come to us. We prevent strain to aging backs, which the dean will appreciate, and we get to stay in one place."

"Good idea," said Rhys. His half-cocked smile told Kurian that he was no longer sore about the morning match.

Aposford nestled into a bend in the riverbed where the water had once slowed to a shallow crawl, though nobody in the village remembered a time when the river flowed. The persistent clouds that hung low over the plain offered just enough rain and light for a meager crop from the orchards, but the village had slowly died along with the river. Before that, it boomed from the trade that flowed with the water. All the towns and villages of the delta had brought their goods through Aposford on their way to the king's city at Fin. As the town expanded, it straddled the river, reaching close to Capric hill, and many of the merchants could do just as well selling in Aposford than continuing to the capital. A bridge stood as the only reminder of the western side of the town, which had burned down in the same year of drought that dried up the water. The destruction of Fin had been a blow to trade, but the death of the river brought the town to squalor. Only one small road passed through Aposford—not counting the riverbed—making it difficult to transport goods in large quantities. The drought had decimated the fruit and cattle that were their only resources. In two generations, what was left of the town shrank by half. The people scattered among the ten cities. Those that remained were too old to begin again. They lived out their days in crumbling houses, without the materials or strength to repair them.

The boys had crossed the stone bridge and gone directly to the well near the village center. At first, their task seemed minor—a few villagers came to draw water and were grateful for the help. But word spread quickly and soon they had a line of people waiting for them to fill whatever containers they had brought. The growl in their stomachs told them they had worked through lunch before the crowd finally drifted away. Rhys amused himself by drawing two buckets at a time to show off for the few stragglers who came later. Tobin made him break out in laughter when he caught a full bucket on the stone edge of the well and dumped the water on himself and the woman next to him. Kurian sat on the edge of an empty fountain, eating a roll of bread.

"I think it's time to retrieve our package," he said and stood up. "I'll return shortly."

"Why do you get to go?" asked Rhys.

"Because I know where the tanner lives."

Rhys opened his mouth, and then closed it with no response. "Let him go," said Tobin, "he's been moody all day. I think that blow to the head this morning knocked the humor from him."

Rhys laughed, then slapped himself on the side of the head and put on his best pout.

"If you need me," said Kurian, "it's just down this street, then the third left." He walked off in the direction he had pointed, hearing his friends talking and laughing until he made the turn. His suggestion to draw water at the well gave him the best chance to slip away for his own errand.

He stopped at the tanner's house only long enough to pick up the parchment, but he noticed the light fading when he came out. Hurrying, he jogged further down the street until he came to his father's house. In ten years, he had not come back to his childhood home and had only seen his father in passing when he had been allowed to come on his first mercy visit at twelve. A few other times he had seen him from a distance, but during the last few years, his father had not ventured out on days when Kurian came to Aposford. He took it as a necessary part of his new life, and his oath to the order. But frustration with the order had only grown after his conversation with the stranger; he needed to speak to his father again, to ask him why he had given his son to an order that was nothing like his stories.

Surely, his father knew that the order was a shadow of its former strength and honor. He must have seen that they made only the occasional visit to the village, and no grand quests. Or maybe his father was too simple to understand, blinded by the stories and legends about the Caprics. Perhaps he believed that their tutelage would lead to his son's greatness, or at least let him avoid the life of a cobbler's son in a dying town, or conscription into Lord Evasius' army at Pallingham castle. He needed to know. He would ask his father and find the answer in his face.

Before lifting his hand to knock, he heard someone running toward him and then Tobin shouted his name. His face was white with panic. As soon as their eyes met, he waved his arm for Kurian to follow, and ran back down the street. Kurian took off after him, fearing what might have happened with Rhys and Tobin alone. If Rhys had been goaded into a fight, they would all be cast to wander and slowly go mad as *gyrovagues*.

The thought tore at his heart that he might lose his home, and more importantly, his life as a guardian because Rhys couldn't control his temper. As he turned back onto the main street, he looked up and his heart sank. His legs refused to run, slowing until he stood unmoving in the street. At the edge of sight, black smoke rose from Capric hill.

Attack on Capric Hill

Lord Evasius looked east from his window in Pallingham Castle, trying to peer through the haze covering the plain. This late in the day, the setting sun turned the air into a sea of shifting colors and lights as it filtered through clouds and fog banks. He would have had a better view from the ground, yet he stared as if his gaze could transmit his will through the golden clouds before him. "Soon," he whispered, "soon."

Pallingham Castle stood on a tall outcropping of rock at the western edge of the plain of Apos, where the flat ground rose in sloping hills on the way to the sea. The castle's stones were quarried from the outcropping on which it stood, so that the spire looked like a single carved rock formation. Lord Evasius' family had ruled from this castle for seven generations, seizing control of the flailing kingdom after the final king died at Fin. He most admired Shadrick, the first of his line, who used his position as the king's most trusted advisor to gain control of the military and bring the ten cities under his rule. All of Evasius' predecessors had the fortitude to maintain that territory, and some had the strength to enlarge it. But none of them had his vision and ambition. None of them would defy God himself to secure the throne forever and wipe the stories of Fin from the people's memory. Evasius smiled when he heard a knock at the door.

"Enter," he said. The guard stepped in first, followed by a tall woman in a ragged black cloak. A shawl covered the left side of her pale face and straight raven hair poured over the opposite shoulder. She stepped past the guard, who spit on the floor of the hall and closed the door. Evasius met her at a large table covered with a map of Pallingham.

"Mouna," he said gladly. "I thought you would keep me waiting until nightfall."

"My lord," she said, "the king will return before I intentionally slow your plans."

"You know how I dislike that perverse idiom."

She bowed her head. "I waited only until your men had arrived at their destination, when I could provide you with the most information."

"How was your night with Captain Fallon, then? He is my most loyal man, my best soldier. I trust your seduction was complete."

"No seduction was needed after my lord's order." Mouna bowed. "He enthusiastically obeyed."

"Then you were able to bind his soul to yours?"

"My lord," Mouna almost seemed demure. "That happens whenever a man lies with a woman. My power simply makes me more sensitive to it, so that I can feel him from afar. And on occasions when the bond is strong enough, make him feel me."

"What do you feel now?" Lord Evasius stared intently at the witch as she walked to the window. She closed her eyes and took a slow breath, then looked out to the east, toward Capric Hill. Evasius walked to her side. His straight brown hair moved in the breeze from the window and tickled his freshly shaven face. Looking at her standing in the window, he could understand a man succumbing to this woman's allure. The last golden light illuminating her face showed a great beauty, but Evasius knew the disfigured horror hidden under the shawl that covered the other side. He also knew of the body under the robes that should have been any man's delight, except for the scars that crisscrossed her skin from terrible rituals and unknown torment. He would never allow himself to come under her persuasion, but she and her kind were powerful tools for his ambitions. She was a link to his commanders in the field, in addition to her other talents.

"They have arrived," Mouna said, breaking the silence. "I feel the hill, the weak old monks in their musty robes, and the heat. Capric is aflame!" A terrifying smile flashed across her face, briefly showing scarred lips under the shawl.

Evasius' heart beat faster. His clear blue eyes narrowed and his honest faced suddenly looked shrewd. "What else?"

"He's anxious, eager," she said, closing her eyes. "I'm trying to understand all of the sensations." Mouna turned her head as if listening to whispered conversation.

"Are they resisting?"

"I don't feel the urgency of a fight, but Fallon is on his guard." Mouna was quiet again. Evasius wanted to grab her and demand answers, but even a man of his power would be foolish to be violent with a witch. "It's changed," she finally said. "He's excited. I sense gold, more gold than he has ever seen. He is overwhelmed."

"Is it there?" Evasius looked at the witch with a desperate hunger. "Is the treasure intact?"

"Is he looking for something specific?"

"The treasure that the Caprics protect. I don't care about all the gold they've collected from pilgrims, just their treasure——the original treasure. Is it there?"

"Does Captain Fallon know what he's looking for? Would he recognize it?"

Evasius knew the worry showed on his face. He had told his men to bring everything in the treasury. Fallon might be loyal and clever, but Evasius wasn't ready to share his plans for a treasure of such myth and legend, the one thing that could bring him more power than any army or bloodline.

"My lord," Mouna said, "I cannot see through his eyes." She glanced knowingly at Evasius. "I see only through his emotions, through his desire. Fallon's desire is to complete the mission you gave him, and he thinks he has succeeded."

"Thank you, Mouna. That will be all." Evasius recovered himself and bowed graciously. "Without you I would be as blind as the kings of Fin." The witch bowed her head and left.

He returned to the table and sat down, staring intently at the little drawing of Capric Hill on his map of Pallingham. So, he would have to wait. It had already taken several years to consolidate enough power and men to take this risk. He had waited patiently through it all. A few more hours meant nothing. Taking a sip of wine, he sat back in his chair until darkness filled the room.

Kurian and his friends reached the gate of the compound after dark, but the glow of flames lit the sky around the hill. The smell of smoke had reached them as soon as they left the village, running as fast as their legs could move. All of them stumbled as they crossed the uneven grasses. Kurian reached the gates out of breath and pounded on the small access door. His mouth was too dry and his cry to the porter came out only as a rough croak.

"Open the gate," Rhys yelled. He threw his shoulder into the wood and the entire gate swung open, unlocked. Inside, thick smoke poured from the teaching rooms. Little was left but smoldering ashes.

The boys saw flames further up the hill and set out at a run again. When they reached the top of the hill, they saw Ward Farrow, the order's guardian, standing in front of a flaming dormitory. He directed the monks scurrying to put out the fire with buckets of water from the well. The Blacksmith's massive frame was silhouetted for a moment, running faster than any other to throw water on the blaze. The abbot, Sage Marten, walked back and forth in front of the dining hall across the training circle. His hand swung repeatedly above his head. Bodies lay on the ground around his feet, and it was clear he was blessing those who were beyond healing. They stood in shock, trying to find someone who could tell them what had happened, when Noeman stepped out of the dining hall. He had removed his robes and stood in his blood-covered tunic. Sweat shimmered on the bald top of his head. His short, gray beard was suddenly dark with soot.

"Dean," Tobin shouted, and trotted over to him. Kurian and Rhys followed. Their teacher looked tired, as if he were older than the abbot. "What happened?" Tobin asked. His wavering voice barely carried over the roar of the flames and the shouting men behind them.

Noeman wiped his hands on a rag tucked into his belt. "Evasius," he said. Kurian had never seen such fury on the dean's face. His small eyes narrowed, and his large nose flared.

"The treasury," Kurian said quietly.

"Yes," Noeman nodded. "They said they had come to collect taxes due from this land. They took everything."

"The treasure is gone?" Rhys said.

"Couldn't you protect it?" Tobin asked.

Noeman shook his head. "They came with the colors of a peaceful delegation. We thought that perhaps Evasius had finally taken the abbot's invitation to discuss ways to alleviate the burden of the drought. Once the gate was open, they showed their true purpose. There were too many for us to fight inside the walls, and after they had injured or killed twenty of us, the abbot ordered us to surrender."

"It was not worth the lives," Sage Marten said, stepping up behind Noeman. "Gold and silver cannot be counted enough for our brothers." The old abbot's skin looked even more like stained parchment in the firelight, and his shoulders were hunched.

"But we swore!" Kurian shouted. He felt hot tears pooling in his eyes. "It was our one charge."

"The decision was made," Sage yelled back. Fear gripped the boys again; they had never seen Sage Marten lose his temper or raise his voice in any situation. He took a breath before continuing in his quiet, measured tone. "All is not lost. Treasure may always be recovered, even from violent hands." They bowed their heads in respect. Kurian could not see how they could recover anything from the hands that had for years claimed too much from a wasting countryside. He did not understand why the abbot had not fought until the order prevailed or fell.

"Tobin," Noeman said, "I could use your help tending to the wounded."

"No," Sage Marten interrupted. "I have higher plans for these young men."

"Abbot?" Noeman said, bowing.

"I am sending you three to Evasius."

Noeman looked most shocked. "Sage," he said, "these boys are unprepared for such a responsibility."

"I believe they are precisely prepared," said the abbot. He called the Blacksmith as he passed nearby. "We need somebody to go to Pallingham and negotiate the return of at least some of our treasury, in payment for the lives taken and the damage to the compound. We are stretched too thin between the wounded and the fire. These three are the only ones not occupied." Tobin nudged Kurian and whispered to him. Kurian shook his head almost imperceptibly.

"But two of them are my most troublesome students," Noeman objected.

"Whom you saw fit to send to the village alone," Sage replied. "I have observed them, and in my estimation, they have the combined skills to negotiate a settlement. Young Tobin has a mind sharp enough to detect any deception in a legal arrangement. Rhys has the strength and size to prevent attacks from any but the clumsiest of highwaymen. Kurian speaks well, if eagerly. He might impress our lord with his negotiation skills, and he is clever enough for his friend Tobin to coach him about the possible pitfalls. We cannot wait, or all *will* be lost."

"Abbot," Noeman tried to object again.

"Dean Goodman," Sage Marten held out a hand to stop him. "They have one other thing that I believe will work in their favor. They are young, clearly inexperienced. While I do not trust that Evasius holds any compassion, I think their youth will catch him off guard. He will be giddy with his prize and will expect a stronger response. The surprise could make him less demanding."

"He will be offended that we have sent child novices to plead with him." Again, Tobin nudged Kurian and nodded his head toward the abbot. Kurian knew that now was the best time to make Tobin's request known, though he saw no chance of success.

"Abbot Marten," Kurian said. They all looked at him. "I know the rules of our order, and I agree with Dean Goodman." The two men stared at him with confused looks. "What I mean is, I believe the lord of the ten cities will be offended if novices are sent to negotiate with him." Noeman folded his arms, looking self-satisfied.

Kurian cleared his throat, not certain his voice would carry him through. The compound was certainly less glorious than he had left it this morning, but this might be his chance to become a full guardian and priest—and the thought made his heart race with hope. "I also understand that this is a diplomatic assignment," he continued, his voice wavering. "An assignment reserved for ordained brothers. If we are to fulfill this task, I would respectfully ask that we receive ordination before we leave for Pallingham Castle." The last sentence came out almost too fast to understand.

"Never!" Noeman reeled as if Abbot Marten had struck him.

"Precisely the quick thinking and willingness to negotiate that I have observed," said Abbot Marten. He stood nodding his head slowly without looking directly at them, considering the request. Rhys kept glancing at the fires, wanting to rush into the action. Tobin stared at the abbot, the yearning on his face clear. It had been a gamble and Kurian expected immediate rejection, but the longer the abbot delayed in answering, the more he felt the desire well up in his heart.

The abbot stopped nodding. "However, my answer is no," he said quietly, "I do not think that is the best course." The hope in

Kurian's heart poured like lead into his belly. He saw Tobin close his eyes, as if in pain. The abbot placed his hand on Tobin's shoulder. "As talented as you may be, you are not yet ready for the full responsibilities of a priest." He turned to Noeman and said, "However, our lord does not need to know we send novitiates to parlay with him."

"If you do what I think you are planning, you will disgrace this order," Noeman said ominously.

"More disgraced than we already are?" Sage replied. Kurian was glad the abbot said it first. "Humphrey," he said, turning to the Blacksmith, "equip these boys with staves—not the practice ones. Bestow the other marks of our order and fill packs with enough supplies for a two-day journey."

"They're not trained properly," Noeman said. "If they're attacked, they won't be able to defend themselves."

"If I may," said the Blacksmith. "The image of strength may be a greater defense than the arms themselves. The more common type of predator will see three men of our order as a threat, no matter how young."

"Humphrey has a point," said the abbot, "and I trust it will not make these boys prideful. After all, clothes and weapons do not make the man. Whether any man is worthy of wearing the signs of our order is only proved in his actions."

"But the giving of those signs normally occurs after there has been some proof of the man's worth, and their dedication to the purposes of our order," Noeman argued. "It is a symbol of being chosen by God as a protector of our sacred trust."

When the abbot did not respond, Noeman threw his arms up and walked back into the dining hall. "This will end poorly," he shouted over his shoulder.

"It's settled, then," Sage Marten said. "Go with Master Humphrey and he will get you all dressed up." The abbot smiled at them like a grandfather patting children on the head and returned to blessing the fallen. Kurian twitched the edges of his mouth as a reflex acknowledgment. He wasn't sure why the abbot chose to send them, but the condescension with which he looked at them did not give him confidence. *Yes, let's play dress up and let our boys pretend at being monks*, he thought. *Then we'll send them into the dragon's lair to beg for some gold from his latest prize.* Something about this felt more dangerous than the abbot's plan suggested. Perhaps Tobin could help him figure it out while they traveled.

Passing by the scorching heat of the dormitory fire, they followed the Blacksmith to the armory. None of them had ever been inside. It was a room just bigger than their troop's sleeping quarters that stuck out from the main storehouse. All the training weapons, as well as a stockpile of real ones, were stored inside under lock and key. On the right side, Kurian recognized the plain ash staves they practiced with leaning against the wall. Small wooden daggers stuck out of a crate. Wooden short swords hung on the wall above, with padded maces and practice versions of spears and falchions. Those practice weapons were primarily used to learn how to defend against them. Few of the monks mastered them.

The opposite wall held the weapons issued to monks at ordination. The Capric staves had a pointed iron tip on the bottom and an egg-shaped bronze headpiece with a red enamel band at its base. Master Humphrey handed a staff to each of them without a word. Rhys felt the weight and smiled at his friends. Kurian knew he was imagining how many heads he could smash with the little metal egg.

The Blacksmith fitted them for traveling boots next, and handed each of them a dagger, showing them how to conceal them comfortably inside their boots, without any danger to themselves. "These are weapons of last resort," he said. "Few people know we carry them, so use them only if you must."

From a peg on the wall, he pulled down a belt for each of them. Kurian could see Tobin's eyes glimmer in the torchlight at the sight of the scarlet and white braided cords. As the only piece of equipment that the brothers wore daily, this was the official sign of priesthood that he craved.

"This is more than you think," their trainer said. "Rhys, come at me with your staff." Rhys looked at his friends and shrugged. He pulled the staff back to swing, but hit the wall. When that didn't work, he lunged forward and jabbed with the headpiece. Michael leaned his head out of the way and stepped inside Rhys' reach. He looped a belt around Rhys' head and yanked to the side, pulling the youth off balance. Once Rhys was on the ground, Michael held the cord tight around his neck and threw the knotted end of another belt at Kurian's face, making him flinch.

"Your belts may be the sign that you are priests of this order, but they can distract, bind, or even strangle your enemy if necessary. They are probably our most versatile weapon and may save your life one day. Just remember the old story of the brothers who escaped from a window using cords like these." He let go of the cord around Rhys' neck.

"Be aware of your surroundings and the proper weapon will reveal itself to you." Michael helped Rhys to his feet and handed each of them a belt. Then he opened a small cupboard at the back wall of the room and pulled out three light chains with vials dangling from them. "Most people think we keep holy relics or sanctified water around our necks—which works to its own advantage with the simple minded—but a fine powder is inside these vials. If you can get it into your enemy's eyes, he will be blind for days. Throw it into a fire and thick smoke will conceal you. Mix it into a drink, and even a surgeon will think the victim dead. This powder is the reason we do not bury our brothers immediately as the rest of the world does." He chuckled. "There were a few embarrassing mistakes during its creation."

Kurian held the vial in front of his face. He hadn't known about this powder, and he had never thought to connect their training and their weapons with deliberately harming another person. It was easier to think their training was for self-defense, and defense of the compound or the treasure. Suddenly, the reality of having to harm other people came to his mind with brutal clarity. This mission would indeed be more dangerous than their teachers let on, but now Kurian wondered if Noeman might be more right about their abilities than Sage Marten. "Master Humphrey," he said, but couldn't ask the question in his mind.

The Blacksmith looked at him with sympathy, an expression the trainer had never shown. "No," he finally said, "I do not expect that you will need to use any of these weapons on a two-day journey to Pallingham. But if you are to look the part, you should carry the full arsenal of our order, and I would never send a man with weapons he knows nothing about. The little knowledge I have given you will make you as dangerous to yourselves as to any foe." He looked sternly at Rhys, who returned a face of blank innocence. "Forget about them, except at the greatest need," he said pointedly. Kurian knew Rhys would not hesitate to use his weapons, and he determined that he, too, would act quickly to protect his friends.

Soon the three novitiates stood alone outside the compound gate. Humphrey had given them packs with a small supply of food, skins of water, and blankets. Sage Marten had told them how to get to Pallingham, although the fresh trail of dozens of horses would be easy to follow through the grassy plain. With a final word of prayer and blessing, he had allowed them to walk themselves to the bottom of the hill, without ceremony or even announcement.

Kurian looked out at the impenetrable darkness and felt both the unending expanse of an unknown world, and panic, as if being smothered in a wardrobe. Behind them, they still heard the chaos of men fighting fire, but it didn't feel real anymore. The still night of the world outside the compound felt like all that mattered.

"Let's get on with it," Rhys said, and they took their first steps west from Capric hill.

Lord Evasius was already awake when the news came that the men had returned from Capric. He had not really slept. Still, he kept his composure and dressed slowly before meeting Captain Fallon in his lower offices. Light was just beginning to brighten the windows, and the soldier was already waiting for him. "I assume it was a success," Evasius said as he entered the room.

Captain Fallon bowed low. His tall, strong form imposing in his mail and uniform. He had sharp features and deep set crystal blue eyes with a hawkish nose. A scar cut through the close-cropped sandy soldier's hair above his left ear.

"We emptied their treasury, my lord," Fallon said.

"Excellent," Evasius smiled. It was finally his, and now he would be the most powerful ruler the ten cities had seen for generations, powerful enough to expand his kingdom across the continent—maybe even across the sea. "Bring it in."

Fallon opened the side door and snapped his fingers. Soon, men came from the hall carrying chests that two of them could barely lift. They kept coming until Evasius was not sure his office would hold them all. He sat casually on the edge of his desk until all of the men had filed out and Fallon took out a ring of keys. "I could not believe it myself, lord," Fallon said with a gravely voice. "Gold." He flung open one of the lids. "More than I have ever seen, although I'm sure it will not surprise your lordship." The man was visibly restraining his wonder, averting his large, deep set eyes instead of staring.

"You have done well, Fallon." Evasius scooped up a handful of gold coins and smiled. "Your reliability shall be rewarded." When he held the gold out, Fallon cautiously stretched out his own hands. Evasius poured it into his palms—more than he paid the man in a year—and a few coins spilled over and rolled across the floor.

"My Lord, while I am grateful for your favor, my men deserve the reward more than I do."

"Then enjoy the night with your men, Captain. Celebrate your success and your new position as head of my personal guard."

"You are too kind, Lord," Fallon bowed low, and Evasius could still see his smile creeping across narrow lips. Fallon was too easy to control with his ideas about duty, and glory in battle. But he was a loyal man, and a good soldier. Giving him more acclaim as Evasius gained power would only secure his loyalty and that of the men he led.

"Leave me the keys. I must begin tallying our new income."

Evasius snatched the keys from the lock and began opening chests as soon as Fallon left. Gold and silver coins, trinkets, and jewelry filled each one. Some held piles of gems. He dug through the metal searching, but could not find the fabled object that the Caprics protected. With each chest, he became more frantic. It had to be here—unless Fallon had missed it, thinking it worthless. In desperation, he dumped several chests onto the floor to search again. Treasure surrounded him, but none of it was worth anything without that one relic.

Finally, he opened a chest with a smaller box inside. The box was overlaid with gold and cut jewels. Inlaid in silver across the top was an inscription in the ancient tongue that told him this was what he desired. Of course, it was so beautiful. Nothing so valuable would be stored in a simple trunk and covered with common coins. He found a smaller key on the ring and used it to unlock the box—but when he opened it, he saw only silk lining. It was empty, except for a scrap of parchment.

"No!" he yelled. "It must be here."

Snatching up the parchment, he threw the priceless box against the wall.

On the other side was a note. In a clear, but simple hand it read:

"Removed for safekeeping to my personal collection."

It was signed with a small icon.

CHAPTER THREE

Pallingham Castle

Kurian felt his belly grumbling well before it was light, but he didn't want to be the one to stop them because he was tired and hungry. Even in the dark, it was easy enough to follow the horse tracks from Evasius' army. He could feel the difference in the ground under his feet where the horses had beaten the grass into a pockmarked trail. Nothing else moved in the night, and they walked in silence.

Their footsteps wove together into a rhythm that called him toward sleep—the long, heavy gait of Rhys, his own steady tread, and Tobin's soft, quick padding. They continually drifted closer, then further from a matching cadence. It comforted Kurian to know that his friends were with him on this lonely walk through the silent, dark plain. Their presence made the chaos they had just left feel like a dream. Memories of their years training together seemed more real than the smoke he could still smell on his robes. These friends were what made the order worth the sacrifice. They were why he wanted so badly to gain ordination, and why the threat of losing that troubled him so much. Exile would mean losing his home, his purpose, and his brothers, whom he had known longer than any family.

Tobin spoke first, asking to rest and drink some water as dawn slowly filtered light down on the plain. They did not stop to eat until well into the morning. Their last meal had been the afternoon before, in Aposford, and that had been a meager lunch. Kurian felt like he could eat the entire sack of rations that Master Humphrey had given them, but he restrained himself to eat just enough to curb his hunger. With any luck, they would eat better at the castle than they ever did at their order's compound. It was possible that Lord Evasius had enough wealth to make even his rudeness seem like lavish hospitality. The Lord of Pallingham had an extravagant but violent reputation.

Through lunch, Tobin and Rhys tried to recall whom they recognized among the fallen the night before. Kurian spoke little. The look that the abbot had given them remained in his mind, and he wondered whether there was a greater purpose to their mission. Each time he thought about the rejection of his request for ordination, it stirred his anger again. It seemed as if Sage Marten had been playing with them by delaying his answer. The anger of Noeman only made it more suspicious. They had given each other strange looks, as if they had been having an entirely different conversation without speaking a word.

Kurian wanted to know what that conversation was, and why the abbot was willing to break the rules of their order so flagrantly over such an important issue as the treasure they protected.

"What do you think was happening last night?" Kurian asked after they had been walking again for a while. "That is, between the dean and the abbot?"

"All I know is Dean Goodman got his tassels tangled," Rhys said. "Usually, that makes me happy." His voice trailed off.

"But why did Sage Marten send us out here without ordination?"

"It doesn't bother me," said Rhys. "I know I'm not making it for another year at least. This is just something special because the compound got attacked. If they want to give me a real weapon because of that, it's all right by me." He kissed the bronze headpiece on his new staff.

"I don't think so," Kurian said. "Sage Marten had no reason to send us instead of a full brother, or going himself. We could have easily taken over somebody else's post helping to fight the fire or tend the wounded."

"He thought Evasius would go easy on us," Rhys said, "on account of we're so young and innocent looking."

"That's hard to believe," Kurian scoffed.

Tobin trotted up from behind. "You're right to wonder. I've been thinking about the problem myself. This sort of breach of the Rule is well beyond a loose interpretation during a crisis. The abbot broke one of the major points of the order clean through." His hair flapped across his brow as he shook his head.

"What do I care?" asked Rhys. "Nobody's going to know that, unless you open your big mouth."

Tobin scoffed. Kurian knew it meant a lecture was coming. "You should care!" Tobin answered, stabbing a finger toward Rhys. "It calls into question everything about this mission and the abbot's motives. Even in previous crises, novitiates have always been ordained before undertaking *any* priestly task—though an abbreviated ceremony is usually used." Tobin's voice rose almost to a screech. "There is no reason why Sage Marten could not have taken a few minutes to perform the rite with us."

"I can think of one," Kurian said. He still felt the disappointment burning in his gut like hot lead.

"I can think of several," Tobin almost screamed. Tears carved streaks of pale flesh through the grime on his cheeks.

"They don't think we're able to become monks," said Kurian. "Noeman threatened just a day ago to make us *gyrovagues*." He felt the hot liquid in his belly churning into anger. "I'm not sure they ever intend to ordain me. Maybe Noeman just wants to torture me for a few more months before he rejects me outright. Then what will I do?"

Rhys wrapped an arm around Kurian's shoulder. "The dean can't do it over the abbot, and he likes you."

"I saw how the abbot looked at us last night," Kurian said through his teeth. "He thinks we're hopeless children, and he's sending us to play with a snake."

"That is the more worrying prospect," Tobin said quietly.

Kurian and Rhys stopped walking and stared at him. "What do you mean?" Kurian asked.

"I might know our history and law inside and out, but diplomatic training doesn't start until after ordination. And while you might have a knack for convincing people to go your way, I doubt you can outwit a leader like Evasius, even with my help."

"I'm still not following," Rhys said.

"Abbot Marten may have sent us *because* we would fail."

"And what does that mean?" Kurian asked.

"It could mean a lot of things," Tobin said, shaking his head. "Maybe Sage Marten has given up on the order; it's been waning for generations." Tobin paused. A cool wind from the west caused him to shiver. "Or it could mean he's working with Evasius."

"What?" Rhys said. "You've lost it, mate."

"No," said Kurian, "it makes some sense. However, that would mean that the abbot was planning for the fall of the entire order by Evasius' hand. I can't believe that."

"Even if Evasius promised him a large portion of our treasury, or lands and titles?" Tobin asked. The wind blew harder, pushing aside a bank of fog, and Pallingham castle came into view for the first time. The stout gray tower perched on its outcropping of rock was the largest structure any of them had ever seen. But from a distance, the castle looked empty and cold.

Kurian could not imagine the abbot joining with a man like Lord Evasius, who had such a cruel reputation. The abbot might think of them as children, but he had always been the kindest of the old monks—until last night. "It just feels too wrong," he said to Tobin. "I think he really does expect us to fail, and then he can banish us." The anger simmering inside of him suddenly boiled into rage. "He as good as cursed us!" Kurian yelled.

"No," said Tobin, shaking his head. "It's not as bad as that. Perhaps he's given us the perfect opportunity. If we succeed, he can't help but ordain us. It would be just like Simon the younger, when he saved a whole troop of brothers by killing a den of lions."

"Now you're dreaming," Rhys laughed.

"Perhaps if we pray before we continue, God will give us a miracle," Tobin said hopefully.

"I don't know if those happen anymore," Kurian whispered, but he joined hands with his friends and bowed his head.

This close to the castle, the plain turned into small hills dotted with large boulders. The soft grass now hid sharp rocks that tripped them, and Kurian kicked them more than once, letting out a grunt of pain. Soon, Lord Evasius' castle stood before them, jutting from the hills like the hilt of a blade thrust into the earth. They approached from the north, where a narrow road led up the rock face toward a large gate in the main wall. Guards stood beside a smaller gate where the road began its ascent. They asked only a few questions before they let Kurian and his friends through to follow the winding road to the top.

Pallingham Castle looked even larger when standing directly below it in the late afternoon. The stout tower rose far above their heads, and it hurt to crane their necks back to try to see the top. At the north gate, a slick black moss clung to every stone, making the walls look more like the hide of a filthy, sweating giant than of quarried stone. An odor of peat smoke saturated each breath as they got close to the walls. Standing at the gate, it seemed as if they should be able to see farther out over the plain, but the hills and boulders strewn below dissolved into a gray sheet only a couple miles in the distance. Kurian felt like he was going blind looking back toward his home.

Once inside the main wall, the castle did not look much different from the compound at Capric. Thatched roof stone buildings stood on either side of a narrow street and people walked up and down the street on various chores. However, the details of the place were very different. Unlike at Capric, the people did not greet each other as they passed, and garbage littered the streets. The smell of human and animal waste mingled with the peat smoke to assault their senses, and as they walked to the tower entrance, they passed more than one man lying drunk against a wall. According to the teachings of the order, such men should hide themselves in shame. But of course, the order also taught that their commission gave them special protection in the world and that had proven false already. He didn't want to think of what happened here at night. Kurian could not believe this was the seat of power in Pallingham. He wondered how the ten cities could allow themselves to be ruled from a single small castle where such debauchery was on display in the middle of the afternoon. He had long suspected there was a reason the order had lost power and influence for decades, and now he thought part of that reason was the condition of the people outside of their local influence.

He tried to keep a vague, unreadable expression on his face. He wasn't sure that even a priest could help the people he saw here, but he didn't want them to see that. He had to elbow Tobin, who gawked at everything that his training had taught him was offensive.

"Try not to react so much," Kurian said quietly. "How are we supposed to win over Evasius when even the drunks can read your thoughts?"

Tobin blushed and raised the hood on his robe to cover his face. Kurian heard him praying softly and hoped that it would help them to survive this place. It didn't matter what was waiting for them. They would be unprepared.

When they reached the tower, the porter called an armed escort. Three tall men in tarnished armor walked close behind them, their hands lingering on the hilts of their swords. Kurian was surprised that they were allowed to keep their staves, but after such a successful attack, Evasius probably thought they posed no threat. While the porter led them through identical passages toward an unknown destination, he stammered about how infrequently monks had visited the castle. The porter promised that they would see Lord Evasius, but after the fourth turn down an indistinguishable hallway, Kurian began to wonder if he weren't leading them toward the dungeon.

He finally stopped and opened a small door that Rhys had to stoop to get through. "Please wait here until my Lord calls for you. Feel free to refresh yourselves with anything you find." He bowed lightly and left before they could thank him. Their armed escort closed the door, but remained outside.

Kurian looked around the small waiting room. There were two chairs and a stone bench in front of a window. Next to it was a table with a jug of water and a plate of bread and cheese. The condition of the food convinced him that the room was infrequently used. Any hidden hopes for a robust meal vanished. Rhys picked up the bread and offered some to Tobin before dropping it back on the plate with a clang. "What hospitality," he said dryly.

"Fortunately, we have no need of it," Kurian said. "Do you suppose we are prisoners, or just unwelcome guests?"

"In either case," Tobin answered, "I suggest we review our strategy before we are summoned."

Tobin reviewed which laws and ordinances of the old kingdom might best make their case while Rhys stretched out on the stone bench and snored. Kurian was amazed at his ability to sleep anywhere. They waited over an hour before the door opened and a man dressed in embroidered silks entered the room.

"I am Lord Evasius' attendant," the man said. "He apologizes for the condition of the room, and he hopes that you will understand it is merely an indication of how poorly our land fares and not a slight against you or your venerated order."

Kurian wanted to point out the irony of such respectful words from the man who had just set fire to their home, but he restrained himself and adopted the posture that he had seen the monks take in Aposford. "We gratefully accept whatever hospitality our host offers and do not wish to be a burden," he said, bowing slightly.

"Lord Evasius will see you now," said the attendant, and stepped out of the room. This time, they ascended what seemed like unending stairways, even for boys who had grown up climbing the steep slope of Capric. Their armed shadows followed closely behind so that they could only move forward. The attendant reached the top of the stairs and stopped at a large set of double doors. "It is nearly time for supper, so my master has asked me to bring you to his private chambers. He often eats here while conducting business in the evenings." He opened the doors and raised his voice slightly. "My Lord, the three Caprics who have come to see you."

They entered a room dominated by a desk on one side. In a long, curved wall, large windows behind the desk let in the fading evening light and showed the hunched silhouette of a man writing. Across from the windows was a door that Kurian assumed led to the bedroom. "One moment," said the figure, who made one more brusque flourish with his quill before setting it aside and standing up. He moved quickly toward them with a long stride that made the open robes he wore flow softly behind him.

"Very good, Geoffrey," he said to his attendant, before turning his attention toward the boys. The ruler's youth surprised Kurian. Evasius couldn't be over forty, but for some reason, he had been expecting a man almost as old as Sage Marten, and perhaps more bent and stooped with cruelty, but he had a vitality and strength about him that was almost appealing, and the surprise on his face when he looked at his visitors was disarming. The man looked honest enough that in different circumstances Kurian would want to trust him. "You didn't tell me they were so young, Geoffrey."

"Forgive the oversight, my Lord," Geoffrey said. He bowed and stepped back to stand by the door.

"Farran Evasius," he smiled at the boys and bowed deeply.

"Kurian Abramson, my lord," Kurian bowed in return. "Allow me to introduce my companions, Rhys Brock and Tobin Hart. You honor us with an audience."

Evasius clapped his hand on Kurian's back. "There is no need for such formalities. You boys must be exhausted and hungry after your long walk. Please sit and eat with me." He guided them over to another table and waved to Geoffrey. At his signal, servants brought in trays of steaming food and jugs of wine. The room suddenly filled with the scent of freshly baked bread and roasted meat. There was also a plate with fresh cheese, butter, and honey, along with several dishes of roasted squash from the recent harvest. Kurian could feel his mouth begin to water. He waited for his host to sit down first, and then all three of them found chairs around the table. From the way he eyed the food, it was obvious that Rhys could barely restrain himself from eating the first thing he could grab.

"I know some of the customs of your order," Evasius said cheerfully. "Would you please offer a blessing for our humble fare?"

Kurian tried to study his face, but could not read anything sinister in it. Of course, Evasius had reason to be cheerful with the new riches he had stolen. Kurian bowed his head cautiously, leaving his eyes just the tiniest bit open so that he was not entirely blind. If only he could ask Tobin to handle this part, but Evasius had asked him, and he could not refuse. "God, we thank you for the generosity of our host, and the meal you have provided. We pray that you bless this food to secure our health, and that you give back to this household a blessing that multiplies the kindness shown to us." Kurian paused. The formula that he had learned for blessing a meal was complete, but he felt an urge to add a few more thoughts. He glanced quickly at Evasius. Confidence seemed to pour out of the man, even with his head bowed. "We also thank you, God, that you have brought us before a man with an open and gracious heart, and we pray that you guide our conversation toward a just conclusion that is within your revealed will." It felt like a risky, presumptuous move, and he glanced at Evasius again but saw no effect. "Let it be."

The other men echoed his final words and Evasius reached for Kurian's cup to fill it with wine. Then he stopped. "Forgive me; does your order drink wine?"

"We are allowed whatever our host offers us, except during a fast," Tobin said.

"Excellent," Evasius said, and filled Kurian's cup to the brim. Rhys reached for a tray of meat and filled his plate, then tore off almost half a loaf of bread for himself. Tobin carefully followed their training in etiquette and took only a small amount of food, waiting to eat only as much as their host. Kurian decided to follow his example, and mimic Evasius as he ate.

"Lord Evasius," Kurian said, "we appreciate your hospitality, especially since you must know why we came."

Evasius took a portion of meat and set down the tray, then folded his hands together on the table. His slender figure made it clear that the man was disciplined with his food and his body. "Yes," he said. "It is obvious you have come about that unfortunate misunderstanding yesterday evening."

"Would my lord be kind enough to enlighten me on what was misunderstood?" Kurian looked for irony in his face, but he showed a perfectly measured expression of contrition.

"I sent my men to speak with your abbot about the drastic needs in our land. As you must know, there has been a prolonged drought and the people struggle just to survive." He paused as if waiting for agreement. Kurian only nodded. "For my part, it is almost impossible to supply enough men to keep the peace and protect the people with what little taxes come in. Vagabonds roam the countryside freely in some areas." An expression of deep concern accompanied the speech. "And that is not even to speak of the other costs of governing."

"Forgive my ignorance," Kurian said, "but how exactly does this relate to yesterday eve?"

"Taxes, my dear boy," Evasius smiled kindly, as one speaking to an ignorant child. It was almost the same look the abbot gave them the night before. "I wanted to ask your abbot for aid in bolstering the tax rolls. After all, your order does retain the largest collection of wealth in Pallingham—larger than my treasury has ever been."

"That was the case," Kurian said flatly.

"That was the misunderstanding," Evasius boomed, ignoring the attempt at goading him. "My men were overeager and thought that my orders were to take the treasure, when only a little bit freely shared would ease the burden of us all. I thought that your Sage Marten would understand the necessity of providing for the public with peace and welfare. I am, in the end, simply a servant, as he is."

"My lord, you do understand that our treasury primarily holds gifts given to God," Tobin said. Kurian could hear the slight tremble of fear in his voice, and was sure that Evasius heard it, too.

"I do," said Evasius, lowering his voice. "However, you must understand that my aim was for the good of the people." Kurian saw an instant where the façade cracked in Evasius' expression. He was angry with Tobin for challenging his motives, but it was gone as soon as Kurian noticed it. "Certainly, God would agree that a little bit of treasure is better used for a noble cause than just sitting in an old monastery gathering dust." He looked almost like a merchant at a stall, trying to sell inferior goods to a discriminating buyer.

"Our abbot would know better than we would regarding God's preferences," Kurian said. "Are you also aware that several of our brothers are dead after last night, and that half of our compound was damaged?"

Evasius looked down with every indication of sadness. "I was told that there was a struggle. I believe it only made my men more determined to bring back as much as they could. However, I am happy that your abbot was sensible and intervened before there was more bloodshed." He picked up his cup and sipped at it. Kurian was certain that he fully understood his mind about whose blood would have been shed. None of them said anything. Rhys had already cleared his plate and was piling on more food. Kurian looked at Tobin in the silence, trying to find some guidance to get through Evasius' defenses, but Tobin only shrugged.

Evasius swallowed loudly. "Don't worry, my friends. I will send some men back to your compound to return the bulk of your treasury tomorrow. I only wish to retain a small portion to pay my armies through the winter. However, I must still humbly request that your abbot be willing to offer a portion of any future gifts he receives for matters of state. In difficult times, we must all struggle together." At that, he shoved a forkful of meat into his mouth and took a gulp from his cup.

Kurian noticed the emphasis on paying soldiers. "Perhaps my knowledge of the law is incomplete," he said, "but I believe all monastic orders have been exempt from taxation since the time of Fin." Evasius set his mug down too firmly and rattled the plates on the table. Kurian had uncovered his anger again. The rest must be a deception, but Kurian was unsure what he was hiding.

"Unfortunately, my young friend, things must sometimes change." Evasius was smiling, but his eyes looked as if he wanted to burn Kurian to ashes.

Kurian lowered his eyes and feigned deference. "We are grateful that you are willing to return much of our treasury, and we apologize for our order's part in the misunderstanding, my lord." Evasius had time to restore his mask of kindness, and he shook his head as if no apology were needed. "If my lord knows anything about our order, then he must know that we protect a very particular item above all else in our treasury. My lord may keep whatever else of the treasury he wishes if we might receive this one item and return it safely to our brothers tonight."

"Ah," Evasius nodded. "The fabled treasure of the Caprics—that is an enigma."

"In what way?" asked Kurian.

"Boys, I must let you in on a secret. When my men returned and told me what had happened, I searched all the chests and boxes they brought for that most important of treasures. I wanted to secure it in my own vaults to ensure its safety, since I assumed that your order would send someone to retrieve it. It was not there."

Kurian suddenly felt like he would vomit. Rhys dropped his fork, his mouth hanging open. "What?" said Kurian. "How? That treasure has been protected by our order for centuries."

"Believe me, I was as surprised as you were," Evasius said. He rose from the table and walked over to his desk. When he returned, he dropped a scrap of parchment in front of Kurian. "There was one chest that held only an ornate box. I had never seen such a beautiful piece, so I assumed that the treasure was inside; it was only fitting to store it in such splendor. When I opened it, all that I found was this note."

Kurian realized that he was clenching his fists. He had to struggle to open his hands to pass the yellowed parchment to Tobin. It was impossible to hide that his hands were shaking. "I don't understand."

"I'm sorry to tell you that your treasure was taken." Evasius looked genuinely concerned again. It was clear to Kurian that this was the secret he was hiding, but he was uncertain about Evasius' reaction. "How long ago, I don't know, but if the note is true, I do know who took it, and I know that it is imperative that it be returned. If the visions that inspired your order were true, then the security of our land rests on your treasure."

"Who took it?" Rhys growled.

"I recognized the symbol immediately. There has been a bandit raiding my supply carts almost every month. In each case, no more than one or two of my men return alive. The stories about him are horrifying. Most of the men who return to me never speak again, but they all draw that symbol. A few have come back muttering, calling him the King of the Caves. He strikes at any place he chooses and vanishes like a phantom. We have never been able to discover his camp."

"Is that all you know about him?" Kurian asked. "We have never heard any stories about this bandit."

"I try to keep the stories from spreading when he attacks," Evasius said. "The people would panic to learn that there was a villain pillaging the most heavily guarded supply transports at will, leaving almost no survivors."

"If he is a ghost, then it would seem the treasure is lost," Kurian said. He had to fight back the anger and tears that wanted to well up, and he looked out the window where night had fallen. One question burned in his mind until he almost forgot about the man he was supposed to be negotiating with—*did Sage Marten know?*

Evasius looked intently at Kurian. He was smiling again, but this time he looked like a cat about to pounce on his prey. "Perhaps it is not yet lost. I would like to offer you young men a deal."

"What sort of deal?"

"It is vital to the realm that the treasure be returned. Obviously, my men have looked for leads and interrogated people thought to have information about this thief, but we have not discovered his whereabouts." Evasius brought his fingers together under his lips. "We have one piece of information about a man whom we think knows where this King of the Caves is located. Perhaps, if monks from a celebrated order were to question him, they would have more success than my soldiers."

"You want us to find the treasure. What do you get from it?"

"You only need to get me the information, and my men will do the rest. As for what I get—I get to restore order to my people when my troops bring him to me for justice. However, I also want the treasure to remain in my castle——under the guard of brothers from your order, of course."

"But that would go against the prophecy of God, and centuries of law and tradition," Tobin said, horrified.

"Clearly the order has not been able to protect it within their compound," Evasius said calmly. "I merely want to help ensure that it is never stolen again."

"Forgive our reluctance," said Kurian, "but I am not certain that we have the authority to make such a decision."

"From what I understand of your order, any monk sent on a diplomatic mission has the full authority of the abbot."

Kurian looked at Tobin, who nodded slowly as his face went pale. Evasius had cornered them into making an impossible decision. It looked as if they would fail in returning to Capric with the treasure they had sworn to protect. Kurian felt his throat tightening at the prospect and took a sip of wine to clear it. "This deal sounds rather one-sided, my lord. From the time we were seven years old we all took an oath to protect the treasure where it lay.”

“As you have seen, I can be gracious,” Evasius said, gesturing toward the table of food. “In return for your services, I will order my men to assist in rebuilding your compound, and I will revoke my request for a portion of your income. In fact, I will issue an edict that confirms my own commitment to your order’s exemption from all taxes as long as my line rules.” He raised his glass as if to make a toast. “And if your oath is that important to you, then I will insist that Abbot Marten make you three my personal delegates to lead the guardians posted here.”

Rhys looked as if he thought this was a fair deal. The position and chance for honor were what mattered to him, and the food was better here. Tobin shook his head slightly, trying to hide it from Evasius. While Kurian had expected to be unprepared, the circumstances seemed to make their original mission meaningless. Evasius had talked them into a corner, especially since he knew the Rule’s teaching about diplomatic missions. Now he was attempting to bribe and manipulate them into promising the impossible. However, the fact that they weren’t monks might mean he could agree to anything and the abbot could rescind any of it. Of course, he would have to break the Rule’s orders about promises and oaths to do it, but the Rule offered no guidance in such a contorted situation. In the end, finding that treasured item was all that mattered. It was his only chance to remain in the order and fulfill his purpose to be a guardian. And perhaps Tobin was right—if the abbot didn’t know the treasure had been missing, they would instantly gain

ordination by snatching it from the hands of a notorious criminal. He took a deep breath before speaking again.

"It appears our only choice is to accept your offer if we hope
to keep our order intact, however, our abbot may need further
assurances," Kurian said. Once the decision was made, he felt
lighter, and he was able to take the last bite from his plate.

"Wonderful," Evasius said. "I have a room prepared for you,
and I will send you on a carriage in the morning to find the
man we suspect." He stood up, and the boys rose as well. Tobin
looked at Kurian, and he knew that there would be a long discussion once they were alone.

Geoffrey opened the door to lead them to their room, but
Evasius called them before they were gone. "Just out of curiosity, would you know the treasure if you saw it? I wouldn't want
the King of the Caves to deceive us when we capture him."

"Only the abbot is allowed to view the treasure."

"Well then, just in case you get close, I will tell you that I have
had scribes dig up what they could about your treasure from
the royal archives. They tell me that the treasure is probably a
book." The boys each looked surprised.

"This won't be an ordinary book, by any means," Evasius
continued. "It will obviously be very old, but its contents are
unknown. Based on the stories that surround it—like the one
about the founding of your order—it must be a thing of great
power. Personally, I believe that it may hold the answers to all
the mysteries of the world. Truly, that would be a power worth
protecting. We cannot know what the King of the Caves might
do with it, and so we must retrieve it to keep all of Pallingham
safe."

Kurian was speechless, unsure whether he even believed what he was hearing. He could only nod as Evasius spoke.

"Certainly, your order would not want a thief and a murderer to wield the power to control everything." Before any of them could respond, Lord Evasius nodded to Geoffrey, who closed the door and hurried them back down the tower stairs.

CHAPTER FOUR

Mystery in Downriver Town

Louise Prescott scrambled up the bank of one of the dry streams of the Apos delta. Dry was a loose description here in Downriver Town, where mud seemed to ooze from the ground and the estuaries where the river used to meet the sea were soaked twice a day by the ocean tide. The fog was heavy this morning, and she pulled her ragged clothes tighter to keep out the damp. Even though it was cold, she found it safer to sleep under the bridge outside of town instead of risk the nighttime hazards of Pallingham's southern port town. It didn't matter that she was clothed in rags and slept in mud; men were still men—and the foreign sailors twice so.

At the top of the bank, she crouched next to the bridge and checked to see that nobody was on the road before heading to her normal spot sitting just inside the town gate. A few roosters made their morning calls in the distance, and she knew that the baker's wife would soon step outside to offer her a few pieces of day-old bread before going inside the warm bakery with the usual statement of pity for the "poor disheveled girl". Most days, Louise ate her fill from the pity of a few neighbors. She never asked for anything from them, but always took what they offered. She didn't mind the shame; it was the only coin she had to pay them, and they accepted it as readily as a few coppers. It didn't hurt that her matted black hair and the mud on her face and clothes made them feel superior.

This morning was so cold that she couldn't sit out in the open as usual. She leaned against the outside of the baker's chimney, trying to feel any heat that might seep through the mortar. Whether any warmth did reach through, she was out of the wind. It was several hours before the day would warm up. She could then take her place at the foot of the gates, but she would miss her breakfast. It didn't matter. She had a feeling that something big was going to happen today, so a little hunger would only help her to stay sharp for whatever was coming.

Almost as soon as she moved to her spot, a coach rolled through the gates and stopped in front of the stables. She recognized the driver. He usually drove the mail coach on the route from Pallingham Castle to Downriver Town. However, he did not usually have three Capric monks riding on top of his coach on a cold, foggy morning. Everybody had heard the stories about heroes from Capric, and how they had secured the ten cities for King Frederick, who had created the most prosperous and peaceful kingdom the world had ever seen. She had never actually seen one. This was something bigger than she expected, and she had to get a closer look. As the monks climbed down the ladder on the side of the coach, she snuck to the opposite side and found a place to sit where she might overhear their conversation.

Once they were all down with their packs and staves, they exchanged a few words with the driver and then began walking toward the Briny Mug, the inn where she expected they would stop first. What she could not tell was what they were doing in Downriver Town. She had not been here long, but she knew that Caprics had not come here for many years. In fact, she hadn't heard of them traveling to most places in Pallingham in decades. Only town elders had stories about the monks of Capric, and often their stories were hazy memories from childhood.

She could hear the largest one speaking as they approached. "When he said he would put us on a coach, I didn't think he literally meant *on* it," he said, stretching and rubbing the small of his back.

"It didn't stop you from sleeping most of the way," said the smallest one. They all had their hoods up against the cold, so she couldn't see their faces.

"If you expected comfort, then perhaps you should have asked to take some of the treasury with us," said the third. "We could have hired our own ride, or maybe just asked for his personal carriage." The sarcasm was juvenile—*Amateur*, she thought. Louise couldn't tell whom they were talking about, but based on where she expected the mail coach had come from, they might be talking about Lord Evasius, which made this trio even stranger—the only traveling Caprics she had ever seen, coming from the last place she would have expected.

"You're in a foul mood," the largest one said.

"I'm sorry," said the third, "I'm tired from an uncomfortable ride, and I want to find our man and get back on the road." They passed Louise, and she followed them slowly to hear the rest of their conversation. It was obvious they were looking for somebody in Downriver Town, but she wanted to know who, and for what.

The smallest one was speaking again. He had a higher voice, making her assume he was younger as well. "Evasius told us to look for him in the inn. I think our best bet would be to go there and wait for him to arrive." So, they had come from the castle, and directly on Evasius' word!

"But how do we find out what we want to know?" the big one asked.

"I'll take care of that part," said the third. "You just look intimidating, so nobody interrupts. Even if he won't tell us, we'll figure out a way to find this King of the Caves." Louise didn't need to hear anymore. She knew who they were looking for, and she had to warn him. These were strange monks indeed, working with a ruler who had never been friendly with *any* religious order.

She sped up, but there was no way to beat them to the Briny Mug at this point, and it was most likely that Alden, the man they were looking for, would already be playing his flute by the fireplace there. Just before they reached the door, she fell to her knees and grabbed the robe of the sarcastic one. She pulled on the tassels sewn into the hem, pressing her face against them, and cried out loudly, "Please, good sirs, have pity on me. I'm a poor orphan who's had nothing to eat all day."

The monk stopped, and when he turned it pulled the robe from her hands, but she kept looking down. "What do you think we can do for you?" he asked.

"You must have some food, or money that you could spare," she said. "Surely you wouldn't leave your order without a little extra for the poor and weak to share." She hoped the loud scene would get Alden's attention and give him a clue that he should leave before they found him. "Please, before you go inside and listen to the music and eat your fill, please spare a bite for a poor, cursed orphan." This *was* almost more shame than she could bear, to beg so garishly.

"Certainly," the monk stuttered. Good, she had caught them by surprise. He reached into his friend's pack and handed her a piece of bread.

"Thank you, good brothers," she shouted. "Thank you. May God bless you for your generosity and sacrifice." She held the bread up toward heaven. "Bless you," she continued to say, until they stepped inside. People in the street were staring at her, but once the monks were inside, she looked in the window and saw Alden sitting in the corner with an empty breakfast plate and his wooden flute. The deaf old fool hadn't noticed—too many nights spent in loud taverns. Now the monks were talking to the innkeeper, and he still didn't see.

She tapped on the window, and he squinted at her through the wavy glass. He smiled and nodded slightly in recognition.

He wasn't getting it, so she pointed to the monks, then back to him. He shrugged his shoulders and put his flute back into his satchel as they walked toward him. It was too late for him to get away now. Something about this felt off. She had to figure out a way to get him away from them.

One of the local men opened the tavern door, and she slipped in behind him, keeping to the back wall and trying to stay out of the view of the monks. Alden was already talking to them, and looked directly at her when he shook his head at one of their questions. After a moment, he pointed toward the stairs that led up to the rooms of the inn. She immediately ducked into the kitchen, sneaked past the innkeeper, and ran up the back stairs. At the top, she opened a storage closet and pushed aside a panel in the back that revealed a hidden passage. Before she climbed inside, she grabbed a mallet from a toolbox, and felt the weight in her hands. It might be enough to knock one of them out from behind. If she could drop the big one, she and Alden could probably escape while the other two were still surprised. Satisfied with her choice of weapon, she slipped into the passage and moved silently down the dark, narrow hall until she came to a hidden doorway in the last room, Alden's room. At the end of the passage was a stairway that led down to a door that opened at the back alley. If she could get him away from the monks, they could escape that way.

There were voices on the other side of the wall, and if she stood on her toes, she could peer through a tiny crack in the wall. Alden stood in the far corner of the room. She thought he was keeping the monks' attention on himself so that she might be able to sneak in through the hidden door and attack if he was in danger. He glanced briefly at the crack in the wall and shook his head again. All right, not yet. She didn't know if she could wait long, but his interrogators seemed to be oblivious that he was signaling somebody else.

The monks spoke kindly enough, asking him to help them with a problem their order was having. They weren't giving any specifics, however, until the leader came out and asked directly. "We were told you might know the location of the King of the Caves, and we think he is the only one who can help us with our problem."

"Who told you that?" Alden asked innocently. "I'm just a musician here, and I clean up the rooms to earn a place to sleep."

"It really doesn't matter," said the monk. "We are on a mission that is important to the peace of all the ten cities, so if you know anything about this man, we would appreciate your help."

Alden nodded; it was time. "I might know something, if it's that important." Louise pulled the latch and the hidden door swung open silently. "But I still want to know who sent you. How do I know you're really Caprics and I can trust you?" Alden continued to talk while she snuck around the bed. She raised the mallet to hit the biggest monk on the back of the head when one of the floorboards creaked. Already committed to the attack, she screamed and swung, but he was turning around. The blow glanced off his upper arm instead.

"Ow!" he shouted, looking surprised, but he quickly raised his staff to counter her next swing. The other monks were surprised as well, and Alden stepped in to grapple with the leader while he was distracted. Once he understood the danger, he was as quick as his friend was to retaliate, and easily tossed the old man to the ground.

The larger monk caught the mallet on his staff and yanked it out of Louise's grip. When he stepped forward, she tried to retreat and fell backward on the bed. He leaned forward and grabbed her by the throat, while the leader kneeled on Alden's chest. "Don't tell them anything, Alden," she screamed, struggling to get free. While the man held her firmly, he was not trying to suffocate her or cause pain. He still had his hood up, and the shadows made his face look dark and ugly. Alden shushed her.

"We don't want to hurt you," the leader said. "We only want your help to find this bandit."

"Bandit," Louise laughed. "You don't even know who you're looking for."

"We know we're looking for a man whose spies are willing to ambush monks who are merely asking questions," he said. "It certainly lends credence to his reputation."

"You are ignorant fools sent by that despot, Evasius," she spat.

The monk grabbed Alden by the shoulder, raised him up, and pushed him into a chair. The big one picked her up by the collar and held her so that her feet barely scraped the ground. She tried to swing and get free of his grip, but his arms were like steel. With better light, she saw it wasn't just the shadows; he was ugly, with a thick, bony chin and narrow eyes.

"Watch him," the leader said to the smallest one, who had barely moved in the struggle. At the order, the young one raised the pointed end of his staff and held it against Alden's chest. "Then enlighten me," the leader said, turning to face her.

When she saw his face, she felt as if she had lost control of every muscle in her body, and she slumped forward in the big one's grip. She stared at the young monk's face as if she could see nothing else: the intensity of his gaze, the long thin nose with an old break, the dark brown hair that hung in wild waves to his jaw, the condescending tightness of his lips. In surprise, she couldn't stop herself from letting one word slip.

"You," she whispered.

Noeman woke late on the second morning after the attack. He was somewhat surprised that he had slept at all, but after caring for his injured and dying brothers the previous night and the next day, he had drifted off the moment he laid down. He had left his robes on, so he could rise immediately, but fortunately, no call had come for him in the night. It was either hopeful for the brothers lying in the dining hall, or it was too late for him to help them.

Birds sang in the large oak at the top of the hill as if it were any other day, as if the treasury buried under the tree's roots was not empty, and the compound not burned. From his cell, the permeating smell of smoke was the only hint that the birds were wrong. The entire compound would likely smell of smoke even after the damage was repaired, reminding them of how vulnerable they really were. Of course, Sage Marten had stopped the fighting before the monks had a chance to mount a defense. If he had rallied them to battle, they could have driven back the force Evasius had sent. The hill was naturally defensible, and the soldier's horses lost their advantage in the narrow alleys between the compound's buildings. Men on foot had greater maneuverability there, and the low roofs against the hillside allowed the monks to gain some height over the riders. They would have lost more men by fighting, certainly, but he couldn't think about what they had lost by surrendering. The treasure, their trust. The protection of God. The order. Everything might be lost.

Someone had left a small pitcher of goat's milk and a roll of bread on a tray outside his door. Beside it was a note instructing him to see the abbot when he had finished his meal. He broke the bread into small pieces and dipped it into the milk while he thought about what he would say to the abbot. The issue of surrender could wait until the next council meeting, which would obviously come sooner than planned to determine if they should remove Sage Marten from being abbot. What weighed more heavily on his mind now were the boys. Sending them was a major breach of the Rule, which Dean Humphrey, their combat trainer, had obviously forgotten in the excitement—he had never been a very capable student. The abbot couldn't have thought they had a chance against Evasius. If they had actually arrived at the castle, would he let them return? They would find out soon enough; the earliest they might come back would be this evening. But how long would the order wait before they were counted as lost, imprisoned, or killed? Confronting Sage Marten was the only way to know why he had sent them. However, after his actions, Noeman was uncertain if he could trust the answer.

Satisfied that he had thought of the best way to broach the subject, he left the empty breakfast tray at his door and walked across the training field to the abbot's dwelling. It was on the eastern side of the hilltop in a small block of four buildings close to the oak tree—the only buildings of dressed stone in the compound. The four buildings were essential symbols of the order—the Sage's apartment, with the treasury façade next door, followed by the Ward's rooms, and then the storehouse and armory.

There were no training exercises this morning, but groups of his brothers were still busy cleaning up the fire-damaged buildings. He realized that for the first time in his life, novitiates were not attending lessons in the rooms on the south face of the hill and the thought made him think of the three that were missing, out alone in the world with no protection. He was angry with himself for letting them go. As frustrated as they made him, he was still responsible for their safety and training. And he was as much to blame for anything that happened to them as the abbot was, since he had not challenged the order that was so blatantly against the Rule. He prayed under his breath for their safety before knocking on the abbot's door.

Inside, the abbot sat at his desk with piles of parchment in front of him. The candles had burned out without being replaced and the abbot stared at him with eyes that looked blind with fatigue. "It's good to see you, old friend," he said with a sigh. "I've been up all night writing letters, requesting aid from other orders. We will need help to rebuild quickly."

"I pray they are received well," Noeman said.

"As much as some of them disagree with us theologically, they still serve God, and none of them wants to see the treasure that built the ten cities in the hands of that snake, Evasius."

"I assume it's also in our favor that an attack on a monastic order is unprecedented," Noeman agreed. "If he risked attacking us, then none of them is safe."

"Quite right," the abbot nodded. "I will have to add that to these before they go out." Noeman did not respond, but waited for the abbot to bring up his reason for calling him. When the silence dragged on, the abbot sighed again, moved his letters to one side, and let the mask of congeniality fall. His face revealed an overwhelming weariness and concern. Noeman had never seen his friend look so old, or so distraught. His skin looked thin and brittle, like an onion skin, and his eyes were dry and red from exhaustion. "I must apologize for the other night," he finally said. "I did not wish to challenge you in front of your charges, or Humphrey."

"Forgive my impertinence," Noeman responded coldly, "but I believe the ones who deserve the apology are absent."

"Again, you show your wisdom, my friend." The abbot looked nervous. "I called you here to explain myself."

"I welcome it, although I doubt any explanation would excuse whatever harm might come to them."

"You're right to be angry," Sage Marten said. Noeman saw shame on his face. His light blue eyes darkened like storm clouds ready to drop a torrent of rain. So, Noeman thought, he knew that he had probably doomed them to torture at the castle. "Three days ago, a man came to see me. Actually, he was a famous prophet; for years, numerous abbots have confirmed his visions to be from God."

Noeman tried to tell if he was lying, but since all of them trained at uncovering deceit, it was that much easier for them to show the obvious signs of honesty. Even in the small details, the abbot gave no hint of deception, despite his nervousness. He was genuinely afraid. "What did this prophet tell you?"

"He had a vision. A vision of our order." The abbot paused as if the details were too horrible to tell. "He said he saw the great oak ablaze. The only way for that to happen would be if our order had fallen."

"If he was talking only about this attack, then he was obviously wrong," Noeman said. His voice had cracked slightly. "We can rebuild from this, especially if the boys can get the treasure back."

"It's about the boys," the abbot said quietly.

"I was going to ask how this explained you sending them away."

"He told me I had to," Sage Marten whimpered. "You know I would never want to hurt any of our boys, but he told me it was God's will. I had to send them away at the first opportunity. When the fires started, I thought I was too late, but when they returned, I saw a way I could follow his instructions. God was gracious enough to give us another chance."

"What was the vision, exactly?" Noeman asked.

"He said that he saw the Treasured Oak ablaze, raining ashes over our hill." The abbot's eyes drifted out of the window toward the oak. "I asked how this could be avoided. I wasn't certain he heard me, because he seemed to be in a trance, as if the vision were playing out before him again. But he finally responded. He said he heard a voice in the vision call out:

Those walking in darkness will see a great light.
Release the Deer, the Brute, even the Princely Son.
On those living in the land of shadow, a light will dawn.'

"After that, his vision ends. You can see now, why it had to be done."

Noeman considered the words for a moment. "If you start by thinking of young Tobin Hart, then I can see how Mr. Brock would be the brute. If there must be three in the group, then of course, Mr. Abramson might begin to look a little princelier."

"Precisely my conclusion," the abbot began. Relief washed over his face when Noeman found the same interpretation of the riddle.

"Did he offer any instructions other than sending them away?" Noeman asked. The abbot only shook his head. "So, it was your choice to send them to Pallingham." The pain of guilt was instantly on the abbot's face. "You could have taken this before the council and sent them to another order, or back to their homes—but you chose to send them to Evasius?" Noeman didn't try to hide his anger. Prophecies were often open to interpretation, or allowed some freedom in how you chose to obey, but you were still expected to conduct yourself in a godly manner. This was unacceptable, and might bring down God's wrath on the entire order for essentially sacrificing these young men. He couldn't stay here, or he might attack his mentor himself.

Tears streaked down the abbot's face. "I panicked. It happened so fast." Noeman stood and turned to leave. "Forgive me," Sage moaned, as Noeman opened the door.

"No," Noeman said, "God forgive you." Before closing the door, he looked at the leader of their order for a moment. The old man was barely sensible. Obviously, he was remorseful, but Noeman was too furious to give him any grace now. "I'm going to town. Somebody needs to tell the people there that we still stand. Send for me if they return," he said, and closed the door. He went back to his apartment to collect his things.

A walk to town would calm him down and give him the chance to focus on something other than the troubles that loomed so far above him. Service always helped him to think and see problems in perspective. It would do him good.

Kurian stared at the filthy beggar girl who had ambushed them from a secret passage.

"Do you know me?" he asked, surprised. The girl did not respond, and it was difficult to see her eyes through the dark, matted hair that hung down over them. "Let her sit on the bed, Rhys." Rhys dropped the girl onto the bed; she seemed to have lost all the fight that she had shown a moment before.

"How do you know me?" he asked again. The girl turned away, and he kneeled down to look into her face again. There were no women at the compound, and she couldn't be from Aposford, because the youngest person who lived there was nearly forty. She couldn't have been at Pallingham, because nobody could have arrived before them. Those were the only choices, so there was no way she could know him, but the shock of recognition on her face was real.

"It's just a trick," Rhys said, "there's no way she could know you."

"He's right," the girl said, "I don't know you. But the King told me to expect Capric monks to come asking about him, and I only just remembered."

"No," Kurian said, "I saw it on your face—you recognized me."

"I forgot, and I just remembered when you looked at me," she said, turning her face away again.

The old man—Alden, if he had heard right—sat on the chair looking stunned at the sudden change of circumstances. Tobin still held the end of his staff pointed at the man's chest, but Kurian could see he was tempted to lower his guard. "You can lower your staff, Tobin. I think we can handle them for now." Kurian picked up another chair and set it down where he could see Alden and the girl. "Can we have a civilized conversation now?"

"Nothing civilized comes from Pallingham Castle," the girl said. Kurian had never seen anybody look so disgusted to say the name of a place.

"What makes you think we came from there?"

"You came on the mail coach, and I heard you talking about Lord Evasius," she said.

"Then you are not without some wits, spy, even if you are hasty to reach conclusions," he replied. It was obvious now that she was the girl who had stopped them at the door, trying to overhear their conversation and delay them so that Alden could escape. Still, she was only a beggar; she shouldn't be too hard to outsmart. "We are, in truth, on a mission from our abbot. Pallingham was merely our first stop, and Lord Evasius was willing to provide a small measure of assistance."

"Please forgive my young friend," Alden said. "She sometimes lets her passions get the better of her."

If Alden would be civil, he would focus his attention there. "No harm was done. All is forgiven," said Kurian. At least he was clean; the girl looked as if she had slept in a pigsty. Alden, by comparison, looked like a modestly successful merchant, dressed in a colorful and well-fitting coat over a slim form. The close-cropped silver hair that ringed his head reminded Kurian of the monk who supervised the fields where the order grew their food. This man could surprise you with his wisdom, as well as his vigor. "However," Kurian continued their negotiation, "if you do know anything about the King of the Caves, it would help us to prevent all of Pallingham from falling to chaos."

"Don't trust them, Alden."

Kurian looked at the girl. "You've already done well to introduce your friend. May I ask your name?"

"Pardon me," said Alden, "this young lady is Louise Prescott."

"Delighted," Rhys muttered. Kurian shot him a look that told him he wasn't being helpful.

"Forgive my friend, Rhys," Kurian said. "He sometimes suffers from the same malady of passions." Alden laughed. Perhaps the scuffle had convinced him of who they were because it looked as if he were lowering his guard. "Tobin, however, is steadier in temperament than Rhys is strong. I am Kurian and I often fall somewhere between the two."

"Can I ask what this mission is about?"

"We would prefer to keep that to ourselves, Alden." Kurian said.

"I need to know if your mission is as important as you say before I reveal anything."

"You've already confirmed that you know something about the King of the Caves," Kurian challenged, "and you are obviously willing to protect him. Is there some other way I can convince you to help us?"

"That's hard to say. If you know I'm willing to protect him, you should guess that I won't tell you anything if I think you're a threat."

"You think three monks would be a threat to a dangerous bandit?" Kurian asked and laughed.

"That answer tells me that you might be. The truth is he is no bandit."

"He robs guarded supply carriages, doesn't he?" Rhys asked.

"Stop," Louise said. "Alden, you don't have to tell them anything." She pushed her hair away from her face and looked directly at Kurian for the first time. She was older than he first thought, perhaps as old as twenty. Her eyes made him shudder. They were bright and clear, the green-gray color of foam on ocean waves, and within them, he saw the same beauty and danger he had seen as they rode past the sea that morning. This young woman was unpredictable and could draw men to their doom if she chose. Most chilling was the sense that they would love her while she did it.

"I won't know until I hear them out," Alden said.

"You won't have to," she said. "I will take them to the King."

"No." Alden shook his head. "I won't allow that."

Louise held up her hand, her face calm, but sad. "The King told me that Capric monks would come and ask about him. Then he told me that I must bring them to him."

"It's too dangerous," Alden said. He looked as if he might jump out of his chair.

"Yet that was his order." Her tone silenced him. "You know him, and you trust him more than anybody, except maybe Xander. He must have a reason for this." Alden studied the floor.

Kurian watched the exchange with wonder. Both of them were determined to protect the bandit and each other, if they could. He had read books about devoted men serving their ruler, but he had never seen a leader inspire such dedication, and certainly not to one so notorious. Either Evasius was not being truthful about the King being a bandit, or the man was even more dangerous than he had said. Images of men returning to the castle after the raids entered his mind, muttering to themselves like lunatics or struck dumb with horror. The King of the Caves was no ordinary bandit, whatever he was, but they would at least have a guide to show them where he was hiding, and that got them closer to the treasure. Of course, it would also mean they would have to be more watchful on their journey. This might all be a ruse to lure them away from the King and into a trap. Why wasn't there ever time to consult with Tobin with these choices, he wondered.

After a few moments, Alden looked at Louise again. "Can I come with you?" he asked.

"He didn't say that it had to be alone," she replied, "but you have important work here."

"It will still be here when I get back. Part of my work is to protect you."

"We can't take both of you," Kurian said.

"And I can't risk sending her alone with you," Alden said, standing up from his chair. Rhys stood up too, and Tobin surprised Kurian by shifting his stance to prepare for a fight.

Kurian remained seated, but held out his hands to stop everyone. "Hold on," he said softly. He waited until Alden and Rhys sat back down before he continued. "Alden, we have all taken oaths, and I will promise you that no harm will come to her from our hands."

"As I said before, I have no way of knowing you are who you claim," Alden responded. "It seems unlikely considering that no Caprics have been to Downriver Town in recent memory."

"It's all right," Louise said. "They are Caprics. It's as he told me." Alden only looked at her, clearly trying to think of a way to persuade her not to go. "Alden, you're thinking about it all wrong—I'm not going with them, they're coming with me." She smiled at him playfully, but the older man was not willing to joke about the circumstances. "They'd be lost without me."

Kurian thought this felt too easy. Yes, the King should be expecting Caprics to come asking about his location; he had stolen the treasure they had kept for centuries. However, he couldn't figure out why the man would tell his followers to bring back the monks to meet him. Kurian rubbed his chin, feeling the few small hairs growing on his otherwise smooth skin. Tobin looked just as confused, and shrugged when Kurian met his gaze. The girl was being truthful, as far as he could tell, but Evasius had quickly taught him to be wary of his judgment when things seemed too easy.

"Why would you be willing to take us?" he asked. "Why would the King of the Caves want to meet with us?"

"I don't know," Louise said, looking at him with her dangerous eyes again. He could see that she didn't trust him. She might be hiding something, but it was difficult to tell. "He told me that three Caprics would arrive asking where to find him, that I should take them to him, and that they would be important to his plans."

"Can you guess what he intends for us?" Tobin finally spoke.

"He won't harm you, if that's what you're asking," she said.

"If anything, he's particular about hospitality," Alden said with a smirk. "Even toward enemies."

Kurian thought that might also describe Evasius after their unusual dinner. "How many men typically camp with him?" he asked.

"Actually," Louise said, "he spends a lot of time alone. Yes, we have a camp with several dozen men," her eyes darted to Alden, who seemed displeased with her giving so much information, "but the King often goes off by himself, sometimes for long stretches." Her face looked both puzzled and filled with admiration. "He always knows exactly what to do when he returns."

"Why can't you just tell us where to find him?" Rhys asked. Kurian heard the frustration in his voice; he did not want to take her with them.

She looked at him as if she were answering a pestering child. "Right, just tell you where he is and send you on your way. That would solve everything. He lives in the Crags of the Wild Goats. You're welcome to go look for him yourself."

"See," Rhys said to Kurian, "all we had to do was ask."

Tobin laughed now. "We're welcome to look if we don't mind wandering through the most confusing maze of ridges and valleys on the continent. There are a thousand canyons or caves perfect for staging an ambush and wild animals roam the entire country—and who knows what else. If we aren't attacked by man or beast, we would most likely lose our way and die of thirst." Rhys' face fell at the description, and Louise gave him a big smile.

That's a useless lead, Kurian thought. Apparently, they were left once more without a real choice. If they wanted to find the treasure and return it to the order's protection, they would have to follow this girl out into the wilderness. She was no threat by herself——if she really would take them to the King of the Caves—but the men at the camp would be. Of course, the Crags of the Wild Goats were far to the north. They ranged along the top of the Northland cliffs, a sheer wall of granite that ran from the ocean in the west to the eastern border of the ten cities of Pallingham. It was notorious for being impassable. If they followed the riverbed on foot, they would be in Aposford in about three days at a normal pace, but it would be another twelve days beyond that to reach the foot of the cliffs and what had been the head of the river Apos. Of course, that would put them almost at the center of the cliff face with no way to reach the top. They would have to go around, either by walking into the Northlands by the eastern end of the plain, or by sailing around the last bit of the cliff that jutted out into a large bay to the west. Either direction would add almost a week to their journey before they worked around the Northland cliffs and could reach the Crags of the Wild Goats. There was no telling how much farther it would be to the King's hiding place. The journey would give him plenty of time to consult with Tobin on the best strategy to reclaim the treasure, but offered no other advantages.

Whichever direction they chose, Aposford was not the most direct route, which worked in their favor. They wanted to avoid their compound in case the abbot decided to punish them for their failure, or even reassign the task to full brothers. This was their best chance at proving their worth to the abbot and the rest of the order, as well as keeping the treasure from Evasius. Going around the compound only helped them to move forward. They would, however, need more supplies, and the few coins they had would not buy enough for such a journey.

"Following Miss Prescott seems to be our best chance," he said. Tobin nodded, but Rhys wrinkled his nose at Kurian's choice. "Alden, if you want to help your friend, we could use some help with provisions."

"That I can do," the old musician said. "It will take me some time to gather enough for all of you, but I will make arrangements with the innkeeper for you to have a room tonight." He stood up and closed the secret door through which Louise had come, and walked out of the bedroom door and down the hall. Kurian looked at Louise one more time before he followed Alden into the hall. He could not sense any deception in her offer to lead them to the King, but he still knew that she had recognized him at their first meeting. How, he could not know, but hiding it was enough of a deception to prevent him from trusting her.

CHAPTER FIVE

Trouble in Downriver Town

Kurian found Alden downstairs, talking to the innkeeper. He didn't want to give the old musician too much freedom, since he had proved to be a spy for the King of the Caves, and there was no way to know the dangers posed by anybody in his trust. The innkeeper was a short, slight man, barely bigger than Tobin, who took notes in his ledger as Alden rattled off a list of supplies. Apparently, the trip was frequent enough that he knew exactly what they needed to make it to their camp in the north.

There were few patrons in the tavern on the ground floor of the Briny Mug. Of course, it was only late morning, and he expected that dockworkers wouldn't arrive for a meal until later in the afternoon. There were still wisps of fog outside, which made the room feel cool and damp, even with the large fire in the back wall where they had first found Alden. He could imagine it as a busy, noisy place to eat with friends, much like the dining hall at their compound. There were many pleasant memories of eating in the hall with his troop. Unlike other orders, they could speak during meals, and their discussions frequently became loud and boisterous, either from Tobin arguing the deeper points of their lessons with the other boys, or from Rhys joking and teasing them. One day, shortly after Tobin had arrived, Noeman reprimanded them for being too loud when Earl had challenged Rhys to see who could eat the most radishes. Both of them were in tears before Dean Goodman stopped the contest. They never got to see who won, but Kurian had always thought Earl, though smaller, would have pulled off a victory.

The memory made him miss home. That was how he thought of the compound. It was home, not Aposford, where his father lived. Even though it was challenging, and childlike moments were rare, he had few complaints about daily life with the order. Still, it gnawed at him that it was only a shadow of its former glory. Then the attack happened and his whole world was uprooted. The treasure was missing, and he didn't know if he could trust the abbot if they were somehow able to return it. If they were successful, the ordeal might reinvigorate the order—but there seemed such a small chance for success.

A murmuring broke through his thoughts. He had sat down at a long table at the foot of the stairs with his back to the wall.

A man at the opposite end kept babbling. "The king, the king," he muttered to himself in a singsong way. Kurian had thought he was asleep on the table with a mug of ale by his head, but his eyes were open, and his face was turned toward him. His speech was slurred and hard to understand at first, but it slowly became clearer. "Into the wild to see the king, following that pretty thing." The man suddenly sat up, making Kurian jump. He stared right at him, but looked through him. "His spies, his spies! They see you. They watch you. Be quick like a deer, strong like an ox, smart like a son with golden socks." The man shrieked in laughter after his rhyme.

"Hush, now," Alden said firmly, stepping up from behind. "You cannot speak to this one." He touched the man on the forehead, and he promptly sank back down to lay his head on the table again, closed his eyes, and looked as if he had never stirred. Alden motioned for Kurian to follow him upstairs.

"What was that?" The encounter had rattled him.

Alden said, "He's harmless. Just tries to spook visitors sometimes. He won't do it again."

"But how did he know we were going to find the king?"

"Don't worry about that. He probably saw us go upstairs together, and he knows my true loyalties," Alden explained.

"Was that some sort of magic you performed on him?"

Alden laughed. "Not quite magic, just a firm hand. I've known old Henry there for a long time. Almost had him recruited to our cause when soldiers picked him up for questioning. Their interviews can sometimes be...aggressive, but something else happened to Henry. When he came back, he wasn't himself; it was as if something else had taken over." Kurian looked back at the drunken man asleep on the table, but he hadn't stirred. "Nothing seems to make him better, so we try to keep him comfortable."

"Is he possessed?" Kurian had read about demons possessing people in his studies. He assumed it might still happen.

"Possessed, cursed, mad," Alden shrugged his shoulders, "whatever it is, it's beyond my skill to heal."

Could Evasius have really created that shell of a man? He acted like one of the *gyrovagues*. One had stumbled into the compound in the spring. He moved like a walking corpse, wearing only an old sack and grinning a toothless, manic smile. He also muttered like this Henry, and it had frightened the novitiates. Kurian couldn't help but feeling as if he was being drawn between two warring powers much larger than himself—and he didn't think he wanted to align himself with either.

"I've got your provisions arranged," Alden said, returning to their mission. "The King will cover the expenses, including a bed for the night and a pony for your food. Shall we see how the others are getting along?"

Kurian only nodded, and followed him back to the room. "You've got two weeks of provisions ready," Alden said as he entered.

"Thank you, but will that be enough?" Kurian asked.

"Certainly," Alden replied. "That will get you to Dury with a day to spare, and with the ways we know, the King's camp is a few hours from there."

"That's impossible," Tobin said, "unless you can fly over the Northland cliffs."

"We know a shortcut."

If Alden was telling the truth, then Kurian's original guess about the length of their journey was too long. They might be able to complete their task rather quickly. Then he remembered that traveling north to Smithfield and then the cliffs at Dury would take them past Capric Hill along the riverbed. "We can't go that way," he said.

"It's either that or take a more dangerous route that's thrice the length," Louise said with a smirk.

"She's right," said Tobin, speaking up again. Kurian knew he could draw a map of Pallingham, and many other realms, from memory. "If they know a way up the cliffs, it's the fastest and easiest path. Otherwise, we head to Whalesand and have to sail around Syrene Bay or head east into the Northlands through Aven, where there have always been rumors of giants."

"I'd rather not pass the compound until we've finished our task," Kurian told them.

"The river curves more eastward a bit before reaching Aposford," Tobin said, but he gave Kurian an understanding look. "If we leave the riverbed at Smithfield, we should be able to head north and find it again near the ruins of Fin. It won't take us much out of the way, but far enough that we could pass unnoticed between the compound and Pallingham Castle."

"You sure you don't want to see giants?" Rhys teased. Kurian, however, was feeling relieved that he finally had a chance to consult Tobin on something that felt important.

"I think that's as good a plan as we can get," he said.

Louise nodded her assent, and Alden rubbed his hands together. "That's settled," he said. "Now, I suggest you lot rest up before your long journey. And perhaps bathe; it may be your last chance for a while."

Captain Fallon approached the stables of the Briny Mug around midday. He had left Pallingham Castle shortly after the monks, giving them just enough time to arrive and find their target, but not enough to move on. From what Lord Evasius had told him, it would be easy to find and follow the three inexperienced monks as they looked for the man who knew the whereabouts of the King of the Caves. He hoped to listen in on their conversation to find out the location of the bandit and lead the castle's garrison there to capture him in whatever hole he had dug into. If he missed that opportunity, he could ask the monks directly and send them back home.

He felt woozy as he dismounted and knew that it was the witch back at Pallingham, checking in on him. As he had approached Downriver Town, he sometimes felt her focusing her magic on him, learning what information she could through the connection they had forged in his bed. Most of the time, it felt like a mild anxiety, as if he had forgotten something and was trying to remember it, so the sudden force of her searching caught him off guard.

"Easy," he said, though he didn't know if she could hear him. "I've only just gotten here."

He found the inn's tavern crowded, and overheard several people talking to each other about the exciting news of the day. People had seen three Caprics heading toward the inn. However, they had not shown themselves again since late morning. As he pushed through the crowd, he overheard several speculations about their business in town. While some patrons doubted the rumor, it seemed everyone who had heard about them had come to see for themselves.

A man carrying three drinks turned around and bumped into him, splashing him with ale and moving on with an absentminded apology. Fallon was a little unnerved at the way people ignored him without his uniform, but he understood the need for him to go unnoticed on this delicate task. If the man that the monks were questioning saw one of Evasius' soldiers, he might not talk to them at all. Being invisible was an unfortunate necessity for this mission. Usually, in a room full of people, everyone kept one eye on him and he could pass through the crowd without being touched, as if some force went before him to clear a path. It was the authority he carried from Lord Evasius, he knew, and he missed it in his disguise. Being crowded together with all these people made him appreciate the respect his position afforded even more. After all, he had earned that position through the sacrifice of dedication.

Dedication was the only gift his father had given him, and with his new promotion, he knew he had become the man his father taught him to be. He had fulfilled every order, knowing that even when his superiors seemed misguided, they were asking only that he put his country first. Because of his loyalty, he had risen quickly in the ranks and discovered that he was a skilled leader, inspiring his men to follow his example—place duty above everything. Through this, he had lifted himself from a person nobody noticed—the son of a crippled, booze-soaked veteran—to a man in the personal confidence of the Lord of Pallingham.

He found the slight innkeeper and requested a room for the night before casually asking what was happening that had the whole town at their door. "Caprics," said the owner, "came in this morning and got everybody stirred up." Before Fallon could reply, the man retreated into the kitchen.

Fallon waited in the front room, listening to the rumors about the Caprics and their reason for coming to Downriver Town. Several people had creative ideas about plots against Evasius, or the return of the line of Fin, and even about the end of the world. The more reasonable members of the crowd mocked them or offered less spectacular ideas. One popular joke was that the city's mayor wanted them to pray for his soul. The crowd laughed at that one, and it was repeated often with some new twist about the mayor's vices. The older patrons frequently used the figures of speech that Fallon had banned from the barracks because he found them disloyal to Lord Evasius. There were several variations of, "Oh, bless me! I didn't think to see Caprics again until the Apos flowed and the king returned," but he kept silent each time.

Almost hourly, Fallon would get the disorienting feeling of the witch breaking into his mind and felt for a moment as if he were drunk. It was very late, and the fire had died down to a soft glow when the last of the crowd left the inn, grumbling about the Caprics' failure to appear. Fallon waited a while longer to be sure no guests came down for a late meal, and then retired to his own room for the night.

He slept fitfully, having dreams, both arousing and terrifying, of his night with the witch. He suspected that she was looking in on him with each one. After waking from one vivid example, he thought for a moment that it was unnecessary for Lord Evasius to use her magic on him with such persistence, but then he remembered the importance of the mission and fell back into restless slumber. Even with the poor sleep, he arose before dawn and returned to the front room to watch for the Caprics to leave the inn.

One of the young monks soon came downstairs and spoke with the innkeeper, requesting that they receive breakfast in their room. He looked like many of the recruits Fallon had trained—seventeen or eighteen, with unruly brown hair. Speaking to one of them alone might be the easiest way to find out whether they had succeeded, and he was about to stop the boy from heading back upstairs when another one came down the narrow stairwell. If he were patient, perhaps he wouldn't have to reveal himself. They might speak openly, thinking they were safe in the quiet tavern. He was surprised by how young they both were. Either his attack on their compound a few nights before was more devastating to the order than he realized, or they were weaker than he originally thought, to have sent children to bargain with Lord Evasius. Their wizened little abbot might have had the wit to converse successfully with the Lord of Pallingham but lacked the boldness to make a true opponent. What could these boys offer but mild amusement? It was no wonder that Evasius had easily turned them into his errand boys.

"I think it would be prudent to bring a few more days of rations if we can spare the money," said the new one, who was smaller and blond—he reminded Fallon of Evasius' scribes. "Even with a guide, I fear losing our way in the crags." *Definitely a scribe*, he thought—*scrawny and fearful*. Captain Fallon focused on his plate, straining to hear their hushed conversation. Apparently, they hadn't gathered the information, but the informant was willing to take them to the criminal's location.

"We don't have much," said the recruit. "We were supposed to return to the compound directly from Pallingham."

"I suppose I don't trust them entirely, and I don't want to be lost in the wilderness without any food," the scribe said. Fallon didn't know who else was part of "they", other than the suspected spy, but he was sure he understood the situation. The young monks had never left the safety of their compound and now, out in the wide world they had no idea whom they could trust. Yet they had shown some trust in Lord Evasius, enough to agree to his terms. A plan formed in his mind: he would offer a solution to their dilemma as an emissary of Evasius, ready to see their mission successful and take news back to him.

"I don't trust them either," the recruit began.

"Friends," Captain Fallon interrupted. "I believe I could help, if I may." They both turned to face him, and he saw them stiffen. Fallon raised one hand to calm them. "Forgive me for not revealing myself earlier; I am Captain Fallon, head of Lord Evasius' personal guard. I came from Pallingham to see if your mission was successful. Lord Evasius eagerly awaits news, and I was asked to bring it to him."

"I am Kurian," the recruit said, "and no, we have not been entirely successful."

"I overheard you preparing for a journey," said Fallon. "I hope you understand that our Lord didn't intend for you to take such a perilous road yourselves."

"We did," Kurian said. "However, the man you sent us to question won't tell us where to find the King of the Caves. He is apparently well hidden, and a guide must show us the way."

Fallon nodded thoughtfully. "Are you certain he could not be convinced?"

"I'm sorry, Captain, but I don't believe it is a matter of convincing. The man claims that the way can only be shown, not told."

"That's a problem," Fallon said. "Lord Evasius will not be happy."

"I think that if we follow our guide we will eventually find the man."

"Lord Evasius didn't expect you to take on the danger of the task yourself," Fallon said smiling. "Who knows how many vagrants the cur has in hiding with him?"

The monk looked at him with concern. "I've come to question Lord Evasius' methods and expectations since our meeting," he said. Fallon detected a bitter tone in his voice. "There was a man in here yesterday who had clearly lost his mind, apparently from the interrogation of Pallingham's soldiers. As servants of God, we find this report troubling."

"The man was probably suspected of colluding with that madman in the caves," Fallon replied with calm. "My men have returned from his attacks with results as severe. Most don't return. If the man you saw was innocent, then he was an unfortunate casualty of an already bloody conflict. I understand your concern, but I hope this has not made you reconsider your agreement with Lord Evasius. Surely as men of God, you are true to your word."

Kurian nodded. "We are. We will pursue the lost treasure and fulfill our order's vows. However, as we told your master, we might not have the authority to fulfill his wishes to secure the treasure at Pallingham."

"Unacceptable. If you won't keep the agreement, I must ask you and your guide to come with me."

"If we do that, the treasure may be lost to all of us," Kurian argued.

"Then we have another problem," Fallon said, slowly pulling a narrow dagger from beneath his tunic.

"I understand," Kurian replied, glancing at the dagger but returning his gaze to Fallon's eyes.

Fallon saw fear there, but much less than he had anticipated. He may have turned to using a threat too soon. It was too late to retract it. "You must find a way to get the location of the hideout from your guide or I bring you all in."

"I believe the man when he says we cannot find the way alone," Kurian said, then looked briefly at his silent friend. "Though we may be able to offer another solution." Like an overconfident fool, Fallon had followed the monk's gaze to his friend and noticed too late that Kurian had shifted his feet to attack. As a soldier, he was fast, but the young monk darted in so quickly that he could barely react. He started to swing the dagger, but the boy was already close in against his body and had grabbed his wrist.

He had thought they were only playing at combat training, since they had barely offered any resistance a few nights before. Obviously, the monks had trained more thoroughly than he thought they would have in their sheltered compound. With incredible speed, the monk jabbed him in the throat, causing him to choke and grab for his neck involuntarily. Before he could recover his senses, he was on his knees with the hand holding the dagger twisted behind his back in great pain. He knew that he was stronger than these boys, but he was held firm in a grip that he knew could break his arm.

As he was about to lunge backward to slam his head into the monk, the scribe hit him in the side of the head with an elbow, dazzling his vision. When he dropped the blade, Kurian threw him forward where he fell into a tangle of chairs.

The monks' feet thudded up the stairs and he heard Kurian yell, "Rhys!" as they reached the top. Fallon pulled himself to his feet and shook his head. They had caught him by surprise, but now that he knew their strength he would not underestimate them again. They were still boys, but he was a combat veteran. The untested young monks would fight based on training exercises and might panic when faced with a true opponent. In a moment, he was steady on his feet and vaulted up the stairs. He heard raised voices further down the corridor, and stopped for a moment at his own room, grabbing his sword from beside the bed before continuing his pursuit.

"We must go now!" he heard from an open door as he pulled his blade from its scabbard. In the narrow passage, they would have to fight him one at a time. The scribe peeked out of the doorway as he was nearing it, and called out to the others, "He's coming!"

Fallon strode the rest of the way to the door, holding his sword ready. Inside the room, he saw Kurian standing ready next to an older man. A young woman, about the age of the monks was by the bed. Standing beside her was the third monk, as large in stature as Fallon and holding one of their staves ready to defend the group. The younger one leapt from beside the door and threw some dirt or sand in his face. It burned and grated his eyes and he punched at the boy with the pommel of his sword as his vision blurred.

His blow landed, and he lifted his sword to swing down on him, but the larger monk stepped forward and parried with his staff. The burning in his eyes grew unbearable and Fallon clawed at them with his free hand, falling to his knees again. All he could see was white light and dim shadows of shapes. He felt another painful blow to the back of his head and all sense disappeared.

Kurian's blood thudded in his ears. He had reacted solely on instinct when Captain Fallon pulled the dagger on them. He didn't know that he could move that swiftly during a real fight. It felt as if his body moved before he thought about it. Tobin had held back again when Kurian attacked, but his clear mind had been there when he needed it, setting up an ambush and throwing the powder from the vial around his neck into the soldier's eyes. If their trainer had been right, and Tobin had made a good throw, he would be blind for a couple of days.

"We have to go," Kurian grunted.

"What happened?" Alden asked, looking concerned.

"We just assaulted the head of Evasius' personal guard," Kurian said.

Louise laughed. "You make friends everywhere, don't you?"

"Well, when somebody pulls out a knife to shake hands, a kick to the head sounds reasonable," Kurian responded. "*Now do you believe we're not working with Evasius?*" She smiled and nodded. He turned to Alden. "What's the fastest way out of here?"

"Your supplies should be ready soon," Alden said, rubbing the smooth patch on top of his head. "But what do we do with him? He won't stay unconscious for long."

"He shouldn't be too much of a threat," said Tobin. "The powder I threw in his face should blind him for a couple days."

"He's out," Rhys said, lifting up the captain's head and letting it clunk back onto the floorboards. "I say we leg it."

"I agree," Alden added, "however I think it would be wise to exit through the rear passage Louise used yesterday. You don't know if there are other guards waiting outside for you." He picked up a small pack and started filling it with personal items scattered around the room. "I will ride ahead and tell the King you are coming. He'll want to know Evasius' newest plot to find him, and he may be able to send you some help."

"Be safe," Louise said.

"I believe your road will be much more perilous than mine," Alden said. "Do not fear. If the King truly gave you this task, then you are ready to see it through. I only wish I could offer you more guidance." He embraced her and then grabbed Kurian by the shoulder. "I will not forget—you promised her safety." With that, he rushed out of the room with the bag slung over his shoulder.

Tobin and Kurian retrieved their bags and weapons from the next room, where the two of them had slept. When they returned, Louise reached behind the bed. They heard the soft click of a latch and the hidden door swung silently open, showing them a dark corridor. She led them inside, where they followed it toward the back of the inn to a set of descending stairs. At the bottom, she opened a door and looked out into the alley. "It looks clear," she said, and they all filed out, making their way to the stables on the corner. The innkeeper was putting the last pack on a pony when they entered from the side door.

"Alden told me you'd be sneaking off in a hurry," he said, clearly annoyed. "Nothing better be broken from your scuffle." He wagged a finger at Kurian and Tobin, and then turned back to securing the load, muttering about being caught up in so much trouble. When he finished, he handed the reins to Kurian. "Don't you work Greta too hard," he scolded, "Greta's a stubborn one, and if you're not kind she'll bolt with all your goods."

"Thank you," was all Kurian could say. The innkeeper scoffed and went back inside. Kurian paused and looked at his friends, suddenly reluctant to take the first step of the long journey to find the King of the Caves. In two days he had already made so many mistakes that he wondered whether the abbot wasn't right about his ability to become a full brother. He was overwhelmed with the feeling that their task was impossible. Planting his staff firmly, as if to pin down his fleeting courage, he finally spoke to the others, "I suppose we'd better hurry."

Tobin insisted that they pray before setting out, and even Louise consented. Kurian only stared at his feet until it was over.

Following Louise, they stepped out into the alleyway again, turning away from the main street. She wound through Downriver Town using alleys and side streets as much as possible, but always heading east and north. Kurian listened for pursuit, but heard only the sounds of the waking city; a rooster crowed late and men called to each other from the docks to the south, but they encountered no people as they hurried down the alleys between the tall, cramped buildings. As the excitement of his earlier fight wore off, he shivered in the cool autumn air. Louise eventually turned left onto a wide street. A few people gawked at them as they passed, having never seen Capric monks. Passing a guard asleep at his post, they hurried through the north gate and disappeared into the gloom of the plain.

CHAPTER SIX

A Dark Fate

Captain Fallon woke to the surly little innkeeper slapping his face. "Wake up, you drunk. This isn't your room, and I don't like weapons in my inn." He knew that he was lying face down on the floor, but everything was white—no shapes, shadows, or colors came to his eyes.

His hand shot out and grabbed the man's tunic, then he pulled him down until he could feel his breath on his face and stared at him with blind eyes. "Call the guard," he growled. He felt the man begin to tremble.

"I will," he whined.

"I am Captain Fallon, head of Lord Evasius' personal guard, and the monks who were staying here attacked me. If you don't do all you can to aid me in capturing these fugitives, you may take their place at the gallows."

"Yes, yes sir," the innkeeper stuttered. Fallon suddenly smelled the sour tinge of urine and he knew he had made his point.

Pushing himself upright made the back of his head ache, and made him feel nauseous. "Wait. How long have I laid here?"

"Four hours, I suppose," said the innkeeper. "Those monks left early this morning, when I was cleaning out the stables. Then I came inside to start cooking for lunch, and eventually made it up here to tidy their rooms for new guests and found you on the floor with your sword. Sorry for the rude waking, but normally men sprawled on the floor is drunk round here, and you isn't wearing a uniform."

"Those monks did something to me, and I can't see." Fallon said. "You need to lead me downstairs, and then alert the nearest guards you find that their Captain requires them to muster at your tavern in a quarter hour. Tell them to bring as many as they can gather."

The innkeeper grabbed him by the hand and helped him to his feet. He was dizzy at first, but quickly regained his balance. This was not the first time he'd taken a blow to the head in combat. Whatever poison the monks had thrown in his face must be worsening the effects of their attack. He told the man to grab his sword and scabbard, and they carefully made their way down the narrow stairs.

Fallon rubbed his eyes, and then his head while he waited for the innkeeper at one of the tables. The man had been smart enough to hurry his customers out before going to find the guard, so Fallon was alone. The dizziness and weariness might be from the blow or his blindness—maybe even from the witch checking on him. Evasius was going to be furious at his failure, and he knew Mouna would have been trying to sense him during the time he was unconscious. Whether she could do that, he didn't know. Suddenly, with the thoughts of her, he was overwhelmed with desire for her. He felt compelled to return to Pallingham Castle to lie with her, to feel her scarred flesh against his own again. A shudder ran through his body. Was this some sort of effect from the tie they had formed, or was this her way of drawing him, calling him back on his lord's orders?

He could not return to the castle immediately. Returning empty handed would be humiliating enough. Perhaps beginning the search for these rogue pawns would do something to redeem him. They could not oppose his master. And even though his blindness prevented him from pursuing them personally, he had the power to get men on their trail. He prayed the spell would wear off and he could be there for their capture. He rubbed his eyes again, and thought that he might be seeing a shadow in his white-blind vision when he turned his head back toward the stairs.

The tavern door opened, and he heard several men enter the room. "I've brought them," the innkeeper said. "Should I bring anything to drink or eat?"

Fallon shook his head. "Who is highest ranking, and how many are you?" he asked the men.

"Captain Fallon, sir, it's Lieutenant Wilson," a clear voice spoke. "Five men are with me, and several more are on the way. Are you all right, sir?"

"I'm not your concern, Lieutenant," Fallon smiled. "Is old Griggs on duty? If not, get him. He's the best tracker I know."

Kurian and the others stopped a mile beyond the gates. The road dissolved into a thick fog only a few yards ahead, so they left it and headed east, climbing in and out of the estuaries of the old river delta. Pursuit might not be likely yet, but they didn't want to offer an easy trail for the soldiers to follow. One rut proved deep enough to hide them from ground level unless someone stood directly on the bank, and they followed it as it wound northeast toward the avenue of the dry riverbed. Even though they were essentially invisible, they did not slow down, and kept a quick pace until the heat of the day tired them and the fear of pursuit waned.

They rested only briefly, eating a light meal and allowing the pony to graze before they continued walking throughout the day. The soft, dusty floor of the riverbed made walking harder, slowing them down, and taxing their endurance in the morning, so they left the riverbed to cover more ground on their second march. The fog lifted in the afternoon, but there was nothing to see on the empty plain. Soft grass stretched out before them, broken here and there by trenches dug out by the river long before. No farms or homesteads remained this far out of town, and there were no resources to draw people to settle in the flat green sea of the plains. They had travelled longer and faster than they had planned, and their feet slowed with exhaustion as the light slowly faded. They climbed back into the deep estuary they had followed that morning to rest for the night. A cold meal of dried meat and fruit served as their dinner, since they did not want to risk a fire if Lord Evasius' soldiers were looking for them. The night was cold, and the second day was much like the first: walking long hours over the plains, following their estuary until it merged with the main bed of the Apos.

As evening neared, they approached the village of Smithfield. Small cottages with fallen roofs stood beside abandoned fields and broken animal pens. Nothing stirred as they stepped onto a narrow lane that led to the small cluster of houses that made up the village ahead. The riverbed on their left bent closer to the road as it neared the town, and then turned sharply east after passing the village. A well stood at the center of town. Beside it towered a large oak tree, its leaves fallen and scattered early before the coming winter, or else already dead. Its roots had broken through the stones of the well, trying to find water. No birds nested in its dry, empty branches, blackened in the failing light from dark moss and lichen. Kurian looked at the tree and the rotting buildings and thought that Aposford was not far from the same fate.

"I wonder if any of these houses still have beds," said Rhys.

"They may," Kurian replied. "But I fear what we may find in them. This is no longer a place for the living, and we should leave whatever is here to its rest."

"Bridges provide more shelter than you might think," Louise said, pointing to the arched stone bridge at the end of the street.

Kurian agreed. "At least we'll be more protected than last night, and since we've already come so far, we may be able to travel a bit beyond Aposford tomorrow and hide in the emptiness of the plains again. I don't want to be caught between Capric hill and Pallingham. I have a feeling there may be more travel between them than is normal."

They found a rope coiled among Greta's packs, so they lowered their water skins into the well to refill them, and then walked to the bridge. The road continued for a short distance before the grasses of the plain began to reclaim it from disuse. Just where their vision failed in the dusk, the road seemed to disappear altogether, as if it never had a destination.

After climbing under the bridge, they unburdened the pony and settled in for the night. Kurian looked at his companions, preparing their blankets for rest. Rhys laid himself at the westward opening, from which pursuit was most likely to come. Tobin moved further under the cover of the bridge, with Louise next, and Kurian closer to the eastern opening. The long, wearying walk had even driven thought from his mind as he struggled just to keep his feet moving. Now, though his body cried for rest, his mind began to run. They had spoken little during their travels, and Kurian suddenly felt the need to talk, as if the loneliness of the abandoned town had stirred his need for speech more than the empty gray of the plain. He sat down with his back against the stones of the bridge, but too many questions crowded his head to know what to say or ask. "Do you love him, Ms. Prescott?" he finally said quietly.

"Do I love whom?" Louise asked.

"The King of the Caves."

Louise raised herself up on one elbow and searched Kurian's face before answering. "Yes."

Kurian nodded. It was the first time she had spoken to him without her guard of sarcasm and contempt.

"But not in the sense you mean, I think," she added. Behind her, Tobin sat up and crossed his legs.

"Then how?" Tobin asked. "Whether the reports we heard are exaggerated or not, the man is clearly hiding for a reason, and we know from personal experience that he is not above theft."

"If it's not love," said Kurian, "then what drives you to follow the man, what makes you do as he asks when there is no sense in the request?"

"Such as escorting three young monks through the wilderness?" she said.

"That would be the first example to come to mind." He did not know why he couldn't help but answer her with the same feigned impertinence that she usually offered.

"I already said it *is* love," she said, and again there was no affectation in her voice or expression. "What I said when I grabbed you in the street wasn't a lie, or just a part I play to be his spy. I was an orphan. My parents lived in a town much like this one, and as it died around them, they decided to move somewhere that was still alive, at least for a while." She paused for a moment. He could barely see her face now, but he heard her sigh. "They were killed on the road by a group of highwaymen, and the last thing my father did was put me on a horse and send it running. A young couple found me wandering and took me in, until I ran away a month later. I was confused and scared. As much as I wanted to find my parents, I had nightmares of the highwaymen finding me. I spent the next two years wandering between small towns on the coast, learning to live off scraps and hide from all the people who take an interest in frightened little girls on the street."

"I'm sorry," Kurian said.

"You don't have to be," she said, but there was no scorn for his meaningless sentiment in her voice. "Eventually I decided to move inland, and when I passed through Dury, the King found me. He found me and taught me and made me part of a new family, and it was enough. It was more than I had ever had.

"Those men in his camp that you're so afraid of cared for me like a sister. None of them would let any harm come to me, least of all the King. I love him as I loved my father—only more so. I would fulfill any of his requests because I trust him, which is why I willingly went back to wandering, playing an orphan for a time so that I could be invisible, to see and hear what others could not and then pass that information to people like Alden to help the King. But because of him, it was only acting. I am no longer an orphan. Can you say as much about your order?"

Her comparison to his own father leaving him stung. She was obviously ignorant of the way the order worked. "We were all left at the order by our parents, if you want to call that orphaning," Kurian said. "It is an honor to be accepted, and since coming there, I have at least found these two who are truly like brothers. As for commitment, I would die to carry out the oath I took to God."

"Commitment is not love," Tobin said. His tone was sad, and Kurian couldn't help thinking the sadness was for him.

"Very true," Louise almost whispered.

"Our brothers care for each other," he said defensively. "We would die for each other. Some of us have."

"It sounds as if you will all do your duty," Louise said calmly, "and that is more faithfulness than I have seen in most throughout Pallingham."

Kurian was about to respond when Louise breathed in sharply. "Someone's coming," she whispered. Kurian turned his head to listen and raised himself to a crouch.

"I don't hear anything," he said.

"Neither did I. Somehow, I just feel it."

Tobin tapped Rhys, who had fallen asleep while they talked, and they both picked up their staves and hid deep in the shadows of the bridge, waiting and listening. Kurian did the same and crept past the pony toward his end of the bridge, peering into the dark beyond their shelter. He could not hear or see anything in the riverbed or on the road, but Greta shook her head and pawed the ground nervously.

Kurian listened until it seemed his own breathing and the shifting of his robes were the only sounds under the dark bridge. Nothing came from beyond their shelter. His heart had slowed down from the initial tension when he turned to tell the others it was a false alarm.

As soon as his back faced the riverbed, he heard a gentle shuffling behind him. He ducked behind Greta and listened.

The sound of carefully treading feet came again, like somebody groping along in the darkness. Greta sidestepped away from the noise and the shuffling stopped.

A voice came from the night. "Hello?"

Kurian's heart raced again. There was no way of knowing who was out there. It could be robbers using the abandoned town to hide, or soldiers set on their trail by Captain Fallon.

"Hello?" the voice called feebly. The fear he heard in the voice might be a ruse to gain their confidence. He didn't know whether to answer or not.

Tobin crept up to his side and whispered in his ear. "Rhys is checking the bridge." At almost the same moment, he heard movement above him. Rhys was never good at sneaking. The accidental tap of his staff on the stones made the cautious steps stop again.

The voice trembled as it called out again. "Is somebody there?"

"Don't come any further," Kurian said in the deepest voice he could manage. "We have you outnumbered, and it's best if you go back from where you came."

"I don't want to hurt anyone, and I don't want any trouble," said the voice.

"I know that voice," Tobin whispered. Then he stood up before Kurian could stop him, "Noeman?"

"How...how do you know me?"

"It's us," said Tobin, "Tobin, Kurian, and Rhys."

"Praise God," Noeman shouted. "Can it be true?" He rushed forward and fell to his knees in front of Kurian and Tobin. "You're alive. I didn't want to hope for it, but you're alive!"

"Of course, we're alive," Tobin laughed. "You only sent us on our mission a few days ago." Rhys jumped down from the bank and landed next to Tobin.

"Yes, your mission." Noeman grabbed Tobin's robe and almost pulled him over. "Did you get it? Did you?"

"No," Kurian said flatly. "Not yet."

Noeman let go of Tobin and fell onto his side. "Then it's gone," he wailed. "It's all lost!"

"Not completely," Kurian said. "We're on our way to retrieve it now."

"It doesn't matter, everything's gone." Their dean rolled on the ground, wailing like a child. "All lost. Everything."

"What do you mean?" Tobin asked. "Dean, what are you doing all the way out here?"

"He burned it. He killed them all," they made out through the sobs. Soon he regained control of himself and spoke plainly. "Evasius murdered them all. He burned the entire compound, the buildings—the Oak. I only survived because I was in town. When I saw the fire and the soldiers, I hid. The soldiers roamed around all night looking for survivors. I hid in the tanner's attic until they left the next evening, and then I ran."

"No," Tobin whispered, and his legs crumpled beneath him. Kurian felt like Noeman had stabbed him in the gut. He screamed with rage and pounded his fist on the stones of the bridge.

"We have lost the treasure, and our order has been destroyed," Noeman said as if in a trance. "The Caprics are no more."

The boys stared at their teacher. The only home they remembered was gone, everyone they knew dead. Any chance of a future disappeared from thought. Louise finally broke the stillness. Walking forward from her hiding place under the bridge, she lightly touched each of them on the shoulder and paused for a moment.

"You can't mourn this loss in a single night," she said. "We should sleep. It will quiet the pain for now."

Sacrifices

Kurian slept fitfully. Memories of his brothers rushing to put out fires around the compound played out whether his eyes were open or closed. When he nodded off, the memories turned into nightmares in which the monks burned along with their home. Tobin sobbing nearby woke him as often as the dreams did, and the twitching muscles of his legs prevented him from reaching a deep sleep, despite his exhaustion.

It reminded him of the first time he had experienced that feeling—another time of loss and confusion. When he first arrived at the order, the young novitiates ran up and down the hill every day until they vomited, and their legs collapsed under them. Then they wrestled and sparred, learning the soft points of the body that allowed a child to escape an adult attacker. The twitching had kept him awake, giving him the only time to think about why his father had abandoned him to the strangers who worked young boys beyond exhaustion and punished every misstep with a swat from the rod. He wept often in those first months, before he accepted the oath of the order. Eventually, the nighttime muscle spasms faded, replaced with the feeling of movement even when lying still in his bunk. The spasms returned after they passed ten years of age, when every twelfth week was devoted to battle. They slept in shifts, ate siege rations, and faced random attacks by brothers acting as an enemy force. They did not pull their punches. It was all to prepare them for their task as protectors. Every siege week, his muscles would twitch again at night. Eventually he grew accustomed to it. He knew his body would also adapt to the new strain of walking such a great distance each day with a full pack.

None of them stirred when the sky started to lighten. Kurian knew that he did not want to be the first one up on this morning. To his surprise, Noeman was the first to move. The dean did not look like he had slept well either. His whole face was swollen, and he glared out through bloodshot eyes. His short gray hair, normally combed down neatly, stuck out at all angles like a bramble bush. Seeing his teacher so disheveled rekindled the fire of terror in Kurian's gut. Noeman had always been orderly and neat in everything. "Discipline is the key to a peaceful spirit," was his favorite phrase when correcting an impulsive novitiate, and he proved it through his stoicism. Now Kurian had seen him lose all control of his emotions. More proof that the order had lost its power long before, and that their show of strength was a fragile façade waiting for the shattering blow from Evasius.

Noeman cleared his throat and smoothed down his hair with his hand. "Boys," he said softly, "I know you are awake. We must talk." Rhys propped himself up against the bridge and Tobin sat up and crossed his legs.

"What's there to talk about?" Kurian said as he started rolling up his blanket.

"To start, I would like to hear about your mission to Pallingham," Noeman answered. He had the same tone he used when he asked them to recite a passage of important script from memory.

"We're still working on it."

"What happened at your meeting with Lord Evasius?"

"He claimed the raid on the compound was all a misunderstanding about trying to collect taxes." Kurian said, and began to load packs onto Greta.

"But our order is exempt from taxes," said Noeman in surprise.

"He was going to change that," Tobin said. "He claimed it was necessary to help during the drought."

"When we finally got around to talking about the treasure, he claimed it wasn't in the treasury." Kurian smiled at the shock on Noeman's face. "He told us a bandit called the King of the Caves had taken it, and asked us to find out where he was hiding. In exchange, he would reinstate our exemption."

"He exempted us from taxes all right," muttered Rhys, "for good."

"That's not helping, Mr. Brock," Noeman said.

"He also insisted that the treasure be secured at his castle when it was recovered," Kurian continued. "Under a guard of our brothers, of course." He slung a bag hard over Greta's back, and she snorted and skittered away from him.

"Obviously he was attempting to use you for his own purposes." Noeman leaned forward and patted Tobin's shoulder. "You boys did nothing to make him attack us again. He simply lied to you."

"I thought that anything we agreed to could be cancelled by the abbot, since we're not ordained," Kurian said.

"Very shrewd," Noeman nodded. "It would allow you to gain his confidence, while moving nearer to the treasure yourselves. Unfortunately, he was equally cunning. But, how did you end up here?"

Kurian pointed to Louise, who was still lying down and listening to them. "Evasius sent us to Downriver Town to question her friend. After that, she volunteered to take us to her bandit king." Louise wrinkled her nose at the description.

"But before we could leave, the captain of Evasius' guard attacked us," Tobin added.

Noeman furrowed his brows and sat silently when he heard this. "That may be good news," he said after a few moments.

"So, you're all right with your students almost being killed, then?" asked Rhys.

"No," Noeman glared at him. "But if he sent a captain to follow you, then obviously he was telling the truth about one thing—he does not have the treasure."

Tobin let out a relieved sigh. "So we still have a chance. Now what do we do?"

"We retrieve the treasure and we try to rebuild," Noeman said firmly.

Kurian turned back toward the pony, closed his eyes, and shook his head. Noeman made it sound like running an errand to Aposford. They might be able to steal back the treasure from the King of the Caves—if God were still on their side—but there would be no rebuilding against the strength of Evasius. At least not in Pallingham.

Thinking about the King reminded him that Alden had promised to send help if he could. Was that a promise to all of them, or just Louise? Louise and Alden were still spies. They had to be on their guard.

He finished loading their supplies in silence while Tobin introduced Louise and gave Noeman more details about their ordeal. Noeman nodded and asked questions with feigned wisdom. Kurian could see through the cracks in his shell; their wise teacher was a coward in the end. Dean Goodman had run when his brothers were dying. Kurian would not trust the dean for protection or guidance against their enemies. Hopefully, he would fight when necessary, and otherwise let them alone.

They had barely left the shelter of the bridge before Noeman interfered in the plan. "We're heading too northerly," he said. "We ought to follow the riverbed back toward the compound."

"That's not the shortest route to Dury," Louise answered, "although the river is easier to follow without getting lost. I've got a sunstone to help us keep straight."

"I don't think we should get too close to the compound or Pallingham," Kurian added.

"But we have to return," Noeman explained. "We must perform the final rites for our brothers. They deserve that, even if we cannot bury them all."

Kurian's face grew hot. He wanted to lash out at Noeman for treating them like his old students when nothing existed of their former home. "That would be the most dangerous thing we could do right now," he said, trying to keep his voice calm.

"He's right," said Louise. "It's likely that Evasius has men watching the compound for survivors—even for these three to return."

"But the rites must be performed. Our dead must be laid to rest with the proper blessings and honors."

"Didn't you ask anyone in town for help?" Kurian asked.

"No." Noeman bowed his head. "I didn't know whom to trust. And I could not further endanger the one friend who risked hiding me overnight."

"Dean," Tobin said, placing a hand on his teacher's shoulder, "doesn't the Rule allow for the rites to be delayed during times of crisis?" Noeman nodded. "I believe this qualifies. If they capture or kill us trying to do this now, our order dies. However, if we survive this adventure to the crags, we can return to bless our fallen brothers in time. It may not be what we want, but our duty and our oath require it in my opinion."

Noeman walked away and stared into the fog in the direction of Capric Hill. "Of course, you are right about the Rule, Mr. Hart. But I will never forgive myself for leaving them there, necessity or not."

"Then go, if you must," Kurian blurted out.

The dean turned toward him with a blank expression. "You would like that, wouldn't you Mr. Abramson? However, I will not abandon you. Whether you believe me or not, I could not forgive myself for that either—and it would be the more grievous sin." *Of course*, thought Kurian, *the coward has to pretend he's protecting us. We're still children in his eyes, not ready for responsibilities in the order—and certainly not prepared to be the last hope of recovering the treasure.*

"Or follow—it makes no difference to me." Kurian grabbed Greta's lead and started North at a rapid pace. Louise caught up quickly, followed by Rhys and then Tobin. Noeman lingered for a moment and sent a prayer in the direction of their old home. Then he turned after the others and dissolved into the mist with the road.

Captain Fallon followed the attendant, Geoffrey, into Lord Evasius' offices and was led to a seat. He knew that he was in front of the large desk that nearly spanned the narrow room, but his vision had not yet returned. Sometimes he saw a blurred image from his left eye when he blinked, but otherwise light and shadows told him where something might be in his path.

His blindness meant that he had to ask a guard from Downriver Town to guide him back to Pallingham. The guard sounded no older than the monks, and his inane questions were inappropriate for a superior. It had been a slow and degrading trip.

The door clicked closed as Geoffrey left. Fallon assumed that Evasius was waiting across the desk, but he heard no sound that told him anyone was in the room. There was no greeting, no wisp of breath or accidental sweep of cloth. Yet, he felt eyes watching him, the same feeling as before an ambush. Even though he was tempted to speak, he trusted his discipline—never speak until spoken to by your superiors, and never trust that you were safe from curious ears. If Evasius were watching him, then he knew this was a test.

The silence remained for what felt like minutes, but Fallon only stared forward. His heart began to beat faster and louder in his ears. There was a faint scent of incense just distinguishable from the burning tallow in the lamps. It was probably lingering on his watcher's clothing. His instincts were telling him a threat was near, but the soldier inside willed him to remain motionless.

"Good day, Captain Fallon." He felt the breath on his ear and nearly lashed out before he recognized the voice. Lord Evasius had been standing so close behind him that he could have killed Fallon instantly.

"My Lord." He saluted from his seat.

"I'm glad to see you have not lost your wits along with your sight," Evasius said, and moved around Fallon's back, toward the desk. Fallon turned his face in the direction of the sound, but did not answer.

"I want no excuses or explanations," Evasius continued. "Give me answers. Find my treasure."

"My Lord, I dispatched seven guards from Downriver Town to track the monks with their guide. More importantly, I discovered that the highwayman is somewhere in the Crags of the Wild Goats atop the Northland Cliffs. Their only known paths are through Aven or Whalesand. Six patrols were ready immediately, and I sent two to each city—and since we have suspected for some time that they might have a secret passage through the cliffs, two should also go to Dury. Three Caprics won't be able to hide with twenty men on the perimeter of the smaller cities."

He heard Evasius click his tongue. "A fair plan, Captain. As soon as your eyes improve, I want you to follow the most likely trail with a full company. When you find the thief's camp, crush them. Return with the treasure, and you will be rewarded well."

"Thank you, my Lord."

"Fail and I may hand you over to the witch." He could hear that Lord Evasius said it with a smile. "She hasn't had a puppet of her own for some time." It took Fallon a moment to realize his breath had stopped. He nodded to show that he understood.

"In the meantime, I want you to see her for another ritual. Our current method of gathering information is clearly inadequate. She may be able to do something about your eyes, as well. See her immediately." Evasius chuckled as if he had made a joke. Fallon did not stand for a moment, and heard the swishing of fabric behind him again. "You're dismissed," Evasius whispered in his ear.

One of his own men led Fallon by hand toward the dungeons carved deep into the rock on which Pallingham castle stood. The white mist before his eyes turned black as they descended. A cold, musty smell at the entrance quickly turned into a nauseating wall of odor from the diseased and rotting people in the cells. He felt moments of heat and light as they passed the torches spaced along the narrow hallway. The witch worked much of her magic here, surrounded by misery and pain. It kept her out of sight, so she wouldn't frighten superstitious soldiers. Fallon suspected she also enjoyed it.

"Hello, Captain," Mouna said, touching his face. He flinched away, and she laughed. "Help him onto the table," she said. Private Mason led Fallon to a low table where he knew that she cut up the bodies of dead prisoners. She had also healed some of his men there. He pulled his arm from the private's grasp and dismissed him before he climbed onto the table on his own. At least it was dry.

The witch prodded him around the face and chest before speaking again. "Being connected with you has been interesting, Captain. I know you feel me when I reach out."

"I think so."

"It's your willingness that makes the bond so strong—your loyalty that makes you do whatever is asked. I need that for this new method to work."

"I was ordered, and I am here."

"Good. If you fight me on this, you will not like the results."

"What are you going to do?" he asked.

"I'm going to enter your dreams, dear Captain. But first, let's take care of those eyes."

She grabbed his forehead, pulled back his eyelids, and poured a burning liquid over his face. The pain was as bad as the monks' powder, but he did not cry out. He tensed his body and pressed his head hard against the wood of the table until she had finished. This was his duty, his only way of regaining his honor. After blinking a few times, the mist faded, and a blurry image of the dungeon room came into view.

"You'll see clearly by morning. Nothing new for a soldier." For now, all he saw was a shadowy mass where she stood. It was better than seeing her mutilated body again.

"When we're done, you will see me in your sleep, and you can give me the information our lord requires." She placed a small metal object in his hand. His skin crawled when she touched him, but he had to follow his orders. He hated that a part of him wanted more. "This talisman will go under your skin, here." She pressed one of her long nails into his flesh between two ribs.

"What is it?" His stomach turned. His heart raced, and he felt on the verge of panic—the same feeling he'd had before his first battle.

"Why do you ask questions you don't want to know the answer to?" She laughed again. "I'll just say you'll always have a piece of me close to you."

Kurian knew they were passing the most dangerous point of the day's march when they crossed the path of frayed turf from Evasius' horsemen. If they followed the path to the right, by his guess, they were only five miles or so from Capric Hill. If any of the soldiers had stayed to wait for them, they might return to Pallingham Castle at any time. They hurried their pace into the afternoon to get several miles from the trail before stopping to rest.

As they were preparing to stop for the night, they came upon a small grove of trees on the plain. A few of the trees had late apples hanging on them that were still edible, and Kurian was grateful to have something fresh to eat instead of the salted meat and dried fruits in their packs.

In the morning, they woke to a cold, dense fog that gave the small grove the feeling of a cave. The thin trees stood like carved pillars holding up the stone-gray ceiling. Before breakfast, the Caprics gathered for prayer. Tobin had encouraged Kurian and Rhys that they needed to recite at least the minimum prayers prescribed during times of travel, and had led them in the practice each morning and evening. This morning, the dean took over from Tobin. Tears fell down his cheeks as he recited the first-hour prayer in his flat voice. The morning under the bridge had been the first time they had forgotten it, and Tobin had begged Noeman for forgiveness when he remembered. Kurian laughed to himself because Tobin overlooked that the dean had forgotten as well. He expected that they would not forget again, and that would make Tobin happy.

He tired of the dean's voice quickly, and he felt like he should keep an eye on Louise, so he peered out from his hood. Louise was kneeling down by the bags. Her body was rigid, and she stared intently into the thick fog just beyond the trees. She cocked her head to one side and cupped a hand to her ear. When he saw the fear on her face, he reached out and touched the dean's arm.

Noeman jumped when he touched him. "Wha...what?" He sputtered. "Mr. Abramson, I cannot believe," he started in his classroom tone, but Kurian cupped his hand over the dean's mouth. Noeman slapped his hand away and looked furious. Kurian jerked his finger to his own lips, and then pointed to Louise. The dean finally stopped trying to argue. At the same time, they all heard the soft thudding of horses approaching on the plain.

Louise scurried over to their circle in a crouch and gestured for them all to kneel down to hear her. "Hide in the fog," she whispered, and motioned to indicate that they should spread out. "Lay down. Your robes," she covered her eyes with one hand, "hard to see."

She moved away and grabbed her blanket, wrapped it around Greta's leads, and took the pony behind a large shrub that had grown up on the edge of the grove. Then she somehow convinced Greta to kneel and threw the blanket over her back and head. Louise hid herself by climbing under the shrub where it grew against one of the trees. The others scattered. Kurian moved quickly to the other side of the grove and lay down in a small depression in the grass beyond. He did not want to get too far from Louise and give her a chance to escape while they hid from the approaching horsemen.

As soon as he was still, he heard the jingle of harnesses and the thumping of one of the horses as it sped up to a canter. He laid still on his stomach with his hood over his head while his breath blew out against the grass. Seeing his breath, he realized he was cold. The horse came up quickly, and stopped abruptly.

Kurian felt the hair bristling at the back of his neck. He could see the silhouette of the rider in the fog to his left. Ten steps closer and the man would be clearly visible. He tried to steady his breath.

Another rider trotted up behind the first and they both stopped.

"I swear I heard voices," one of them said.

"We're probably close," said the other, "but you can never tell where sound is coming from in a fog like this. We could run around in circles and pass them right by."

One of them whistled loudly, and a moment later, Kurian heard other horses come running. He felt the earth trembling beneath his body, and the hoofs of one came so loudly in his ears that he thought the horse might trample him. When the hoof beats stopped, Kurian could see at least three other riders—the fog made it difficult to be certain of their number.

"I think we're close," the voice said again. "They can't get too far on foot, so we'll go back to where we can see the trail and wait for this fog to clear up."

"Yes, sir," said the others.

"Stay alert, boys. We may get promoted to the castle if we catch the ones who slipped through Captain Fallon's grip." The lead rider kicked his horse hard and they rode back in the direction from which they had come.

When they were gone, Kurian rolled over onto his back and let out a long sigh.

Battle of the Apple Grove

Kurian watched from beneath a pile of leaves as Noeman poked at the fire with a dry stick. The dean sat near the center of the grove of trees where they had camped the night before, with Greta tied to the nearest tree. He had covered his robes with a blanket; it wasn't a perfect disguise, but he could easily be confused for someone trying to escape a dying village like Aposford.

When the riders left, they had decided quickly that confronting the pursuers was their only option. If they had been tracked across the plains, then they could not run fast enough to escape. Kurian had proposed an ambush, and Tobin had immediately offered a plan.

Now, Louise hid behind Noeman in her original place while the boys hid beneath leaves that had naturally piled up against the tree trunks at the south end of the grove. With luck, the riders would approach the dean, leaving their backs exposed. At first, it felt cold and damp, but the longer they waited for the riders to return, the warmer Kurian's hiding place became. The leaf pile smelled of rot and mold, stifling his breath. As the fog lifted, steam rose even from the piles that weren't hiding anyone, making them excellent camouflage. Now they waited.

Kurian had felt the nerves of an impending attack during his training, but he had always known that nobody would be seriously hurt. Waiting in ambush for real enemies made him feel jittery. It wasn't the intense energy he had felt after fighting Captain Fallon—it was the expectation of that feeling. Except that now the odds were less in their favor. The ambush made him feel more confident, while also feeling more afraid for the outcome. Once they sprang from hiding, there was no controlling the results. He understood Rhys' love for the fight, the eagerness for struggle, but in his own heart, he also feared the danger. He loved and hated the creeping vibrations that started in his belly and worked out toward his limbs.

Carefully, he turned his head to look toward the plains. Waiting without moving for almost two hours was becoming painful. The fog had burned off an hour before, and he could see for at least a half-mile now. It was unlikely that the day would clear much more.

With his body pressed to the ground, he felt the horses coming before he saw them. After several minutes of steady hoof beats, they came into view one by one. Seven—two more than he had counted that morning. Kurian's heart suddenly boomed in his chest.

They rode spread out in a line, their heads moving to scan the ground before them. He saw now that they were dressed in the uniforms of the guards he had seen in Downriver Town. Each wore a tunic covered with a heavy jerkin of dark leather and a studded cap. Riding in the center of the line, their leader wore a mail shirt and a brimmed helmet. As they passed his hiding place, Kurian saw that the leader carried a long sword, while his men had short swords and daggers. This wasn't going to be anything like siege week at the compound.

"Good day," called the leader to Noeman. Kurian recognized his voice from that morning. He turned his head again to watch them walk into the trap, and waited for Noeman's signal. The guards brought their horses together in a small semicircle around the dean's fire. It was a poor formation for defense. God might finally be in their favor today.

Noeman waved a hand at them, but kept silent.

"Are you traveling alone, old man?"

"No," Noeman answered. "I have my pony." He gestured at Greta.

The guard dismounted from his horse and walked over to where Greta was tied. "And how long have you had this pony?" he asked as he looked over the bags tied to her back.

"Not long. I lost everything, so I gathered what I could to find a new home."

"We've been tracking three young men and a woman across the plain. They also have a pony." He picked up one of Greta's hoofs and studied it. "You haven't seen anybody have you?"

Noeman shook his head. "I saw the trees and decided to stop to warm myself with a fire. Haven't had fresh apples in a long time, either. You should try one." Kurian thought he could hear the dean's voice waver. He wasn't accustomed to deception, and it went against everything he taught.

"You said you lost everything."

Noeman nodded and looked down. "Fire," he grunted.

"Seems you were able to gather quite a lot," the guard said innocently.

"God provides." Noeman poked at the fire again with his stick.

"This is a puzzle." The guard scratched his chin. "You say you're traveling alone, and that you only just got this pony, but we've rode all around this part of the plains this morning and there's only one set of pony tracks leading up to this place." Kurian's muscles started to burn. The guard knew Noeman was lying, and they needed to attack now if they were to have surprise on their side.

Noeman stared at his interrogator.

"I don't know who you are, but I don't believe your story."

"Maybe you mixed up trails somewhere," Noeman said. "Or maybe those other people moved on from here." The dean looked nervous, even from a distance. He needed to give the signal soon.

"I think maybe you stole that pony from some poor soul, and a patrol of guards makes you nervous." The man crossed his arms, standing over Noeman.

"That's ridiculous!"

The guard leaned further over Noeman. "But it's your lucky day. I'm after those other four, and I don't have time to drag you in. I might confiscate your pony, but it'd just slow me down."

"What are you going to do then?" the dean asked.

"I'm going to let you go," said the guard. Kurian saw the dean relax. "As long as you give me anything valuable you might be carrying."

"You'd take everything from an old man?" The dean seemed appalled at the very concept, more than being personally affronted.

"Gold, silver, copper, whatever you've got. Consider it a discount on justice." His men laughed.

"You're a pack of wolves," Noeman shouted, waving his stick at the guard. Then he gave the signal and threw the stick into the fire.

The small fire exploded with a flash of flame and smoke from the monk's powder that had also been in his hand. The horses screamed and reared, throwing three of the guards to the ground. The leader tried to jump back, and Noeman knocked him over with a kick to the knee. When Kurian, Rhys, and Tobin leapt from their hiding places in a cloud of leaves, the remaining riders wheeled about in panic. Smoke continued to billow from the fire, pouring out in every direction and obscuring the entire grove.

"What magic is this?" shouted the mounted guard to Kurian's right, and drew his sword. Rhys thrust his staff at him, and knocked him off his horse. The middle horse bolted, and Rhys swung his staff again, flipping the rider over its tail. The man landed on his head with a loud crack.

Kurian rushed forward, trailing leaves and smashed the knob of his staff against the head of a man on the ground. Another guard was trying to draw his sword even though he was still laying on it. Kurian jabbed at him with the pointed end of his staff. It pierced the leather jerkin and the man screamed and fell limp on his back. Seeing the blood made Kurian stop. The sound of fighting around him faded, as if he were going deaf. His body suddenly felt heavy. His stomach churned, and he was dizzy. He had drawn blood before, but it had always been one of the hazards of training—never on purpose. It was only scrapes and sprains. None of his friends was ever injured.

He turned to look at the first man he had hit. A dimple in the leather cap told him he was probably dead, too. Smoke washed over the body, blocking him from view. After preparing to defend his order in battle for ten years, he had now killed two men in seconds and realized how little prepared he was for bringing death. He fell to his knees and vomited.

The third grounded man had now gained his feet and rushed toward Kurian's back with his weapon raised. As he swung, Tobin jumped out from the smoke and parried with his staff, then swung back at the man with a ferocity that Kurian had never seen from him before. Pushing the man back with every swing, Tobin ended up fighting beside Rhys against the man he had unhorsed. Only their torsos were visible in the thick smoke from the powder, making them appear to float as they battled with the guards.

One man remained on horseback. Kurian watched as his horse wheeled, and he surveyed the situation. He didn't see Kurian kneeling in the smoke. Finally, the guard drew his sword and prepared to charge toward Rhys and Tobin, still fighting with his comrades. Coming to his senses, Kurian picked up his staff and swung wildly as the horse sped by. He saw the rider fall back into the fire, but the horse's flank slammed into Kurian, knocking him to the side. When he stood up, the guard was almost on top of him with a naked blade and flames leaping from his back. The padded cloth of his shirt seemed to be protecting him.

"You're on fire!" Kurian yelled. The guard turned to look and began beating himself with his free hand. Then Kurian swung his staff and flinched when it thumped into the distracted man's head. When he turned, Rhys and Tobin stood together, looking for other threats.

Noeman had drawn the dagger from his boot and was wrestling on the ground with the leader of the guards. While the dean had caught them by surprise, the leader fought with a calm precision that his men did not have. He threw Noeman against a tree and took the opportunity to arm himself. Behind him, he didn't see Louise creeping out of her hiding spot. She swung Noeman's staff at his legs, buckling one knee. He crumpled to the ground, and Noeman jumped forward with his dagger.

Kurian looked around him at the dead guards appearing through the rapidly dissipating cloud. His throat felt closed off—he couldn't breathe until violent sobs racked his body and his feet carried him stumbling from the grove.

❧

He was glad it wasn't Noeman who came to him first. Tobin approached slowly and waited a moment before sitting down next to where he had fallen. Kurian didn't look at him. He lay on his side, staring over the grass. Tobin sat in silence for several minutes before placing his hand on Kurian's head.

"It hurts," Tobin finally said. Kurian did not answer, but he sat up and looked at his friend. "I imagine it will fade."

"They were going to leave," Kurian said after a long pause.

"Maybe," Tobin nodded, "but how long would it have taken them to catch our trail again? They might have set their own ambush ahead of us, or pulled back just out of sight and waited for us to reveal ourselves. You remember the blacksmith's reminder: 'attack no man if it be in your power.' We could never avoid this fight, or one like it."

"I killed two of them without a struggle. They were just lying on the ground." Kurian felt warm tears streaming down his face. "It didn't feel like defense; it felt like murder."

"We know who sent them, and what he intends," said Tobin firmly. There was a stern resolve in the look he gave Kurian. "His actions have already proved that he is a dangerous threat. What we did fulfills our oaths to protect our brothers from harm, and gets us closer to reclaiming the treasure."

Kurian felt a pain in his chest over his heart, and struggled to breathe again. "I'm not fit for that oath. This day—this whole journey——shows I probably never was. I agreed to give the treasure to the man who destroyed our home. I just killed two men who were already down, and then lost my wits during the fight. I'm not just a monster; I'm a coward." He turned his face away from Tobin as he felt the sobs coming again.

"God will forgive the killing," Tobin said, grasping his shoulder.

"You know him better than I do."

"Your guilt is not just to shame you. It's one of the ways he calls to you." Tobin sighed and squeezed his shoulder again. "Turn to him and you'll feel it eventually. But you also must forgive yourself."

Kurian felt like that was something he could never do.

"In the meantime," Tobin said, standing up and holding out his hand, "there is work to be done."

He didn't believe Tobin, didn't think God would simply forget what he had done. The order had lost His favor for some reason, but he and his friends were still alive. Perhaps they could find a secluded place where He would ignore them and their faults. They might be able to hide the treasure where it would be safe, and somehow lead quiet lives. The guilt was something he would have to figure out later.

He grabbed Tobin's hand and stood up. Hopefully, his friend would still want to join him in hiding. "Thanks for saving me," he said as they walked back together.

Rhys and Noeman had already piled the corpses at one side of the grove and were covering them with leaves when Kurian followed Tobin back to the camp. Louise stood at the opposite side of the circle of trees, arms outstretched, trying to woo the guards' horses with apples. It looked like she had already had some success, since two of them stood beside Greta.

"Welcome back," said Noeman when he saw them. He came over and gripped Kurian's shoulders, looking into his eyes with what seemed like genuine concern. It was the way his father had always comforted him when he was a child. It helped, even coming from the dean. "I'm glad you're all right."

Kurian had an urge to hug him, but he held back. The dean would not think it appropriate.

Rhys, on the other hand, grabbed Kurian in his thick arms and lifted him from the ground. "We did it," he said with a crazy grin on his face. "We survived our first real battle." He put Kurian down and slugged Tobin in the shoulder. "And our little scholar has some tricks up his sleeves, eh?"

"Now what do we do?" asked Kurian.

"We keep going," Tobin said, "only now we have extra supplies, which we needed after running into the dean. And we have horses. They can cut days off our traveling."

Rhys cleared his throat. "I guess all that reading also made you a horse expert?"

"Well we can't just let them go," said Tobin. "They'll go straight back to their stables and Evasius will hear that his guards have disappeared. He'll guess that we made them disappear. But we can send Greta back home and the innkeeper will know—maybe he'll spread rumors that we have disappeared." Louise cocked an eyebrow and shook her head behind his back.

"Tricky," Rhys said, wagging a finger at Tobin. He was still giddy from the fight.

Kurian watched Louise grab a third horse's bridle and pointed so that the others would look. "I think we brought the horse expert with us."

They determined to stay another night in the grove. Since the threat of pursuit was gone for the moment, they lit a fire and the boys sorted through the new supplies while Louise captured the remaining horses. Once she had convinced the leader's horse to trust her, the others came more easily. It was almost dark by the time she had gathered the last one. Riding lessons would wait until morning, when they had all rested.

After a meal of roasted apples, and bread from the guards' packs, Noeman stood up in the firelight. "Ms. Prescott, would you assist me with something, please?" She nodded, and he turned to the boys, smiling. "Boys, if you would, please hand Ms. Prescott your belts and staves." Kurian's mouth dropped open. The dean couldn't be serious.

"Why?" Tobin asked.

"Because after your determination in pursuing the retrieval of our treasure, and because of your courage and resourcefulness today, I know you are ready."

"Ready for what?" Tobin said.

"He wants to ordain us," Kurian said, his voice flat. As smart as Tobin was, sometimes the obvious took a while to sink in. And this was obviously the easiest way for Noeman to take control of the situation and carry out his fantasy of rebuilding the order as it had been.

"I've been thinking," said Noeman, "that to rebuild the order, we will need more than just one monk." He pointed to himself. "And I would be happy to call you my brothers."

"I suppose you would happily be the abbot, as well," Kurian said, crossing his arms. Of course he wanted to be in charge, after running away while the order burned. He may have made it through today's fight, but he ran when everything was at stake.

"Well, that seems like the most logical choice. I am the only one who has studied all the order's subjects, as well as mastered the guardian training. Though, I could wait to take on that role until we have a new cloister."

"Don't you understand what's happening? The order is gone! You said it yourself under the bridge. There's no going back." Kurian stood up from his seat by the fire to face the dean at the same level. "The blacksmith, the abbot, our troop...even little Simon. Everyone we knew is dead." He felt tears welling up again, and fought to keep control of his voice. He almost had to growl to get the rest out. "There's no rebuilding while Evasius is still in power."

"We have to try," Noeman stuttered, looking surprised at Kurian's outburst. "We took an oath."

"But there's no order to swear to anymore. We failed in our charge, and God forsook us."

"How dare you say such a thing!" Noeman stepped forward as if he would strike him, but they were no longer in the classroom and Kurian stood his ground.

"Kurian, stop," Tobin whispered next to him.

He shook his head. "Where have the great heroes been for the last century? Why didn't our brothers ever travel further than Aposford, and why were their missions only mercy visits? Had they collected all the ancient relics, or did all the rules stop them from guiding the people of Pallingham? I've been outside the wall now, Dean. I've seen the way people live outside the influence of our little compound. Nobody respects God or listens to his servants. We had no power, and we let a tyrant like Evasius take control of the people's hearts and minds while we cowered in fear of breaking the Rule. The Caprics are dead, and it's because of men like you." He untied the cords from his waist and dropped them at Noeman's feet. "But I would be free of your Rule." He spat on the red and white cords, then picked up a leather tie from the baggage and wrapped it around his waist.

He knew how the dean would see it—a rejection not just of the offer of ordination, but of his original oath. The dean would see him choosing to be an ordinary person instead of taking the responsibility of their vestments. He waited long enough to be sure it had sunk in, and then stalked toward the emptiness of the plains.

"What would you do instead?" Noeman asked. His face was red, and his cheeks twitched. Kurian had never seen him so angry.

"I'm going to get the treasure, to fulfill that part of my oath. Then I will do whatever it takes to make sure Evasius never touches it. If God helps us pull off that miracle, then maybe we'll get a vision for what comes next." He wheeled around and walked beyond the trees into the darkness.

When the glare of the fire no longer lit his back, he sat down and began tearing off the small tassels sewn into the hem of his robe. They were another sign of the order and the Rule. The fifth abbot, Sage Capric, had authored the Rule and designed what became the uniform of the Monks of the Treasure, as they were once called. After adopting the Rule, and making it the guide for every aspect of life at the order, the Caprics became a nickname that overtook the original. In his scheme, the white and red colored tassels, much like the belts, were supposed to be a constant reminder of their dual oath to God and to the order, as well as their compound mission to protect the treasure and serve the people as spiritual guides. The red was a symbol that they had pledged their lifeblood to God and their brothers; the white signified their vow to be pure and blameless in all they did.

He stopped tearing them off after remembering their meaning. The Rule and its regulations might go overboard, but he could still do his best to fulfill those oaths to God and his brothers, to an upright life—even outside the order. The missing tassels could be his personal reminder that the Rule was not the same as his promises.

Eventually, he lay back on the springy turf and stared up at the blackness of the sky. He tried to block out the thoughts of all the chaos in which he found himself: the order burning, his friends and teachers dead, the fight with Fallon, and the battle that morning.

As soon as he pushed out one terrible thought, another one entered his mind to fill his heart with despair. A soft breeze passed over him, and chilled the wet streaks running down his face. He had been staring blindly at the unchanging black of the sky, until the breeze brought his mind back to where he was. Slowly, he realized that he was looking at a pinpoint of white light in the sky. He had never seen anything like it in his life. It wasn't like the bright area in the clouds that showed where the sun was on lighter days, and it wasn't the similar glow that hinted at the moon. This was a small shimmering point of light, like a candle seen in a distant window—only it was a pure clear white.

He propped himself up on his elbows and squinted. After staring for several moments, he thought he could see other, dimmer points of light near the first one. Suddenly, it occurred to him what it might be. During a series of lectures a couple years before, Noeman had shown them maps of pictures that he said were in the sky. He said they were made of points of light, and called the study of the pictures astronomy. Kurian wasn't sure he could believe his eyes. This was a star—the first one anyone might have seen for generations.

"Are you planning on sleeping out here tonight?" Louise said behind him.

Kurian jumped to his feet and wiped his face with his sleeves. "No. I was just..." He pointed toward the sky. "Did you see it?"

"See what?" she looked up.

He looked back to where the star had been, but it was gone, covered up by the clouds again. "Nothing," he said. Maybe he hadn't seen it. It might have been his imagination. Not that it meant anything if he had seen it. Such things were merely unexplainable weather. When he looked at Louise again, he thought he saw the same knowing look she had given him in the tavern.

"Your friends are fully ordained now. Tobin was very eager, but Rhys was more reluctant. It was a lovely ceremony."

"I suppose that leaves me out, then," he said. He expected her to say something witty and biting, but for a while, she said nothing.

"Do you want to talk about it?"

"No," he said, and started walking back toward the grove with her. He could see the campfire glowing between the trees, and wanted to be near his friends. But, he also felt like holding back and being alone with Louise. She seemed to understand what was happening better than the rest of them, and he wanted to find out more. Not tonight, though. There would be plenty of time during their journey.

"But thank you for the offer," he said as they neared the trees.

"One orphan to another—any time," she said softly.

CHAPTER NINE

The Ruins of Fin

Rhys approached Kurian while he took a moment alone behind a tree the next morning. He always tried to tell Kurian secrets at the most inconvenient and uncomfortable of times. "Sorry about last night," he said, standing shoulder to shoulder with him. Kurian shoved him off balance.

"Don't worry about it."

"We've been working at it for so long, and I was wondering if I would ever make it, like you were." Rhys shrugged. "Didn't think it would hurt anything since Noeman was offering...and with everything that's happened. But, I want you to know that we're still a troop."

"What do you mean?"

"Even though you didn't get ordained with us, I'm still your friend. You can count on me." Rhys smiled the way he had when they would spar to a tie during training. "I'll follow you to the end of this thing, wherever it takes us. Tobin, too. But he might be a little chummier with the dean."

"Thank you," was all Kurian could say.

Rhys slapped him on the back. "Now let's ride some horses!"

Louise had already given them basic instructions about handling the horses. They had divided the baggage between the two most troublesome mounts, including the swords and daggers, and then she had introduced each of them to the horses they would be riding. She would take the lieutenant's horse, because the others were used to following it, and because her experience gave her the ability to control him. When they turned around, Kurian and Rhys were surprised to see the dean already mounted.

"I *have* been on a horse in sixty-two years," he said in response to their expressions. Tobin, however, had one foot stuck in the stirrup. He was hopping on his free leg as the horse skittered around the grove. For a moment, they tried to suppress their laughter with snorts, but after watching Tobin hop about with one leg up in the air, Rhys bent double and roared.

"Don't get cocky, boys," Louise said. "You're next."

There had been a stable at the compound, but other than the few times visitors had brought their own mounts, it had been empty as long as Kurian had been there. Long ago, the Caprics had travelled across the country on horseback, but as they travelled less, they tended to remain on foot. Their horses became too old for work, and they never replaced them.

Louise grabbed the leads on Tobin's horse and steadied her until he had hoisted himself into the saddle. Then she untied the remaining two and walked them to Kurian and Rhys. He had never been close enough to touch a horse, and now their sheer size was intimidating. His side was sore where one of these horses had knocked him over the day before, and he hoped the horse wouldn't remember. She handed Rhys the larger horse, a chestnut brown mare. Kurian's was a mottled gray that shook its mane when he reached out a hand toward him.

"There's no reason to be afraid of him," said Louise. "Show him you are unafraid and deserve respect, and he will do as you ask." The horse turned its head and tried to take an apple that she held out to Kurian. She tossed it to him before the horse could get it, which allowed him to feed the animal. It was satisfying to feel the crunching teeth inches from his hand.

"Let's make a deal, horse," Rhys said, looking into his mare's eyes. "You don't kill me, and I won't kill you." She snuffed at his hand, looking for an apple of her own. He grabbed one from the ground and fed it to her, then stuck his foot in the stirrup and lifted himself smoothly into the saddle. "See? Easy, Kurian." He smiled and patted the horse's neck brusquely. She nipped at him, and Rhys yanked his hand back. It was Tobin's turn to laugh at him. "At least I got up on my own," Rhys said in response.

Kurian mounted without incident. The gray accepted his weight readily, and didn't show any signs of displeasure. "Are we ready, then?" he asked.

Louise untied Greta's leads, pointed her south, and patted her haunches. "Go on home," she said, and the pony started walking toward Downriver Town. Finally, Louise mounted the lead horse and they started north again.

After they were all comfortable with walking, she showed them the basics of steering, and encouraged them to pick up the pace. "We'll not go much faster than walking ourselves if we can't get up to a trot or a canter," she told them. Along the way, they practiced moving quicker for short distances until Kurian thought his rear would never be able to survive the two hundred forty miles to Dury. Louise gave them breaks each hour to let everyone rest—including the horses. Noeman asked that they time their rests to match the liturgical hours and insisted that they return to the full office of prayers to seek God's blessings on their journey. Kurian didn't object, but he also didn't agree to join in.

"Whatever it is, it has to make sense for it to be significant to King Frederick *and* Evasius. Ancient genealogies are likely candidates." Tobin's voice drifted forward where Louise could hear every word. They had been debating Evasius' claims about the treasure being a book for most of the day, and by the afternoon, she could almost make their arguments for them.

Kurian trotted beside her, riding as far from the dean as possible and avoiding the discussion.

"Where did you learn to do this?" he asked her as she slowed to a walk.

"My father," she said. "I was almost twelve when I lost my parents, so I grew up with the horses my father used on his farm. I helped to feed them, I cleaned their stalls, and I prepared them for work or riding."

"And you remember all of that from so long ago?"

"So long?" She lifted an eyebrow. "You've never spoken to a woman, have you?" She saw him squirm in the saddle.

"I don't remember what I learned about cobbling as a boy," he said, defensive.

"You don't really forget," she laughed. "Just as you don't forget how to talk to people. But, when I lived at the King's camp, I helped with the horses sometimes. He keeps a few around for messengers."

"I guess that makes sense." He was embarrassed.

She couldn't tell why she enjoyed making him uncomfortable with her comments, whether it was just for fun, or something more complicated. This time, she knew he was trying to find something to get his mind off the pain of losing so much, and she felt guilty about teasing him.

"Why are you asking?"

"Because riding along in silence is boring."

"And?"

He shrugged his shoulders. "I'm tired of being in my own head. There's not much good there lately."

"Things like that always change," she said, with a half-smile. "Just like the weather."

"If you had something about God in that sentence, you'd sound like Tobin."

"Who says I didn't?"

"So now you're going to start talking about God, too? I didn't know you believed in anything but your King," he said.

It stung a little because he was being defensive without understanding. "You never asked," she said, hoping he wouldn't take it for more sarcasm.

Suddenly, she knew he needed more than just light talk to help him handle his emotions in the moment. She patted her horse's neck and changed her grip on the reins. "My dad used to tell me that the best way to drive away brooding was to go as fast as you could bear on a horse—and then go faster. So, until your mood changes, how would you like to try a gallop?" Kurian grinned and nodded.

"Follow my lead," she said. She looked back at the others, who were lagging behind and then clucked her tongue. The horse sped up to a trot and his horse followed quickly. After they were moving faster, she gave the command and kicked. The battle-trained horse broke into a run in the same instant. In the corner of her vision, she saw Kurian almost fall backward when his horse took off, too. After regaining his balance, he leaned forward, and began to catch up to her. Faintly from behind, she heard Rhys' horse neighing, and him screaming, "Whoa!"

The wind lashed at her face and felt colder than it had a moment before. Soon tears streamed from her eyes, and she laughed for the sheer thrill of moving so fast over the plain. It had been far too long.

After a couple of minutes, she slowed down. Kurian was out of breath, but held a giddy smile and kept laughing. She laughed with him because it was the first unguarded moment of joy she had seen from any of the monks, and she loved being a part of it. The others were just smudges in the distance behind them, probably a mile off.

"That was incredible," he said between breaths.

"You liked it?" she asked. "Let's go back even faster." She kicked with her heels, and sped off toward his friends, her dark hair flowing behind like a banner, and the hoof beats of Kurian's horse chasing after her. She hoped it was the first sound of a new friendship.

They rode on for six days, continually north. At each break, Louise held her sunstone up to the clouds and looked through it to track the sun. Even in the heaviest clouds, the stone always picked out the sun as a bright spot in the sky. On the fourth day, they passed another crumbling village and filled their water pouches from a dirty well. The water was undrinkable, so the next morning, Louise showed them how to gather dew on extra blankets. Each night, they went to bed exhausted and sore, but by the end of the first week of riding, Kurian was finally beginning to adjust to it. He could feel the proper muscles strengthening and hardening, just as they had whenever he began a new phase of his training at the order.

On the morning of the seventh day, they found the riverbed again, and turned to follow it northwest. By noon, they began to see low buildings in the distance. They knew it held no more hope for civilization than any of the other villages they had seen on the plain. These were the ruins of Fin, the ancient city of kings.

Fin had stood as the seat of power for twelve hundred years before King Frederick found the treasure that created the Capric order. At the time, little was known about the history of Fin before Frederick's grandfather, King Heinrich III. But after establishing the order in his fifth year, Frederick ordered them to gather ancient artifacts and texts that revealed the kingdom's past. The Caprics sent many of their finds to the scholars of the academy at Fin. The knowledge they gathered helped Frederick to expand the kingdom across the ten cities of the plain. Fin became a center for learning and culture that drew wise men and artisans from neighboring kingdoms, which further expanded its influence. The cities of the plain became wealthy from the trade that poured into the kingdom as they reached across the seas, and into the North.

However, Frederick's sons were not the charismatic leaders that their father was, and his grandsons fell to quarreling over control of the kingdom. In their disputes, they hired advisors from the wealthy and ambitious Evasius family. When the kingdom found itself at the brink of civil war, Shadrick Evasius, advisor to the sitting king, seized control of the army and destroyed the city from within.

The city of Fin burned to the ground in a single night, and then the siege engines tore down the stones of almost every structure. It had remained empty for over a hundred years. The knowledge stored in the academy was lost, and only scattered pieces of the kingdom's history survived at the Capric order.

The Caprics kept histories of their order, which sometimes overlapped with the happenings of the kingdom, but not a comprehensive account of what the academy had discovered. The history of the kingdom was lost with them. With the order destroyed, the very memory of Fin would fade, and people would only remember Pallingham and the rule of the house of Evasius. As long as they feared or obeyed them, Evasius' fathers left the people alone, but did nothing for their education or their enrichment. Trade had slowed to a trickle even before clouds covered the sun and drought dried up the river. Art and culture were nonexistent. Slowly, the people who hadn't fled adapted to this new way of things, and lived under the gloom of Pallingham and its rulers. The Caprics retreated from an increasingly ambivalent people, and lost what influence they had to make things better. Now, not even the memory of a better time would remain.

They fell silent as they approached the remnants of the city. Grasses from the plain had overgrown the streets in clumpy tufts. A few cobblestones showed through the turf like trail markers to the underworld. Low walls marked the outlines of the city and piles of stone scattered along the riverbank stood as memorials to the grand structures that once towered above the streets. In the North, darker clouds gathered, dimming the light and foretelling rain.

Kurian had grown up reading about the grand city of Fin and hearing stories about King Frederick. He remembered the way that Tobin would study the paintings of the city, pointing out every detail to Kurian with fresh awe. But the kingdom and their order had failed the cities of the plain a long time ago.

Now, the rubble of the city barely looked like it was constructed by men. It might just as easily have been leftover pieces from a giant's game of Tablut, or dropped from the sky by God. He glanced at Tobin, who surveyed the destruction with a look of disbelief. Perhaps the destruction of their own home was hitting him at last, or maybe he was remembering the grandeur of the paintings.

Noeman dismounted before they reached the walls and knelt for a silent prayer. Louise signaled for the others to get down and walk. It felt inappropriate somehow to ride into a place so still and empty, as if it would disturb something that ought to remain untouched.

The stillness in the city was so complete that their own soft footfalls seemed foreign. Kurian strained his ears at the silence, hoping for some sound native to the city. Nothing came to his ears until a crow swooped down from the sky and landed on a crumbled stairway ahead of them. Looking up, he saw half a dozen more circling down from the clouds. He hadn't seen any birds while approaching the city and their arrival made the hair stand out on his neck. The one on the stairs watched him approaching, then let out a single caw and leapt into the air to join its companions.

"I've always wanted to come here, but this is no longer a good place," Tobin whispered beside him. Kurian shook his head and looked back to the sky. The murder circling above had grown to twenty crows, and the first break of the silence had turned into a din of cackles and caws that echoed down among the stones. The noise grated on Kurian's ears, making him cringe.

"Something is wrong here," Louise said. "Be careful."

"How does she do that?" Rhys asked. "She always knows when trouble's up."

"We all feel it," Noeman said. "The place is tainted."

"No, it's different with her. We've got goose pimples, but she looks like she knows before something happens," said Rhys. "She did at the bridge and the apple grove. How do you do it?"

"It's hard to explain," Louise answered. "Maybe you'll understand later. Now be quiet."

As they continued through the city, they passed by a row of buildings with mostly intact facades, but the empty doorways revealed only more crumbled stone behind. In places, the walls rose two stories above their heads, and Kurian was glad that they blocked out the sight of the crows. The wall of the last building rounded the corner of an intersection, and would provide decent shelter for the night. He was about to propose it as a campsite when the crows stopped their cawing. He heard the flapping of many wings on the other side of the building, as if the entire flock were landing together.

When they reached the corner, he looked toward the clouds again, but the crows were gone. A few hopped around on the ground, but nowhere near as many as he'd expected from the noise. Instead, he was surprised to see a rickety wooden shelter constructed against the wall. A small fire burned next to the shack, and soon a heavy, stooped woman shuffled outside. She tossed some crumbs to the birds and mumbled to them as if they were pets.

"Ooh!" she hooted when she saw them. Patches of stringy black hair clung to an otherwise bald scalp, and she squinted at them with one eye while the other drooped down her face. "You startled me. Leave an old woman alone, won't you?"

"We don't mean you any harm," Noeman said first. He was clearly as shocked as the rest of them to find a person living here.

"Harm," she chuckled to herself. "Just leave me alone."

This was both surprising and suspicious, and Kurian had the creeping feeling along his neck again. He didn't want to approach the woman and leave themselves in the same vulnerable position that the guards in the apple grove had taken. Tapping Rhys on the arm, he pointed toward the other side of the intersection. Rhys immediately remounted and moved to watch that corner. He sent Tobin to the same corner they had just turned, and then he moved around the woman's shack so that Noeman and Louise stood between the three of them with their horses and the two pack mounts. From horseback, he hoped they could spot any trouble early enough to defend themselves.

"Wait," said the old woman from the shack, as Noeman stepped closer to speak with her. She shoved a curled hand into her pocket and pulled out a rag that she coughed and spat into, then stuck back in her pocket. Then using her finger and thumb to hold her good eye open wide in a freakish stare, she looked at each of them in turn. "What is they?" she said. "Not phantoms like before—not dead ones with secrets. Such tasty secrets they has here."

"Are you all right?" Noeman asked. "We have some food and water we could share if you require aid."

Kurian turned from watching the street for a moment. "What are you doing, Dean?"

"It's called charity," said Noeman with an unusual bite in his voice. "It's one of those priestly duties you've decided to forego."

The old woman let out a cackling laugh and several of the crows mimicked her in response. "No, not phantoms, darlings," she said to the crows. She studied them again with the eye she held open. "Three young men…monks! And one old one." Her expression changed from intense interest to disappointment when she looked at Noeman, and then turned to a look of expectation. "And a beautiful young woman." The crows hopped toward Louise and made a rapid clicking noise. Kurian couldn't take his eyes off the woman now, and even the dean took a step back. Tobin and Rhys were staring at her as well, instead of watching the road.

"Are you hungry, or sick?" Noeman asked, still trying to play the compassionate priest.

"Yes, very hungry, me and my dears," she said, eyeing Louise again.

"As I said, we have food and water." Noeman opened his pack and started to rummage for something to give the woman. "We can also provide care for any injuries or ailments, and we can pray for you. It must be hard being out here alone." He was rambling as he sometimes did when he was nervous.

"You sure they real?" she said to the birds. One of them snapped its beak at her.

"Noeman," Louise said, tugging on his sleeve. "I think we should leave."

"Why do Caprics come to Fin?" the hag asked, as if to herself.

"That is our business. We are on an important…" Noeman started.

"They come to join these ghosts, bring more secrets for Duana?" she asked, stopping Noeman mid-sentence.

"Fin is dead. Capric is dead."

"Now, Madame, why would you say such a thing?" Noeman stepped away from his horse and strode toward her. Kurian felt a sense of dread and remembered that he was supposed to be watching for danger. However, the danger looked like it was right in front of them.

"We sees the smoke, my darlings enjoy their feast there," she said to the dean, then focused her attention on one of the birds cawing and rattling at her. "They can't be." She pulled at the lids again and eyed Kurian, Rhys, and Tobin more carefully.

Louise stepped up behind Noeman and urged him to leave again.

"Right age. Maybe they is," the crazy old hag said to the crow. "Lord Evasius wants to know these three come to see us."

Kurian wheeled his horse around to face the woman. "What do you mean about Evasius?" he shouted at her, but she still focused on her pets.

"Yes, the Hart looks tasty," she said in response to a caw, "they all do. But Evasius doesn't like if we dally. There's treats for this news, my darlings!" She cackled again, and the crows joined her.

"Tell us what you know about Evasius," said Kurian. When she ignored him again, he urged his horse forward quickly. As soon as he was between her and Noeman, she lunged at him with surprising speed and power.

He lifted his staff to protect himself, but her body exploded into a mass of crows in midair. A blur of wings beat against his shoulders and head with the sound of a windstorm. Their calls were deafening in his ears, and he felt beaks and talons scratching at him for a moment before the cloud of black feathers flew past him. They circled up into the sky as they had before and headed southwest—toward Pallingham Castle.

Kurian's horse was jittery and skipped to the side as the birds flew away. The other horses pulled at their reins and snorted. His heart raced and he was suddenly parched. He patted the gray's neck, and then looked at the dean for some explanation. Noeman looked as shocked as Kurian felt.

"That was unusual," Tobin said, staring at the empty space where the witch had stood.

CHAPTER TEN

Thaumaturgy

They all stood still for several moments, trying to comprehend what they had just seen.

"We should go," Louise said. Nobody objected.

They made their way carefully on the overgrown cobblestones as darkness came over Fin. After passing out of the city, Kurian trotted ahead and set a fast pace away from the river, north and east into the plains. He wanted to get as far from there as possible.

The others followed without asking where he was going, and he finally slowed down and stopped after they had run about five miles. It was empty, and far from any civilization—as good a space as any.

They all dismounted, and pulled down only their blankets and a little food for the night. Rhys thrust a sword into the turf and tied the horses to the hilt, but they left the saddles on, ready to flee if necessary. Nobody spoke as they sat huddled on the ground. Kurian wanted to ask questions, but couldn't think of how to break the silence. Noeman sat across from him, shaking his head and mumbling to himself. Eventually the dean stood up and paced back and forth, a dim figure in the darkness. Kurian could hear him muttering, "No, no, no. It's not possible."

"Dean," Tobin said with a worried look, "what's not possible?"

"That woman," the dean pointed back toward Fin. "There's no way. That doesn't happen anymore."

"I don't think I've ever heard of someone turning into a flock of birds," said Rhys.

"But was it..." Tobin began.

Noeman stopped in front of them. "*Thaumaturgy*. Magic or wonder-working as simpler folks called it, albeit of the darker sort."

"Like Sage Bennett did back when the order started?" Rhys looked impressed.

"Yes and no," Noeman said impatiently. "Sage Bennett performed many wonders and miracles, but he never did them of himself. Every *thaumaturge* in our history was a man of humility and grace. They were often surprised when God chose to answer their prayers in miraculous ways. But there were others who gained something like that power through darker means."

"Well, if it doesn't come from God, what are these darker means?" Tobin asked.

"I'm not certain where it comes from; I never studied it much. I've read about rituals and conjurations that gave them unnatural strength or knowledge. But I've never heard of anything like this." The dean returned to pacing. "And as I said, it doesn't happen anymore. *Thaumaturgy* was common in the early years of our order, when there were wars and missions from the king. Eventually it simply stopped."

"Why?"

"I don't know!" Noeman threw up his hands. "One of the abbots tried to institute a course in *thaumaturgy* for a few years, but nothing ever happened. It seemed like something that couldn't be learned. The brothers generally assumed that God didn't need to use it anymore."

"Then why did you teach us to pray for miracles?" Kurian asked. The more he heard Noeman talk about the order, the more it bothered him. He had never quite viewed the history of the order as a dissipation of their spiritual potency, of God performing fewer miracles through their work, but it offered more evidence of their decline.

Noeman's face showed that he was struggling for an answer. "It's what we've always done. It's part of having faith." He shrugged his shoulders. "And many things are miraculous that may not seem incredible; they're just more...circumstantial than supernatural." Kurian folded his arms, waiting for a better explanation. "Why not ask? Perhaps God will decide to do something astonishing."

"That is just the sort of nonsense you spouted in each of your lectures. 'The brothers generally assumed...'" Kurian mocked Noeman's tone. "'Perhaps God will do something astonishing.'

You aren't certain of anything, are you? Except your rules, of course."

"Kurian, stop," Tobin stood up in front of him.

"I'm sorry," he said, shaking his head. "But even if the dean is right, then where are the miracles? We're caught in the middle of a war over our little treasure, and now it's obvious that one side uses witches."

"Stop!" Louise said. "We're all exhausted, and I think a little scared." She pointed a cautionary finger as Kurian opened his mouth to speak. "You're right that Evasius has witches, but that isn't Noeman's fault. His family has always accomplished their deceptions in unexplained ways. Maybe this has been their way from the beginning."

"And how are we supposed to fight back against that?"

"I bet even thauma-birds can die," Rhys said with a chuckle.

"We must have faith," said Tobin.

Kurian almost left. Tobin was sounding more like the dean since the ordination, and he wasn't sure he could talk as freely with him anymore. Faith was the vague answer the brothers gave for every problem, and he had watched too many faces in Aposford lose hope after hearing that answer to think that it was the great cure-all. There had to be a more realistic way to face this.

"Don't look so disgusted," Noeman said to him. "Brother Hart may be more right than you think. I have told you almost all I know of miracles, and I cannot instruct you in their practice. However, today's events have made me reconsider some other information. I'm afraid something much larger may be happening in our world. We may yet see a resurgence in *thau-*

maturgy if my suspicions are correct." He had stopped pacing, and finally sat down, indicating for them all to do the same. "There is something you should know."

Kurian sat reluctantly.

"Before the order was attacked, I confronted Sage Marten about sending you to negotiate with Evasius. It made no sense, and flaunted some important regulations of the Rule. I feared what Evasius might do to you."

"You were worried?" Kurian said. "I thought you were about to turn us into *gyrovagues*."

"Never!"

Kurian was surprised to see genuine pain on his face.

"Whatever you might believe about our relationship, Mr. Abramson, I only ever did what I believed would push you to excel. You could have been a remarkable brother if you learned to accept discipline. I may have given in to frustration with you at times, and for that I am sorry, but we are straying from my intent."

"I'm sorry," Kurian muttered. "Go on."

"The abbot was distraught, frantic," Noeman continued. "He told me that a prophet had visited him with a vision. He believed that the vision instructed him to send the three of you away, in order to save the order and the compound. When the first attack came, he was terrified that he missed his chance, so he sent you away immediately. That was why I failed to dissuade him that night. It was like talking to a lunatic."

"Can you tell us the vision?" Tobin said, leaning forward.

"The prophet said that he saw the great oak burning atop the hill, and then a voice spoke a short verse:

'Those walking in darkness will see a great light.
Release the Deer, the Brute, even the Princely Son.
On those living in the land of shadow, a light will dawn.'

"The abbot believed that the verse spoke of you three, and that removing you from the compound would prevent the order from falling and the tree from burning. Since that interpretation was erroneous, then perhaps the prophet's vision was meant to save your lives, for sending you away at that moment clearly did. What the rest of it means, I do not know."

"Are you even sure it's about us?" Tobin asked.

"I'll admit, it's vague on the details," Noeman said, "however, if it is about a trio of men at our order, then you three make the most sense, simply by starting with you, Brother Hart. After that witch called you by name, I'm convinced that the prophecy is about you—and somehow, through her demonic arts, she knew it."

"Perhaps the other part is about the treasure," Tobin added. "If it is a book of great power and knowledge, then it would bring hope and light to the people. Evasius would see something like that as a threat. It might even bring the kingdom back to what it was during the time of Fin."

"You'd need a king for a kingdom," Louise said with her best sarcasm.

The verse made Kurian think of the star, and he suddenly felt compelled to say something.

"I think I saw a star the other night," he blurted out. Everyone stared at him as if he had transformed like the witch. "Outside the apple grove. It was only for a moment, and then it was gone."

Louise smiled at him. He thought she knew the moment he was remembering, just before she distracted him.

"Are you certain?" Noeman leaned forward until Kurian saw the wonder on his face.

"It was a pinpoint of light in the sky, the way you described it in the astronomy lectures." He shook his head. "I'm not certain it was really there."

"Nobody still living has seen a star, or the sun, or the sky," Noeman said with awe. Then he laughed deeply. "You wanted to see the miraculous, Mr. Abramson——you've seen it!" Noeman looked toward the sky as if suddenly the clouds would part and reveal gloriously lit heavens. He sighed, and the others followed his gaze.

"This is the best news in weeks," Tobin said, then breathed deeply and lay back with his hands folded behind his head.

"Why is a hole in the clouds so important?" Kurian asked. "I'm not even certain it's what I saw." He didn't understand why Tobin was suddenly so relieved.

"Because, my friend, it means God is still there, when I had feared that he left us."

"How do you know that's what it means?"

"I have faith," Tobin said simply.

"You're becoming impossible." Kurian picked up his blanket and walked a few yards away to go to sleep. This was exactly the sort of response to things that the order had taught them to make. Everything could be a sign or an omen, depending on the interpretation. Now Tobin decided to hope in something that probably wasn't a sign at all. But he was finished looking for meaning in every falling leaf. He only wanted to fulfill his oath and prevent more destruction from Evasius.

He had to focus on calming his breathing after wrapping himself in his blanket. The others also picked spots to sleep, and he heard Tobin and Rhys whispering for several minutes. As he was on the verge of finally falling asleep, Rhys called loud enough for him to hear, "Good night, Princely."

Tobin and Rhys giggled to each other and Kurian rolled over, not knowing if he would ever make it to sleep now. He took a deep breath, realizing that this was their way to make peace. They were still trying to be his friends. "Good night, Deer Brute," he said, to tell them he accepted. Then he slipped into a deep sleep in which he dreamt of a sky covered with innumerable stars that blazed like fire-lit gems, and people who glowed like his star, so bright and clear they lit up the night and hurt his eyes.

As one of the ten cities of the plain, Dury was still uniquely productive, despite its small population. However, its remoteness from other towns and cities meant few residents of Pallingham wanted to live there. It stood at the foot of the Northland cliffs, at the northern edge of the plain, and was almost half way between the ocean to the west, and Aven, the furthest eastern city on the plain of Apos.

People had originally settled in the natural caves found in that part of the cliffs, and eventually built Dury between the river and a small forest that fanned out west and south. Even when the river dried up, the caves still offered ample water supplies for the city through hidden springs and cisterns. The forest provided a rare source of timber, as well as a varied diet that few other cities in Pallingham enjoyed.

A well-maintained road ran parallel to the cliff face between Aven and the sea. Where it passed through Dury, a southerly route headed toward Pallingham Castle. For years, few had travelled these roads besides Lord Evasius' men, either soldiers or lumber carters.

Captain Fallon had come to Dury several times to guard shipments of supplies along the dangerous Cliff Highway. While he had encountered and defeated small gangs of men who tried to waylay the shipments, he had never encountered the King of the Caves who was causing so much trouble. The man seemed to be gaining influence in the area, as well. As his attacks became bolder, the other criminal activity diminished, as if they were afraid. Fallon had searched the caves in the cliff himself, but had never found a clue that he even existed—except for the reports of terrorized men. He longed to meet this king of criminals, but he never attacked when Fallon was present. That could make the difference in finally catching him; if only Fallon could be there to inspire his men and counter the madness that the man seemed to instill in the soldiers.

This time, he felt like he might have the opportunity. He stood outside the guard shack at Dury's southern gate, watching the road with ten of his greenest men. Seventy-five had come with him, in addition to the twenty he had sent the day before. Now he had them spread out between the three gates, and patrolling the roads up to a mile from town. Twenty of them had spread out across the city in two-man teams, questioning citizens and looking for anybody suspicious. Add the score of guards posted to Dury permanently, and he was certain that he would catch the Caprics if they approached the city.

The first real rain of the season had begun that morning, and he smiled to himself as he watched the misery of the young soldiers standing guard with him. They crossed their arms and stomped their feet to keep warm as the water soaked through their uniforms. Of course, he shared part of their discomfort. The first hard autumn rain meant the gloomy season was upon them. The clouds that always covered Pallingham would darken and turn the world into a dim, damp twilight for almost four months. Most of the plain would get rain almost daily, and the eastern cities might have some snow. He didn't expect he would see the sun's strong glow through the blanket of clouds again until late in February. What soldier wouldn't weary in their vigilance under such conditions?

"Here," he said, grabbing blankets from the guard shack and handing them to the nearest man. "Use these until I can get some cloaks sent here. Duty comes before comfort, but I know you'll do it better if you're warm." The recruits thanked him. He nodded curtly and said as he walked away, "and light that watch fire early. I need you alert."

By his guess, he had arrived at Dury at least five days before the Caprics, who had escaped on foot. However, he thought the show of force was necessary to dissuade any potential spies waiting to aid them. A few days of watching the patrols ought to plant a seed of doubt into anybody who might be sympathetic to them.

He was certain he had chosen the right city to reinforce. The King of the Caves would raid the Cliff Highway most frequently, and then seemed to disappear. Now that he knew his camp was in the crags on top of the cliffs, Fallon was convinced that he had a hidden means of ascent. That ruined the cliffs as a defensive feature of the city, but it gave him hope in catching his prey. Somewhere in the caves near Dury was a path to the top, which meant that the monks' guide would lead them here. All he had to do was intercept them on their way, and he would have the spy who could lead him straight to Lord Evasius' treasure.

Fallon supervised the change in the watch and waited for nightfall before he left the gate. He wandered the city streets for hours after dark, avoiding the bunkhouse where the off-duty men stayed. The commanding officer of the guard had given up the attached apartment to him, but going there meant sleep—and he was no longer alone in his dreams.

It was past the second watch when he could avoid sleep no longer. Returning to the apartment, he removed his sword and fell into the bed in sopping wet clothes. His body was numb from the cold rain, and the warm room made his feet and hands tingle in pain. Weariness soon overcame the sensation and he was asleep as soon as his eyes fought their way closed.

Immediately, he felt a body in the bed with him, but when he turned, he was in his bed back in Pallingham. Mouna lay next to him in her black robes, the outline of her body blurred and difficult to see.

"Nicholas," Mouna cooed, "I feel like you've been avoiding me. I've been waiting so long." Her voice echoed in his head just as her body seemed blurred to his eyes.

"Much to do to prepare the search here," he said, standing up from the bed. "I won't let them slip away again." His side itched and burned where she had slid the talisman between his ribs. It was small, but the cut had needed stitching, and now it troubled him when they had these dream meetings.

"I'm certain you're doing a thorough job searching." She propped herself up on one arm, and began to slowly draw her robe up, revealing inch by inch her slender, pale legs.

He stood at attention as if he were giving a report to Lord Evasius.

"My men have secured access to the city, and are patrolling the streets and the roads. That is my report for now." Behind him was the door he needed to walk through to leave the meeting and the dream. He dared not look at it until he was dismissed, but he craved dreamless sleep.

"But I have information for you, this time," she said. "The Caprics are closer than we thought."

"Do you know where?"

"One of my colleagues met them in the ruins of Fin before sundown yesterday. She informed me this morning."

"How did they get there so quickly?" They were moving with almost impossible speed. Perhaps he had underestimated their abilities and training again. Or, something else had happened. "Did they have horses?"

"You're so quick," she smiled at him. "Looks like the guards from Downriver Town were not up to the task. I hope you are, Captain. I do enjoy working together." She beckoned with her fingers and it felt as if she were pulling him toward her with a rope tied to his body. He resisted and stood his ground, and she laughed.

"They could be here as early as tomorrow," he said. "I need to ensure my men are fully alert."

"You do that, Nicholas," she said, and released him from her spell of temptation with a wave. "Maybe the next time we speak, there'll be something to celebrate."

"Give my regards to our lord," he said before turning for the door to his escape.

A Warm Welcome

Soft drops of rain on his face woke Kurian the next morning. He felt calmer than he had during their entire journey, as if the terrible events of the last two weeks had only been a story told by one of the brothers before bed. For a few moments in the refreshing drizzle, the tragedy didn't seem like it touched him. Then he remembered their encounter with the witch. He remembered the feathers beating against his skin and shuddered.

Everyone else rose because of the rain, too, except the others jumped up from where they slept and quickly rolled up their blankets to stow them. By the time they had enjoyed a small breakfast, the rain grew heavier. The cold, hard sheets of water washed away Kurian's waking euphoria.

He dreaded the day's march as they started. The constant din of the rain dragged out the long hours of riding into a damp monotony. The hood of his wool robes saturated quickly, and then dripped water down his face. During the heaviest downpours, they could not see more than a dozen yards, and Kurian knew that the rainy season was officially beginning. He hoped Tobin was right about God being with them, but this seemed like more proof to the contrary. Harsh weather became another obstacle to achieving their goal. To make things more miserable, Noeman still insisted on dismounting and observing the office of prayers at the appropriate rest times. Kurian was sorry that he could no longer join his friends in what had once been a meaningful part of their days together, but he was also glad he didn't have to kneel in the mud.

The rainfall ebbed at times, but continued throughout the day. They slept on the plains again, creating makeshift tents with the extra blankets. It slowed the downpour, but they were still subject to persistent drips that made sleep difficult.

They mounted weary and wet the next morning, expecting to reach Dury before lunch. The weather continued, forcing them to stay close to the riverbank so they wouldn't lose their way. Soon, the road came into view on their left, paralleling the path of the river. A few miles later, they stood before the Dury forest. The undergrowth was thick at the edge, making the forest of beech and oak trees look like an impenetrable wall, except for the passage of the road. The boys had never seen so many trees. The closest growth of trees they could compare it to was the neat rows of small orchards near Aposford.

Before the road entered the shelter of the trees, Louise veered left, across the road, and followed the timberline saying, "I know a place we can dry out."

Eventually, they entered a clearing cut out from the forest. A cottage stood in the center. It looked as if it were constructed largely from the trees cut from the clearing. The windows glowed with firelight, and they were all glad for the opportunity to get warm.

Louise rode up to the cottage while the men held back. She dismounted and knocked at the door. Kurian tried to watch the trees and the cottage. They were getting close to the king's camp—only a day away according to Louise. She had become pleasant enough on the plains, even friendly, but after all they had experienced, he felt he needed to be on guard. Evasius' servants had found them twice, and the King's men might not be as kind as Louise had been.

He heard her shouting over the rain, and then the door swung open and a large man in furs stepped out and lifted her off the ground in a great hug. When he finally stopped shaking her, she gestured back to them and the man walked out to greet them.

"There's a shed for your horses around the other side of the house," he said. "Get them settled in and I'll pour you a bowl of stew." Kurian's stomach nearly howled at the mention of hot food. He saw a smile spread across Rhys' face. Enjoying some hospitality would be a welcome reprieve.

Inside, the cottage was nearly as sparse as the cut clearing it stood in. A straw mattress lay on the dirt floor in one corner. The only furniture was a small table with two chairs. But it was warm, and brightly lit by a large fire and several oil lamps. The warm air felt like a barrier he had to cross to enter the doorway, and with it came the aroma of a heavily herbed stew. His stomach growled again as he took a deep whiff of their first warm meal in a week.

"Gideon Birch," said their host, handing out steaming bowls from the table. He stood even taller than Rhys did, so that he had to duck under the bags of potatoes and squashes hanging from the rafters. A motley collection of thick furs bunched around his shoulders, making him appear bulkier than he truly was, and his bushy, reddish beard created the illusion that the furs were part of him. He was clearly strong and stout, the type of man that Rhys would grow to be. The smile had not left his face since he met them in the rain, and wrinkles from laughing made him look older than he probably was. From where Kurian was standing, Gideon was large enough to block his view of the table, so that he was surprised to see another figure seated there when Gideon finished giving them their stew.

"Alden," Louise said happily, and crossed over to her partner from Downriver Town. "Why haven't you said hello?"

"Well, it's tight quarters in here," said the flute player. "I figured you'd see me soon enough." She laughed and hugged him. Both of the men looked at her with the love of a proud, protective uncle.

"I'm sorry I don't have more seating," Gideon said, "but you lot should be used to eating on the ground by now." Noeman thanked him for the food, and then introduced himself and the boys. Kurian almost forgot to wait for the prayer before devouring the stew. As he scraped the bottom of the bowl, Gideon said, "Don't be shy if you want more."

"It's good to see you," Alden said to Louise after she sat down across from him. Then he looked at Kurian, "and I'm glad you made good on your promise."

"I'm glad to see you again, too," Louise said, smiling.

"I wanted to send help as soon as I got to the king, even though I knew it was a fool's errand. It would be more than a miracle to find anybody out wandering on the plains." Looking at Kurian again, he said, "If you'd stayed to the riverbed, it would be another matter—but I was right about your road being more dangerous."

There was silence.

"I'm sorry about your brothers," Alden said to them all. "We received the news from a friend in Pallingham."

"Thank you," Noeman said.

"It may actually be worse than we've thought," said Louise. "We met a witch in Fin. Somehow she was able to turn into a murder of crows and fly straight to Evasius."

"Then he knows you're coming." Alden paused in thought for a moment. "Of course, we could have surmised that from the company of soldiers that arrived in Dury three days ago, led by that captain you blinded."

"They've been onto us at every turn," Kurian said.

"Evasius and his family did not get where they are by anything except ruthless cunning," Alden sipped at his own stew. "Remember old Henry at the tavern?"

Kurian remembered the insane rant from the man at the Briny Mug. Suddenly, he realized that the nonsense rhyme seemed to match the prophecy that Noeman had told them after meeting the witch. "Wait, you told me that he knew we were going to the king because he saw us together. But he knew things about us, who we were, just like that witch did."

Alden looked uncomfortable for a moment and glanced at Louise. "And what would you have said if I told you that I thought a witch had taken his mind or possessed him with a demon?"

"At the time I would have thought you were overly superstitious, but I did ask if that trick you did to make him quiet was magic." Kurian tried to watch his reaction, but Gideon broke in.

"The king's men are not without their own mysteries," he said. "But right now, we have to figure out how to get you lot past nearly a hundred soldiers and guards."

"Where do you fit into all of this?" Tobin asked.

"I've always been very comfortable alone," Gideon said, still smiling. "In fact, I was recruited while hiding in a cave full of grain outside the city walls. The king asked me to make this place for our friends to move quietly between Dury and Pallingham. I give protection and warm food; I get a quiet place where I can build things."

"So, you're going to get us up the cliff?"

"No, Louise and Alden can do that." Gideon lifted the edge of the furs he was wearing to reveal a sword strapped to his back, and a leather shirt that held enough daggers and knives to make him look like a pincushion. "I have a chat with anybody trying to follow you."

"I see." It was Tobin's turn to look uncomfortable. Even when showing off his weapons, the smile never left Gideon's face.

"The rain will give us some cover if it doesn't let up, but we won't be moving till well after dark." He reached up to a loft built above the door and pulled down a bundle of tied cloth. "Now that you've warmed up a bit, Alden brought you some fresh clothes to wear. Sorry, Noeman, but we didn't know you were coming."

"I have something extra that should fit," Alden said.

"Just until I'm dry, thank you," Noeman replied.

"I've also got a couple of hammocks and some blankets. You can rest until we're ready to leave," said Gideon, pulling down another bundle. "Unfortunately, brother, I'm going to have to insist you change for everyone's safety."

"If I cannot wear my robes when they are dry, then I will sleep in them wet," the dean said.

Alden held up a hand before Gideon opened his mouth again. "I understand. They are symbols of your order. However, the soldiers know your order was destroyed, and they're looking specifically for three monks and a young woman. If they find even one from your order, there will be nowhere to hide. Every soldier in that company will come down on us in a moment."

"I have worn these robes for over fifty years," Noeman said, his eyes sparkling wet in the firelight. "Besides these boys, they are all I have left of my home and my life. Do not ask me to cast them aside so lightly."

Alden leaned forward in his chair and looked long into the dean's eyes. "I will only ask it for a short time, then. Will you consent to a disguise until we have reached the king's camp?"

Noeman stared back at him, looking as uncertain as Kurian felt the first time he had spoken with Alden. The calm, reasonable demeanor was disarming. He made you want to trust him. The dean eventually nodded his head and Alden gave him a comforting smile.

"I will dry them and pack them with care myself," he said. "Now, what about your staves? They're another giveaway."

"We gathered a lot of weapons from some guards that tracked us," said Rhys eagerly. "Swords, daggers."

Noeman patted him on the shoulder like a parent calming an excited child. "If you promise that we may retrieve them on our return, I will consent to whatever replacement you approve."

"They will be safely hidden," Alden nodded his head.

Kurian and the brothers stripped down to the singlets beneath their robes and found places to lie down. Gideon held a blanket out to offer Louise some privacy while she changed, and then she picked her way between them to one of the hammocks he had strung from the corner of the ceiling. Alden claimed the mattress. Only Gideon stayed awake, sitting next to the fire and propping his feet up on the table. The ground was harder than the grass of the plain, but after an exhausting two days in the rain, Kurian fell asleep immediately.

As night approached, Captain Fallon waited for news in the tavern beside the bunkhouse. Strategically, it was his preference for a temporary headquarters. It gave him visibility to the public, and was the closest building to a central point between the three gates of Dury. The main street from the southern gate forked in two directions, one toward each of the northern gates, and the Tavern stood in the fork. If a runner came with a report, he could move quickly, without having to cross the entire city. The tavern was also a likely spot for the monks to come if they were able to sneak past his men.

After he had arrived and spread out a large map of Dury on one of the tables, the patrons quickly finished their ales and left. He enjoyed being alone with his work in the large room; it was more appropriate to the position he enjoyed. The apartment in which he'd slept didn't provide enough room to walk and think. It would have gnawed away at his concentration until he was irritable, and he found that irritability was not conducive to either good tactical decisions, or successfully leading men.

Upon waking from his conference with Mouna that morning, he had rescheduled the watch rotation, ensuring that his veterans would be rested and alert later in the day. It made the greenhorns more listless and tired in the morning, but it ensured a tighter watch after nightfall.

If the monks were smart, they would use darkness to slip by his guards. Fallon would attempt to counter that strategy by sending his patrols further down each of the main roads and hiding lookouts in the woods. With the mayor's help, he had also instituted an immediate curfew. The criers had passed through the streets all day, warning that anybody discovered out after nightfall would be arrested. The only piece of the arena that he couldn't control was the rain; that would still be in his prey's favor. *If Evasius' witches had true power*, he thought, *they would fix that for him as well.*

He stopped beside the large front window of the tavern and noticed that the rain had let up. Perhaps Mouna had more influence than he knew. More likely, it was just a temporary break in the storm. The wind still whipped through the streets, as it had all afternoon.

He scratched lightly at the wound over his ribs. Thinking about the witch was just a distraction. He resumed walking around the room, examining the map on the table from every angle. His instinct told him that they would come tonight. All his intelligence confirmed it. Now, his plans hinged on the moment he heard boots running down the street.

Waiting for the battle was always when he felt most at peace. All the confusion of life fell away. Everything became clear.

Fox and Hound

Kurian woke as soon as Tobin touched his shoulder. It didn't feel like any time had passed at all. The fire had dimmed to embers in the hearth, and the lamps no longer burned, so the darkness convinced him that he had slept for several hours. The room was still warm, but there was a draft when the wind whistled through the shutters. "I've always envied your ability to sleep so soundly," Tobin said, smiling. "Time to go."

"You mean Rhys, don't you?" He blinked his eyes and slapped his cheeks to wake up.

"Rhys sleeps quickly. You sleep hard." For a moment, Tobin looked the way he used to on the morning of an exam—tired and worried. "I almost had to pull your arm off just now."

"No. You only touched my shoulder," Kurian argued. Tobin looked back in disbelief.

Louise and Alden sat at the table whispering to each other. He looked as comfortable and healthy as he had been at the Briny Mug, while Louise was dirty from traveling. Her hair had dried with a slight wave to it that drew Kurian's eye. She had changed from the blouse and skirt they had met her in to tunic and trousers in the same style as the clothes offered to the men. It was shocking to see a woman wearing them, but it might be a convincing disguise if she covered her hair.

Kurian dressed while Rhys helped himself to another bowl of stew, and Noeman kneeled in the corner, praying. He noticed their packs leaning near the door, looking full again. A pair of walking sticks and four short swords also stood against the wall.

"Stopped raining," Gideon said as he opened the door. "Grab your packs. Second watch starts in just over an hour. If we hurry, we can cross the river while they're thinking about their bunks." They did as he told them and filed out into the night. Alden and Noeman took the staves, while the rest grabbed swords. Then Gideon took off his own satchel. "A parting gift for you, from the king," he said, and pulled out light cloaks for each of them. "To help keep the rain off, and to cover up that hair," he said to Louise.

They jogged as quickly and quietly as they could, skirting the forest until they neared the road. "Have to be careful," Gideon whispered. "Patrols are coming down the road all the way through the forest, and the mayor's instituted a curfew, so we're the only ones out tonight."

He paused and looked toward the road. "Wait here a moment," he said, and then moved closer in a crouched run. He kneeled behind a tree, looking toward the road. Kurian wasn't sure how he could see anything under the shadow of the trees.

After a few moments, Gideon made a warbling whistle. "Our turn," Alden said, and led the others forward.

"No sound of patrols," Gideon said to them, creeping out from the underbrush.

He signaled for them to follow and then trotted across the road. The rest of them followed in a line. When they were scrambling down the muddy riverbank, they heard the snapping of bushes behind them.

"Stop!" they heard a voice yell behind them, then, "Here, they're here!"

"Run," Gideon said. "Our only chance is the forest on the other side."

Kurian watched him help Louise, Noeman, and Alden down the last part of the bank. He thought he should position himself at the opposite side to help them back up and was just beginning to move when the long blast of a horn came from the road.

The knock at the door stopped Fallon's walking. The sentry outside opened it and stuck his head inside.

"Sir, you should hear this."

He stepped out of the door and faintly heard a horn blowing in the distance. The pattern of the call told him exactly which lookout it was. "The southern road," he said, and ran to his horse tied at the corner of the tavern. "Take your horse and go to the other posts. Send half their men to me and the rest out on the roads to search. They know my orders. Only three men at each gate. Go!" They both mounted and rode in opposite directions.

Fallon spurred his horse to a gallop. The hunt was on.

He blew through the gates in under a minute, and passed two small squads of men running along the road to reach the horn.

The first had split off from the gate as instructed; the second was one of the patrols on the road. Once they knew the direction their prey had run, they would spread out in a fan to search for the monks. The men from the cliff gates would do the same. If the Caprics persisted in moving toward the cliffs, his men would catch them in the middle. With fifty soldiers performing an orderly search, he was certain they could find these ridiculous monks.

It was almost two miles to the southern edge of the forest, and he was winded from galloping at full speed the entire way. His horse breathed hard as well. The lookout stopped blowing the horn when he saw him.

"What news?" he asked.

"Seven of them, sir, sneaking across the road and into the riverbed. Ran for the trees after I started blowing."

"Good man," Fallon said, "tell your comrades when they arrive, then carry out my previous orders."

The soldier saluted him, and he rode down to the riverbank. Soon, he found the place where they had descended and followed the tracks across the river and toward the forest. There was just enough light filtering through the clouds to see the muddy trail in the open, but he wouldn't be able to track them through the forest in the dark. However, if he could pinpoint where they entered it, he could better position his men to search for them.

The trap had sprung. The Caprics had walked straight into the jaws that would soon close about them.

Fallon smiled. They would pay for the dishonorable trick they had pulled before. They would wish for blindness after he had his turn to strike.

Kurian was breathing heavily by the time they stopped running. They had pushed deep into the forest away from the river. He felt stuck, with no escape. There were, after all, dozens of soldiers searching for them. Thinking about that made it harder to breathe. The horn had stopped a moment before, but that probably meant they were following.

"They are going to come searching for us once they gather their numbers," Gideon said quietly. "Pray they don't have dogs."

"What should we do?" Noeman asked, breathing hard as well.

"We can act as a decoy," Alden said. "You four hide until they follow us, then sneak back to the cottage."

"Then what," said Kurian, "wait for you to come back?"

"Alden's right," Gideon said. "They'll chase whatever is moving in the dark, and I know these woods better than anybody. I can lead them where they'll get more than they bargained for."

"And we're just supposed to trust you'll return?"

Louise grabbed his pack and swung him around. "I've brought you this far. It's time you trust me!" He could barely see her—just an outline—but he thought he knew how she looked at him based on her tone. He wanted to believe it was how she had looked at him when she first saw him; more than recognition, it was knowing. Remembering that, he found he wanted to trust her.

"Ok," he said hoarsely.

"The horses are already packed, just in case," said Gideon. "Plenty of supplies and a stash of money as well, if you take mine."

"If we're not back by morning, head for Whalesand," she told them. "I'll try to catch up, but if I don't, hire a boat to Ramah and find a fisherman named Broadman. He'll take you the rest of the way."

The sound of men crashing through the underbrush at the forest edge hushed them all. "Hide," Gideon told them, "and don't move until they give us chase."

Suddenly, Kurian couldn't see his massive form anymore, and he only heard a whisper of movement heading back toward the riverbed to tell him they had left. Tobin tugged on his shoulder, and together they crawled halfway under a fallen tree trunk where Rhys and Noeman had already disappeared.

The wet ground seeped through his new clothes, making him cold. He focused on trying to steady and quiet his breathing. Feeling Tobin's chest rise and fall against his shoulder helped to calm him. He needed to protect Tobin the same way Tobin had protected him in the apple grove. The wind blew in the treetops, making them creak and sigh, and the sound of heavy footfalls and snapping branches came slowly closer. Finally, he heard a horse galloping at the forest edge, a couple hundred yards away.

"Kurian," he heard faintly over the wind. "I'm tired of chasing you, Kurian." He recognized the voice as Captain Fallon. "Come out now and you'll live."

"Not one for subtlety," he whispered to Tobin, trying to stave off the panic and the bile rising in his throat.

Tobin hushed him.

He saw distant torches, ghostly lights floating between the trees. He could only hear the nearest soldiers. With every step, they sounded only an arm's length away, and then closer with the next. It was impossible to tell where they were until he saw the faint glow on the trees in front of him.

Just as he thought he would see a soldier step into view, there was a commotion toward the river. Somebody was running through the undergrowth quickly. The snap of breaking branches shot through the forest and the torchlight on the trees disappeared as he heard the soldiers take off in the direction of the noise. "Here," some of them called far off, and the sound of running faded away. Captain Fallon's horse also galloped back toward the riverbank. Suddenly, a booming crash filled the forest, as if a tree had fallen over. After a moment of silence, the shrieks of wounded men reached them. Gideon must have left a terrible surprise.

Eight pairs of men had already gone into the forest, and more were arriving from the bunkhouse. The screams of their comrades coming from inside the dark forest was beginning to rattle the newcomers.

"I heard some locals talking about the bear-man in the forest," Fallon overheard one of them saying. He dismounted directly in front of the soldier and received a jittery salute.

"Soldier, button up that lip. It's a dark forest, and obviously some of our men had an accident."

"Yes, sir."

"Now get your torch, and start your search."

Fallon grabbed a torch himself. He needed to see exactly what had happened in there. After giving orders to a corporal to organize the remaining men, he made his way quickly toward the screams.

Half a dozen soldiers stood with torches, surveying two wounded men and one corpse. A large piece of tree trunk, rigged as a trap, had struck all three and knocked the top from a smaller tree on its way down. It had hit the dead man directly, and maimed the others with the ragged ends of hewn branches jutting out from every side. The Caprics were receiving help from somebody who knew this forest well. They had turned his trap against him, but he was not without hope. They were still out here somewhere.

"What are you doing just standing there?" he said to the six men nearby. "Get the wounded to the physician, and the two of you get back to searching." He pointed to the two who looked the least composed at seeing the carnage, and led them further into the forest.

There was no trail to see in the dense undergrowth. The storm had littered the ground with broken branches, ruining another tool for tracking. He would have to rely on his large numbers and a thorough search; eventually they would scare them from hiding. The odds kept turning in this game, and it seemed a powerful force was working against him, protecting the Caprics. It couldn't possibly be their god. He hadn't spared their order from the fire, so it made no sense that these few would be so impossible to capture.

Branches broke further ahead as somebody started running. "The odds turn again," he said, and dashed forward as fast as the torchlight could illuminate his path.

The torches had converged on a distant point, and the screaming men masked any accidental sounds as Kurian snuck away with his friends. At the forest edge, they looked for signs of anybody watching. The plain stretched out to the south, dark and empty. Other soldiers with torches milled about on the road, or between the forest and the riverbed, their night vision probably ruined. Fallon's horse stood in the light as well, but he was not on it. They had a perfect escape.

Another uproar burst from the forest far behind them, causing them to pause and drop to the ground. This time a higher pitched scream filled the air.

"Louise," Kurian said, and began pushing himself off the ground.

Rhys lunged and pushed him back down, laying on top of him. "You do that and we all die," he growled. Kurian tried to shove him off, but Rhys had pinned him. "I don't like it either, but we can't help them. They gave us the chance to get away." He stopped struggling and nodded before Rhys let him up.

With the fading sounds of men tearing through forest behind them, they ran to get as far as they could into the empty plains. Before they were far, a white light blazed from behind them and a sound like a peal of thunder knocked them to the ground. When Kurian looked around, the trees appeared to be aflame with a white light. As he stared, it faded into a central point.

The light dazzled his eyes so that he could not focus after the glow was gone. Without a word, they got up and fled. The sky opened again with a fresh downpour and they escaped into the storm.

They kept going until his lungs burned and his legs stumbled from exhaustion. Kurian felt a muddle of rage, pain, and grief seethe up in his heart as he ran. When they finally stopped, it drained away, leaving him empty and powerless. Louise had sacrificed herself for them. He wondered if this was how the dean felt as he had watched the compound burn from Aposford. He looked at Tobin and shook his head. "We had to," Rhys said from behind, then both his friends put their arms around him and together they wept.

PART TWO

CHAPTER THIRTEEN

Blubber and Bone

Lord Evasius smeared sealing wax on another letter to one of his nobles and impressed it with his signet. The lamp wavered in a draft from a window left open to allow the sound of the rain to drown out other noises and cocoon him in his chambers with only his thoughts. It helped him to concentrate on the mundane task of manipulating lesser men so far off.

He had prepared almost identical letters for the handful of influential men in Pallingham, informing them to prepare for a general conscription and muster in the spring. The nobles had cowered before his ancestors when they first seized power, but Evasius himself had always had to resort to politics—vague promises that could be revoked with the right excuses. They still feared him, which was why they never pressed the issue when he broke a promise, but they resisted him in small ways that prevented him from claiming what was his. Their petty exercises of willfulness had become a predictable irritation, like a nagging splinter that made itself known whenever you tried to use your hands for a meaningful purpose. That would change when he had the treasure. Once he controlled it, they would think that even God validated his rule. He could finally claim the title his family had sought from the beginning. He could become king. And with the fabled treasure in his grasp, they would obey any order. The irksome little nobles would become his fiercest defenders to secure their own survival.

After that, what would stop him from leading the combined forces of Pallingham to conquer the Northlands? He could become Emperor—ruler of a greater power than the kings at Fin had even imagined.

It would soon be past midnight, and his body ached from sitting for so long. He stretched his arms before beginning his final letter for the night. This one would go to his neighbor in the north, King Bagler—an offer to reinstate an ancient trade treaty. He hoped it would reopen the roads north and lure King Bagler into his trust. The cave-dwelling bandit who raided his supply carts and spooked old Bagler would be finished within a week. If he could convince the aging monarch to allow caravans to travel between their lands, then he could quietly slip an advance force into the Northlands to wait for a surprise assault. It only required him to adopt a distasteful mask of subservience in his correspondence with King Bagler for a season.

Before he set pen to paper, he heard Geoffrey knocking at his door. "Enter," he said absently, and was surprised when Mouna charged through the door.

"My Lord, there is trouble at Dury."

Evasius felt a familiar pain begin behind his eyes. Mouna stood above him, her tall figure an imposing sight, despite her gaunt frame. "What new incompetence has the captain perpetrated?"

"I do not know the details," she said, "only that he is terrified." Mouna began to pace in frustration. "The sensation was so intense. It hurt. I could feel his terror within myself. I immediately tried to join his bond with my viewing bell."

"And what did you see?" Evasius was getting impatient with her hysteria.

"I'm not certain I was successful. It is one of the most difficult things in my power to combine two very different magics. The spell may have failed."

"What did you see?" Evasius rose and pounded his desk with a fist.

"Nothing," she said, finally stopping her pacing. "A white light that hurt to look at, and then blackest night." With a word, two soldiers carried in a wooden stand with thick legs on which rested a heavy bell of black iron, inverted so that the mouth opened toward the ceiling. She then showed him the few moments before the light and the dark.

"Is he dead?" Evasius asked.

"I do not believe so," the witch was shaking almost like a common woman in his presence. "I can feel him. He is not asleep either—at least not in the normal sense—for I cannot communicate with him."

Evasius sat back down in his chair and leaned back. "We must assume that he failed to capture the monks. The patrols he sent to Aven and Whalesand will more than likely fail as well." He looked out the window and played with his signet ring for a moment as a new plan formed in his mind. "Mouna," he said gently, "it is clear to me that I can no longer trust my plans to simpleminded men. How willing are you and your sisters to take a more active role in our plans?"

"We are yours to command, my lord." Mouna took a deep breath and appeared to regain her menacing calm.

"I am in your debt," said Evasius. "How quickly can you reach our northern cities? With your powers, I know you can snare these troublesome monks."

"Duana is our fastest. She can be in Aven within a day, and she can send some of her crows to Dury to spy out the roads until another from our coven can arrive. As for myself, I can be in Whalesand in three days, assuming you can sacrifice your fastest horse to the journey."

Evasius allowed himself to look impressed; that road normally took a week or more. "Our quarry could probably get there no faster, coming from Dury." He stroked a finger around the ring of his parted lips as he thought. "Take any horse you wish. And use whatever powers you have available to find our enemy and bring me that treasure. Unfortunately, I must stay and rally what forces I can from our nobles to be ready for the next stage."

"My Lord, there is one more method I might use to find out more about the captain. Sometimes the bell is delayed in its vision—whatever I saw could have happened hours ago. However, I can use the talisman I placed in his body to force him into a sleep, although he might not wake from it, and I would only risk your man with your permission."

"Can you do this and still leave before dawn?"

The witch nodded. "I can speak to him right now if you order it."

"Please enlighten me," Evasius said, waving a hand to encourage haste. "And do try to give Captain Fallon a taste of what his failure will bring."

She pulled a small phial from inside her robes and swallowed its contents—something the dark, rusty color of dried blood. Evasius watched her face intently as her uncovered eye rolled back in its socket, exposing only the yellowed white. Suddenly, she thrust her head back and her veil fell to the floor. With unconscious revulsion, he shivered as he viewed her face fully for the first time. He knew there were scars there, but he did not expect fresh wounds. Pustules bulged along the jaw line, an open cut festered over the left brow, and the normally covered eye rolled back uselessly into a socket with no lids.

A wheezing gasp parted her lips, and then she began to move her lips as if speaking, but no sound came out. The terrible mask before him evoked pure physical disgust, as would the prospect of sharing a bed with a corpse. He was willing to wait and watch because it was necessary. That face was indispensable to his power.

The rain had woken Captain Fallon after the blast of light. At first, he had feared that he might be blinded again, but he quickly discovered that it was only the darkness under the canopy of branches. The wave of energy that had surged through the forest had blown out all the torches and flung him against a tree trunk where he lost consciousness. Since he knew that none of Evasius' witches were nearby, he reasoned that they had not caused the explosion of light that had poured over and through his body like a fire without heat. He settled on the only reasonable explanation to his mind: the king of the caves had conjurers as well—or was one himself.

The soldiers on the road had re-lit their lamps and torches, giving him a direction to head toward as he felt his way out of the undergrowth. Now, back on the road, he was redirecting their search. He pushed all the men he could in a single line that would walk along the face of the cliff, heading east. He even conscripted civilians from the city to fill the gaps, attempting to create a wall of torches and flesh that would prevent his prey from finding their escape. The mice would not be returning to their hole if he could help it.

An hour after the explosion, the men returning from the forest on the western side of the river told him about the cottage hidden in a cut clearing. An image flashed in his mind—the instant of the explosion, before his eyes could close against the unbearably bright light—three silhouettes stood between the trees. But the soldier who sounded the alarm had said he saw seven people.

He clenched his teeth and a shudder ran through his body as rage poured from his core. A part of him did not want to believe it, but he knew that the extravagant light show was only a diversion.

"Take me there," he growled at the soldiers.

He spared only four men to come with him, and they raced back toward Dury's southern gate on horseback. The heavy rain lashed across his face as they rode, and it woke the spirit of battle in him again. These were the times that he felt most alive, and he smiled as he spurred the horse faster. The speed of the horse, and his mastery over its movements made him more confident; he felt in control.

They had not yet reached the edge of the forest when Fallon felt a pain like a spear tip tearing through his ribs. There was no time to react as he lost consciousness and tumbled backward from his horse.

When he opened his eyes, he was on his back in a vast room, so large he could not see the ceiling or the walls in the shadows. The handle of a dagger stood out from his side. Before he could move, Mouna leaped on his chest and twisted the knife. Pain surged through his body and he screamed. Never had pain been so complete. It seemed to seep from his body into his mind and his heart so that it felt complete and eternal, as if nothing else were real, or ever would be.

The next moment, the witch was caressing his face with the back of a bloodied hand.

"Our Lord demands a report, Captain," she said. Her face showed only disgust, and her voice was thick with the accusation of a wounded lover.

The pain receded, leaving what felt like a gaping hole through half his torso. "The enemy," he gasped, "they have magic." His face matched her expression of revulsion and his heart burned with hate for this witch who had such power over him. "And it's a sight more impressive than anything you've conjured," he added with contempt.

"Oh, Nicholas," Mouna said, pouting. "Bright lights and a big boom are nothing compared to my power." She leaned close enough that he could feel her breath and all light in the room vanished. He saw her face only by what seemed like an internal, unearthly glow. "Tell me what happened to them."

Fear passed over Fallon now, as intense and physical as the pain had been. It was almost overwhelming, but this, he thought, he could master.

"It was a diversion," he said. "I've just been told of a cottage to which they likely escaped, and I was on my way there to pursue them when you interrupted. You've probably let them escape by delaying me."

"It's no use trying to hurt my feelings with your taunts."

He gave up on his hate and resigned himself to cooperating to avoid that all-encompassing torment again. "I've forced a line of men against the cliffs for nearly a mile. Since we almost caught them, I believe they'll head for Whalesand. That's the direction of the cottage."

"Lord Evasius is very displeased, but he has not thrown you out with the filth yet."

The witch leaned back and sent a new wave of pain through his body. "You are to pursue them and meet me in Whalesand—

that is, if you wake up from this meeting." Then she wrenched the knife from his flesh and vanished.

Captain Fallon did not wake until daybreak. When he roused, he found himself lying in a bed with a void in himself. It felt as if he had a hole in his side, just below his heart, as if someone had dug a piece of him out with a spade. His body was whole, but he still felt the wound, like veterans who still felt long-severed limbs. There was also a gap in his memory; his men had to remind him where he was and what they had been doing before he recalled his new orders. The hollow in his body took him off balance as he stood and ordered his lieutenant to bring his horse.

The Northland Cliffs had always protected the people on the plain of Apos from any northern enemies, as the ocean had from the South, West, and East. The cliffs towered over two thousand feet in places, and presented a sheer face, except for occasional overhangs or caves, like those found near Dury. They pierced a mile into Syrene Bay in the West, and stretched two hundred twenty-five miles directly east, where the fortified city of Aven protected the narrow stretch of land between the rapidly descending cliffs and the sea. The cliffs turned the plains into a plate-like peninsula almost completely isolated from the rest of the continent.

Kurian knew that the cliffs were awe-inspiring. When they had first seen them in the light of a rainless morning, he had stared at them for several minutes with the others. For that first day, Tobin craned his neck constantly, trying to glimpse the top through the low, dark cloud cover. But the majesty of the cliffs could not hold Kurian's attention. They impressed upon him with incontestable force the sense of his own smallness. Under that feeling, he could not help but doubt their chance of success.

They trotted their horses a hundred yards south of the road, keeping the cliffs in sight, but also wanting to hide their passage. The night after the escape, they had slowly retraced their steps back to the cottage while trying to avoid the soldiers searching the forest on both sides of the road. Once there, they had checked the baggage on their own horses, found the money in Gideon's bags——none of them were brave enough to mount his massive horse—and headed west long before dawn. The rain and clouds had retreated enough to reveal the cliffs on the next morning, and now it was after lunch on the third day from Dury.

Unlike Tobin, Kurian kept his eyes focused on the path ahead to avoid the large puddles—some of them almost ponds—that covered the grass of the plains now. Water filled every low point, proving that the flat perfection of the plains was only an illusion. They were the only bright spot of the rainy season, and they had a new allure this year. When he first came to Capric Hill, he would stand next to the small puddles that formed on the flattened top and stare at his towering reflection. Now they rode through a landscape with a thousand mirrors, and he could watch from a dozen angles as a stretched horse and rider passed by. In these reflections, he hovered above the ground, distant and small, and imagined he could float away from the world and everything that had happened over the past month. He wanted to take it all away—talking to the stranger at the compound, the fire, being fooled by Evasius and chased by Fallon, even meeting Louise. He wished he could go back to the day he had come to the order and beg his father to take him home.

He shook his head and focused on Rhys in the lead. None of those things could be. There was no going back. However, the pain and the injuries all had a cause: Lord Evasius. Kurian told his friends that he was committed to fulfilling his oath to God, but he felt more satisfaction at the prospect of denying Evasius the one thing he wanted. That would probably not erase the pain, but it would justify it. Right now, that purpose burned in his chest and shoved him forward when he noticed the childish desire to escape. The weight of the cliffs driving down his spirit could still not overcome the necessity of their cause, even as it made him doubt their ability to achieve it.

Tobin began singing softly behind him. It was a song the order had always sung for brothers who died, a song of mourning followed by new hope. They had not tried singing it when they learned of the sack of their compound and the murder of their brothers. Their grief and fear had been too great, so they had deferred the rituals of mourning until their errand was complete and they could give their brothers a proper burial. Hearing it now hit his heart like an arrow, but it felt right. He knew that Tobin sang not just for their brothers, but for Louise, and probably for Alden and Gideon, as well.

"Farewell to you, my brothers dear,
I am going far away.

I am bound for God's own Heavenly shore
Where I'll rest 'till that Redeeming Day.

"So, fare thee well, my brothers dear,
I am waning in the brume
And my death, dear brothers, should not grieve you,
But your dimness there in Apos' gloom."

The burning in his heart became an ache to join in, to mourn. They had been foolish to put it off. Louise had been right that they could not mourn their losses in an evening, but to push away the need for mourning had wounded Kurian even more. It became impossible to hold it in any longer, so he joined Tobin with a trembling voice.

"We have taken each our oath and arms,
We have pledged to defend,
Now I pray you'll boldly guard and mend
All that evil seeks to rend.

"So, fare thee well, my brothers dear,
I go beyond the plain.
But for me, 'tis reason to rejoice
As my faith has overcome all pain.

"I stood beside you long in life
And I'll wait for you in Fin,
With my heart, I see you're more than friends;
You're my brothers and my priestly kin.

"So, fare thee well, my brothers dear,
I am passing as the wind.
But I know once more we'll meet again,
After this world's fateful din.

"Now the Treasured Oak sways with the wind
And I wish I could remain,
For I know 'twill be some long time
Before I see you again.

"So, fare thee well, my brothers dear,
And when I see you again,
We'll be washed, dear brothers, in that glorious reign,
And we'll dance through the streets of Fin."

When he heard the dean's clear voice join in, he could not bear it, and he did what Louise had taught him. Spurring his horse, he raced past Rhys until the tears streamed across his face, as much from the wind as from his grief. He pushed, and the horse went faster. He galloped until he didn't think his body could handle more, and then he dropped his head and let his mount settle into its own pace. After some time, the gray stopped and neighed loudly. Kurian wiped his face and looked up to see the ocean just yards ahead of him.

A narrow beach of smooth stones stretched from the cliff on his right and curved southwest to form Syrene Bay. This was the sight he needed. Calm water gently lapped the shore in front of a western sky with a deep orange hue. It was not the violent ocean in Downriver Town that Louise had mimicked in her tempest that first day. This reminded him of her kindness on the night that he had seen the star. The water was the same gray-green of her eyes, but at peace. At that moment, he could not pray, but he hoped she was also at peace. With the same thought, he wanted to curse Evasius and the king for her death, and for dragging all of them into this bloody struggle. She was, in the end, only an innocent victim of their manipulations, like he and his friends.

He dismounted and drank from a nearby puddle, then walked down the beach and stepped into the water with his bare feet. When his friends trotted up behind him, he did not turn around, and they did not speak. They waited until he stepped out of the water, mounted his horse, and turned to follow the shoreline around the bay.

Whalesand sat in the southern crook of Syrene Bay. The locals claimed that the name came from a miraculous accident. The founders had once lived in a nearby village a short walk inland, until a storm one year wiped out all their crops at harvest. In despair, the people sent men to seek help from neighboring villages. One of their parties stumbled upon the carcass of a great whale, beached on the stony shore during the storm. The beast was a godsend, with enough meat to feed the village through winter, and enough oil to heat their homes. They set up temporary shelters near the carcass for the work of butchering, and soon the entire village moved there. The following spring, they settled in and built a dock to begin a life of fishing instead of farming. When the whale had been completely removed, the people were amazed to find that its weight had ground the stony shore to coarse sand where it had lain. The sandbar was still a curiosity for children, over six hundred years later, and old men still loved to tell the tale to whomever would listen.

The local tavern, The Blubber and Bone, was a squat building with a peculiar curved shape that made no distinction between roof and walls. The effect from the interior was like standing under an empty, capsized ship. For several generations, the explanation for the tavern's unusual architecture was that it had several of the original ribs of the whale in its framing. The claim could never be disproved without tearing open the walls, and the owners resorted to brutal retaliation to stop the wagers that patrons would place on the veracity of the story. Soon, they would have a new story to argue over—whether the four men who came into town that night were secretly Capric monks, or had killed them for their trademark staves.

Rumors had already reached Whalesand about the destruction of the Capric monastery. Those who believed that the men were monks in poor disguise were, therefore, in the minority. It was the only reason the strangers were not only left alone, but ignored with conspicuous intensity.

Kurian entered the dark tavern first. The cold had driven all the previous thoughts and worries from his mind, leaving only the hope for a warm fire somewhere in the village lights ahead. Feeling the warm air of the tavern, his next thought was food. He wandered toward a table with an empty bench without noticing the groups of faces dimly lit in the pools of light cast from solitary candles on each table. The roar of talk and laughter which they had heard from outside subsided to a dull murmur when they entered, but Kurian was too weary to pay attention.

As they sat, a robust looking man with patchy blonde stubble asked what he could get them. They ordered dinner with ale. He soon returned with a watery stew that smelled fishy and had large circles of oil floating on top that shimmered in the firelight. Under the broth were chunks of a tough meat that was more fat than flesh. Kurian thought he knew where the first part of the tavern's name came from, and hoped that he wouldn't encounter the second in one of the chunks. The pungent ammonia smell of the fish was new to him, and he almost felt sick from it. Tobin looked like he was feeling queasy as well, but they both had been trained too well by the order to refuse what was set before them.

"Sir," Noeman said before the barman walked away, "could you tell us where we could hire a ship?"

The man looked warily at their staves and scratched his chin. "S'pleny of good cap'ins in Whalesan'," he muttered. Kurian could not tell if the man's speech was so difficult to understand because of an accent, or because he was drunk. "Sorry for you, only 'un 'ere tonight is Bacchus." He cocked his head toward the back of the room and the only well-lit table, directly in front of the fire. The patrons there seemed to be having a lively conversation—or perhaps they were playing a game——it was impossible to tell which. They chose that moment to raise their mugs in unison and crash them together so that the ale sloshed over them like a golden rain.

"Could he get us to Ramah quickly?" Kurian asked urgently.

"He could prolly get there in a dinghy faster'n the others could in a caravel wi' wings—but I would'n sail wi'em."

"Why not?"

"S'not my business," the owner spat on the floor and Noeman looked shocked despite his attempt at a calm facade. "Ask 'im yourself."

When the barman walked back to attend the other customers, Noeman turned to his students. "While it's not a glowing recommendation, this Bacchus appears to be our only option, currently." They nodded and turned to their stews for a moment, but none of them could force themselves to eat more than a few bites. Fortunately, the bread was hearty and warm, and the butter was sweet. Kurian found that he could get more of the stew down by dipping his bread in the broth, and thus fulfilled his obligation to Capric etiquette.

When they had finished eating what they could, the four of them rose and approached the table at the back. Six men straddled the stools on either side, each one with rough, tanned skin and dark, wiry beards. By some trick of the light, they appeared for a moment like very human looking goats as Kurian drew near. He had the impression that he might see horns peeking out of their hair if they removed their caps. Two women also flitted between the men playfully, but retreated as the monks closed in. At the head of the table was the only shaven man among them. His hair was lighter than the other men's and reached down to his shoulders in thick, blonde curls. He wore a strange peaked cap that rose up on either side of his head, furthering the notion of horns. His smile stretched broadly across his face and gave him a very appealing look, despite the deep grooves that tracked along his mouth and eyes. He leaned his chair back against the wall, sitting in the full firelight, looking like he was a wild king holding court with these hairy brutes before him.

"Gentlemen," Noeman said to the table, "which of you is Captain Bacchus?"

The man at the head let his chair fall forward and used the momentum to leap upon the table in one smooth motion. The men around him cheered at this amusement. He strutted down the length of the table and dropped down lightly in front of Noeman. "That would be me," he said, and sat back down on the edge of the table with his arms folded. "Captain Dylan Bacchus." He bowed his head briefly with a tipsy carelessness. "But my friends call me Dilly——and almost anyone with gold is a friend."

Kurian was surprised that he spoke with a clear, bright voice that had a refined tone. The rogue was clearly not unsophisticated, and his clarity of speech, combined with his fascinating appearance made him almost likable.

"Well, yes, Captain Bacchus," Noeman began.

"Dilly."

"Dilly," said the dean, clearly uncomfortable with the familiar attitude.

"We need to get to Ramah as soon as possible," Kurian said to speed things up.

"Ramah," said Bacchus, running his tongue over his teeth and smacking his lips. "Been there plenty of times. Not a brief journey, mind you, but easy enough." Kurian thought he suddenly looked bored, and he seemed not to notice their Capric staves. He appeared so at ease he might fall asleep standing.

"Why wouldn't it be quick," Tobin said, "isn't it right across the bay?"

"Sure, it's close," Bacchus nodded, "but you can't sail straight there."

"Why not?"

Dilly chuckled. "It's not called Syrene Bay for no reason, kid." He stood and threw his arm around Tobin's shoulder, pulling him in to a circle with the others. Suddenly he got a conspiratorial, but intensely excited look in his face. "You can't sail too close to the island. Even though Ramah is directly across the water, you'd have to sail through the fiercest straights in the continent to get there that way. On one side, you have the crumbling edges of the cliffs as they fall into the ocean—rocks and crags that could scuttle even the lightest boat. On the other, there's the island itself." He paused and looked each of them in the eye. "And on the island, there are the Sirens." His intensity convinced Kurian that Dilly would relish such an adventure.

"They're just a myth," said Noeman, "an old superstition."

"No!" Bacchus stood up, finally looking serious. "I've seen a ship get too close to that island. The men go crazy, they leap from the ship and try to swim to shore without care for waves or freezing water. Only the most beautiful and deadly creatures in this wide world could cause a man to dive into a wild sea. On calm nights, some men claim they can even hear their song from the village here—and they can barely stop themselves from going for a swim."

"We must get to Ramah immediately," said Kurian. "Is there any way through?"

"Going through the straights gets you within reach of their song. But I've come up with a few ideas to try and outsmart those vixens." Dilly leaned back on the table again with a satisfied grin. "I'd be willing to consider it—if the price were right."

"What nonsense," Noeman said, bristling. "This scoundrel wants only to scare us into offering him more for passage."

Captain Bacchus looked hurt. "Are you saying I'm lying?"

"Exactly."

"I'd never."

"Cap'n Dilly loves to drink," interjected one of the fellows at the table, "and Dilly dallies with the ladies, but he don't lie."

Captain Bacchus clapped the man on the back. "Poetry!" he shouted. "Pure poetry, Bill." Then he turned back toward them.

"The barman told you not to talk to me, right? That's because no other captain will even consider the straight. They wouldn't take your money if you suggested it." He crossed his arms and looked justified in his position.

"Dean," Kurian whispered, "we don't have time to wait for another option."

"Will this be enough?" Tobin held up the large purse from Gideon's horse.

The look of excitement brought Dilly's face back to life again. His eyes bulged slightly as he watched Tobin drop the bag on the table with a satisfying clank. He nodded almost imperceptibly as he hefted its weight.

"Yes," he said decisively, "I think it will be. And for such distinguished guests as the last remaining Caprics, I'll allow you to stay aboard my ship tonight instead of this dank old whale's gullet."

Kurian was caught off guard, and he could tell the others were too. Apparently, Dilly was more perceptive than he let on. He heard Tobin offer a quick prayer of protection.

Captain Bacchus nodded across the table at the man sitting to the right of his former chair. The most brutal looking man of the bunch stood up. He looked like he hadn't bathed in months. He had a shaved head, and a white scar stood out along his jaw through a heavy beard. "Allow me to introduce my first mate, Jack Darling," Dilly said. "Jack, show our guests to the officer's quarters, and prepare us to cast off in the morning." Jack only nodded and grunted.

Next, Captain Dilly slapped Tobin on the back and whispered to them, "Don't worry, boys, nobody will bother you with Jack by your side. Just don't expect too much in the way of conversation." He cackled and moved back to his own chair.

It looked as if they had completed their business and had no reason to stay in the tavern. On their way out, they paid their tab with the barman, and then followed Jack out into the cold dark.

Captain Dylan Bacchus felt a pleasant glow about the evening after the monks left. It had been a risk on his part to call attention to their identity—it had been a risk to assume that's what they really were—but his instincts had screamed "monk" more than "assassin". He felt the gamble had been effective in finalizing their decision to sail on his boat. Now he had a job—and a very lucrative job it was. That meant a happy crew. Lots of gold and a happy crew meant a happy Dilly. Who could fault him for buying a few rounds for the house and drinking too much himself? There was still time to sleep it off.

The only thing that would have made the night a complete success was some feminine companionship. The girls who had previously been at the table had wandered off with his men.

He sat in a pleasant fog of ale as the night grew old, and the other drinkers went home. He recognized only the enjoyable numbness of drink that felt as if it would continue as long as he stayed at the Blubber and Bone. Eventually, the dying fire and the thought of the money awaiting him on his ship convinced him to leave, but first he headed toward the back of the tavern. Through the hallway that led to the rooms was another door that led outside, where he could dispose of some of the ale he had drunk that night.

His vision rolled like the deck of a ship, but the floor remained steady and he bumped against the walls of the hall. A woman stood in one of the doors. He was certain she was speaking to him. Yes, she was inviting him inside.

Dilly was amazed at how tall and slender this woman was, with long, straight black hair that fell down her back, and dark eyes that were enchanting. She was beautiful, but for some reason she covered half her face. He tried to ask why a beautiful woman would do that, but she only invited him inside again. This night was turning out even better than he thought, but he had to tell her he would be right back. She closed the door and he continued his way down the hall to reach the back exit.

In the doorway of the last room was another woman, also beautiful. She looked younger than the first, but was not as tall.

This was his luckiest night in years. Money and women were showering down on him.

"You don't want to spend the night with that old hag, do you?" she said with a sweet, whispering voice.

Unfortunately, the urgency of reaching the back door still pressed upon him, and as he reached for the latch, he felt like he'd been hit on the head, or maybe he just fell. Whatever the cause, he was on the floor. He laughed at himself and rolled over. Soon, he felt as if he was being dragged, but he couldn't keep his eyes open anymore. The ale finally claimed him.

CHAPTER FOURTEEN

The Right Type of Madman

The hammocks onboard the Osprey were like sleeping on a cloud compared to blankets rolled out on the ground. Slowly, the ship rocked Kurian to sleep while the soft lapping of water against the hull wove the spell of a lullaby. He woke the next morning refreshed and alert, and was surprised to find himself thinking about their voyage with anticipation. Mr. Darling fetched them before dawn for breakfast. As they left the room beneath the stern castle, Kurian saw that Captain Bacchus was only just climbing the gangplank, leaning on a smaller man who wore a hood and cloak against the cold. The captain appeared to be drunk. Even though Bacchus could barely stand, and presented nothing like the genteel captain they had seen the night before, he insisted on joining them for the meal.

Two of the goat-men from the night before were already eating when they walked into a small dining room with unusually curved walls unlike any room the monks had ever seen. To Kurian, it felt more like a cave somebody had covered in wood planks than a fully manmade room. Everywhere they looked were small nooks, crannies, and nets that stowed peculiarly shaped items for which he could not imagine a purpose.

The noise of men working filtered in from outside as the crew banged about the ship. They shouted to one another in a nearly foreign language that would have been easy to ignore for its strangeness, if not for the muddle of familiar words that he caught between the strange ones.

"Hope you had a pleasant evening," Captain Bacchus said, sitting down. "Let me introduce Bill Samuels and Sam Jetters." He indicated the two men already eating. "We call them Flotsam and Jetsam. Brothers of the sea, if not by blood."

"How d'you do?" said the two men together. Kurian assumed that they got the peculiar nickname because they seemed to do everything in unison. Each took a bite or reached for his mug whenever the other did. There was no other resemblance. Bill had the same dark beard that all the crew seemed to have, except that he was heavier, with bright red cheeks and a bulbous nose. Sam had a very straight nose and sallow, sunken cheeks.

"Captain's only joking," said Bill.

"He teases him with the nickname," said Sam, "because he found Bill here floating in the sea."

"And then," Bill added, "he tossed old Sam in to fetch me." The two sailors chuckled together, but the joke evaded the monks. Tobin smiled and nodded politely with an expression of confusion he rarely showed.

A thin sailor with a dirty leather apron brought out two chargers filled with fried fish and green beans. "Finally, the beans," said Bill, then the two of them engaged in an almost choreographed passing of dishes between them to refill their plates.

"Bill loves his beans," said Sam as his friend munched away.

"Food of dreams," Bill said, his teeth squeaking against the skins of the beans. "Learned to eat beans from my father. Green beans, long beans, broad beans, red beans, painted ponies, pickled beans, any type you please. Beans can almost make a man live forever, my old dad used to tell me." He studied a particularly long specimen between his fingers as he spoke. "My father—who taught me to rhyme, by the by—even wrote poetry about beans. I'll tell you my favorite."

At this, he stood, and Sam soon followed. Then they began to recite together,

"Beans, beans, they make you fart,
And farting, you know, is good for your heart
'Cause a grown man giggles like a lass
When bubbly air escapes..."

"Bill!" Captain Dilly interrupted, "I don't think our guests are used to that sort of rhyme."

Sam and Bill sat down, laughing together. "That was always my favorite one, too," Sam whispered across the table.

Kurian almost laughed himself. It sounded like some of the jokes he and his friends would have made back at the compound. He found that he liked the men aboard the ship. Though they were crass, and probably illiterate, they were merry. It was a relief from the gloom that seemed to follow his party across the plain. The meal also endeared them to him. After his first experience of fish the night before, the tender, flaky meat on the Osprey was a culinary masterpiece. It redeemed the whole idea of fish as food.

A bell rang outside, and Captain Dilly rose to leave, although he had barely taken a bite.

"Time to cast off," said Sam.

"Hope we don't tear the mast off," rhymed Bill. Then they both shuffled out to their duties.

Captain Fallon arrived in Whalesand well before dawn, but a nagging feeling urged him not to follow the plans he had formed with the witch. She had told him to surround the tavern with men, and then meet her inside. He stopped at the local garrison to gather the force of men he would need, since he had brought only a dozen of his best with him from Dury. Now he had thirty with him, but the whole plan didn't feel right. It was different from the instinct he had when a mission was about to fail, so he began to wonder if the feeling was Mouna trying to force her will on him again. His question was answered when they met her on the main street, outside the tavern.

"Our quarry has already moved on, Captain," she said. "I've been trying to encourage you to head to the docks."

"It's too bad you can't just control me like a marionette."

"Try me," she snapped. "We must get to the docks. They've hired a mad captain to attempt the straights." Without warning, she leapt onto the saddle behind him and spurred the horse forward. His soldiers now knew he was not the final authority here. He resigned himself to accepting it until he found his chance to free himself from her control. Perhaps if he were successful, Evasius would promote him beyond her reach.

They reached the docks of Whalesand in just a few minutes. Men moved everywhere in the yard, and it was impossible to know which ship to go to in the dark. They found the harbormaster's office and asked where Captain Bacchus' ship was. He pointed out the window toward the bay, where they saw a ship just barely illuminated from a few lamps, already under way. Fallon cursed.

Mouna ordered one of his archers to follow her, and they hurried to the end of the dock. After he had nocked an arrow, she cupped her hands over the arrowhead and whispered into them. When she removed her hands, a perfect sphere of roiling fire hung from the end of the arrow. The soldier looked nervously at Captain Fallon and raised his bow.

"Wait," he said. The man lowered his arrow and Mouna turned on Fallon with a snarl.

"We must stop them," she shouted.

"No, we must get the treasure."

The witch folded her arms. "Of course, that is our Lord's first wish."

"If you destroy that ship, they may not survive, and they will certainly know we are on to them."

"And we pick up whoever does survive and make them take us to the treasure."

"Can you guarantee that the right ones will live?" Fallon asked, enjoying the thought that the witch could be carried away by her emotions like any fool. He knew she had no experience away from the castle. In this circumstance, engaged in a mission where things could change instantly, he had an edge.

"What would you do instead? If we follow them, they will see us as soon as the sun rises."

"We stalk them," he said. "Can't you do anything to hide a ship, witch?"

She glared at him, leaving no doubt that she would destroy him if he did not perform. It was still satisfying to get under her skin.

"I can cloak a ship in fog and darkness," she finally agreed. "It will look strange to others within view, but it will protect us from prying eyes. And if we must get close to the island, the Sirens should ignore us. We only need a ship to hide, Nicholas."

"Fortunately for us," the Captain said, "our Lord has a few ships for his future navy here. The prospective admiral and I are old friends."

"Then lead on, Nicholas."

They had to wake the admiral and impress on him the urgency of their mission before he would risk his position and his ship on the chase. After that, his men took their time preparing to sail.

Fortunately, the delay masked their pursuit amidst the normal traffic of the harbor. Fallon was certain that the ship ahead would not notice them until they had separated from the cluster of fishing and trading ships that waited to be towed out of the harbor—and with Mouna's tricks, they might not know it was a ship that followed them. He smiled, fantasizing about the moment when he would reveal himself and they would realize that their running and fighting had been fruitless. Fallon would catch them and give Evasius his prize, or he would die.

On the deck, a cool breeze blew over the Osprey from the direction of the bay, carrying the strong smell of salt to which Kurian was still not accustomed. It mixed with the smoke of the strange oil lamps around the ship to create a unique, but pleasant odor. He watched with fascination as a smaller boat with a dozen rowing men towed them into the bay. When they were almost beyond the sand bar, the crew began to scurry around the deck. They shouted to each other and hauled on a web of ropes that Kurian had difficulty following to any specific connections. Soon, the sail floated up the mast under an invisible power, with the mystery that a ship can only present to the uninitiated. As the wind caught the sail, Kurian felt its strength catch in the ship and carry it forward like the gentle leading of a shepherd. At the same moment, he noticed the first glow of light in the east.

Behind the visible chaos of the crew's movements, he felt the finely coordinated effort of men who had worked together for years. In many ways, it reminded him of the training the brothers had engaged in at the compound. When he first arrived, it had been difficult to know what was happening at any given moment, but with time, he had learned how the small groups cooperated with the whole to achieve a common purpose. He realized that, apart from sharing an altogether different purpose, this company of men was not unlike the one in which he'd grown up. It soothed his spirit to know that such a thing still existed. He smiled, seeing the camaraderie of men working together in strenuous labor, and tried to stay out of the way.

As the wind drove them forward, he was surprised at how quickly they progressed. In a few minutes, they were past the sandbar and the deck began to roll more severely in the open water. He and his friends were unprepared for the experience. The sailors stopped their work to laugh together at the four of them as they stumbled around the deck. Soon, Dilly invited them onto the stern castle where he and Jack Darling stood by the wheel. Ascending the stairs was even more challenging than moving about the deck. Once they were on top—and supported against the railing—Kurian began to feel an even greater rising in his spirit. The salt-wind in his face, and the occasional spray showering back from the bow, built an excitement within him that whispered of daring and adventure.

"Welcome to the sea, gentlemen," Captain Bacchus said, giving Kurian a knowing look. He seemed revived from his earlier state, and the glint of exhilaration was in his eye again.

"How long until we reach Ramah?" Kurian asked.

"Assuming we make the passage, we ought to arrive this evening. Our most dangerous time will come at midday."

"And how do you propose we make our way past these dangerous Sirens?" the dean mocked. It was the most incredulous, sarcastic and disrespectful tone Kurian had ever heard him use. In reply, Dilly presented a ball of beeswax.

"Wax?" said Noeman, "Wax is your brilliant plan?"

"Not entirely," Dilly said, offended. "First, we stuff our ears with the wax to cover up the Siren song, and then we have men go about the ship blowing whistles, banging pots and pans, and, of course, we ring the bell till the clapper falls out. In other words, we make the best damned racket we can. If that doesn't drown out those beauties, then it can't be done."

Noeman shrugged his shoulders. "I'll be in the bunk room praying when it comes time. That would be our only hope, in my mind—if the creatures even exist."

"But if we succeed..." Dilly's eyes shone, and he seemed not to hear Noeman's response. "If we succeed then I'll be the richest captain in these waters." He turned to his first mate. "Just imagine the premium we could charge to transport goods to the Northlands in a day, while the other boats still take over a week—not to mention the danger inherent in it." From Kurian's perspective, the prospect made no visible impact on Mr. Darling. He held his distant stare over the bow as firmly as he held the wheel.

It was late in the morning when they first saw the island in the distance off the port bow. The cliffs towering up on the right side had been visible almost an hour earlier. By that time,

Kurian had found that the rhythm of the waves, combined with a lingering exhaustion, put him into a sort of waking trance. Other than the brief amusement that they all shared when Rhys had turned a little green after breakfast, he had simply stared ahead with the first mate. When Mr. Darling pointed out the island, Kurian could not remember a thought that had entered his head during the preceding hours.

The part of the island they could see was only a shallow slope rising from the bay. A light-colored beach stood out on the point around which they would have to sail. Further in, there were wooded hills that rose quickly into low-lying clouds. It looked like an inviting place, despite the stories that warned them away.

"We'd best plug our ears early," Captain Bacchus said, "Hearing follows quickly after sight in Pallingham."

He let out a piercing whistle and all the sailors gave him their attention. "Mr. Darling has told you our course—and bless you stubborn buggers for sticking with me. If we succeed, they will sing songs about us, and lavish us with anything we want." The men cheered. "But from here on, any man overboard is lost. Each man is responsible for his own body and his own task. If you don't resist those crooning hags, we won't stop you. That goes for me, too. So plug your ears tight, and steel yourselves, boys." The speech dampened the crew's spirits, and they each shoved the wax deep into their ears before solemnly returning to their work.

The wax was another novelty to Kurian, and though he did notice a muffling of the ship's sounds, he was surprised that he could still hear with clarity what those close to him said.

"Do you think it will work?" he asked, feeling like he needed to raise his voice.

"I have no idea," Captain Bacchus shouted with a grin.

His grin quickly changed to a look of curiosity. Dilly tapped Mr. Darling on the arm and pointed behind Kurian, asking a whispered question. Kurian turned around to see a dark fog in the distance. It hovered in a large mass above the water, and spread out from the mass in a broad, low mist. It reminded Kurian of the way buildings or trees would loom out of the fog on the plains when mist rose from the ground. Sometimes it was impossible to tell whether there was something there or if the fog was simply getting thicker until you were almost close enough to touch the thing.

"Looks like a storm brewing back in Whalesand, or some such trouble," Dilly said, still studying the gray mass. He pulled a spyglass from his pocket and looked at the object for a long time before he said, "But not like any I've ever seen."

He closed his glass and replaced it in his pocket. "Well, good thing we're heading the other direction, my monkish friends."

Kurian suddenly felt like talking to Captain Bacchus. He wanted to find out more about him, and more importantly, to tell him what he suspected might be behind them. In the back of his mind, he felt a little guilty for not divulging the reason they had to get to Ramah so quickly before they hired Dilly and his crew.

"Captain Dilly," he said at length, "how did you know that we were Caprics last night?"

"A not-so-wild guess, my friend." Dilly winked at him. "Carrying the staves was a poor disguise."

"But how did you know we hadn't just stolen them? You obviously knew about the sack of our compound."

"You had a good smell about you." The comment confused Kurian. The captain saw his expression and sat on the railing next to him before looking intently into his eyes. "I could tell you were a good lot. Now I may not go in for your ideas about God, but I knew that I could trust you to act out of that goodness."

The speech was not helping to dissipate Kurian's guilt.

"One thing I've learned in my business," Dilly continued, "is that it's altogether easier on me if I know the other man has scruples. If he does, then I don't have to be as creative in thinking about all the ways he can diddle me—and usually I don't have to be ready to do him the same. In sum, I figured you a safe bet."

Now Kurian felt as if he might be getting seasick. He didn't want to be the cause of more pain and death. The dean had counseled them to be tight-lipped about their situation, but Noeman's current absence gave him the courage to speak up. "What if I told you we were being pursued?" he said before the captain changed the subject.

"Ha!" Dilly slapped him hard on the shoulder. "Our glorious Lord Evades-much burned your order to the ground! I'd factored in your fugitivism."

"How about if I told you that cloud might be them?"

"It doesn't look like a ship," Dilly looked again.

"We've already met one of his witches. I think that could be one of their illusions."

"I'm afraid you're probably right," Tobin said.

"Then let's hope they don't have wax!" Captain Bacchus said, with an excited gleam in his eye.

"That's it?" Kurian said, "You're not angry, or worried?"

"I tried both of those once, and I didn't much like them," the captain replied. "I prefer to live in the adventure I'm in now. And I have no cause to be angry—you boys did me a favor. I've wanted to try this passage for some time now, but couldn't convince the crew without your money." He said the last while hooking a thumb toward Jack.

Kurian was astounded at this attitude. He and his friends had run from Evasius' soldiers since they first encountered Captain Fallon in Downriver Town. Now he realized that there was a constant, lingering fear over him that sometimes bordered on terror. This strange, gangly sailor looked at the threat with ambivalence, and it was baffling.

"Do you want to do anything about our pursuers?" Tobin said with a similar confusion.

Captain Dilly shook his head. "There's no way they'll catch us before we reach Ramah. But as soon as we land, I advise you to get your horses and ride like hell if they're still behind us." With that, he turned back to the wheel and told Jack to prepare the crew for their noisemaking.

"What kind of a madman have we hired?" Kurian whispered to Tobin.

Tobin looked at Captain Bacchus and said, "Exactly the kind we needed, I think."

They could not continue their conversation because of the sudden, urgent ringing of the bell, followed by men making noise all over the ship with makeshift instruments. Pots banged

together, wooden pins clapped, and screaming whistles mingled with men's shouting. The effort enveloped the ship in
cacophonous sound. Somewhere in the din, Kurian thought he
caught a group singing a simple melody, but he could not focus
on it. *If the Sirens do not lure us to death,* he thought, *the blare might
drive us all mad.*

CHAPTER FIFTEEN

Siren Song

Kurian was not sure how long it was there before he noticed it. The Song was quiet and distant, but continuous. It snuck through the wall of sound the sailors were trying to create, crawling through the dead space like a persistent draft. Captain Bacchus had spent the last half hour rallying his crew if they lagged in their noisemaking. He dashed across the poop deck, screaming and waving his arms like a crazed conductor, but shortly after the Song began, his attempts faded. Their raucous symphony became a dull pantomime, as if a wave of exhaustion had swept across the deck.

By the time Kurian recognized the music as a new sound in his ears, he could already feel it in his body. It became difficult to focus on watching the crew, and then an intense loneliness crept into his spirit. He looked at Tobin and Rhys, seeing in their faces the same exhaustion and seclusion that brought a desire to weep. Their eyes became distant and vacant. Then Kurian felt as if he were trapped in an invisible cell, separated from his friends by all contact except sight. The sense of isolation grew. It blotted out almost everything from his focus. He was dimly aware of noise and movement nearby, but those things had nothing to do with him. His solitude turned slowly to despair. He understood now that the burden of their journey rested solely on him, and he could not see how he would ever find the King of the Caves, let alone how he could retrieve the treasure. The others would soon fall away, and it was the height of folly to expect that he could confront Evasius alone. He was not a man; the monks had raised him up to be a coward and a failure. His own nature made him a murderer. Even God had turned his back on everything he had once aspired to be. Now Kurian was alone, with no escape from his prison. Sobs broke from deep in his chest as the responsibility weighed on him.

As his eyes observed the men moving all around him, all ignoring each other, it occurred to him that these feelings might be a result of the Siren's cry. He tried to resist it, thinking that making his own noise might help him. He began screaming, letting out any sound that would come from his throat. Tobin fell to his knees and began to pray in a loud voice. Rhys fell next to Tobin, but ranted and tore his clothes. Kurian could not hear their words over the Song.

The desperate loneliness grew into a physical craving deep in his gut. He wanted companionship. He needed it like food, or water, or air. Looking at his friends, and the men aboard the

Osprey, he realized that the company of men could never fulfill his need. This was a deeper hunger, something he had only caught hints of in the middle of the night. Dim, half-remembered dreams had been his only taste. Shame followed every sampling. It was something forbidden to monks, some-thing he had renounced with his oaths. But it still tempted him. Perhaps refusing to be ordained freed him from that re-striction. The physical need moved down from his gut to his groin, and spread up into his chest, so that his entire torso crawled with an irrelievable itch. His body felt as if it might im-plode or explode at the same time. He thought he might die if he did not find relief.

In his mind, the faces of all the women he had ever known began to shuffle before him unbidden. Perhaps somewhere in them he could find the one who could satisfy his desire, and he could give up this foolish quest and go to her. First his mother from long ago, then Mrs. Williams next door when he was a boy, the old women who lived in Aposford, or the slightly younger ones he had seen at the well, then the few he had glimpsed at Pallingham and Downriver Town, even the witch at Fin. None of them could ever be enough. Finally, Louise ap-peared in his mind. She lingered longer than the others did. He could see the eyes he had thought were dangerous, and the dark, wavy hair that tangled so easily. He saw her fair skin, and her knowing smile—but as beautiful as he could now admit she was, he knew that even she was not enough. She could never satisfy such a hunger. And she was dead. He could not go to her. Only the melody flowing in his ears could promise relief and pleasure enough. The creatures that offered such beauty in song might succeed where every woman would fail.

On the main deck, two sailors bumped into each other and started to grapple. The scuffle distracted him briefly from his thoughts, and showed him his danger. As one man hit the other, Kurian saw wax fly across the deck. One sailor stopped fighting immediately. For a moment, he stood stunned, and then he cleared the other ear, dashed toward the railing, and dove into the sea. The sight weakened the spell, and Kurian shoved the wax deeper into his ears. It offered mild relief of his feelings and he believed he could keep himself under control. At the same time, he envied the man.

Other sailors looked over the railing, and then to the island. Two more splashed into the bay, and more were about to follow when their fellows restrained them and tied them to the mast. The effort reduced the level of noise considerably.

"So wondrous," Dilly said in the lull. He sighed deeply. "Hearing that hymn, I feel as though I have never been with a woman. Not a real woman. They have all been girls——no, puppets, imitations! They were merely the dolls girls play with. And I have only been a boy playing at being a man." Another man flew into the water, and Dilly watched him as he swam away from the boat.

A dull horror crept into Kurian's mind as he watched Captain Bacchus pull the spyglass from his coat. He stood as still as the man who first went overboard and slowly raised it to his eye. The gasp that escaped his lips expressed all the longing in Kurian's own heart.

"I have never looked on beauty and my heart has never stirred," said the captain, "until now. What dreams they offer; what secret delicacies." Kurian wanted more than ever to look at the beach himself. He crossed behind the wheel and stood beside the captain to look at his face. He saw his own desire reflected there, with the promise of fulfillment.

"Mr. Darling," Captain Dilly cried, "hard to port! We will have sweet water tonight."

Jack Darling stood as stoically as before, staring straight ahead. When his order was not followed immediately, Captain Bacchus turned to look at his first mate, then stepped toward the railing and vaulted lightly over it.

Kurian watched him with a mixture of envy and shock. The splash threw water against his face. The cold, salty drops felt good, as if they were a foretaste of what lay beyond. His gaze rose slowly, from the railing where Captain Bacchus' hand had lighted for a moment, to the water, and then to the island.

They were now almost directly beside the point with the beach, and being closer, he could make out several figures there. It was still distant, and he squinted to see more clearly. When his eyes refocused, he saw that there were women, and the smoothness of the forms convinced him that they were nude. Even from so far, he knew they were the most striking creatures he would ever gaze upon, and suddenly the Song regained force and overwhelmed everything on the ship.

What had been simply harmonious voices in the distance took on words. Though he did not know the language, the message felt familiar and heavy with promises of consolation and delight. The memories of his dark dreams glowed suddenly with a harsh light that revealed every detail. These distant figures were the ones in his dreams, and now he thought he could see their faces in his memories. Each face he remembered was more beautiful than the last. Some were almost familiar——the perfected form of some beauty he had seen; others were exotic and new with features like a goddess. They repeated the dreams in his mind, and filled it with acts he had never imagined. The available pleasures came so quickly in sequence that he almost felt they happened to him simultaneously.

The experience overcame his will. His shame burned away in the harsh light of realization. The greedy craving in his body filled the void. Dreams were not necessary—now he could enjoy them in person, and never be alone. Why resist something so alluring?

The figures on shore danced together and waved their arms, beckoning him to join them. He found himself stepping forward.

But now somebody was blocking his way. He tried to push forward and was shoved back. It was the small, hooded man who had carried the captain aboard. Kurian stepped forward more forcefully. The little man pushed on his chest, trying to stop him, but could only slow him down. He strode forward until he backed the other man against the railing. He pushed him aside and grabbed the rail, and then felt arms around his waist pulling him back.

"Tobin, Rhys," said a voice, "help me." Kurian thought the voice was familiar, but he couldn't remember where he had heard it. He pulled more forcefully at the railing, gaining a few inches to dive into the bay.

Other hands grabbed his shoulders and arms. His fingers were ripped from the rail, and he was dragged away and thrown to the deck. He tried to get up, but somebody knocked him back down. The sweet music became more urgent. He had to break free and reach the figures on the beach. They begged him to join them soon. Somewhere in his mind, he knew that he could fight his attackers, but he could not remember how. The music made it hard to focus and remember, so he just pushed and moved instinctually. He flailed and was free for a moment.

Again, somebody stopped him and threw him back. This time, a weight was on his chest, and he could not move his arms. He heaved his body to get free, but the hooded man was sitting on his chest. Somebody else held his arms outstretched.

Then the man slapped him in the face. "Kurian," he said, and slapped him again.

Kurian recognized that name, and the voice was familiar, but still he could not place it. Then the man pulled back the hood and he saw the face of a ghost.

The airy music dimmed, and he lay stunned. One word escaped his lips: "How?"

"The King," she said.

Then Louise smiled, and the urging of the Song lost its force. It became something he could willfully reject. Tobin and Rhys released his arms and helped him to his feet. The struggle to restrain him seemed to have helped them get their feelings under control as well.

"I never expected you would be the one saving me," he said to her.

"Did you hope it would be the other way around?" She spread the sarcasm thickly. "Sorry to disappoint you."

"Welcome back," Tobin said. "Now maybe we can prevent more of these men from jumping ship."

Kurian could tell there were fewer men on deck, but he wasn't sure how many they had lost. Few still made any noise. He saw Bill among those unconscious on the deck, while others stood immobile in their personal struggles. "Do you think Louise might have the same effect on them?" he asked.

"It's worth a try," she said. Then she removed the cloak and stood next to the wheel, where everyone could see her. She showed no fear, or any influence from the Sirens.

"Men of the Osprey," she said loudly. "I convinced your captain to bring me aboard today. Unfortunately, he gave his life already in this journey." Several of the men looked up at her, and while their focus changed, their struggle was still clear. "I'm sorry that I could not prevent Captain Bacchus from going overboard," she continued, "but the rest of you can survive. You only have to resist for a short while more. We have already passed the beach, and the Siren's pull is growing weaker. See how it is losing its effect on you as we continue." She was right; the Song was beginning to fade.

The men stirred and looked around them. They were gaining back their wills, but the thirst remained in their eyes. It only had a new target. Kurian saw them gathering at the foot of the stairs to the stern castle, but he did not guess their intent. He was still struggling to retain his own concentration.

"Kurian," Louise said over her shoulder, "you might get that chance to save me now."

He realized what she meant as the first sailor stepped on the stairs, and he jumped forward to stop him. Eight others crowded behind the first man, and Kurian wasn't sure that he and his friends could stop them if they gained the stairs.

"That will be far enough," he said as firmly as he could manage.

"No," said the sailor, "if we can't have the singers, we'll have her."

Rhys called Kurian's name and tossed him his staff, then stood behind him. "Come on!" he said. "After all that, I'm ready for a fight."

The sailor pulled a knife from his belt and tried to climb the stairs. Kurian rapped the man's knife hand with his staff and made him drop it, and then pushed him back hard enough that he fell into the crowd. "If we all go, they can't stop us," he said after his fellows had righted him. "There's only three of them." They made a rush for the stairs.

"Stow that," bellowed a new voice. The sailors looked as shocked as Kurian as he turned to look at Jack Darling. His stern expression had not changed, but his gaze had settled on the crewmen assaulting the stairs. They backed off, looking at their feet, each of them trying to fade into the background.

"Sorry, sir," somebody mumbled.

"There's been enough loss on this boat today," Jack said. "Even though the Captain's gone, this girl is still under his protection. I'll pay you when we land, and you'll have more than enough to satisfy yourselves with the harlots in the Northlands." Kurian doubted that was true.

"Now get back to your posts." Jack did not have to yell this time. The men were cowed enough already, as if his voice were a worse threat than a whip.

As the crew returned to their duties, Kurian noticed that the music had fully subsided. He no longer heard its solemn cries or felt its urgent pull. They had sailed outside of the Siren's reach, and most of them were alive. He was sorry for the loss of Captain Bacchus, but he was also relieved to have survived his own narrow escape.

"Darn," Rhys said beside him. "I really wanted a tussle. My body needs a good stretch to feel right."

Kurian looked behind them and saw the mass of fog still hovering in the distance. "Don't worry," he said, clapping Rhys on the back, "I think we'll have the opportunity to stretch our legs at least before the day is through."

The most eventful moment of the rest of their voyage that day was when Bill woke up. He sat upright suddenly screaming, drawing everyone's attention. He stared around him for a few moments in confusion, until his friend Sam helped him up.

"Sam," he said, "I think I've had the most terrible dream in my life."

"What's that?" said Sam.

"I dreamed I went and got myself a wife."

"You've had it easy then."

"Tell me that when you've got your own old hen."

Sam looked tired and patted him on the cheek with one hand. "That's enough for today, Bill." The other men loomed nearby with clenched fists.

They arrived in Ramah shortly after the exchange. The day was still bright, but the smell of cooking fires from shore suggested that the light would soon fade. Darker clouds over the heights that climbed up to the cliffs promised more rain. The diminished crew performed the reverse operation from that morning, except that there was no dock at which to moor. Kurian had no interest in watching this time. Louise was telling them about her escape from Evasius' soldiers, and how she had followed them to Whalesand.

As soon as the ship had dropped anchor near Ramah, Noeman came out on deck, looking exhausted from his own struggle with the Sirens. He would not speak or meet their gaze. Jack immediately put their horses in a longboat and ordered them aboard.

"You take Captain Bacchus' advice and ride hard," he said to Kurian. "And you remember what it cost to get you here." Then he turned and walked away.

Kurian was tired and wanted to rest. He was certain his friends felt the same way. But there would be no rest in Ramah. They would only pass through. Louise told them they had to climb aboard another boat to cross Lake Hasslemere before nightfall and hide in the wilderness from Fallon. Kurian had some hope again because Louise had returned. Through death and distance, the King of the Caves had sent their guide. Though he did not know the man's motives, he believed Louise's story that he wanted to see them. And he trusted his notion that the man would not go to so much trouble if he intended them immediate harm.

He might not be a friend, but at least the threat had winnowed down to Evasius and Fallon. So far, they had been fortunate enough to stay ahead of them.

Hasslemere

The longboat swayed more heavily in the unprotected harbor than the cog they just left. None of them had yet developed the sea legs necessary to stand in the smaller craft. The five of them sat on two benches, with Rhys' large frame centered between Tobin and Louise. Kurian sat closer to the bow next to Noeman, facing the others. Following closely behind was a second vessel carrying their horses ashore. Over the creaking and splashing made by the oars, Kurian heard the pilot of the trailing boat asking how they had come through the straight. The sailors of the Osprey answered as if the man were delusional. The rumor of their shortcut would travel quickly, and Mr. Darling was not as flamboyant or boastful as Captain Dilly had been.

With Noeman joining them, Tobin asked Louise to retell her story. "Since we'll land soon," she said, "I'll summarize." She took a deep breath and tucked some hair behind her ear before continuing. "As soon as we separated in the woods, Gideon moved us closer to the search parties. Our movement started to draw them toward us, but they weren't coming quickly enough for him. We heard Captain Fallon taunting you as we crept along. Gideon could tell that he was close to you four from the sound, so he readied us to create a distraction. It felt like we had gone about a hundred yards deeper into the forest when Gideon shouted and we all started running toward the cliffs, away from Dury. The soldiers took the bait and set off the first of Gideon's traps.

"I saw three of them chasing us with torches, and then something large flew past and they were gone. The torches went out, and all I could hear was their screaming. The trap probably threw a whole tree at them, knowing Gideon. He stopped us from running much further, and we waited for the next opportunity. He'd placed several traps in the forest in case of trouble. I only hope he didn't leave any in place where an innocent person or some poor animal would trigger them." Noeman waved his hand to urge her along. He was obviously not interested in the details.

"The trap scared the soldiers and they stopped following us. They probably saw it as proof the forest was haunted, but I think Gideon encourages those stories with his behavior. Soon enough, we heard the captain yelling at them and Gideon got us ready to play bait again. This time, I screamed and we started moving."

"We heard that scream," Rhys said, "and Kur..." He stopped when Tobin jabbed him in the ribs with an elbow. He looked at Tobin with an incredulous expression. "Well, we thought that was it for you, I guess."

Louise looked down and hid a smile. "Well, I'm glad you didn't turn hero," she said. Kurian felt his face flush.

"I...we..." he stuttered, "You...you told us not to."

"And then you magically escaped," Noeman said impatiently.

"When I screamed," she continued, "the captain started chasing us. We hadn't gone far when there was a blinding light and a boom like thunder. You heard it. You said it knocked you down?"

"It threw us on our faces," Tobin said. He looked excited. He had always loved the most adventurous stories from their order, the ones with unbelievable escapes. Kurian thought he looked like he was listening to one of them again, even though he had been part of this story.

"Fallon and his men were blown back and knocked out, but it didn't do anything like that to us," she continued. "When the light had dimmed, the King was standing in front of us with a couple other men. He gave Gideon quite the look, but didn't say anything about the traps. He doesn't go for sneaky things like that. I don't care what you've heard," she held up a warning finger at Kurian, but he hadn't been planning to say anything this time.

"After that, it was simple. He set me on a horse and I headed for Whalesand; Alden and Gideon stayed with him. There were soldiers near the cottage, so I stayed away from there, or else I would have met you. I went straight through the plains, instead of following the road, and I arrived yesterday morning, ahead of you.

"I watched you talking to Captain Bacchus, and after you left I waited to convince him to sneak me onto his ship. He wasn't in the best condition that night, but after a few hours of sleep, I was able to wake him and find out your plans. When I heard you were going to try the straits, I convinced him that I could serve as an extra distraction against the Sirens."

"That work out how you expected?" asked Rhys.

"I didn't anticipate that reaction, no," she said, looking embarrassed. "But I'm glad I was there." She tilted an eyebrow at Kurian, who nodded agreement.

"I paid you back," he said.

"We can compare ledgers later," she shrugged. "The rest of the story you know."

"We're glad you're unharmed, dear," Noeman said, not looking at her.

Kurian followed his gaze back to the Osprey. The dean was still dealing with the events of the day. Kurian turned toward the quiet fishing town. A handful of buildings stood close to the water where a shallow quay led directly up to the main street. Fishing boats still moved around the bay, but no other large ships were there.

Ramah might attract the occasional shipment from afar, but in general, it was a solitary place. It was the furthest southern town on the coast of the Northland kingdoms, and had once been contested as an outpost of Pallingham. However, the town was indefensible, stuck on a narrow slice of land between the bay and Hasslemere, a large, liver-shaped lake fed by the trickling runoff of the highlands to the east. It was a town similar to Aposford in that there was nothing visible to outsiders that explained why people remained there to scratch out an existence.

The strangest thing about the scene was the foreign architecture. The rooflines slanted more, and the doors and windows were set deep under large awnings. Instead of whitewash or colors made with clay, the town was almost colorless with dark browns, grays, and black. Only one large building close to the water stood out, painted a deep red color with large brass lamps hanging from the corners of the roof—probably an establishment for the visiting sailors. When he considered the faded paint and the dilapidated condition of many of the buildings in contrast to this one, he found the overall impression of the town depressing.

On landing, the oarsmen allowed them to disembark, tossed their baggage on the quay, and then pushed off to return to the Osprey. The ship's bow had already turned west to escape up the coast.

"Looks like Mr. Darling doesn't want to stop and chat with our pursuers," Kurian said, looking toward the blob of fog hovering on the water in the distance. He guessed they had a three-hour head start before Fallon would be on their trail.

"After our own interview with Captain Fallon, I don't blame him for running," Tobin said.

Turning back toward Ramah, Kurian found that the only bright point of the town was the youth and vitality of the people. Unlike Aposford, the people finishing their work for the day were younger and heartier—not people clinging to their final years. In contrast to those he saw in Pallingham and Downriver

Town, they were working. They were clearly not wealthy, but they didn't appear dejected and slovenly like the people of his own country. And they were friendly enough to greet the strangers with a nod as they led their horses down the main street. It was a welcome feeling to be greeted, but when Kurian looked at the women, he couldn't help thinking of the Sirens. He smiled awkwardly and looked away.

Merchants and traders quickly approached with shouts of "Welcome, friends," and "Excellent prices," as they waved clothing, food, and various merchandise above the crowd. The accents were as varied as the goods. Kurian even heard an offer for their horses—and outrageous proposals from women near the red building. They wore audacious and revealing dresses that left little to the imagination. If Kurian and his friends were still wearing their robes, he doubted the women would have made the effort.

The monks pushed through the sellers as politely as they could, following Louise straight through town, toward the climbing hills and darkening clouds beyond. At the end of the street, less than a quarter mile from the quay, the buildings abruptly stopped at the shore of the lake. There were no merchants or tradesmen at this end of town. The buildings at the water's edge were either storehouses or deserted shacks. The walls that faced the lake were windowless.

In the afternoon light, the view was almost pleasant. Across the water, Kurian made out the far shore rising into wooded foothills. Above them, he knew the Crags of the Wild Goats climbed to the top of the Northland cliffs. In the forefront, however, the water was black and still. It looked more like a bot-

tomless hole than liquid, as if it might swallow anybody stepping foot in it. Dirty foam collected at the gravel shore, lapping
at a slimy, moss-like vegetation that made walking treacherous.
To their left, the lake expanded north, making the far shore invisible. A hundred yards to their right, they saw three small
fishing boats with triangular sails landing on the beach. Louise
turned in their direction. Eight fishermen were hauling each
boat ashore by the time they drew near.

"Broadman," Louise called, and a wiry but strong man left
the group to meet them. The others continued to pull in the
boats and cover them with tarps. He was shorter than Kurian,
and certainly not the man they would have picked based on the
name Broadman. He smiled when he saw Louise, revealing ex-
tremely white teeth behind several days of reddish brown
beard.

"Hello, little turtle," he said to her. "Not hiding your head today, I see. What brings you to Ramah?" He looked at the monks
suspiciously. His glare made it hard to believe he would have
taken their word that Louise sent them.

"You already know I need to cross the lake, James. I'll hide
once I'm on the other side."

"And them?" James Broadman cocked his head toward her
companions. "Don't look at me that way," he said to them, "I
take after my mother's side."

"They would come, too." She handed something to him that
Kurian couldn't see. "He wants to see them."

Whatever she gave him seemed to satisfy his doubts about
them. Perhaps it was payment, or some message from their

leader. James only nodded, then looked back over the water and up at the clouds.

"Can it wait until tomorrow?"

Louise shook her head.

"Hasslemere is not our friend tonight," James said. "If you can hide here, it would be safer, young turtle."

"Enemies are close behind," Louise said. "The far side is the safest place."

"I don't like it," said James, but whistled to the men working on his boat and gestured for them to launch it back into the water. "But if you must go, we cannot waste any time. Even now I am not sure we can make it in time."

"Have some faith," Louise whispered.

James grunted. "I trust your king, but I *believe* in Hasslemere—at least more than any man's claims." He gave her a resigned shrug. "On the bright side, nobody can follow you until light."

"Why not?" Tobin asked. Something about the situation had turned him pale.

"Nobody sails Hasslemere after dark," James answered, "and this storm makes it doubly dangerous." Then he pointed at their horses, "They'll have to stay. I don't have space for them, and you don't have time to carry a larger boat from the quays. Sentries on the other side might be able to help you with new ones."

Without waiting for discussion, he turned to his fellows and spoke hastily while Kurian and his friends pulled the packs from their horses and handed them to the two men waiting in the boat. Next, they struggled to pull themselves through the single gap in the high, scalloped gunwales. James followed quickly, and climbed nimbly into the boat with perfect balance. As soon as he was onboard, he covered the gap with a shield-like plank. When Kurian saw this, he realized that the railing was not truly scalloped, but that the whole boat was surrounded with removable, eye-shaped planks. Each fit into an iron catch and had a handle facing inward. Other than permitting entry to the boat, he could not tell what purpose they served.

Benches crossed the hull, like in the longboat, except that box frames covered in netting were stowed beneath them. The passengers sat down facing the bow, and James stood directly in the front. With the two fishers who sat in back with oars, they filled the craft.

"Now boys, this is Seamus, and that's Tully," James said, pointing to the other fishermen who began rowing away from the shore. "You do anything they say and we'll be fine." Louise and the Caprics nodded. "Hasslemere's an unusual lake. How can I explain it?" He rubbed his chin and looked up, thinking. "It's not haunted, per se. But there is a knack to crossing safely—especially under conditions like these." His words did not encourage Kurian.

Tobin raised a hand as if he were in the dean's class. The hand trembled slightly. "Why exactly don't you sail at night?"

"Because you can't see the hasslefish," James answered flatly.

"That's what I thought you'd say." Tobin was sweating in the cool air.

"What's a hasslefish?" Kurian asked.

"Scuttle me!" James muttered, "I shouldn't have said anything. Listen, we have enough light to see them coming. Just do what we say if we come across them and we'll make it. I've dealt with them a dozen times. Of course, we'd do better to avoid them altogether." James did not gesture in excess while he talked, but his frustration at his passengers was clear. "As I was saying, Hasslemere is tricky, even in daylight. It senses your moods, and it tries to make you lose your bearings."

"I thought you said it wasn't haunted," Tobin said, his voice cracking.

"*Per se*," James added.

Tobin nodded manically.

"It's not haunted in the normal sense," James struggled to explain. "It just...has a personality. I don't know how it works; I only know what it does to people who head out unprepared. If everybody onboard isn't completely certain about their destination, fogs and storms brew up out of nowhere. If somebody is in a foul mood, we don't let them sail because the lake turns foul—and that's when the hasslefish hunt."

"Sounds like more silly superstition to me," Noeman grumbled. "As least, that's what I would have thought this morning." He looked up for the first time since they had left the Osprey, and his face had changed. Kurian thought he looked less certain of himself. The dean who had always known everything was beginning to doubt his convictions. Kurian knew it had started with the witch at Fin. Noeman had to rebuild his whole world after that revelation. Now, after being wrong about the Sirens, the truth of the world around him had shaken him to his core. Kurian liked the change. He looked humbled, and that made him look kinder.

"Now," James said loudly, and pulled a hand down his face, "maybe we can quit the interruptions and avoid dying today, yes? Good." He took a deep breath and composed himself. "If we sail and row, we'll shave off some time and reach the far shore in about an hour.

"Look at that gap in the trees," he said, turning and pointing over the bow. "See where the shoreline is visible and clear? That is where we're going. When we get closer, you'll see two markers that will make it easier to see.

"Focus on that point, know that's where we're going—but just as importantly, believe that we can get there. Any seed of doubt or distraction in your mind will only agitate the lake, and then it will try to befuddle us. Does everyone understand?" He waited for them to show they did. "Focus and believe—we get across easy."

After James' speech, Tobin and Noeman began praying immediately, along the same lines as his instructions. They asked for focus and confidence in their arrival, as well as protection from God. Rhys leaned forward on his bench, propping an arm against the removable planks and staring hard at their destination. He had never excelled at performing multiple tasks, so singular concentration was his best chance of success. Louise also stared toward the landing site, but her gaze wandered toward the hills above with a satisfied and expectant smile.

Kurian couldn't join in prayer with Tobin and the dean. His mind never wandered as much as it did during prayer. For fifteen minutes, he tried Rhys' method of staring at their goal, but his mind raced with unanswered questions, predictions of their immediate future, and memories of the last month's horrors. Even as he looked at the far-off beach, his mind jumped hundreds of miles away in a second.

The water of the lake was still, except for the wrinkled chevron in their wake. Only the fluttering of the sail and the rhythmic dipping of the oars broke the silence. With each stroke, they groaned with protest in their slots, as if the boat itself did not want to continue the journey. Between light puffs of breeze from the ocean, the smell of coming rain poured down from the hills with the resinous scent of evergreens and juniper. The combination was a somber song from a lonely boat in a more solemn landscape.

At the same time, the accumulated weariness of traveling throbbed behind Kurian's eyes and made concentration difficult. He tried to shake himself into wakefulness, and finally decided that he needed to talk to somebody. With the others trying to focus in their own ways, James looked like the safest choice. He slid between the two rowing fishermen to where James had moved to take the tiller at the stern.

"Why do you call Louise turtle?" he asked.

"When I met her," James answered, "she was cowering inside a hood, trying to hide her head like a turtle."

Kurian nodded, not sure he understood the motivation for the nickname, and decided to change the subject. "With all the danger," he said, "why do you sail this lake?"

"Don't get distracted," James warned.

"I won't," Kurian said, "talking a little will keep my mind from wandering too much."

James nodded. "We're on the lake because it's lucrative. Not ferrying people for the king, so much," he said, nodding toward Louise, "but the everyday work."

"What would that be?"

"Crabbing," James said. "Those boxes under the seats are crab traps. The noble women up north pay handsomely for a powder made from the shells of crabs found only in this lake. The meat's worthless, except for feeding pigs, but we grind the shells and mix them with oils. When the mixture is cooked, it turns a deep red color and they paint their faces with it in King Bagler's court."

"You still haven't told us what a hasslefish is," Kurian said, trying to get his original question answered.

"They're a small fish—usually no more than ten inches." James held his up his index fingers to indicate the length. "Ugly things. Teeth pointing out every direction."

"Why would you be worried about a little fish?"

"Because they hunt in packs," James said quietly, keeping his eyes on the far shore. "Usually over fifty of them come together near the surface. When the lake turns foul and it's difficult to get your bearings, the brutes will leap out of the water—some of them fly over the boat. They also have a row of spines on either side, like a porcupine. Once they're in the air, they throw them like little poisoned needles. The men who are hit go mad, usually fling themselves into the water and become lunch. Those shields along the gunwale are good protection if we need them."

Kurian sighed heavily. "Sirens, storms, poisoned fish—why does anybody ever get into a boat?"

"It wasn't always this way," James said incredulously. "Story goes a witch cursed the lake when her children got lost in a fog and drowned." He began to sing.

"A voice is heard in Ramah,
Lamentation and bitter weeping.
Rachel is weeping for her children
Because they are no more."

"At least, that's what the songs say. The water has been calm ever since, only disturbed by the strongest storms, and something breaking the surface. It took on her animosity and pain then, and the hasslefish started to appear."

"A curse. One more reason to stay off it...wait, what are you doing?" Kurian's anxiety about the boat sharpened as James turned away from their destination. More surprising, the sail and its heavy wooden boom shot across the boat, over the heads of the two men rowing, nearly catching Kurian in the stomach.

"I'm only jibing," James said calmly.

"But I thought we were heading for the gap in the trees."

"Yes, but we go faster if we zigzag a bit to better catch the wind." James looked at Kurian and laughed at his shocked expression. "You should sit down and try to focus, before I give you a nickname. In five minutes, we should be able to see the pillars marking the trail and then it will be easier."

Kurian nodded and gingerly stepped back to his seat beside Noeman. While his curiosity was sated, apprehension about the dangers of the lake gnawed at his mind. He truly hoped they had a safe journey, but a cloud of fear hung over him with the idea of fending off the darts of the hasslefish. Was his stubborn insistence on retrieving the treasure going to kill them all in the end? Even though they had survived this far, others had paid the ultimate price, and he and his friends had killed for it. Could this really be what God wanted from them, despite their oaths?

He looked up between the shields when the boat turned again and had trouble finding the beach. The light was fading surprisingly fast now, and the shore looked further away, not closer. The markers should be visible, according to James, but they weren't there. Even the lighter colored beach was harder to see when he found it. It was like looking through old glass.

"Everybody needs to check their minds and hearts," James called from the stern, caution in his voice. "There's a mist gathering, but we're almost there." He pointed to the shore. "Remember, we're going there. Look at the fires on the pillars."

The mention of a fog confirmed Kurian's fear that they might be sailing into trouble. He couldn't see the pillars or the fires, and this worried him even more. The fog thickened, and darkness settled at the edge of his vision. Slowly, the darkness closed in so that the beach was the only thing visible, and it was shrinking as if he were traveling down a long tunnel. Everything outside the confines of the boat was dissolving from his vision.

"Disturbance," James said. "Port side." They all looked where he pointed and saw several ripples spreading across the surface a hundred yards away. A soft bubbling sound like many oars dipping into the water moved toward the boat.

"Take two shields," James told them, grabbing two of the planks himself. "Protect your side and your front. The person next to you will cover your other side. Press the two shields together above you." He tied the tiller to the rail so the boat would stay on course, and then pointed once more at the beach. "Above all, remember that beach and we'll make it. Shields up and ignore the chaos. Remember the beach!"

James kneeled behind Seamus and Tully on their bench. They pulled up the oars and grabbed their own shields. Between the three of them, they formed a cone shape with the planks that covered them on all sides and overlapped on top. Tobin saw their formation and copied it with Rhys and Louise. Kurian and Noeman did their best, sitting back to back and holding up four shields. The planks were heavy and difficult to hold in position, and hiding in the dark shell made it even more challenging to think of the beach.

Everything was still for almost a minute. Huddled in the small shelter with Noeman, the echoing staccato of their breathing took Kurian to the verge of panic. The silence outside dragged on until he was tempted to lower his shield and peek out.

Suddenly, something struck his right shield with a thump. In a moment, three more strikes hit together. He heard the projectiles hitting elsewhere on the boat, but most landed on his shield as far as he could tell.

"It's Kurian," James yelled, "for all our sakes, knock him out!"

The order surprised him, and he looked over his shoulder at the dean. Noeman looked surprised too, and didn't look like he intended to follow it.

"I'm serious," James yelled.

"If I'm drawing them," Kurian said to the dean, but he looked back with a pained look.

"Rhys," Noeman called, "you can reach him easier. You do it."

They shuffled around to regroup while the spines thudded into the shields and the ship. Before they had all their shields propped up, one of the fish landed in the bottom of the boat at Kurian's feet. In an instant, he saw the dull gray scales of the fish, the sharp ridge along its back and the riot of pointed teeth in its mouth.

It looked at him with eyes like jet. Then the fish flopped against the deck and the quills on its side shot up like arrows. Kurian felt them pierce his chest and arm, and he fell between the two benches. Other than the immediate pain on impact, he didn't cry out, and he didn't feel anything but shock.

Louise screamed, but Noeman and Rhys immediately closed the circle of shields to cover Kurian between them.

"James," Tobin yelled, "they hit Kurian."

"Put him out now or he's dead," James roared.

Rhys lifted his fist and grimaced, then slammed it down on Kurian's forehead. The back of his head smacked against the hull and everything went black.

CHAPTER SEVENTEEN

The Signpost

The last hints of light had faded from the sky over the bay before the ship dropped anchor, so Captain Fallon landed with his men in complete darkness. All thirty of those he had gathered at Whalesand were with him, along with ten sailors borrowed from the Admiral. However, in his judgment, Mouna's presence almost doubled the effective strength of his force. While he did not know the size of the band of thieves led by the king of the caves, he doubted they would offer significant resistance. Criminals, he'd found, were often cowards and would run at the first sign of a fight.

Of course, with the revelation that the thugs were using magic, Mouna's presence would be essential to neutralize that effect. Things appeared to be working out better than he had feared at Dury. However, he knew how quickly a battle could turn. The only thing he truly controlled was his own resolve and he had never felt so committed; he would succeed in his mission and redeem himself, or die in the effort.

The smell of oncoming rain gradually strengthened as they unloaded the boats, overtaking the odors of salt and seaweed around the tiny quay at Ramah. Fallon watched the new soldiers carefully as they passed the local tavern, the only building with any outside lighting. The prostitutes leaning against the gilded doorway called out to them, but the men remained in formation. Fallon walked over and questioned them about the monks. He flashed two gold coins as incentive, and they quickly told him his prey had gone toward the lake. *With Admiral Shea's crew coming ashore, it's probably the easiest money they'll make tonight,* he thought.

Lifting himself back onto his horse, he took off at a trot and quickly reached the lakeside. It was so dark, some of the men only stopped when their horses' forelegs splashed in the water.

"Torches," he ordered, and his men produced several lights.

Mouna, still riding behind him, gasped when she saw the water. He craned his neck around and was surprised to see fear in her face.

"They have crossed over," she said. "You must follow them, but I cannot come with you." She squirmed in the saddle, and then dropped awkwardly to the ground.

"It's just a lake," he said, "why can't you come?"

"I cannot cross that lake!" She shook her head violently. Her mood was going to affect his men quickly if he didn't intervene.

Fallon jumped down beside her and led her away from the shore. "Why not?" he asked, his voice hushed.

"Because I see my future there, you stupid little toy soldier!" Her shout carried in the calm air. "There is something ancient beyond that water. Even now, it pushes me away and prevents me from going any further. My destruction will follow if I attempt to cross."

"Then what will you do?" Fallon massaged his temples with one hand. With the other, he wanted to strike her, but he controlled his anger.

"I will return to Pallingham. When I arrive, I will contact you, and you can report your progress for Lord Evasius." The witch took a tone that did not allow for argument.

"And what am I supposed to do against the thief's magic?"

"You have nothing to fear," she said, running a hand down his cheek. He turned away, his face burning with anger. "I have put you under my protection, so you should be immune to the madness we have seen in other men who have encountered him. You also have a strong mind, Captain; do not underestimate your own power to resist when your mission is threatened."

"What about my men?"

"They will follow your leading. In many ways, leadership is a magic of its own." Her tender tone disappeared and now she spoke to him with certainty. "Be firm in your resolve, and they will not falter."

"Hurry then. Do what you must." He turned back toward his men, calling over his shoulder, "our lord cannot go without his information for long." He did not look back to see where the witch went, and assumed she would return to Admiral Shea's ship. As he remounted, he hoped it was the last time he would see her. Deeper in his heart, he knew that he feared facing the magic he had seen at Dury again, but he pushed that down and covered it with anger as he would smother a fire.

"The witch balks at every shadow when she is not safe in Pallingham castle," he said to the nervously shifting soldiers. "We must press on."

There was only one building near the shore with any signs of life, and it matched the description from the prostitutes. Several small fishing boats were nestled against it, and light shone from the single window that looked onto an alleyway. The clouds opened as his platoon neared the building and rain poured down without warning. The soldiers doused the torches, and Captain Fallon knocked on the door of the fishermen's workshop.

A bearded, sinewy man opened the door and peered out into the rain. Inside, Fallon saw other men of similar build stirring large, steaming cauldrons with wooden paddles. They were all shirtless in the steam-filled room and ignored the visitor at the door.

"Yes?" said the man in the doorway. His eyes inspected Fallon's armor and weapons without concern.

"I must get across the lake," Captain Fallon said.

"Come back tomorrow," the man said, and began to shut the door.

Fallon stepped forward and shoved it back open. "Price is no concern."

"Not for me neither," said the fisherman. "We're done sailing tonight."

His rage flared. In an instant, he pulled his dagger and stabbed the man in the throat. He pushed his way inside and threw the body to the ground before the vats at which his colleagues worked. Three soldiers entered behind him before the last weak gurgle escaped the man's throat. The other fishermen stood shocked for a moment, then lifted their paddles as if to defend themselves.

"Your colleague refused me crossing," Fallon yelled, walking around the end of the row of cooking vessels. "Unless you want to end up like him, one of you will ferry us across the lake tonight."

They stared at each other, then the one closest to him spoke. "Crossing at night would be worse. It's suicide. The hasslefish would kill everyone on board."

"Nonsense!" Fallon roared. He drew his sword, knocked the paddle from the man's hands, and hewed half way through his neck. As he fell, the others backed up into a corner.

"It's true," another cried. "The fish kill men every year. Nobody goes at night."

Fallon stopped short of attacking him as well. They were telling the truth. He saw it on their faces. They were more afraid of the lake than they were of him. More damned magic. And without Mouna, he had no way to cross without risking his men. Since he had met her, he could not escape the supernatural, and he fumed because of it. The sorcery should have made his mission easier—given him more strength and honor—but it only tricked him, stealing the competence he had always enjoyed.

The witch toyed with him, and every time he closed on the monks, some invisible hand scooped them away. Why was he unable to catch them?

He felt trapped by things he could not explain—stuck in this cat-and-mouse game with the monks, ensnared by Mouna and her magic. But across the lake, in the canyons and caves above, he had a chance to prove his loyalty and free himself from her noose. He would not waver in that pursuit, but he had to be cautious. As much as it enraged him, he would wait until it was light so he could cross safely. Risking his men would mean failure—and potentially his own death, before even seeing his prey.

"You," he pointed his sword at the man who had spoken, "show my men where they can sleep tonight. At dawn, you will take us across." He was the youngest of the six remaining men, and he stepped hesitantly toward the soldiers by the door. They grabbed him by the arms, and Fallon nodded for his men to take him outside.

As soon as the door closed, Fallon kicked one of the boiling cauldrons toward the remaining barefoot fishermen. A burning tide of water and half-cooked crabs poured across the floor. They scrambled to leap out of the way, shouting in pain as it washed over their feet.

In their mad dash to escape the scalding flood, they forgot Fallon and his sword, until they landed within his reach.

His fury was partially sated when he stepped back out in the rain.

Tobin and Rhys dropped their shields as soon as the boat scraped the pebbly shore. Together, they lifted Kurian over the railing, refusing the help of James and his comrades. Louise hovered next to them, concern furrowing her brow as none of them had ever seen. Moreover, she looked confused, or so Tobin thought.

This didn't surprise him; he felt confused himself, and scared. His best friend lay unconscious—at the hands of another friend—on the rocks of a strange beach in a country more distant than any of them had dreamed they would travel. Then there was the poison from the hasslefish. For all his studying, he didn't know what to do next. His head rocked up and down repeatedly, as if the movement would jostle the answer from his mind.

Without thinking, his eyes scanned Kurian's limp form, and when they set upon the wound in his chest, his medical training suddenly sprang to the forefront of his mind. One of the spines from the fish had lodged near the left armpit. Tobin lifted the arm for a better look and discovered a second spot of blood on the back of the sleeve, with the last sliver of a second quill just showing above the fabric.

"You'd better tie him up," James said from behind while he unloaded their luggage, "and keep him away from the water. That's all the advice I can offer." James dropped a pack, then cupped his hands and made a bird call toward the woods. Seamus and Tully labored to pull the boat ashore.

Tobin looked up for a moment, recalling the danger if Kurian should wake under the influence of the poison. He told

Rhys to get their corded belts and tie Kurian's legs. Tobin knew that if he were conscious he would hate the idea—being tied with the symbol he had chosen to reject in front of Noeman—but it was for his own good. Of course, if he also knew that Tobin was tending his wounds, he would have to thank him for all the extra study in healing.

Pulling the knife from his boot, Tobin cut the sleeve off and exposed the wound on Kurian's chest. The sharp spine passed just beneath the skin of his arm, sticking in the flesh like a large splinter. However, the tine in his chest stood straight out almost two inches. They were no thicker than a small twig and looked like polished bone needles.

Tobin grabbed the first between the knife and his thumb and pulled it from beneath the skin. As soon as he did, blood flowed out from the wound. Rhys winced, and Louise stifled a yelp next to him.

"Rhys, how is it you've always been so eager to cause pain, yet so squeamish at its remediation?" he asked to break the tension. Nobody laughed.

He ripped the torn sleeve into strips and tied it tightly around Kurian's arm. Then he carefully pulled at the quill in Kurian's chest. There was a soft snap and it came out short, leaving the fragile tip inside the wound. The broken end revealed that the quill was hollow——*probably as a reservoir for the poison,* he thought.

"God have mercy," he said. "We don't have the means to treat this here. He needs surgery to get out the last piece, and we should be breathing a vein to remove the poison."

"That wouldn't help," said a cracked old voice above them.

Tobin looked up to see a man standing at Kurian's head. Rhys jumped to his feet, ready to fight. The man appeared older than the dean, but surprisingly, in better physical condition. He held his hands in front of him, showing he was unarmed. Deep lines scored his face and his skin was the dark color of earth, darker than Rhys' tan complexion. He wore a rough tunic made of hair and an oiled cloak lined with silky furs. It was a more refined outfit than the piles of skins that Gideon wore, though it had the same wild character. Tobin had never seen anybody who looked like him, but the sudden appearance and even more surprising declaration infuriated him.

"How would you know?" he shouted.

"Because I've seen it before," the old man croaked. "Normal medicine won't help."

"I won't just let him die," Tobin's own voice cracked, and he suddenly had to fight back tears.

"You have to take him to the King's camp—if you can get there in time. Their healers can help him, but the chest is the worst place for a hasslefish sting...goes straight for the heart." The old man tapped his own chest with a gnarled finger and let out an awkward chuckle.

"Who are you?" Noeman said, stepping forward until he almost shoved the man with his chest, "and what right do you have to scare these boys?"

"No harm meant," the newcomer skipped backward lightly. "But I wonder at the state of the world when monks are so rude."

"This is the sentry," said James before Noeman could respond.

"Right, right," chirped the old man. "I am the Watcher. I am also sometimes the Signpost." He bowed deeply with a flourish of his hand. "I can point you to the narrow path." His flourish ended with a finger pointed toward a dense cluster of trees.

"We're headed there already, Xander," Louise said, still kneeling beside Kurian.

"Ah, Miss Prescott," the watcher said, "I didn't recognize you amongst so many strangers. And in such masculine clothing." He paused with his mouth open, holding a finger at his temple.

"And you startled me," she said.

"Now I remember," Xander said, as if he hadn't heard her, "your coming changes things."

Quickly, he made a different bird call and four other men appeared at the tree line.

"Gentlemen, we have distinguished guests—the last remaining Caprics. Two of you make a sledge for that one, and we'll escort them home. The other two, cover our trail and give Evasius' men a false lead. I don't care who comes with me—draw straws if you must." He turned toward the boat. "James, would you mind helping them?" Xander's mysterious manner disappeared as he gave the orders, which only made Tobin think him stranger than before.

"We're not going home tonight," James shrugged his shoulders, and helped Seamus and Tully pull in the boat.

The rain pelted down, dripping off Tobin's hood as they followed the trail through the forest. He and Noeman had decided to don their old robes since they no longer needed stealth. They were within reach of the King of the Caves, whoever he was, and disguise would not profit them. Rhys kept the clothes from Dury, claiming they were easier to ride in.

Xander and the other sentries brought enough horses from their scouting camp for them all to ride. For Kurian, they constructed a sledge of two long poles, with blankets tied between them to support him. The ends of the poles were lashed to Xander's saddle so that the sledge dragged behind his horse. Their two escorts, introduced as Elwell and Briggs, followed behind, helping the rain to obscure their trail. The narrowness of the track made it easy in the beginning, where they had to ride single file, but further up the hill the trees spread out, and so did the riders. Elwell and Briggs were soon crisscrossing the back of their path to blot out any trace of their passing. The rain was their expert assistant.

Tobin rode beside Kurian's litter, keeping a careful eye on his friend. Xander was setting a quick pace on the sloping trail, and he did not want Kurian to fall and suffer another injury. Louise followed close behind him, and when he looked back at her, he saw the same grief and fear he felt. More surprising than her show of emotions, he thought he could see her lips moving in silent prayer.

It spurred him to pray for Kurian as well; the depth of his concern had made him forget. Tobin spoke with Kurian on the plains about the possible dangers at the king's camp, but neither of them imagined at the time that magic would be one of them. They thought it was only a threat from Evasius' side, but Louise's story of her escape had made Tobin uneasy—until now. She was still the king's spy, but the concern on her face was enough to win his trust.

Noeman trotted around him and sidled up next to Xander. Tobin could barely make out their conversation over the patter of the rain.

"I would like you to apologize to those boys," the dean said.

"Are you certain you don't want an apology for hurting your pride?" Xander replied.

Noeman scoffed. "I see that only insults come from the one who pronounces others as rude. My pride has nothing to do with it. You scared them unnecessarily while their friend lay wounded."

"Do you cut down a signpost for directing you, 'this way to this town, that way to another one'?" Xander pointed in opposite directions.

"What kind of nonsense is that?" the dean asked sardonically.

"Then why attack the signpost for speaking the truth?"

Noeman stared at their guide. Tobin recognized the expression from the classroom; it came out when one of the novices gave a painfully ignorant answer. He realized that the dean could not deal with anything but the most explicit statements—and the answers always had to fit his expectations. He had no imagination to see the new insult leveled at him through Xander's questions.

"Are all of your master's servants so inane?" the dean finally said. "I certainly hope the thief can speak better for himself."

"Accusing a man of robbery on his own doorstep," Xander mused, "very rude."

"Now you attack me for the truth," the dean raised his voice and jabbed his finger at him. "He took our most valuable treasure——the one our order was founded to protect—and admitted the theft when he left his seal in our treasury."

Xander shook with silent laughter.

"What is so funny?" Noeman shouted at him.

"You scream about treasure," Xander said with amusement, "but you have no conception of true riches."

CHAPTER EIGHTEEN

A Secret Shared

Despite all the warnings from the young fisherman, Fallon's troops had no trouble crossing the lake. His primary concern was that the rain would wipe away the monks' trail, but they found signs of a small camp on the far shore. Beyond that was a broad trail through the forest, marked by two short columns with censers on top. The small signal fires they contained had run out of oil and burned out.

The trail, however, had several signs of use. He quickly found areas of churned up mud, including a clear hoof print filled with water. Another few hours, and even the ongoing drizzle might obliterate them. He dashed forward with his men to follow the tracks, leaving the boats on shore with their new owner.

They followed the signs left behind by the careless monks until mid-afternoon. Then the forest ended abruptly, thirty feet from several steep ridges and canyons that sprang from the earth without warning. They had reached the Crags of the Wild Goats. Before him, Fallon saw three forks just beyond the main entrance. A smaller canyon opening was visible a short way to the north. But the trail disappeared with the trees.

Fallon sent another man to scout out the smaller canyon, and then scoured the ground of the larger entry. He crossed the gap between the forest and the crags repeatedly looking for the slightest hint, but it was impossible to discern which path the Caprics had taken.

He swore under his breath.

For the first time since he was promoted to head a small patrol, he felt the eyes of his men watching him, scrutinizing him. They had to know he would keep them alive and bring them home after a successful mission, or else they would not respect his authority. Mouna was right about leadership—it was like its own magic in the way it held sway over men——and he had always been a natural leader. However, he had always had the resources and information to make good decisions. Now he faced a blind decision with a small chance of success. The soldiers knew they lacked the provisions to wander in the maze of the crags for long, and even the newest recruit could see the potential for ambush in such a place. Any uncertainty on his part would make them doubt, leading either to desertion or death.

The scout returned. There was no trail. The smaller canyon was more barren than the larger one.

Where had they escaped to, and which path should he take? He had to decide. *No,* said the voice of doubt in his mind, *you must draw out the decision without appearing hesitant.* He needed more information. Maybe they had missed something while they hurried through the forest.

Perhaps the monks were not being so careless.

"We missed something," he said forcefully. "They must have made this false trail, then gone back and branched off on another path." There was no grumbling from the soldiers; no nervous glances from face to face. He held them—at least for now.

He lifted himself back onto his horse and wheeled about. "Keep your eyes open as we go back. Look for anything unusual in the forest. Do not hurry. We cannot afford to miss anything."

While they traveled, Xander would not allow the monks to keep watch. They were in the King's territory now, and the monks did not know the land or the passwords. It meant most of them slept well when they camped, except for Tobin and Louise, who shared responsibility for watching over Kurian. As far as Louise could tell, Rhys had no stomach for it, and Noeman was more interested in quizzing Xander about the King, so the job fell to her and Tobin as much from duty as from concern.

Louise nursed Kurian through the final hours of their third night so that Tobin could sleep. She admired his dedication to his friend, and welcomed the way his concern relieved some of her own. If he weren't there, she would be the one needing re-lief from watching and worrying. Of course, unlike Tobin, she had confidence that the healers at camp could save him, if they could only get there soon enough. Though she knew nothing of medicine, she saw that he was getting worse with every passing hour. Her anxiety and dread spread with his illness.

He had woken once in the first night, but only for a few moments, and by that morning, he had developed a fever. He sweated even in the chill forest air of the first day. When they left the forest and entered the crags, she was grateful for the cold autumn rain that consistently fell. It might be the only thing keeping him cool, buying them time to reach the camp.

Occasionally, his muscles tensed, and he thrashed about as if he were in a fight. In the middle of the night, he let out sudden, mournful wails that broke the silence of the wilderness. It sent a shiver down her spine each time.

She sat in the rain outside of the cave they had camped in, holding his hand. It was all they could do to sooth his fitful bouts. It was a balm to her spirit as well. Alleviating his pain—even a little—gave her more hope. *If it would help, she thought, I would cradle his body in my arms instead of just holding his hand. Of course, the others would stop that in a moment.*

"I'll look after him now," Tobin said behind her. He crowded his way into the spot by the litter, leaving no room for her, and picked up the same hand she had held. Standing up, she saw his exhaustion, as if he hadn't slept for days—and maybe he hadn't. His blue eyes were bloodshot, and he could barely hold them open. Mud stained his robe up to the red and white belt he had reclaimed from Kurian's ankles when they left the lake.

Inside the cave, she could make out the other men moving around the small fire, packing up the bags. Briggs had only just returned from watching the canyon to their rear.

"You sure you don't want to sleep a little more?" she asked, hoping he might leave her alone for a moment longer.

Tobin looked at the top of a ridge to the west. "It's past dawn. We'll be leaving soon." He let out a deep sigh, and tossed one of the millions of pebbles strewn through the narrow canyon. It skittered across the mud and loose gravel like an escaping rodent. "I'll get to sleep soon enough, whatever the outcome."

"We'll be in camp this afternoon," she said, trying to encourage him.

"After the journey we have had since leaving home, I anticipate nothing but more horror from any change in location."

It wasn't a fair thing for him to say. The trouble had always come from Evasius' soldiers following them, and he knew that. But he was exhausted and angry, and she understood how hopeless he felt.

"They can heal him," she said, her throat tightening. "I've seen the king's men do incredible things. Once there was a man caught under a rockslide..."

"Why are you trying to persuade me?" he asked, as if harangued. "I believe only God can heal him now."

"Because I hate seeing him like this, too," she said, tears flowing freely. "And because it gives me hope."

"And if your hope is misplaced?"

The scorn on his face bit deeper than the words. She wanted to hide from him, but there was nowhere to go. "When you thought I was dead, I know it pained you, and I know you were all happy I survived. It's different with Kurian. He's still here, so hope is possible. I hope because I ... care about him—I've come to care about all of you." She wasn't sure if it was because of the pause in her words, but she saw the insight on his face.

"That's right. You have a secret. From the first day, you've kept it from us, but we all saw it on your face. You knew him already."

She shook her head, looking at her feet.

"Yes. I saw your surprise and recognition. You may not have been expecting him, but you recognized Kurian in Downriver Town."

"No. Yes." Her face flushed, and she wiped her eyes. "Yes, I recognized him. But no, I didn't know him."

"Tell me how," Tobin said. "I've come to trust you. I believe that your King is not the man Evasius told us about, even though I don't know what sort of man he is. Tell me how you recognized my best friend. In ten years, we never saw a girl or a woman close to our age. How did you know him?"

"I didn't lie to you in the tavern. The King told me to expect three Caprics."

"You didn't tell us the whole truth, either."

She shook her head again.

"So, tell me now," he urged.

"The King showed me Kurian's face. Older, but it was him."

"How?"

She hesitated. She had held this in her heart for years as a private longing, always looking for evidence that it would someday happen. Now she feared that if she told somebody her secret, it might never become true. "It was like a vision," she finally whispered.

"You're saying he showed you Kurian's face. In a vision." Tobin sat back, looking humored. "Why?"

"He told me that the man he showed me would be important—him and his friends." His smirk made her defensive. "He said I would be the one to find him and bring him to our camp, and that he would be among three Capric monks."

"Do you know why your king thinks he's important, or for what?" He leaned forward, as he would when he discussed the treasure with Noeman. She had piqued his curiosity.

"I don't know exactly why any of you are important to the King. He didn't give me details." She hesitated again. Could she share her secret hope? Tobin had been kind and caring to her from the beginning, and she knew he was a trustworthy confidant. If anybody could hear it with compassion, it was Tobin, whether he hoped for the same thing or not. She took a deep breath before letting it spill out of her heart. "The King said he would be important to me, as well. He told me that someday that man would bring justice for my family and others like them. He said that someday..."

Tobin nodded and raised his eyebrows. "Nothing ever brings out Kurian's wrath like injustice." He stopped. "I'm sorry. You had more to say."

"Someday," she said and closed her eyes, speaking quickly before she lost the courage. "He said that someday that man would be my husband."

Tobin's mouth fell open. Then he blushed. A grin spread across his face like a little boy who has just heard something scandalous. Louise shook her head and sighed, knowing he was not going to take her seriously. She saw it coming: "You know he took some vows that will make that difficult," or some other joke that trivialized everything about her vision and her hope.

"So now you think you love him?" Tobin asked. It was a better question than she had braced for.

"As I said, I care about him—about all of you—but, I don't know."

"Well, do you believe him?"

"Who?"

"Your king."

"Yes," she said, and combed her fingers through her wet hair. "He has a gift for knowing things, and I did always believe it. Now I'm afraid I may have ruined it by telling you. Not about the marriage—that's the furthest thing from my mind. But I have always wanted something like justice for my parents."

"God will punish the ones who killed them."

"At the end, maybe." Her passions were instantly aflame. "That's what you believe, isn't it? What happens until then? Do they continue murdering innocent people and selling their children as slaves, or worse? The King promised that justice would come in this life, through that man."

She pointed at Kurian and the action stopped her cold. Suddenly it was all real. Talking about it—admitting it—broke through the possibilities of someday and embedded it firmly in her heart. Seeing the face from her vision before her meant someday could be now. How could she doubt the King's word, especially with the vision to confirm it? Things would be put right.

As for Kurian, she already knew he was a man who would fight against evil. In time, he might become the man she would love.

The King's Camp

There was nothing to see, no hidden clues in the forest to tell Fallon where the monks had gone. They returned to the beach at Hasslemere at dusk and hastily set up camp. One of the boats was missing, along with the young fisherman. A wise choice to run, he thought, while hoping the man met his greatest fear on the lake.

He was the first to rise the next morning. His sleep was fitful after being in a bed for a couple of nights. He studied the pillars and the path that led away to the northeast, looking for hints, thinking about the possibilities. It was impossible that the monks could cover their tracks so successfully in a forest when they had lived their entire lives on the plain—unless they had help. Some of the brigands must have been waiting for them.

The young boys might be captives even now. The thought made him smile, although he wished they were captives in Pallingham's dungeon, under Mouna's supervision.

Stepping away from the trailhead, he wandered back to the shore, letting his mind work through his memory of the previous day. Had he missed anything? The foam undulating at the water's edge caught his attention for a moment, and then he turned left to walk around the entire landing area. As he reached the end of the beach, and turned back toward the forest, he noticed a dense cluster of pines, and behind them, what looked like a large game trail.

He pulled back branches and squeezed behind the trees, stepping into the forest. On the other side of the family of trees, the trail exited cleanly onto the beach so that it was invisible from the shore. Curious.

Nothing moved under the canopy of trees, but the unending hiss of soft rain was broken up into heavy, irregular drips falling from leaves and needles. There was no sign of human use along the trail, but he followed it on a whim.

The trail split a few hundred yards inside, with one leg heading uphill to the right. He turned with it, and felt the hair on his neck stand up.

Something he had not yet noticed pricked at his instincts.

He increased his pace, pushing up the slope until his breath came in short bursts and his heart raced. As he came over the crest, he saw a small clearing in the trees that looked over the lake and the landing beach. Something gnawed at the back of his mind, a sense to keep looking, and as he inspected the clearing, his suspicions were confirmed. On the further side of the hill, hidden from the water, was a small permanent shelter nestled among the trees.

It had only recently been deserted, and as he searched the grounds, he felt as if hidden eyes watched him. No matter. Even if they had left a lookout, he had found a clue.

He trotted down a second trail leading away from the shelter until he was certain it led back toward the game trail he had first discovered. This had to be the true escape route. Whoever was at this observation post had taken the monks onward, while a second party had created a false trail. He had to admire the skill with which they covered their tracks.

It crossed his mind that he might be overreaching to create a plausible story that fit his discovery, but he felt certain in his gut that he was right.

Rushing back down to the beach, he surprised his men by bursting from the copse of trees.

"We're moving," he ordered, and the camp exploded with activity.

Tobin was tired of moving, and it was only noon. The novelty of riding rather than walking had worn off for him back on the plains, as soon as he had realized that it involved pain and soreness. He couldn't seem to get used to the feel of a saddle.

He was tired of riding, and moving, tired from watching Kurian slip away from him—even before the hasslefish left a bony quill in his chest.

Looking down at the litter dragging behind Xander, he could tell that Kurian's condition was deteriorating. He had turned from pale to ashen gray, and a light foam like that on the beach of Hasslemere gathered around his mouth. The sight of his friend lying helpless tugged at Tobin's heart and made him want to lash out at the same time. It just couldn't be real; it wasn't fair. However, he could not deny what his eyes saw.

He prayed constantly over Kurian, but he was losing hope. Even after learning about *thaumaturgy* and the miracles some monks used to perform, it was difficult to believe that God would do something incredible this time.

Louise kept encouraging him. She had hope, and she offered it to him in the form of the healers at their camp. He admired her for it, but he was tired of that, too. She had begun as their guide to an enemy camp. Somewhere between Smithfield and Dury, he had begun to think of her as a friend. But she was the one who told them to go to Ramah. It was her advice that might end in Kurian's death, and it was difficult not to blame her, despite trusting her intentions.

She had also saved him from the sirens. Which made her what?

He wanted to be angry with her, while at the same time, he saw something in her that he knew he should have. She was afraid and worried about Fallon and Evasius, however she did not despair the way Kurian did. She was concerned about Kurian's wounds, but she did not share Tobin's doubt that healing was possible. Her confidence in facing their troubles was somehow stronger than his own, or Noeman's. In some ways, she was braver than Rhys was. He couldn't figure out what it was, and her admission about Kurian that morning only complicated things. After weeks of suspicion and hiding, he was simply tired, and he wanted to be finished with all of it. In the end, his judgment told him Kurian's injuries were not her fault, and that she had proven trustworthy, and his judgment rarely failed him.

On their third day from the lake, he was also tired of the arguments between Noeman and the peculiar old man, Xander. Each day, he found creative ways to insult Noeman and his faith, but Noeman continued to pursue debates and conversation with him. Flustered, the dean would let his horse wander toward the back of the group, and then come back abreast with Xander a short time later with some new topic. Perhaps the dean missed the company of somebody his own age, or else he was intrigued by the intellectual challenge.

The only time that Xander really insulted him clearly was when he called him a viper the day before. That had left the dean in silence for hours. Tobin expected Kurian would like him.

To Tobin and Rhys, he spoke more kindly, telling them that there was still a chance for them to avoid the dean's folly. They only had to turn about, he said. The twirling motion he made with his finger made it look like he was telling them to spin in circles, which made less sense than much of what he said. Ultimately, he was still telling them that their order and their faith were flawed.

Something about the exchange got under his skin. Xander said it with the same calm confidence that drew him to Louise.

That observation made him doubt his own sanity. The man was wild.

Xander continued to lead them through the afternoon, hurrying only slightly when Kurian began moaning and flailing in his stupor, and would not be comforted. Tobin had no idea how he knew where he was going. Every turn in the canyon looked like any other.

Then Xander made a hairpin turn to the right and led them down a narrow ravine that closed in the further they went. Tobin and Louise had to drop back from either side of Kurian's litter and ride single file. As he looked forward, Tobin thought they were heading directly into a dead end, but suddenly, Xander made a sharp left turn. He followed, and then looked back. From this side, the passage looked like it dead-ended again, and the remaining riders seemed to materialize from the straight wall of rock.

Quickly, the crack spread out again into a natural amphitheater. On the far side, a broad stone arch spanned the only exit, and standing within the arch was a wooden gate studded with iron. It looked as sturdy as any he had seen in woodcuts of castles and forts. Tobin expected sentries were watching from the arrow slits on either side.

"Maran," a voice challenged from the gate.

"Atha," Xander replied, and the gates opened for them to pass.

They had found the King's Camp, and Tobin suddenly remembered all the dangers they had imagined when they sat back in Downriver Town.

The gates creaked open slowly, and standing in the center to greet them was Alden.

"By the King, you made it," he said, smiling broadly. Louise leapt from her horse and ran to embrace him. Soon, he was rushing them all inside the gate and directing them as if he knew exactly what had happened, and what Kurian's injuries were.

"I don't suspect you'll want to be separated from Kurian," he said as he led them through the camp, "so we have made space in the healing house for you."

After passing through the gate, they found themselves in a large, level area. Tobin looked to the right and left, seeing that the walls of the canyon spread out to a width of several hundred yards. They narrowed again about half a mile to the east. Unlike the rest of the canyons, a few clusters of trees grew near the steep walls. The camp itself seemed to be a semi-permanent settlement within the canyon. Houses stood at random intervals, with no apparent organization, but then, there were no streets. Interspersed between them were small shacks and lean-tos. Three larger buildings sat at the center, and he assumed that at least one of them was a meeting area; however, he could not determine the purpose of the other two. Beyond them, he saw pens with goats and sheep, as well as a small farm plot.

They had all been expecting a group of large, surly men who reeked of lawlessness. Instead, Tobin saw many elderly people, as in Aposford. Most of the inhabitants were closer to Alden or Noeman's age, and he was beginning to think that their silent protectors, Elwell and Briggs were the youngest men in the King's employ. Then he heard a sudden outburst of high, squealing laughter. Three children chased each other through the puddles between houses, weaving through the rain.

A lump caught in his throat. One of them had sounded like their youngest friend, Simon, who had turned eleven a week before the attack. When he looked more closely around the camp, he saw women and men of all ages. The place was nothing like they had feared; it wasn't a hideout, it was a burgeoning village.

Alden took them along the northern wall of the canyon toward a house that stood beside a pool of water. As they drew nearer, a small spring was visible, spouting from the cliff and filling a small, carved fountain that spilled over into the pool. A large cave gaped open like a mouth on the opposite side of the water from the house. It was identical to the dozens they had seen in the canyon, but he suspected this one was a storage place.

"I hope you are comfortable," said Alden. "I would have preferred meeting again under more pleasant circumstances. We will do everything we can to help Kurian. If you'd like, I can come this evening and play my flute for you."

"We would like that," Louise said.

Alden gave her a confused look. "I assumed you would take your normal room."

"Oh, yes." She paused and smiled awkwardly. "Of course, I will. It's only that it's been so long since I've heard you play...I just didn't think before speaking."

"Where's Gideon?" Rhys asked.

"He returned to Dury to reclaim his cottage."

Rhys grunted, and his shoulders drooped.

Tobin wanted to ask questions about the camp, but he felt safe with what he had seen, and he was exhausted. It could wait until they had slept. For now, he made sure that Kurian was in a bed, under the care of a healer, and then he stretched out in a chair at the foot of his bed and closed his eyes.

He had not meant to fall asleep in the chair, but when he opened his eyes, Tobin saw Xander speaking to a short woman in hushed tones. Lamps burned in the small room, and outside night had fallen.

"How is he?" he asked.

"Your friend is still asleep," said the woman, giving him a warm smile. She looked to be almost as old as Noeman, and deep lines spread across her plump face when she smiled. But her eyes were keen and alert. They shone in the lamplight.

"This is Charissa Fairchild, our chief healer," Xander said.

"Thank you for your help, Ma'am."

"I'll do what I can," she said, "but I'm not certain how much help I can be at the moment."

"Why?"

"Well, child, he was struck twice, which means twice the poison. My guess is that is why he's not woken. For now, I've given him my favorite poultice. It's a bit sticky, but it should chase that nasty venom right out—and it smells divine." She inhaled deeply and closed her eyes with a blissful grin.

Tobin noticed the pleasant aroma for the first time, sweet and floral with a tang of resin. It definitely emanated from Kurian, where a golden, syrupy smear stained the bandages on his arm and torso. Sweat also beaded on his brow, but he at least appeared to be resting quietly.

"So, will he recover?" he asked.

Charissa shook her head. "Can't say for sure. That stinger in his chest went in sideways. It's burrowed deep, between the ribs already, where we can't reach it."

"Straight for the heart, like I said," Xander interjected.

"Can't you get it out?" Tobin's worst fears were beginning to become real.

"If it hadn't broken off, we could cut it out, but it's too deep for my skill," said the healer. "He needs the King."

Now their mysterious leader was a healer? Tobin didn't know what to believe about him—or this place—anymore. But if they thought the King of the Caves could help Kurian, he wanted it to happen immediately. Neither of them moved to go get him.

"Well, isn't he here?" he asked.

"No," Xander said. "He often goes off alone for a time. Communing, as he says, searching things out."

"Then go get him. This is his camp, isn't it?"

"I said he goes alone. Nobody knows where he is unless he calls."

Tobin felt as ready to fight Xander as Noeman did, except he was ready to skip over arguing and go straight to fists. He took a deep breath to calm himself enough to try for a straight answer.

"How does he do that, if he's alone?"

"How can you tell if it's raining?" Xander said in his usual way, returning an obscure question for a question. "When he calls, you know."

"Can you call him, then?" Tobin raised his voice, and it also rose in pitch. "My friend is dying."

Maybe it was a myth, Tobin thought, *and there is no King of the Caves.* He couldn't rule it out if they had come all the way to his camp and he was absent.

Xander shrugged his shoulders, but looked on him with compassion. The weathered old man lifted the hood of his cloak and opened the door before saying softly, "Can you command the wind?"

When he had left, Charissa patted his arm and said, "Don't worry about Xander's drama, child, our King knows he's here."

CHAPTER TWENTY

The Calling

*K*urian.

His eyes opened to a dark room.

Had someone called him?

He was in a soft bed, but he didn't remember how he got there. The last thing he remembered was sailing, but the memory was confused. The boat was large and small at the same time, and the light was both full and dim. There was music and shouting, but also complete silence.

He yawned and a stab of pain in his chest put the memories in order. There had been two boats. Then he remembered the hideous fish and the sharp tines flying toward him. With his right hand, he touched the spot and felt a bandage. His fingers came away sticky and he wiped them on the bed sheets.

Nearby, he heard the rhythmic breath of someone sleeping. It sounded like Tobin, soft and quick, rather than the long, forceful breaths of Rhys. It definitely wasn't the dean's snore.

He felt his eyes drooping closed again, ready to fall back into, hopefully, a dreamless sleep.

Kurian.

He started awake again. The whisper was so soft, it seemed to come out of the air; it couldn't be a real voice. It had to be the remnant of a dream.

As he moved his head to look around the room, something was wrong with his vision. The bed and blankets, Tobin asleep in a chair, everything was outlined in a light that offered no illumination. The room was dark, but every corner and edge shimmered like fire glinting off metal, except white and blue instead of orange and red.

James said the fish were poisonous. This must be an effect of the poison, or else a dream caused by it.

The voice called him again, the slightest bit louder. *Kurian.*

"I'm here," he said.

He listened, but no further whispers came. *I'm going insane,* he thought, and almost laughed at himself.

Suddenly, he felt compelled to leave the bed, to dress and step outside. He was certain there was something vitally important for him out there.

Pain shot through his chest and left arm as he lifted himself out of the bed. It was dizzying, and he had to hold himself against the wall until the lights rocking at the edges of the room stilled. Then he pulled his clothes on with stiff muscles and quietly shuffled out of the door.

The cold night air shocked him out of his groggy haze. But the sight that met him froze him in place. Every drop of rain flashed with the same glittering light. Blue and silver droplets cascaded around him. They exploded into luminous fountains in the puddles at his feet. The drops shone like the star he had seen on the plain, and now he stood in a flood of stars, as if the heavens had descended to frolic on earth.

It was some seconds before he breathed again, and it came with a great sob. His heart yearned for this moment to continue. He wished he could stop time and live in it forever.

Through the falling, splashing stars, he could see the lighted outlines of buildings. This must be the King's Camp. With the realization, he knew why he needed to leave so urgently. He had to look for the King of the Caves. He had to retrieve the treasure, regardless of his injuries. It could not wait.

Still, he stared about in wonder at the twinkling rain.

After bringing himself to move, he found a fountain in the cliff wall, spilling down into a pool beside the house, and drank. The water was cold and refreshing.

As soon as he looked up, something shot skyward in the distance. Above the canyon wall, he saw an enormous column of fire that whipped around like a rope mooring the earth to heaven. It, too, glittered in his vision, as if lightning rode the flames. He knew it was a beacon meant for him.

Then he heard it again, this time so subtly he could barely distinguish it from his own thought.

Come.

Fallon knew his men were tired. He was tired. However, since he could not sleep, neither would they. He had roused them four hours before sunrise, even though they had searched well into the night. His plan was always to bear right, toward the cliffs. They marked every intersection, indicating the direction they had traveled from, and then took the other fork if they came back around. There had been no trail, but he was confident there would be a clue somewhere.

In a day and a half of steady riding, they had only found three branches to the right. Each had quickly dead-ended.

Now the canyon looked as if it would run straight for miles, with only small caves that they could search in a moment. If it weren't for the rain limiting their vision, he would gallop through the narrow valleys until his horse collapsed, or he found the monks.

Then, for a moment, the sky lit up like daylight ahead.

"There!" Fallon shouted.

He pointed to the hills in the east, where a tongue of fire climbed into the sky. It wasn't a clue; it was a signal fire unlike any he had ever seen, as if their prey wanted to be found. More likely, it was overconfidence, trusting that their false trail and the winding canyons would ward off any pursuit.

"What is it?" asked his lieutenant, stifling a yawn.

"An invitation," he said, smiling. Pressing on had paid off. If they had been sleeping with only a lookout awake, they might have missed the fire shooting up from the crags.

Then he turned to face the column of riders behind and shouted above the rain. "Our enemies have given away their position. We must reach them before that flame goes out."

"At every fork, I want two men to search the canyon that moves away from the fire. Continue to mark searched canyons with stones. If you find something, sound your horn, start a smoking fire—do anything to signal the rest of us. Then send one man to find the main force. We will mark our path with torches or spears planted in the ground."

"Sir, won't that also signal the bandits?" said the lieutenant.

"Let them know we're coming," he growled.

"But sir, might they not also escape?"

"Does it matter? That beacon is close. If one of our scouts finds them, the rest of us will be on them within minutes. If they panic and run, they will not be able to hide their trail." His horse snorted and spun nervously under his rage.

"We will follow them into any corner of these hills and destroy them," he yelled to his soldiers. "Ride hard. For Lord Evasius. For your fellows. For Pallingham!"

His horse reared with an ear-splitting scream and then leapt eastward. A moment later, forty horses thundered after him.

Kurian stumbled through the canyons for what felt like hours, following the fiery beacon. Sometimes he fell, and each time it was harder, more painful, to stand and continue. His tongue clove to the roof of his mouth and he began to feel hot, even though he walked without a cloak in the cold mountain rain. In his poison-tainted vision, he saw shadowy figures dashing along the ridges to either side. They increased the urgency he felt, as if they were racing to cheat him of his goal. But his strength faded quickly. Eventually, he had to crawl. Each movement shot through his chest like another quill from the hasslefish until he feared his heart would burst. Every breath was a cloud of thorns.

Then it was in front of him. The fire raged within its column, as if encased in glass. It rose directly from the ridge, roiling together with smoke and shot through with lightning. Beneath it yawned the black mouth of a cave, the only thing not lit at the edges. The dark opening seemed to swallow up all light, and it looked to him like the mouth of death. He knew this was his journey's end.

He knew the King was inside.

With his last strength, he stood and staggered into the darkness as the poison tried to reclaim him.

He collapsed, but did not hit the ground. He felt as though he floated into the cave on a bed of air until the dark walls engulfed him and all light failed.

CHAPTER TWENTY-ONE

Revelations

Tobin woke to Rhys shaking him. Light filtered in through the open shutters, telling him it was already past dawn. Rhys held his staff as if ready for danger.

"What is it?" he asked.

Rhys pointed to Kurian's empty bed. "He's gone, and everybody in the house is dead asleep."

Tobin jumped up from the chair, instantly alert. He touched the blankets on the bed for a moment. Cold. Then, he scanned the room for anything out of place. Kurian's clothes were missing, but nothing else. His staff was still propped in the corner with Tobin's own.

"Maybe he's feeling better?" Rhys asked hopefully.

Tobin frowned, shrugged his shoulders, and walked to the next room, where Rhys and Noeman had slept. The dean still sprawled on a bed, snoring heavily. Next, he moved across the hallway and opened the door of Charissa's room enough to peek inside. She, too, breathed steadily in her bed.

"They won't know what happened to him," he said, turning to Rhys. Then he hurried down the hallway and stepped out into the camp. He hoped deeply that he would see Kurian sitting with Louise next to a fire, but he didn't believe that would happen. Outside, the heavy rain had lifted, but a gentle mist continued to fall. Smoke from cooking fires immediately hit his nose, followed by the scent of breakfast. Xander was already walking toward the house, and called out a greeting.

Tobin knew already that he had nothing to do with Kurian's disappearance. There was no feigned innocence in the greeting. "Kurian's missing," he said. "All of us slept right through whatever happened to him."

Xander lifted the corners of his mouth as if he were speaking to rambunctious children. "The answer to his location is simple: he was summoned."

"How do you know that?" Rhys asked.

The Signpost, as he liked to call himself, merely pointed through camp to the eastern sky where a thick shaft of smoke rose straight up from the canyons. It appeared to have no interference from the wind, and simply disappeared into the blanket of clouds. Rhys immediately jogged a few steps in that direction before Xander called him back.

"I am going to see my brother," he said. "You can't stop me!"

Xander shook his head. "You have not yet been called," he said sternly.

Rhys whirled on Xander, pushing him in the chest with his staff.

"Brother Brock!" Noeman shouted, stepping from the house. As if it triggered a primal response, Rhys lowered the staff and turned to his teacher. The struggle for control rolled across his face like a tremor in the earth.

"I do not believe Kurian is in danger," Noeman said calmly, "and we gain nothing by fighting them, do we?"

His pupil violently shook his head while looking at the ground.

"I'm sorry," Rhys said to his feet. "We've just been through so much and I panicked."

"When can we see him?" Tobin asked.

"When you are called, or he returns," Xander said, as if it were obvious, and then breathed deeply. He smiled at Rhys—everything forgiven. "Now, I had intended to invite you for breakfast, but if you would prefer, I can have something sent to you in the healing house."

"Thank you," said Noeman, "I think we would prefer to be alone for the moment." The dean bowed deeply and shepherded the young monks back toward the house with a hand on each of their backs.

"Do you really think Kurian is safe?" said Tobin.

"I do," Noeman replied. "Didn't the healer say that only their leader could heal him?"

"She did. However, I assumed he would come to us."

"Nothing about our experience tells me that Xander or the other men bear us ill will. I trust Kurian is where he must be."

"But you fought with him the entire way here," Rhys said. His tone suggested he was complaining about being scolded.

"We had our…discussions. I may have been frustrated with him. However, he is an exceedingly wise man. More than that, he is a man of peace. Each of his antagonizations was ultimately for my good." The dean looked back over his shoulder at the retreating figure of Xander. "In other circumstances, he would have made a fine Sage for our order. We could have been great friends."

Tobin saw the grief on his face and knew the dean thought of Sage Marten, and the fight they had before his death.

The dean's words were shocking in the extreme. However, before he could ponder them, Louise trotted up from behind and entered the house with them.

She beamed.

"I heard Kurian went to the King," she said. "It's wonderful. I told you everything would be all right."

"You might have come a bit sooner," Rhys blurted, "before I almost took off Xander's head."

Tobin nearly laughed. He knew Rhys would be cross the rest of the morning, but would only mention all the wrong reasons. "Do you know when we can see him?" he asked her.

"You'll get your turn. Be patient."

Rhys and Louise sat on Kurian's bed, while Noeman sat in the only chair. Tobin couldn't help but notice the similarity to their placement on the day they first met her—except that Kurian was absent. And this time they were companions in hope instead of adversaries.

Charissa suddenly stepped into the room, bleary eyed and wobbly, as if she had just woken from a deep sleep. She let out a squeak and her ample arms flapped about as she stretched.

"Morning, darlings. What'd I miss?"

Kurian heard a man singing. He didn't know the language, but it was a strong, pleasant voice. The song tugged at his heart in a way he could not explain. It made him want to give himself over to a cathartic weeping that promised to soothe the pains of the past month, and those before.

Then he opened his eyes and again found himself in a small room. This one looked like a cave, but the light was so bright, he could barely tolerate looking around. He thought it might be the same effect from the hasslefish poison, so he rubbed his eyes.

When he opened them again, they were beginning to adjust to the light. He lay in a bed again. It was, indeed, a small cave. There was one exit that opened into a dark passage. Candles stood around the room in nooks and on natural rock shelves, and a good-sized fire burned in the middle of the floor, its smoke disappearing through a hole in the ceiling. Across the room, the singing man faced away from him, and stood over a small, high table like a reading stand. It held a candelabrum on either end. The peculiar thing was that the brightness in the room came not from the candles or the fire, but from the man.

It was pure white, and so dazzling that he wished he could gaze for hours at that light, but it was also painful and frightening. When he blinked, there were rays of other colors of light blazing from the source. He wondered how long he could live if the poison were so strong.

The man stopped singing and spoke, still facing the table. "You have woken early."

"How long have I been asleep?" Kurian asked, stifling a yawn from habit. His voice felt rough from disuse.

"Perhaps an hour," the man said. His voice still carried the hint of a song as he worked with unseen things at the table. "For many hours before, you were beyond sleep. However, I did not expect you to rise until late this evening, and it is still before the midday meal."

Kurian's head was foggy. He was not certain he understood everything the man said. He only knew he had the feeling of having taken a long journey, and finally arriving at his destination. Or did it feel like he had returned home? In either case, he felt like he could finally rest. Part of him wanted to fall back in the bed and sleep until the man expected him to wake. But suddenly, there was an urgency to complete his business here.

"How are you feeling?" the man asked, and then faced him. When he turned around, the light seemed magnified. It poured forth from his face like the heat from the fire, blinding and beautiful.

Kurian squinted, holding up a hand to shield his face from the glow. As he raised his arm, he noticed that the pain from his wounds was almost gone. "The poison has done something to my eyes."

"Was it the poison, or something else? Some get a glimpse behind the veil after an experience like yours." The man stepped around the fire and cupped a hand over Kurian's eyes. He muttered something under his breath, and when he pulled the hand away, the light returned to that of a normal fire-lit cave.

The glorious figure had disappeared. Standing before him was a man wearing simple clothing with no distinctive ornamentation. There were no weapons on display, and he looked the part of a farmer or tradesman, rather than a bandit lord. The hint of a smile played constantly on his lips, as if he might laugh at any moment. He wore a short, dark beard with neatly trimmed hair, more akin to Alden, the flute player than the wild man, Gideon—yet somehow both men followed him. When Kurian looked into his brown eyes, the piercing gaze stunned him, and there he saw the same intensity that Gideon had shown. He could keep no secrets from those eyes.

He stared in silence for a moment, recognition dawning on him, and then found the courage to speak.

"You're the man I met at our compound," he whispered, "the day Evasius first attacked. You asked me about our history."

"I'm glad you recognize me. It means I chose well." The King sat down on the floor next to the bed, his arm resting on one upright knee. His posture was one of complete confidence and relaxation. As in their first meeting, he exuded signs of both vivacious youth and the experience of many years. This time, Kurian got the impression that he was enjoying himself, even that he liked Kurian's company.

"What do you mean you chose well?"

"You may think you came here for the treasure of Capric, but you are here because I called you."

"You are the King of the Caves, then?"

He nodded. "I have many names. That one is common for the moment." He lifted his hands and glanced toward the ceiling. "The reason should be obvious."

"I came because you stole our treasure," Kurian said, "and because a prophet told our abbot we had to leave." He was beginning to feel bolder now that he met the man. The King seemed less like the terrifying raider of caravans the more that they spoke—more like the man Louise described. He almost added, "God sent us on this quest," but his recent doubts made him hold back.

"Yes," said the King, and the smile faded into an expression of grief, "it saddened me to see Sage Marten so fearful. It was too easy to convince him of the necessity. Still, we barely got you out in time."

Kurian's mouth opened, and his eyes bulged. "You're saying you were the prophet? You showed that terrible vision to the abbot?"

"What I showed your abbot was exactly what Lord Evasius did."

"And you've also healed my wounds. How did you do these things? If this is all magic, I've seen that evil from Evasius' witches." Kurian spoke with more bravado than he intended. Yet in the thousand times he had rehearsed this conversation, that had always been the attitude he imagined—show no fear, demand what was yours, fight if necessary. In the face of this quiet man with healing hands, it was an unnecessary facade.

He cleared his throat and asked less accusingly, "Are you some sort of wizard?"

"Nothing so simple," the King rose and stepped back to the table where Kurian now saw there was a large book.

It was bound in dark leather. Along the raised bands of the spine and on the corners, it had worn to a dusty tan. It was a book like any other that Kurian had studied at the monastery—except perhaps older. The King laid his fingers gently on the cover. The room felt suddenly charged, as if the lights from the night before were surging through Kurian's nerves.

"The prophecy which I gave to Sage Marten was part of something larger, something he should have known," said the King, then he lifted his head and spoke in such a way that his voice reverberated in the cave, like the sound of many voices speaking as one. It was terrible and glorious at once.

"Those walking in darkness will see a great light.
Release the Deer, the Brute, even the Princely Son.
On those living in the land of shadow, a light will dawn.
The moon will shine like the sun
And the light of the sun will be as seven days.
Rivers will open on the bare heights,
And the dry land will spout fountains of water.
Fragrant and fruited trees will spring from barren wilderness;
Wild beasts will no longer threaten the pastures;
The people will rejoice, and justice will reign
When the king returns to the shadowed lands
And the waters of Apos flow again."

Kurian was silent for a few moments. The words struck something in him. They felt like old words, like those from Fin, and they brought to mind his vows. They spoke of the desire every one of his brothers had shared: the return of the kings, the restoration of Fin, of knowledge and peace, and the blessings of God.

Again, he wanted to weep.

Except this time, he wanted to throw himself at the feet of this man whose voice threatened to unravel his soul. He wanted to beg him to illuminate these words, to explain all that had happened, and offer him some glimmer of hope. If this short lyric was from the treasure, he wanted more, and something told him the King of the Caves could give it to him.

He searched his mind for a wise question, something worthy of the answers he sought. But he could not break through the storm of thoughts that raged in his mind. "I thought that was only a joke with the townspeople," he said, "a saying about things that would never happen—when the Apos flowed, or when the king returned." He knew it was trivial and foolish before it left his lips, but it was the only thought clear enough to speak.

"It is a memory so old that they have forgotten what it meant," the King said solemnly, "and so it became a joke for fools. As do many mysteries."

The King picked up the book and turned to face Kurian.

"Is that it? Our treasure?" His voice shook, and he felt as if he was atop a great cliff, looking over the edge. The air felt thick, as if his past were in the room with them, his entire life whirling around this moment. There was the most intense sense of expectation he had ever felt, mixed with fear.

And then, surging to the forefront like a lion leaping from the shadows—*Reverence*.

The vertigo washed away, and all his focus bent sharply onto the book. Had they really come so far for something so plain? Was it possible that their order's primary mission was to protect this crumbling stack of parchment and leather?

The King gingerly stroked the book's cover and nodded. "It is."

"What is it—magic?" Kurian whispered.

"Again, you think too simply."

The King of the Caves kneeled before him and looked up from the book. "You regaled me with your order's history when first we met," he said, "but do you remember anything older?"

Kurian shrugged. "Legends, myths. Stories that have no time...if they happened at all."

"Then I will let you discover for yourself what it is," said the King. He placed the book in Kurian's lap and walked silently to the darkened passage. "I will return when you have decided. But do not tarry, for time is short." Then he turned and faded into the shadows of the tunnel.

Louise harangued them through breakfast to leave the house of healing and see the camp. Noeman acquiesced first, seeming almost as eager to go as she was, once he had made up his mind. He even tried to convince Tobin it might be like the mercy visits to Aposford, although from what he had observed so far, these people needed no help from a few orphaned monks.

They stepped out into a cool October day with the fresh smell of rain on the ground. Unlike the plains, the water had quickly sluiced to the lowest point of the canyon and disappeared, leaving the paths muddy, but free of large puddles.

At this elevation, Tobin thought the dark clouds still hanging overhead looked almost close enough to touch. If it were possible to reach them, would his fingertip loose a deluge?

In this place, anything might be possible. He had already seen an impossible column of smoke that morning, except that had now disappeared as cleanly as Kurian.

As they walked around, his previous day's observations about the camp proved true. It was almost a small village, a permanent settlement. It contained its share of young and old, although every person seemed to have a certain vitality that was missing in Pallingham.

A group of children followed them with curiosity, darting between tents and houses to snatch glimpses of the strange monks. The elderly left their chores to greet them warmly, and the younger workers, busy with more strenuous tasks, offered words of welcome as they passed. Tobin noticed that most of them still wore swords at their sides, and that a handful of men were always within a few quick strides of the monks. There was trust, but also caution here.

They could have walked through the site's entirety in a quarter hour, except that the inhabitants—especially the older ones—kept stopping them. They wanted to know about the monks, and to tell their own stories about the King and his camp. Every one of them offered a morsel of food or a cup of tea while they spoke. By the end of the afternoon, Tobin began to wonder if the camp and their order shared similar rules about hospitality. He had never learned how to refuse such sincere offers with grace and dignity, so he accepted each time, until his stomach was overfull, and he walked uncomfortably.

Despite their graciousness, it was obvious they had very little. This, more than anything, convinced him that these people were not the vicious criminals that Lord Evasius had described. They were castoffs from all over Pallingham and the Northland Kingdoms, trying to scratch out a living in hidden exile.

That did not mean there wasn't more going on. For some reason, Evasius felt threatened by them—perhaps only because he thought they had the treasure. He expected they would find out in time. But for now, he knew the people were good and honest.

"I know nothing about their king," Noeman said as they approached the large buildings at the center of camp, "but I could live with these people, and serve them."

"And give up the order?" Tobin and Rhys asked at the same time.

"If the treasure is here, and there is opportunity to serve God by ministering to a community, why could the order not be here?" The dean shrugged his shoulders with unusual levity. "Or anywhere?"

Rhys leaned close to Tobin and whispered, "If we get to vote for abbot, the dean's prospects are getting shaky." Tobin jabbed him in the ribs.

"Then you see it?" Louise asked with hope in her eyes.

The dean looked around him, smiling, nodding almost unconsciously.

"If only Dean Goodman understood the full weight of his words," said Xander as he stepped out of the large building that looked like a meeting hall. "I am happy you have concluded that we are not kidnappers and thieves."

They looked at each other, not knowing how to respond.

"I'm uncertain whether I can tell all that you are in a day," Tobin said, trying to give Xander a taste of his own mystification.

"Another understatement," Xander said in his enigmatic way. An implied question—*Was it part of your studies? —*seemed to hang behind his words.

He bowed toward Tobin and Rhys. "My friends, if you would permit me, I would speak with your dean alone. I believe there are some things he is ready to hear that are for him alone." He stretched out an arm to invite the dean into the building.

"It would be my pleasure," Noeman said, stepping inside. Rhys was clearly uncomfortable, and Tobin was about to object, but the dean agreed too quickly, and was gone.

Xander asked Louise to take the boys back to the house of healing to wait for dinner, and then entered the large empty hall and shut the vast double doors. Tobin stared at them for several moments, focusing on a large relief carved into the wood. It was a symbol he had seen once before, a symbol that he was told stood for crime and horror, standing against their order, against the Rule. Seeing it now in such contrast brought a riot of emotions to his heart. The mouth of a cave was on the door, topped with a crown——the signature of the King of the Caves.

CHAPTER TWENTY-TWO

The Treasure

Kurian read with ravenous speed. He read without regard for the Capric Order's restrictions—there was no longer an abbot to look upon this treasure, and besides, he had rejected that life. He was now as much in violation of the Rule as the man who had taken the book, and it didn't matter. The hunger to read, to know and be enlightened about the object of his oath drove him on. Each pause forced by the turning of an ancient page only prodded that desire to greater urgency.

In the back of his mind, a thought tried to push its way forward. *Take the book and run. Now, before the thief returns.* But there were no weapons available, and he had no idea how many guards waited within the cave. He did not know whether the way out would be obvious, or if he would become lost in a subterranean maze. More importantly, he did not want to run, and he did not believe the King was a simple thief. So, he continued to read, slowed only by the archaic language and the ancient vellum. The treasure drew him deeper into its pages with stories amazing and incredible, joyful and tragic. Some of them felt familiar, as if he had heard them before with the details changed. Most of them included enough of what Noeman had called *thaumaturgy* that they would probably make the dean's head spin.

But while the stories summoned an almost magical attraction within him, he was confused. They were just stories. There were no instructions on how to perform similar signs and wonders. There were no spells or incantations. Only stories. And the more he read, the more it impressed in his heart that they were the stories of real people, often confused and frightened, as he had been that month. Many made worse mistakes than he ever had. But in each case, there were opportunities for redemption, for honor, courage, and hope to redeem those mistakes. And when a hero rose up in the stories, each one reminded him of the heroes of the Caprics, who never did their miraculous feats under their own strength, but always with God. With each story about imperfect people doing extraordinary things through faith, he began to wonder if he did not have something in common with them—if God's assistance might be the only reason he had reached his destination.

"Had your fill?" The King's voice coming from the passage surprised him.

"Not by far," he said, and then blushed at his own honesty. He had read less than a quarter of the book's thickness and he wished for more time.

"Three hours is all we can spare." The King laughed quietly. "But before we can come to our purpose, I see you have questions."

"I don't understand," he said, "why was this so valuable to Frederick that he created our order to protect it? So far, it's just old stories. Incredible, yes, but I don't see why Evasius desires it so greatly. What could he possibly gain from it?"

The King stepped into the room and stirred the fire before stretching out beside it. "Lord Evasius' motives depend on how much he knows. If he believes it is an ancient book of magic, then it offers him more power to conquer and subdue. It promises him the ability to rule without contest. Whoever possesses it is a threat to his ambition.

"If he knows what it truly is, as King Frederick did, then the book has its own perils. The Evasius family has been cunning and ruthless for generations, and they have always understood the power of story and memory in guiding the nation. For many years, their goal has been to wipe history from the minds of the people, to imprison them in a story that begins and ends with the name Evasius. It's why your order, and the other monasteries, have always been dangerous to them. Your histories and your acts of compassion kept Fin in the people's memory, even as the older things faded or turned into myths."

"Then what is it truly?" he asked, holding the book close. "What did King Frederick believe it was?"

"It is the history of your land before it became the land of the pall, the land cursed to be always in shadow. It tells of the time when the skies were as blue as the mountain iris, as you once said, but also it tells of greater days. It is Pallingham's history, and its destiny. That is what Frederick believed, and it inspired everything he did."

The King pointed to the book in Kurian's arms and gazed fiercely into his eyes. "That is the story that made Fin possible."

Kurian looked at the treasure with a new sense of awe. What he read amazed him, even though he did not understand all of it. His mind was a tangled mass, but only one certainty was in his heart: he would redouble his commitment to protecting this book.

As the afternoon wore on, Louise began to form her own concerns for Kurian. When she had first lived in the camp, the magnificent call would come down in the same way, but the person would return shortly after it had receded. The fire or smoke remained visible only while the King held conference with them. It had disappeared this morning, but Kurian had not returned for many hours. Part of her worried that he might not have made it to the King. His condition had been dire. Still, she believed the King would not have let the Caprics come so far only to fall short. She trusted that, if he had to, the King would find Kurian to complete his purpose. But Tobin's anxiety, and his pacing, prodded deeper in her heart with every minute.

She decided not to tell the monks about her concerns. Doing so would only worry them further.

That left little for them to discuss. They waited in silence for an hour before she heard the lilting song of Alden's flute floating through the camp outside. It was the sign that dinner would begin shortly.

She fetched a washing basin and water from Charissa and laid them down in front of the two young men. Then Alden entered, playing his flute and dancing around the front room. He only stopped when he came between them.

"Good evening, friends," he said in his most poetic tone, "Xander has requested your attendance at a special feast as honored guests." He bowed deeply, then took the washing basin and kneeled at their feet. Tobin and Rhys gave each other uncomfortable glances as he removed their boots and rinsed their feet in the water. After that, he poured water from the pitcher for them to wash their hands.

"Indulge me, please," he said when they had finished. "I think that whenever possible, a feast deserves new clothes, and currently it is possible." A young man entered carrying two sets of clothes. They were as fine in quality as Alden's own dress—Louise suspected they came from his collection—and they appeared as if they were tailored specifically to the monk's sizes. Each consisted of a white silk tunic and an embroidered coat over strong, but soft leather pants that matched their boots.

"Are we allowed to accept gifts?" Rhys asked.

"It's unusual for us," Tobin answered. "But we are taught to accept whatever hospitality is offered." He shrugged his shoulders as if he had no better answer, and then the two monks went into a room to change.

When they emerged, Louise thought they looked like fine young men of good breeding and status, and said so.

Tobin cleared his throat, and thanked Alden, and then Alden led them all out toward the meeting hall where light and song already poured from the open door, prepared against the coming dark of night.

The smoke was only a half-mile distant when it disappeared. It behaved like no smoke Captain Fallon had ever seen. Rather than dispersing in the wind, it appeared as if the source suddenly ceased, and the tail end of the column rose quickly to meet the clouds like a rope drawn through a trap door in the sky.

He stopped his tired men and had them mark the direction in which they had last seen their only clue. They had ridden since well before dawn, and the signal had been deceptively close in the twisting canyons. What may have been a few miles for the crow was close to twenty confusing miles on the ground. Pairs of riders had split off as they encountered new paths, leaving him with only ten men by late morning. The larger canyon that he had followed had narrowed and held several surprise switchbacks that drew it gradually toward the north, away from the beacon they had originally seen in the east. By the time it disappeared, he had ridden beyond it, and it stood slightly south and west from his position. The canyon, however, continued away from the beacon, further east until the next northward bend.

He swore. In his haste, he had considered only the plan to mark the trail of his main force, but had neglected to tell his men when to return if they had not found anything. Now, his men were spread out over a score of miles, and were likely to wander further apart—easy targets for the criminals they hunted, who knew the territory.

After a few moments of thought, he ordered the column of riders back to the last intersection. There was room there for a camp that the returning riders could not miss.

They pitched camp in time to eat lunch.

The soldiers performed their tasks with few words. Fallon saw their exhaustion, knew the silence was a warning sign. If he continued to push them, there would be trouble.

To relieve some of the strain, he broke the watch into shorter segments. With men stationed along each path, he made sure the rest of his men had settled in before finding his own place to nap. *Hopefully, the others will return before morning*, he thought as he lay down—though he hated to waste so much time.

It felt like his eyes had just closed when they snapped open again.

It was dusk. He had slept for almost five hours, and he had been dreaming. The witch was watching him again, not engaging him in his dreams yet, but watching. Even in his sleep, he felt her cyclopean gaze dragging across his body, felt her horrific presence as if she rode just behind him in the endless, indistinguishable canyons of his nightmare. He could not bring himself to turn and look at her, and she did not speak, but the threat of pain lingered always in his mind. Something else had broken in on the dream enough to wake him, and in the moment of waking, he had felt the connection between them shudder like a plucked bowstring.

He brought himself up to a crouch and looked around cautiously. The watch was on alert as well, heads raised to the west while the rest of the men remained in deep sleep. Then he heard it again, the faint cry of a horn in the distance.

His men had found it, and the witch would know. That meant Evasius would know.

Fallon stood and roused his men, knowing that the chance to recover his honor and his freedom would come by dawn.

Lord Evasius yawned deeply. He was bored after an hour of listening to the complaints of the Duke of Adaminster. As the nearest of Evasius' nobles, Adaminster was also his most persistent nuisance, so he was indifferent to any offense the duke might take at the breach of etiquette. At the least, it relieved some of his boredom to watch the flush of indignation climb the duke's neck and blossom on his cheeks.

"I simply do not grasp how you expect me to build you a respectable capital when all of the funds I create go toward armies without a war to fight," Adaminster whined.

Adaminster showed a proficiency in creating prosperity—even a hint of luxury—as governor of the lands just north of Pallingham Castle, and that meant desperately needed revenue for Evasius. But as a man, the duke was too self-absorbed to present either a useful ally or a competent enemy. He had no true ambition. The luxuries afforded with wealth and titles were his only cravings, making him as soft and demanding as an infant.

His skill was useful. The man was not.

"My dear Duke," Evasius said, the title slick with condescension. "Do you not think that, as Lord of Pallingham, I am not privy to greater information about threats to our land than you would be? Trust me when I say that the army will be necessary. Soon."

"And this springtime muster," Adaminster began. He had come immediately upon receiving Evasius' letter.

Evasius held up a hand. "Your last report pleased me. Four thousand in the barracks there is an excellent start."

"However, training two thousand more in five months...and during the rainy season." The duke sputtered to show his outrage, as if the topic were too ridiculous for him to make the effort at words or argument.

Evasius was about to make the same offer that his ancestors had often made to the nobles: do as I ask, or I will find one who will. The existing nobles understood the implications. First, he let the silence between them ripen. He took a sip from his cup and pulled back his lips to reveal teeth stained crimson with wine. But before he could speak, there was an urgent knocking at the door.

"Enter," he boomed, not taking his eyes off the duke until a flustered and winded guard stepped through the door. "Speak."

"My Lord, one of the prisoners—one that Mouna was working with—he's gone mad. Claims he *is* Mouna, and has a message for you." The guard stood at attention, except for the thumb burnishing the seam of his coat.

"The message?"

"He says Nicholas...apologies, his words; Captain Fallon has found the camp, and that he...I mean, she, will report to you in person by morning."

"Dismissed." It was curious news. Good that Fallon had found the camp, but troubling that Mouna was not still with him. She was supposed to ensure his success. Another runner came before the door closed. This one carried a letter. He recognized the seal immediately as that of the garrison commander at Dury. He dismissed the runner and read the letter. It sealed Captain Fallon's fate—assuming he were foolish enough to return.

The monks were not at the bandit camp. They had left a challenge on the garrison door in Dury, demanding Evasius answer for the slaughter of their order, taunting him into open battle at the site of his treachery—Capric Hill.

It was arrogant posturing—or foolish miscalculation of his strength. Even if they had joined forces with the bandits, they might be able to gather a few hundred ragged fighters. They stood no chance against him. He relished the opportunity to answer the challenge, to see the terror on their faces as thousands of his soldiers surrounded them. Or, perhaps he would finally reveal the greater power he wielded and let Mouna destroy them by herself. Either prospect would please him.

According to the commander's note, they were seen leaving Dury a week before, traveling through the plains toward Aposford.

There was little time—perhaps a day—to get ahead of them.

"Damn the spring," he said to the duke, who blanched. "How many men did you bring with you?

"Only fifty."

"I'm engaging them now," said Evasius. "Take ten back to Adaminster, and ride like the devil is upon you."

"My Lord?"

"I want three thousand of your men in Aposford by evening tomorrow. Supplies can follow, but those men must be there, ready for battle." Evasius rose and Adaminster fumbled to get out of his chair. "I will meet you there with another three thousand from my garrison here."

"My Lord, why?"

"A rebellion is upon us, Adaminster," Evasius said quietly. "I tried to remove its head at Capric, but it appears to have grown another. Now, I intend to crush it." He strode from the room before the confused nobleman could reply, the rapid click of his boot heels demanding that the duke follow.

CHAPTER TWENTY-THREE

Interview with the King

"If all you've said is true," Kurian said, still holding the precious book, "that doesn't explain why you took the treasure."

The King of the Caves nodded and tossed a stick into the fire, mumbling something Kurian couldn't hear. It sounded like, "Now to the point of decision."

"What does any of this have to do with you?" Kurian asked.

The King said, "This time, I will tell *you* a story." He paused and cleared his throat. "There was another man called the King of the Caves, many centuries ago. For years, he, too, hid among the Crags of the Wild Goats and was declared an outlaw by the sitting king."

"I was just beginning to read about him," Kurian interrupted.

"Then you know that he was promised the throne, and that he was a great warrior and musician," said the King, and Kurian nodded. "What you have not yet read is that the prophets declared that his line would always be on the throne, that someday one of his sons would rule forever."

"Then the prophets must have been wrong, because the Evasius family has ruled Pallingham for generations."

"You have not heard the full story," the King said. He glared at Kurian and the way the fire reflected in his eyes made Kurian fall silent and regret interrupting. "There were many prophecies about this greatest of sons, and for long years the people of the plain yearned for his coming. But in their waiting, they were not vigilant, and when the time came for the fulfillment of many of the prophecies, they did not take heed. Many had turned away from the promises and could not see what was happening before them. For others, a train of corrupt rulers and painful losses made them forget. The rulers themselves became infatuated with their own power and wealth, much like Evasius.

"Long before King Frederick built the Kingdom of Fin—long enough that your treasure was the only remaining memory of that time—the child was born into a hostile nation that had forgotten the previous times of honor and glory that the first King of the Caves built, a nation that ignored the prophecies of his coming and the new kingdom that he would bring." He paused and turned away, closing his eyes as if recounting a painful memory. "They were further lost than the people of Pallingham are now. No fulfillment of prophecy, and no miraculous signs—what you call *thaumaturgy*—could change their minds.

"When the son became a man, and the time came for him to claim his throne...they killed him."

Kurian realized that he was sitting fully upright for the first time since he had woken. He leaned back while the ageless man paused. Something about the story had caught his attention, something he was sure the King was trying to imply, but he could not separate it in his thoughts. It slid from his mind like a shard of eggshell stuck in the whites.

"You are of the same line; the first King of the Caves was your ancestor," Kurian said. It was the closest he could bring the slippery thought to words.

"More than that," said the King. "I am that same son." His gaze was steady; there was no lie in his face.

Kurian knew the man believed every word. *Am I dealing with a madman?* he wondered.

Inside the meeting hall, Tobin was sweating. When they were led through the carved doors, he realized that it was barely larger than the dining area back at the monastery; but where the dining hall had been at least half-empty while he resided there, this place was filled with bodies. Their speech was a roar, combining with the steady drumbeats and instruments from the far corner to make a constant, chaotic din that pierced his ears. Down the center of the room, three large fires filled the place with light and flickering shadows. Many danced around the fires, but even the shadows of those who stood still celebrated on the walls behind them. The riot of movement joined the storm front of sound to overwhelm him. Soon, the fires and the crowd made the air thick and hot, and his intense sweating darkened the clean, light clothes that Alden had given them to wear.

It was the first civilian celebration Tobin remembered witnessing, although it stirred something deep in his memory, from the vague time before the order. His training told him that this might be the carousing that the righteous were supposed to avoid, but then, he had never seen so many people look so overjoyed. Could wickedness truly make people think they were this happy? Before the noise and jostling engulfed his senses, he considered a new theory: this might be only the early stages of the sin, and the street drunks he had seen in Pallingham Castle were the latter. It still didn't align with the goodness he had seen in these people that day.

The crowd had parted as Alden walked them toward a long table on a dais. He saw Xander and Noeman standing at the center of the table, and Noeman stepped down to meet them. Xander raised his hands high and the drums sounded twice more, then stopped. All eyes turned toward him.

"Quite a reception," Rhys whispered as the dean stepped between them.

"Friends," Xander said to the crowd, "our honored guests have all arrived." He lowered his arms and held them out toward the three monks while the entire camp cheered and bellowed.

"We have awaited this day for many years," he continued. "It is a sign for the beginning of a new age. A sign that God will keep His promises. That we were right to trust the King." Another roar from the crowd filled the room, blasting all thoughts from Tobin's mind.

"Soon, all your sacrifices will be rewarded. You will see the beginning for yourselves, and soon after, our neighbors on the plain—those we had to leave behind. All will see the fullest measure of life, but we will *know* it. That is cause for celebration!" Another roar, accompanied by the musicians, filled the room. Xander had to work to quiet the crowd again. Finally, when all was silent but the crackling fires, he lifted his cup from the table. "A toast," he said, but he could not finish the speech.

Outside came the call of a horn, loud enough for all to hear.

Every head turned to the door and the sound of a gate watchman shouting as he ran toward the hall.

"We are discovered!"

Captain Fallon pushed his horse through the canyons at breakneck speed. The tight hairpin turns nearly threw him from the saddle, but he continued as quickly as the horse and the terrain would allow.

The horn sounded twice more in the hour it took him to find the source.

Thirteen of his soldiers had already arrived, and the ones he had briefly camped with came up behind at sporadic intervals. Seventeen others would be coming soon.

He was winded from the ride, but the thrill of impending battle was upon him, and he felt no fatigue. "Show me," he gasped at the soldier as soon as he had stopped.

"Sir, we almost missed the turn, it was so sharp," he pointed to a narrow crack that doubled back from the main path. "It looks like a dead-end, until you walk right up to the next bend."

The two soldiers who had sounded the alarm had already set up a small fire and prepared torches for the larger force. Fallon leaped from his mount and grabbed one. He waved for his lieutenant to follow and trotted down the dark crag until it appeared to end in solid rock. When he saw the corner of the turn on his left, he stopped and peered around it. Across a wide space, he saw a gate built into a natural stone archway. Large fires from behind offered enough light to show its size. The camp was better fortified than he expected, which meant his prey were less likely to flee into the maze of the Crags. They would trust in the gate and the high canyon walls. But he had ways to break through their defenses.

"How shall we prepare, Captain?" asked his second.

"We'll burn them out like rodents," Fallon said. "With any luck, this will be their only exit."

In a brief time, the gate would be a charred heap, and he would charge through leading his men. Then he could repay the monks for all the trouble they had caused, and this King of the Caves, as well. He imagined what their faces would look like as he took their treasure and opened their bellies. It made the corner of his mouth twitch.

Neither of them moved or spoke. Kurian studied the King's face while the smoke from the fire continued its flight toward the hole in the ceiling. Time seemed to slow and draw out until he was not sure how long they sat in silence. Seconds felt like minutes, and then hours, as his mind tried to make sense of what he had heard. The logical reaction was to dismiss it as pure fantasy. However, the King's firm resolution was something he could not ignore. It stopped him from simply objecting. The ethereal vision he had seen upon waking might have made him think the King was a ghost, but he had touched him, watched him eat. There was a possibility that the whole experience was a vision or a dream, but so much of it was physical that he could not deny they were both sitting in this cave together. Kurian's mind knew it was not possible for the King to be alive after so long, but after all he had seen, he knew remarkable things could happen.

"How could that be possible?" was all he could ask.

"It was God's will," the King answered.

"You just told me they killed that man."

"Yet here I am."

The King folded his hands and gazed gently upon Kurian like a patient teacher waiting for his student to discover the lesson.

"If your story is true," Kurian said slowly, "then you cheated death somehow. I guess you're also the rightful King of Pallingham."

The King only nodded.

Kurian realized the implications almost immediately; this man's quarrel was with Evasius, and he could have made his claim at any time over several centuries without bothering the Order. The biting lump of anger that had cooled in his stomach while he slept heated to molten fury again. "If God wanted you to rule so badly that he brought you back to life, then why couldn't you just challenge Evasius yourself? Why did you have to bring our order into it?"

"Your order was not created to be left out of it, and you know it!" the King bellowed with unexpected strength. He did not move, but with the greater volume came an imposing appearance of physical power and dignity that belied his reputation as a brigand. His was not the presence of a criminal; it was the terrifying demeanor of a sovereign conqueror. "You pledged an oath to God to protect the truth you now hold in your hands, and to defend the people from evil. Even if the oath were something only constructed by men, as you have come to believe, in your heart you pledged to God. You should not have been surprised that a man like Evasius would oppose that. If you wanted to be spared, you should have abandoned the order before taking the oath and wandered into obscurity instead of recanting under the apple trees. But you know this would not have saved you from Evasius in the end, for you have seen how the people suffer."

Kurian cowered against the rough wall in his bed, wondering how this man knew his private thoughts and his actions in the apple grove. The book lay at his feet. His anger poured out in hot streaks down his face.

"They were good men," he said.

The light in the room seemed to diminish as the King stood and sloughed off the commanding presence. Then he kneeled beside the bed and wiped a thumb across Kurian's cheeks. Instantly, he felt relief of the pain in his heart.

"Many were," the King said. "However, being good has never been sufficient armor against evil men. The Caprics did much good in their time, and for long years they pushed back the spread of evil, but you knew even before we met that they were diminished and failing their purpose in this time."

Kurian laughed humorlessly. "So God let them be slaughtered?"

"You may not understand all in the moment because of your grief," the King said, "though I will still tell you: He sometimes allows good things to be removed so that greater things may be built."

The King rose and stretched out a hand to him. "May I show you what I mean?"

Kurian took his hand and stood on unsteady legs. He followed because the King held a surety of conviction that swayed him, and because he had opened the secrets of the treasure to him. Even the most studied of monks could not speak with such convincing belief. What would have come across as arrogance from the dean—claims to know God's will——this man spoke with simple but powerful authority.

Once Kurian was certain of his footing, the King picked up the book from the bed and led him by the hand toward the passage. As the King deftly guided him through the uneven tunnel, Kurian realized that he wanted to believe it all. He wanted to believe that the kings would return and restore the glory of Fin. It had always been one of the most thrilling tenets of the Order's teachings. Now he thought he was looking at the type of man who could do it, if only he could overcome Evasius.

What spilled from his heart next shocked him. *It was the singing,* he thought. *He held my heart the moment I heard him singing.*

Greater Things

The King led Kurian into a larger cave that was dark, except for a single lamp burning in a wall nook. He released Kurian's hand and lit two torches from the lamp, placing them in nearby sconces that flanked a rough wooden door. In the light, Kurian saw that this cave was large indeed, larger than the Order's outdoor training circle, though almost bare. It was round, with a domed ceiling that climbed higher than the torchlight. A large stack of firewood sat in the center, ready to be lit. The only furniture was an altar against one section of wall that had been carved flat and smooth. Above it, a large circular window was cut into the rock, and the dim light coming through told him that it reached to the outside, and that it was almost night. Within the cutout was a stained-glass window that presented the King's symbol—the cave a dark indigo, and the crown above only a dull orange with a ray pattern spreading from it.

"This is our *hagiary*," said the King, "where we celebrate and welcome those who would join us. It is a place of choosing and oath making, much like the canopy of your Treasured Oak." The King took on some of his formal bearing before adding, "I promised to show you something, and I have more to tell you. If you are willing to see and hear, you need only open the door."

After coming so far and listening to so much of this mysterious story, this was not the time to turn away. Kurian took a few slow steps toward the door between the torches and reached out with a shaking hand. He slid back the bolt and pulled on the handle.

Bright light poured through the doorway, causing him to shield his eyes and step backward. Slowly, his sight adjusted and he looked through the door upon a grassy plain bathed in the brilliant light. It was purer than any natural light he had ever seen—though not so white as his previous vision—and so intense that even the grass before him reflected an emerald gloss. Scattered over the plain were patches of intense, colored foliage that he believed were flowers. In the distance, he saw an enormous orchard that stretched beyond the edge of the door's frame. Close by was a town bustling with life and activity. It appeared newly built, but in a moment, he realized why it felt familiar. It was Aposford, restored with fresh mortar, paint, and thatch. The whitewash gleamed brighter than fresh snow. Like the buildings, the people also looked restored. He did not recognize anybody from this distance, but he was certain the crowd was larger, with a greater population of the young and healthy. None of them sat in the filth of the gutters, begging for scraps from those who had nothing to give. They moved about happy and unafraid.

Somehow, he knew—as he would have known if the sight were a dream—that Evasius did not rule over this prosperous and growing town. He knew that the people were free and good, as they had been at the height of Fin's influence. Then he looked up and saw for the first time where the great light was coming from. The sky was blue, and shining in it, just before the top of the door, was a round, blazing circle: the sun.

Another glint of light caught his eye, and between the town and the orchard, he saw a band of blue bending behind the buildings like a road. Again, with the prescient knowledge of a dream, he knew this was the river glittering in the sun, and he stood breathless.

"What is this?" he asked after a few moments.

"You know the place."

"It looks like Aposford, but not now."

"I told you I would show you greater things," the King said. He stood by the altar with folded arms, smiling at Kurian's wonder.

Kurian stared until time again lost meaning. As he gazed through the doorway, Kurian wished to lie in the grass and bask in the light, to stare into that beautiful blue sky for weeks, to swim in the water and live in peace with those people. Almost on their own, his feet stepped forward, and then he craned his head around the wooden frame to get a better look. Finally, he could hold back no longer, and he stepped through the door completely. At once, the vision disappeared, and he stood inside the entrance to another tunnel. Subterranean blackness yawned without end before him.

He backed out of the tunnel, into the torchlight. "What happened?"

"I chose you, in part, because you trusted your heart when it said the Caprics were failing," the King said. "Now you have proven your willingness to join in Pallingham's destiny."

"What do you mean?" Kurian asked.

"Many have seen visions here. Always, I am the one who brings them to the door. Some wish to linger, enjoying the vision for its goodness, and they are disappointed when the door must be shut. Only those willing to step through ever see the vision fulfilled. Because of your boldness, I am pleased to call you my friend and fellow traveler."

Kurian watched him shut the door, feeling as if he had passed a test, much like the first time he met the King. It pleased him, and he knew that he desired this man's approval. In that moment, he suspected his heart had made an oath that his mouth simply waited to voice.

"Do not be deceived," the King continued. "Passing through the door is only the first step in a long and difficult journey."

Kurian heard a loud roaring sound through the stained-glass window and looked up to see it flickering with strong firelight. The crown in the stained glass now glowed like living gold. The beacon that had called him here was shining again.

"As usual," said the King, "you have made your decision just in time. Your friends will arrive soon, and we have more to discuss."

Four hours passed after the horn first sounded outside the gates. The horn had blown three more times, and with each blast, Tobin expected to see Captain Fallon come out with a long string of soldiers, emerging like a serpent from its lair. Still, the watchers at the gate had not seen any sign of Fallon or the horn blower. He glanced once more over the archway of rock that stood above the gate, where he perched on a carved ledge. From there, he looked over the wide natural courtyard he had passed through the evening before.

Nothing.

Dark had fallen shortly after the first horn, and the bonfires now behind him made it impossible to see in the blackness outside. He stepped back and shook his arms, looking at the basket of heavy stones that he was supposed to rain down on enemies approaching the gate. This was a job for Rhys' strength, not his small limbs.

Helping to determine strategy would have been a better task for him, but as soon as the threat was present, Noeman had volunteered them for any hole in the defenses.

No, he was letting his nerves cloud his judgment. They had all volunteered, and he most eagerly. In a strange moment of decisiveness, he felt brave enough to step forward for these people because he had seen their gentle kindness, and he hoped for a peaceful future in such a place. Fallon and Evasius threatened that. If nothing else, he wanted to fight to protect the innocent children who lived and played in the camp. Right now, they were going with the oldest and weakest to safety in a remote cavern. Louise had left camp with them without saying goodbye.

If he thought clearly and ignored the jitters, he was right where he ought to be. Dropping heavy stones was something he could keep up for hours with his strength. Rhys' greater bulk, bravery, and skill at fighting helped more on the ground to brace the gate or repel soldiers who broke through. Tobin could continue dropping stones on the backs of those who breached the gate. And Noeman was the one who should counsel Xander and the other leaders.

Still, he wished the terrible waiting would end.

It was worse than the ambush at the apple grove because he saw no possibility of talking their way out of armed conflict.

Hiding along the ledge with him were a half-dozen archers—all that the camp could arm—and one other man with a basket of stones. Between him and the other man were three boys younger than he was, between twelve and thirteen. Armed with buckets and barrels, their job was to pour water through sluices cut into the stone arch that would help douse any flames that caught on the wooden gate. Tobin didn't want to think of how uncomfortable it would become on the archway if the gate caught fire.

The boy next to him chewed on his lip, and gave an overconfident smile when Tobin caught his eye. "Don't be too afraid," the boy whispered. "The King will save us before it gets too bad. None of Evasius' soldiers has ever stood up to him."

"And I was trying to think of a way to reassure you," Tobin said. Again, he was surprised at the depth of trust these people had in their leader, and he admired the kid's bravery.

Silently, he prayed that bravery and trust would be enough.

"Any sign?" Xander called up from below.

"It's too dark to see anything," the lead archer replied.

Xander gave an order, and the archers threw several lit torches into the darkness. In their small circles of light, they revealed only bare ground.

"Nothing," the archer said. Xander nodded.

"I still think it is safe to assume that Evasius' man has found us, and is gathering a force to attack," Noeman's voice came faint against the wind picking up atop the gate.

Then an answer to the torches came.

Thunk, went the first arrow that slammed into the gate. It hit so hard, Tobin thought he felt it under his feet. The next three thudded into the wood in quick staccato and everyone ducked below the wall.

No report from the archers was necessary after that sound. Xander leaped forward, his thin, aged form silhouetted in the firelight. "Archers ready!" Six bows creaked as they drew taught.

Tobin heard the soldiers before he dared peek out to see them. The sound of marching poured out from the narrow crack and echoed in the natural amphitheater. He looked at Rhys, who raised his staff in one of his signs of encouragement, then he finally lifted his eyes over the edge. The serpent he feared was coming around the corner of the gorge. Their shields shone dimly in the torchlight and they held them close together, covering each other so that they truly appeared like an enormous scaled beast. They were only able to fit two men abreast through the narrow crack, so it was impossible to tell how many waited to file through. The serpent might be long enough to swallow the small camp whole.

As they reached the threshold of the gorge, the first two pairs spread across the opening in a v-shape and planted their shields low. Three more stepped behind them to cover their heads and created a diamond that formed the snake's head. Behind them, Tobin saw Fallon standing without cover, as if he rode the monster. At such a close range, even a poor archer could take him down. It showed a confidence that was both foolish and terrifying.

It was too far to see the expression on his face, but Tobin imagined it held the same condescending boredom that confronted him and Kurian in the Briny Mug. When that face loomed in his dreams, he realized the expression was a thin veil for unquestioning loyalty and depthless malice. The Captain behaved as if killing them would be a waste of his time and skill.

"Hello," Fallon's voice boomed from the hollow. "I am Captain Nicholas Fallon, leader of the personal guard of Lord Farran Evasius, ruler of Pallingham. I would speak to whomever is in charge."

Xander stepped to one of the arrow-slits that flanked the gate and shouted through it. "You are above the Northland Cliffs, Captain. If Pallingham has power here, then up is down and dark is light."

"My presence and that of my soldiers says otherwise, stranger. Please tell me your name, and whether we have found the camp of the criminal known as the King of the Caves."

"Aye, this is the King's camp, and I am his servant, Xander."

"Three monks came to your camp recently," Fallon said, obviously beginning his same rough attempt at negotiations that he had in the tavern. "Tell your master he may hand them over, along with the treasure he took from them, and I will spare everyone else behind your gate."

"You mean, until you can return with a larger force to root us out," Xander said in the same way that had so frustrated the dean.

"I believe I have a large enough force already. Yet I am willing to avoid unnecessary bloodshed if he is."

"My master is tenacious. He does not relinquish what he has claimed as his own."

A few of the archers on the wall chuckled to themselves. Tobin did not comprehend Xander's strategy yet, but he was grateful he was protecting them instead of handing them over. His quirky answers were confusing or frustrating the captain, who was probably used to more formal battlefield negotiations. The laughter lightened Tobin's mood. *These would be good men to fight beside, and dying with them would be honorable.*

The thought shocked him, and for the first time, he began to think he might have as much courage as Kurian or Rhys.

"If you refuse my offer, you will see how much power Evasius wields in this hellish waste," the Captain yelled.

"And if you try to overcome the King's men with arms," Xander almost sang, "you will see that his command is over more than just a few canyons and caves."

The men inside the gate shouted in defiance of the invaders, and then began singing a hymn of victory against overwhelming odds. In tune and lyrics, it was nearly identical to one of the battle hymns Tobin learned at the compound. Hearing it sung in the face of enemies roused a will to fight within his spirit, and he knew that they had made the right decision to help. In that moment, he almost understood the dean's growing infatuation with these people. Then he heard the order roared from outside the walls that made everything else disappear.

"Fire!"

Fallon's lips pulled back in a satisfied snarl when the first wave of flaming arrows slammed into the gate and silenced the singing. He was glad it had come to a fight; for weeks, he had desired an open struggle instead of the endless hiding and chasing. Now there would be fire and blood, and if he had his way, plenty of both.

He raised his own shield just in time to catch the first volley of arrows from the archers above the gate. The weight of the arrows slammed the shield against his shoulder with satisfying force. Immediately, it set the thrill of battle coursing through his blood, and the intense focusing of his senses allowed him to see everything. First, he saw the water pouring down over the gate and extinguishing the arrows lodged there. So, their fortifications were not entirely primitive. Next, he saw a single shaft flying past his head and piercing the leg of the man behind him.

"Hunker down," he shouted. "Shields up! They have only a few bowmen, and we can wait them out." Of course, he was right. The archers sent only three more volleys, and then quit. They most likely had no arrows to waste, and wanted to wait for a clear shot.

"Bring forward the horse," he told his lieutenant. The order passed down the line, and the men stood to either side as a heavily laden horse strode forward. The smell wafting from the creature made his eyes water as it passed. From its head to its haunches hung dripping blankets that reeked of the oily resin that Mouna had created on Admiral Shea's ship. More of the stuff was in thick earthen jugs slung over its back. In normal circumstances, he would consider it a waste to sacrifice a healthy animal, but he had no time to spare—and he could not risk men by attacking the gate directly.

The animal gazed at him with wild eyes and its nostrils flared as it wavered on the verge of panic. He only needed it to remain in control for a moment longer. As soon as the horse was ahead of his front line, it saw the dying torches at their flanks and reared. He swatted its hindquarters with the flat of his sword and it launched itself into the open space.

The defenders did exactly as he expected. With a galloping horse heading directly for them, presumably with a rider, they fired a barrage of arrows. The horse stumbled, flipped end over end, and slid to a stop at the foot of the gates. It lifted its head and pawed weakly at the air.

"Fire," he said in a low growl.

Another volley of flaming arrows carved a shallow arc through the night and found their target. They hit the blankets with wet slapping sounds, and instantly, a wall of flame engulfed the gate. The size and intensity of the conflagration was unlike anything he had ever used to burn out a criminal. A single scream from the horse erupted above the roar of the flames, and then faded. A few seconds later, the jugs unbroken in the horse's tumble exploded and showered fire out into the courtyard.

He laughed in surprise. The witch knew how to make fireworks!

Behind the wall, he heard shouts of fear and urgent calls for water, but he knew they would never be able to stop the blaze. The slots they had cut out to pour water on the gates would never allow enough water to put out those greedy flames—and who could stand the choking smoke that poured over the archway?

There would be no more resistance while they attempted to save the gate. His fight would come soon.

He clapped a hand on his lieutenant's shoulder. "That is how you get foxes out of their dens!"

Tobin saw the horse barreling toward the gate and felt his heart sink with dread. He let out a sigh when the carcass touched the gate without effect. But when the archers knocked more flaming arrows, he acted on instinct and pulled the boy beside him to the floor, shielding him with his own body.

Fire shot up through the sluice where the boy's face had been a moment before. It jetted through the hole with such intensity, that Tobin feared it would scorch him through his clothes. The defending archers were already running down the stairs on either side of the gate. One of the other young boys fell backward and landed on the men below.

The smoke began billowing up on either side of him and the boy, surrounding them and obscuring everything. He rose to hands and knees, but he could not see over the side, or to the stairs.

"Tobin!" he heard Noeman's terror stricken voice through the smoke.

"I'm all right," he shouted. "But, I can't see the way out."

"Jump toward my voice," Rhys yelled. "We'll catch you."

"The boy first!" he managed before the smoke choked him and made him cough.

The boy who had encouraged him before looked no less courageous. He winked, then leaped and disappeared through the billowing wall of soot.

"We've got him," Noeman said.

He held his breath and jumped. Scalding grit peppered his face before he felt cool air, and then he opened his eyes to see Rhys flying toward him. The Brute did his job, taking only a couple staggering steps when their bodies slammed together. Rhys set him down and Noeman pulled him close, whispering prayers of thanks.

"Next time you stay on the ground, where it's safe," Rhys said.

The line of defenders had fallen back from the blaze. Xander stepped up from behind them. "It won't be safe for long," he said. "There's magic in those flames." He stepped aside and put his arm around the boy, who grinned and held out a cup of water. "This is Crispin, the one you saved."

"Thank you," Tobin croaked, taking the cup and gulping it down.

"Thank *you*," the boy said. "If you hadn't pushed me down, my friends would be calling me Crispy."

"I like this kid," said Rhys.

"Brother Hart, I thank you as well," Xander said, bowing. "You have performed the first act of bravery on a night that will likely see many."

"It was my duty, part of my oath," Tobin said. He turned to look back at the gate, engulfed in flame and smoke.

"What do we do now?" Rhys asked. "It's our first siege."

Noeman slapped the back of his head. "You've trained for this."

"We do what we can to prepare," Xander replied. "The gate should hold up for a couple of hours. If we're lucky, they'll wait until it's burned most of the way before attempting to breach."

"Do we have anything to form a barricade?" said Tobin.

"Exactly what I was thinking," Xander said. He called a few men forward and told them to find all the carts and spare lumber around the camp. Then he turned back to Tobin. "Would you do me the honor of supervising the construction, Brother?"

"I'd be honored," Tobin said. "I'd also like a few shovels and picks."

"What do you have in mind?"

"Maybe a way to slow down our invaders, and press them against their own bonfire." Tobin borrowed Rhys' staff, then drew in the dirt.

An hour after midnight, Tobin and his team upturned the final cart for the barricade. They had dug a semi-circular trench behind the burning gate, heaping the dirt into a makeshift rampart before constructing the wall of debris on top. It gave them cover and a height advantage for when the gate crumbled. And that would happen soon. Already, there were holes and gaps where the intense fire had burned through. In another hour, the charred wood would fall under its own weight.

"An excellent job for hasty fortifications," Xander said more plainly than usual.

"I hope it holds them back long enough to thin them out," Tobin said. "Thank you for trusting me."

"You showed you deserve it."

"If I might make another suggestion." Xander nodded, and Tobin continued, "When they come through, the fire will be low enough that we can access the lower stairs again. Post your archers on the flanks and Captain Fallon will be caught in a very tight trap."

"For such a gentle man, you have a dangerous mind for tactics," Xander said, giving him a conspiratorial look. "I wish I had a dozen like you and your friends." Tobin felt a rush of pride at the compliment. "Unfortunately for me, your battle is over tonight."

"What?" Tobin was taken aback. "But they could come through at any moment," he objected. Then he saw the flaming pillar over the strange old man's shoulder and understood.

"Yes," Xander said, "you are called."

"But we must stay and fight! Captain Fallon pursued us here, and we brought this danger on you."

"I appreciate your sense of duty, but this is no longer your fight," Xander argued. "Even in the heat of battle, the King's call must be answered." There was no room for discussion in his bearing.

Tobin hesitated, looking at Rhys and Noeman.

"Do not think that your presence will sway the battle, for we were never defenseless." Xander saluted both Tobin and Rhys, and then waved a hand as if to shoo them away. "Go, or I will have you bound and carried to the King."

Rhys tugged on his arm. "Let's go. We still haven't met this King we've been looking for."

Tobin turned to follow, and realized that Noeman remained standing beside Xander.

"Dean Goodman?" Tobin said, searching his teacher's face for an explanation.

"I have been your teacher, but now I am only your friend," Noeman said. He took a deep breath before speaking again. "I pledged my life in ignorance to a purpose and to a God whom I did not know. I had gazed upon the shadow, but not the figure that cast it. I spent my life searching for answers to questions I did not understand, and teaching my fumbling knowledge to young men like you so they could also pledge their lives to that God and that purpose. And where I thought I had travelled so far down this path that the answers must be just over the next rise, I see that I was caught in a thick brier that I had planted myself. All along, what I was searching for lay under my feet, buried where I could not reach it. But Xander has shown me a different way, and I intend to follow it."

"That is a long way to say you're not coming with us," Tobin said. He would have seen this coming if he weren't so worried about Kurian, but he was not entirely surprised. Still, it pained him.

"No," Noeman said, "I am not. I can teach you no more, because I am just as much a student here as you are. After speaking long with Xander, I feel almost like a child again...like a new man. In fact, I think it would be a fitting name. How do you like the sound of Newman?" The Dean spoke with a wistfulness Tobin had never heard, as if he were distracted or dreaming. Then he shook his head and focused on Tobin and Rhys again.

"What about rebuilding the Order?" asked Tobin, stifling a sob.

"Xander has convinced me of a better plan. You will understand more when you find Kurian, and I think you will see why I should not join you. I am still too much a man of the Order for what comes next." Noeman came close and embraced them both, then gently took their staves, saying, "You will not need these where you go."

"We will miss you, Dean," Tobin said.

"As long as I survive tonight, we will soon be reunited."

Rhys pulled on Tobin's arm again, and they turned toward the beacon, then jogged into the dark, away from one fire and toward another.

CHAPTER TWENTY-FIVE

The Steward King

The aroma of oily smoke saturated the air of the canyons. Captain Fallon breathed deep and thought fondly of the many times he had torched the home of a rebel or thief and waited for them to run out into the arms of his soldiers. Always, he felt satisfied to have completed his mission, whether he captured the criminal, or burned them alive. The method was so familiar to him, that he could see the gate burning in his mind, even though he had withdrawn his men around the corner of the gorge. No reason to expose his men to the possibility of random arrow fire.

The light flickering on the walls of the narrow crack told him how intense the blaze was. It waned by midnight, and he peered around the corner to assess the damage. Though he saw gaps between planks, the fire was still too high, and the wood might still be very tough to break through. He decided to wait another hour.

In the meantime, he sought out the soldier that was injured by an arrow in the first volley. He was no older than Fallon was when he had volunteered for the army. Someone had already pushed the arrowhead through and bandaged the leg, but he could tell he was in pain from the panting and thick sweat.

"What's your name, soldier?"

"Irving, sir."

"I know you joined me in Whalesand," Fallon said, kneeling so he could see his face. "Are you from there?"

"Yes, sir," Irving said through short breaths.

"Then I can be honest with you, young Irving. You know what a wound like this does to a man when a surgeon is not available." It wasn't a question.

Irving nodded. "He gets a stick leg. If he's lucky."

"That's right," Fallon agreed. "And I want you to be lucky, Private Irving, but I need your help."

"How's that, sir?"

"Surgeons are expensive, and the taxes coming to our Lord can barely keep the healthy soldiers provisioned. However, he would spare no expense to save a hero, a man who risked his life to save his companions. That man would be invaluable as an inspiration to others. Can you be that man, Irving?"

Irving laughed a little through his pain. "I figured I'd die out here regardless, sir. What'd you need?"

"Good man," Fallon smiled. "I need that gate brought down."

Shortly after one in the morning, Fallon helped Irving to mount a horse. "Better to risk an injured man and another beast than a good sword," he told his Lieutenant quietly. He tied a piece of blanket over the horse's head, then led it around the corner and handed the reins to Irving. The remaining soldiers waited behind them on horseback, ready to charge.

"You'd do best to jump at the last moment, Private."

"If I'm lucky, sir," Irving replied. Then he kicked the horse into a gallop.

Fallon leapt onto his own mount and watched in anticipation as horse and rider barreled toward the fiery gate.

Irving did try to jump from the horse, but his bad leg ruined his balance. He rolled to the right and bounced once on the ground before crashing against the stone archway. In the same instant, the blinded horse crashed into the barrier. The burnt wood shattered, and the gates flew open at the impact of a half-ton of horsemeat. Exactly to Fallon's plan.

"Charge," Fallon yelled, then spurred his own horse full speed toward the same burning portal.

The King walked Kurian through a wider tunnel, into a cave the size of a large common room. It was filled with cabinets, chests, and other furniture, and looked, for all intents and purposes, like the hiding place for a successful highwayman. Kurian shivered when he felt the warmth of the large fire in the center of the room, not realizing that he had felt chilled in the *hagiary*.

"You keep saying you chose me," he said, "and now you say I've chosen some path, but I don't understand it. I doubt you would have taken so much trouble just to have me walk through some mystical vision door. Tell me to what purpose you chose me."

The King watched him for a moment, as if sizing up a sparring partner. Then he held out a hand, inviting Kurian to sit at a table. "The answer to that is wrapped up with the other questions that have been treading the halls of your mind for the last hour."

When Kurian did not reply, the King continued, "How did Pallingham become as it is now? Why is the sun covered and the river dry? Why are the Evasians ruling instead of the kings—instead of me?"

Kurian had not voiced the questions, but they were on his mind. He nodded agreement.

"From what I know of you, your mind is habitually more dexterous than this," said the King, breaking his gaze. "Yet, the deep mysteries confound even the wise."

"Does it have to do with the prophecy you spoke before?" Kurian shivered again when he remembered the reverberation of the King's voice in the small cave.

The King nodded, appearing pleased. "The answer begins with leadership, for the people will follow their shepherds. Thus, it is more important to know who, or what, shepherds the leaders. Fin rose because King Frederick was a righteous man devoted to justice, truth, and freedom, rooted in the Treasure, and protected on your hill." Kurian did not need further explanation. Frederick's shepherds were the founders of the Order:

Sage Bennett and Ward Finlay, both men of unimpeachable character. Each performed with the skill and wisdom that qualified them to guide a King, and their *thaumaturgy* only confirmed it. The King asked, "Did you know that Capric Hill was once called Shepherd's Knoll?" but did not wait for an answer. "It is why the vision of the treasure and the oak was given there, and why Frederick made it the Order's home—so you would be shepherds of the people. From atop the hill, the monks were intended to be an example of holiness lifted up, and a place from which learning and blessings could spread out to all the people, even to the king himself.

"The blessings stopped flowing when the book was locked away, and the order became increasingly focused only on the happenings of the hill. The Rule created by Sage Capric merely codified the chill settling in their hearts. In time, it froze them solid.

"As the Rule overshadowed the Treasure, the shepherds stopped leading. They became blind guides if they were guides at all. The results were first visible in Frederick's grandsons who lacked wisdom and weakened the kingdom through incompetence. The sickness spread in their sons, who became shrewd, perverting knowledge and justice for their own gain. That was when politicians like the Evasius family suddenly appeared and gained influence. When the leaders lost their bearings, the people followed.

"Corruption and evil ruled in their hearts, and God allowed that corruption to pollute the land to show them the product of their desires. They lived for darkness, so darkness came upon them. They could not slake their thirst for wealth or power or pleasure, so the river dried up and the land went thirsty. It was only through God's compassion that enough rainwater and filtered light remained to grow food. Otherwise, the plains would have perished altogether, becoming as desolate as these canyons."

The King wept without shame, showing the same emotion he had when telling his own story, except that this time Kurian found himself weeping as well. The story astonished him, and tears of sorrow and compassion flowed freely for his country. He understood now that the man had not been weeping for his own death, but for a people he loved who had fallen so low.

Forty soldiers galloped behind Fallon with sword, shield, and bow. A warning cry came from within the gates, and then the shout pouring from his men overpowered all other sound. Across the open courtyard, he saw the hastily constructed barricade silhouetted by two large bonfires inside. The bandits were not stupid; they had prepared. Without thinking, he counted the points of firelight reflecting on metal that hovered above the secondary defenses. Twelve. Others might be hiding further behind cover. Maybe double. Plus a handful of archers, likely hiding on the flanks just behind the wall. Odds were good.

He heard an arrow fly overhead and one of the bright metal points fell with a clatter. His own archers had stopped before reaching the gate to suppress the defenders for a moment. They took down another. He closed his eyes tight as he approached the smoke and fire.

Then he was through the gate.

Only yards to the barricade. He ducked as he passed the threshold, and felt the whistling wind of another arrow cross over his shoulder. Hidden archers on the flanks, as expected.

"Fan out!" he roared. "Take the wall!"

He saw the dark trench in front of the barrier, and meant to stand in the saddle and vault himself over the top with his momentum. A blow from behind caught him by surprise and he faltered. Speed drew him off balance as the horse veered away from the wall of carts and wagons. He rolled over one shoulder, landing on hands and knees in the trench.

A shout of rage began deep in Fallon's chest. He sprang up to attack the unseen foe, and the shout died on his lips. His men had vanished, and so had the defenders. He was alone in the circle between gate and barricade. The demolished gate still burned on its sagging hinges, but he heard no sound from it. Then he thought there was movement or noise around him, but it was like wisps of dust blowing by. He turned around and saw nobody on top of the wagon at his back, either. Turning once more, a white light suddenly shone through the stone archway, blinding him, and filling the smoky air with light brighter than day. It seemed as if a more intense fire of red and gold hovered in the air above the arch. It held the shape of a crown.

"There were warnings that the people would suffer for their injustices," the King said when both of their tears had dried, "warnings repeated over an age. However, this time your order locked them away underground. That was, until I brought them out again, because the time has come."

"Time for what?" Kurian asked.

"For new shepherds: Shepherds ready to fight against the darkness by feeding the people with knowledge and understanding instead of terror and avarice. Ones who know the darkness for what it is and choose the light."

"You want me and my friends to be these shepherds? Shall we reestablish the Order and rebuild?" The prospect thrilled Kurian more than he would have expected. Finally, the Order could return to its former purpose and glory. They might even live up to the stories his father had always told him.

"You will be shepherds," the King said, "but not as monks."

"Then what?" Kurian asked, confused. "The brotherhood is all we know."

"Are your ears still closed to the prophecy, or is it your heart?" the King said gently. "The time has come for this part to be fulfilled. The land has been dark and thirsty for a long time, but it will not be forever. It requires only the release of the Three. You know the Deer, and you know the Brute. You can explain those with your mind. Tell me what is left."

Kurian wanted to look away, but the King's firm gaze held him. "The Princely Son," he said quickly and turned his head. He did not know why everyone assumed that title was his, but he did not like the implications that went with it.

"Did you think that your surname meant nothing, Kurian Abramson? Prince is a fitting title for a son of the Exalted Father."

Kurian closed his eyes and listened to his own rough breathing and speeding heart.

"Do not forget that you stepped through the door, despite your fear."

"What would you have me do?" Kurian shouted. "Speak plainly, I beg you."

"I wish you to rule," the King said with some of the regal presence from before, "to be king in my stead."

"You are the rightful king," said Kurian.

"Yet you also have a distant claim to the throne. The proof is secured within in a safe place, for the time it is needed." The King rose from his chair and stood by the fire. "I understand your hesitation. It will cost you much."

Kurian also rose, but paced. "You're asking me to sit in your place. I could never rule half as well as you! I couldn't inspire people the way you do with Louise, Alden, and Gideon. I can't heal the way you do. I only know the Rule, and you seem to know even God's will. And I thought I had lost faith in God until today—until I met you."

"I'm not asking you to be me, and you will not be alone. I am asking you to take on my authority," the King responded. "Would you begrudge me the right to give what is mine as I see fit?" Kurian paused mid-stride, then shook his head and continued pacing. "Then allow me to give you this trust, for the people need a king and it is not yet time for me to return to Pallingham's throne. In truth, my Kingdom is much greater than the plains, and in many lands, I have already enlisted the help of others to rule. At the appointed time, when all my enemies are brought low, I will return as King over them all." As he spoke, the imperial bearing returned completely, but without the threatening manifestation from before. Though he stood still, the King's presence filled the room with graceful majesty.

"Until then," the King continued just above a whisper, "this is the purpose for which I chose you, and the reason I called you out from your former life."

Kurian stopped pacing when he realized that by stepping through the door, he had already agreed to the King's vision. His heart had committed his feet before his mind could object. Going back on that decision would be the same as renouncing his oath to protect the Treasure—especially now that he knew its true value. This time, an act of will was required to persist in his choice. He kneeled before the King, who reached out and laid a hand on his bowed head.

Then Kurian spoke the words that always completed a prayer in the Order, words that combined request, hope, and submission to God's will: "Let it be."

Fallon staggered back against the wagon because of the great light and held his sword up in defense as a figure stepped through the gate. Soft footsteps were the only sound he heard. Immediately, he thought he knew what had happened and lowered his sword. "Am I dead? Was I hit by an arrow, or struck down from behind like cattle?"

"No, you're not dead," the figure said. "You're simply experiencing what my servant, Xander, warned you of."

"You're the King of the Caves," Fallon said.

"Yes," said the figure, and then he came into full view as he stepped forward. He wore an armor of white metal above a radiant linen robe. Crimson stains had wicked up from the hem as if he had waded through the blood of an army, but he carried no visible weapons. Fallon lifted his sword, intending to charge, but his hand came up empty. The sword was simply gone.

"I thought you wanted to avoid unnecessary bloodshed," the King said.

"You're the one who killed so many of our soldiers, or made them crazy," Fallon said. He tried to lift his arms and step forward to fight hand-to-hand, but found he had no strength to move.

"According to muddled reports from your spies," said the King. "A person who disappears is not necessarily dead, Captain. Sometimes they wish not to be found."

"Then what did you do to them?"

"I simply spoke with them, as we are. And while we are speaking, I am having similar conversations with the men who came with you. To those who want my help, I give it."

"What about the maniacs who returned like animals?" Fallon asked with scorn. He would not let this man pretend he acted out of compassion. The criminal studied him for a moment with a gaze that seemed to pierce his thoughts. Not even Mouna could see so deeply into him. Unintentionally, memories of his life began to flash in his mind, particularly those of cruelty and hatred. A multitude of faces in the pain of death. A myriad of naked bodies never capable of patching up his soul the night after.

"I have a knack for destroying self-deception," the bandit said, "and revealing what men truly fear about themselves."

Fallon remembered with uncanny vividness his blind meeting in Lord Evasius' office. He felt again his master's hot breath whispering in his ear.

"They were reminded of their darkest deeds," said the King of the Caves. "Your men did not lose their minds because of anything I did; their own consciences drove them mad with guilt because they were unwilling to renounce the evil they had done. The ones who did went free and began new lives. The ones who didn't sided with their own madness." He stepped closer until he was face to face with Fallon. "I can sense the same struggle within you, Captain."

Fallon felt a knot in his throat as he realized that he was as helpless now as he was to resist Mouna. "This is the worst sorcery yet," he said, straining against invisible bonds.

"It is power, yes, but not the sort of magic to which you have become accustomed." He was surprised when his interrogator looked thoughtfully at his right side, where Mouna had slipped her talisman between his ribs.

"I will not beg for my life, or my mind," Fallon spat.

"Then how may I help you?" the sorcerer said with a mocking expression of innocence on his face.

"You are a criminal; there is nothing you could offer me."

"What about freedom?" The fiend gestured to the fresh scar in his side.

Fallon did not answer.

"If you wish, I can break the tie that binds you to her."

The lump in his throat tightened, making breathing difficult. The thought of sleeping without dreaming of the witch, and the things she asked of him—it almost broke him. But he would not be turned. He stared into the eyes of his new tormenter and let him see all the hate built up behind them. Silently, he dared the King to release him. The magician climbed easily to the top of the barricade, and Fallon found he could move again. He turned to face his enemy, and the sensation of surrounding movement returned. There were phantoms all around, and the sound of clashing metal.

"I see you are not ready to be free," he said, looking down on Fallon, "and yet you are strong enough to face your own depravity. Therefore, I will grant you the bondage you desire. However, I think you will find my friends infinitely more tolerable as captors."

The King dropped behind the barrier, and the light disappeared, returning Fallon to a night lit by the fires of war. Around him, his soldiers were in disarray. Some had fled, but most writhed and blubbered on the ground like the lunatics who had returned from the outlaw's raids. A few were on their knees in a position of surrender, and several more fought with manic rage against foes real and imaginary. Finding his sword back in his hand, he intended to join those still fighting and take as many with him to death as possible.

Before he could move, three bodies landed on him from behind and knocked him to the ground. He thrashed with wild fury, but more men grabbed at his limbs. In a few moments, they had him disarmed and bound. They also bound the remainder of his men and forced them to the ground beside him, and then an old man in a dirty tunic made of hair approached them.

"I warned you," said Xander.

Fallon bowed his head, and the victorious cheers of the defenders drowned out the stream of curses spewing from his mouth.

CHAPTER TWENTY-SIX

Gifts

As soon as he voiced his prayer, a sharp intake of breath told Kurian they were not alone. He rose and turned to see Tobin and Rhys standing in another passage, which he assumed led to the entrance of the caves.

"Hi," he said breathlessly, and then cleared his throat. "How long have you been standing there?"

"Long enough to bear witness," said the King, and moved to embrace them both. "Welcome valiant warriors!"

As soon as the King released them, they thanked him, and both rushed forward to greet Kurian. Rhys grabbed both of his friends and lifted them in a great bear hug that squeezed out all of Kurian's breath. "We were worried when you disappeared," Tobin said. Rhys offered a gruff, "Good to see you on your feet."

"Where's Noeman?" Kurian asked, looking behind them to the tunnel.

"He decided to stay behind at the camp," Rhys said, shaking his head and cocking his eyebrows.

Tobin's gaze flitted between the King and Kurian. "Is this him?"

"Yes," Kurian said. "This is the King of the Caves, my friends. The true King of Pallingham." He did not feel the need to say anything about Lord Evasius' stories of the King being a criminal. That statement eliminated them all.

"And what we just saw…" Tobin tried to prompt him in his gentle way.

"He was the one who showed the vision to Sage Marten. He called us all out from the Order. I have decided to answer his call and join him." Kurian looked at the King for a moment and received a small nod. "You may come with me if you wish, or you are free to go where you please."

"You know we won't leave you," Tobin said.

"I told you we were still a troop," Rhys echoed.

"I had to give you the choice," Kurian said, and then realizing why he offered it, he added, "it's the way he works."

"One of the other ways that I 'work'," said the King with a smile, "is by offering gifts. I once told a story about a new set of clothes, and some of the men in camp took the allegory to heart, as you have seen." He tugged on Tobin's new coat. "However, in this case, I shall give Alden a run for his money."

He turned away from them toward a large cabinet against the far wall and flung the doors wide. Inside were three sets of armor that gleamed in the firelight like no metal they had ever seen. Rather than reflecting, they appeared as if they cast their own glow. The silver colored breastplates were inlaid with gold along the edges. Fine castings of noble animals and rich fruits embellished the shoulders and chest, appearing to move in the flickering shadows. Hanging above them, glinting as if gems stood out from every edge, were matching helmets that could have served as crowns for ancient kings.

The King opened a second cabinet, revealing arms of equal beauty. Three swords rested horizontally on hooks. Kurian could just make out inscriptions where the blades met their hilts, written in the same arcane script as the Treasure. Small kite shields leaned against the back of the cabinet, also coated in a metal that looked like still water. In the center of each was a symbol in relief: a strong, noble stag on one, the next with a ferocious badger, and the last the King's own symbol. Someone had embellished the reliefs with paint, giving them a lifelike brilliance. At the bottom of the cabinet lay scabbards and belts made of fine lambskin dyed red and white like the belts of the Caprics.

"Dress quickly," said the King, "for I have arranged a meeting with Evasius, and Aposford hangs in the balance."

"What do you mean?" Tobin asked. "If we meet him wearing that, he'll think we mean to do battle."

"And you must," the King said to him, while holding out the smallest breastplate. "All rulers, however small a territory they maintain, must fight to exercise their rule, else they lose all. There is always resistance, though some must contend with arms and some in other realms. For you, I believe it will be both, or Pallingham will never be free of Evasius."

They helped each other to secure their arms and armor. Kurian thought their fighting skills would be hindered, but not useless with the armor, and he was surprised at how light it was and how much movement it allowed, as if the armor had been forged for them. He longed for the now familiar staff instead of the sword with which he had rarely practiced. Yet, the sword was beautiful and deadly, and he eagerly wanted to learn its secrets.

Finally, the King wrapped the Treasure in thick leathers, placed it into a satchel, and led them back to the *hagiary*. Tobin pulled up next to Kurian in the wide passage and whispered, "Are you sure about this?"

"I've never been more certain of anything," Kurian smiled back. "I read part of the Treasure."

"You did what?" Tobin nearly screamed.

"He let me read it, and I found out why it is so valuable to the whole plain of Apos."

Tobin waited, speechless.

"It tells of the great kings of old, and of the glorious king who will restore Fin," Kurian said, turning his head to include Rhys. "And I believe that it's him." He gestured toward the King, walking ahead. "I'm still terrified, and I can't fully explain it, but he has my oath of allegiance. No, more than that—now that I have seen him, I want to spend my life learning to be like him."

He shrugged his shoulders. "That probably sounds insane."

"Not entirely," Tobin said as they stepped into the enormous round cave. "I think I'm beginning to see it, too. And I think all of our new friends would agree."

The King unbolted the door through which Kurian had seen the vision, and then turned toward them. "Kurian, my friend, you have accepted your call, and I will leave you with this reminder: the road will be longer and more difficult than you now imagine. Do not lose hope. You do not travel alone." He blew into his cupped hands and lifted them above Kurian's head where he spread them out as if he were anointing him with oil as they had the ancient kings. Kurian immediately felt all of the anxiety leave his mind and body, and he was filled with a new strength of courage and conviction to see the vision come to pass. "Go forth King of Pallingham."

Turning to Tobin, he held out the satchel carrying the Treasure. "Studious Tobin, I call you to the task of the Sages." Tobin took the bag with wide eyes. It was his secret desire, only shared in greatest confidence with Kurian. "However," said the King, "I will give you a clue to their one great error. Remember the oak. How does it protect its life?"

"By spreading its fruit, the acorn?" Tobin asked in a moment.

"Very wise, and very quick. Learning its wisdom will require more time."

"My King," Kurian said. "Are we all to protect the Treasure now, as before?"

"Do not worry about the task assigned to him," the King said. "I have put the book in here." He pointed to Kurian's heart. "Mr. Hart will help it get in here." He pointed at Kurian's head. "As he will help many."

He stepped to the right and faced Rhys, and his stature became rigid and formal. "Mr. Brock, I know that you do not understand all you have seen on your journey, and that you persist first because of loyalty. It is a quality that brings you honor. Use it to protect your friends well."

"Is that it?" Rhys asked, looking confused.

"That is all you are ready to hear. However, that does not mean you are not also called to great purpose. You will discover yours when you truly decide to join your friends. For now, stand firm in your loyalty, for it will be tested."

The King then stepped beside the open door and held out the torches to them. "This way, you will find the hidden path back to the plain near Dury. A friend will meet you below."

"You're not coming with us?" Kurian asked.

"It is not my time. Do not lose hope, Kurian, and trust that when you need it, help will come."

There was no vision within the doorway as they stepped through—only darkness. It retreated enough for them to see the next few steps in the tunnel, no more. Kurian turned and caught a final glimpse of the King before the door shut. Then they were trotting through the blackest night he had ever known with only the torches to find their way.

PART THREE

CHAPTER TWENTY-SEVEN

Morning in Pallingham

urian, Rhys, and Tobin traveled through dark, narrow passages in the earth for hours. It didn't matter whether they were just below the surface of the Crags of the Wild Goats, or deep in the heart of the Northland Cliffs—the three friends could not tell the difference in the dark underground. The torches miraculously endured, but their light could tell them nothing about the world beyond the stone.

During the first hour, Tobin and Rhys told Kurian their story of reaching the King's camp, including his illness and disappearance. They told him of the people at the camp, and of their teacher's change of heart. Tobin gave his best guess at Noeman's reasons for staying behind, and Rhys recounted the siege by Captain Fallon before the King called them. He did not leave out his disappointment at missing the final action. Then, Kurian told them about his time with the King, answering all their questions—mostly Tobin's—about what he had learned about Pallingham, their Order, and the Treasure that they now carried in a leather satchel. Eventually their conversation died off, as if the long tunnel, pulling their voices into nothingness without any echo, also stifled their desire to speak.

In the front, Kurian was the first to notice when the passage began descending rapidly, just after a sharp turn. Tobin quickly pointed out that the walls were changing from the rough, biscuit-colored sandstone to the cold, mottled gray of granite.

"We must be going down into the Northland cliffs," he said.

Kurian was quick to agree. He touched the stone where rough tool marks ran across a seam in the rock. Parts of the passage were natural, but somebody had gone to the trouble of enlarging or lengthening the tunnel for their own purposes. *Possibly the King*, he thought—*or he could just be the latest benefactor*. It obviously made sneaking on and off the plains very simple. A slight breeze cooled his face, and he noticed that the air was fresher here.

"Could we be close to the end?" he asked.

Tobin and Rhys both shrugged as if to say, "How should we know? We've never been in a cave before, either."

Shortly after the passage began its descent, they took the first switchback and entered a small cavern with a large hole in one wall that opened to the outside. Wind whistled past the opening, and dim light filtered through, illuminating what looked like a small sitting room. Two chairs and a table sat against the wall opposite the opening, and a metal brazier stood ready for a fire. When Kurian stepped to the edge of the natural window, he understood what it was.

"It's a lookout post," he said. The other two stepped up to the precipice beside him.

"Very sneaky," Rhys said with an approving grin.

The edge of the cliffs dropped nearly two thousand feet from their toes. Far below, they saw the lights of Dury off to the right, surrounded by its dark forest canopy. Before them, the plain spread like a gray-green carpet in the dim light of dawn. However, when Kurian looked up, he realized that it was not the same dawning light he had grown up with. Instead of a gradation of gray, lightening in the east but still charcoal in the west, the sky over Dury was a deep indigo. On the furthest horizon, it was almost black, like the darkest sapphire, and in it, he saw a faint pinprick of light, then a few more. Stars.

They were as beautiful as he remembered, shimmering like distant gems, multiplied in their beauty by each new one he saw.

"Oh, my," Tobin said, breathless. Kurian followed his gaze east. The sky grew lighter in shades of blue instead of gray, from darkest sapphire to indigo, then cobalt, chalcedony, and finally the translucent, liquid shade of an aquamarine. At the eastern horizon was a line so bright all color was washed away to tones of palest yellow.

As they watched in silence, the line expanded, condensing into a round bump, mounding up on the horizon like a new sprout pushing up through the earth. The light intensified as it grew until it formed a half-circle with rays of piercing light bristling from it like spears. Kurian watched in wonder, suspecting what it was long before he saw that rising orb. In the east, where the light was strongest, the sky looked exactly as it had in his vision, and that could mean only one thing: this was the sun. He wasn't certain he would have recognized it before the vision, and even now it shocked him with its beauty and intensity. From so high on the cliff, the light made it seem as if he could see forever. He thought he could make out the ruins of Fin over sixty miles to the south. The horizon itself was like looking into the future. He could only imagine what the people on the plain were feeling, being the first in generations to look upon this miracle.

The rays of light drifted higher, and in the moment that it topped the lip of the cave's window, it poured on their faces with full intensity, blinding their dark-accustomed eyes. It was almost as bright as the moment that he woke and first saw the King, and seeing it now reminded him of everything. He suddenly understood—no, wholeheartedly believed—everything the King had told him would come. This was proof, and it gave him hope.

Rhys stepped into the shadow of the cave wall, rubbing his eyes.

Tobin gasped. "I feel as if I have never seen daylight until now," he said, still staring at the horizon.

"I suspect we will soon see many new things," Kurian said with a smile.

Tobin turned to face him, and the sun reflected off his armor and flashed over Kurian's face, making him squint. The light was less intense, but still the same pure color of the sun. "You shine like the sun, Tobin."

"So do you," Tobin said.

Then, he noticed that he also reflected the sunlight like a walking mirror. He twisted his shoulders and a beam of light flashed across Tobin's face. They both laughed. Rhys drew his polished sword and held it in the light, moving the reflected light over his friends' faces. For a few moments, they were boys again, with a new toy. With flashing swords, they flung darts of light at each other, and deflected those coming their way with their shields. A matching light show played across the walls while the boys danced around the cave in mock battle. They laughed for pure joy, as they had not done for weeks, because the exorbitant beauty of the light was as intoxicating as wine, and they drank it in like men dying of thirst.

Finally, Kurian realized what they were doing, and recalled their purpose. He stopped the play, and let his laughter run out. "This is good," he said, "and we needed it. But we still have a mission, and our time is running out."

"It's too bad we can't get rid of Evasius with a few glints of light," Tobin said.

"It's more fun the old-fashioned way," said Rhys, then swung his sword in his bold, passionate way.

"In any case, I suspect this new change in the world won't serve his ends," Tobin added.

"And I believe it's only the beginning of the help the King promised," Kurian said. He sheathed his own sword and glanced over the edge of the cliffs again. "It's a long way down, and even longer to Aposford. We'd better get moving."

They found fresh torches and dashed into the dark tunnel leading down to the plains.

Something was wrong with the sky. The pure black of night, which usually turned into a dirty, dim glow at morning, was changing to an ever-lightening blue, scattered with a few strange dots like far off candles. Lord Evasius noticed them about an hour before dawn, and he almost feared that something was wrong with his eyes. White spots floated in his father's vision before he finally went blind in old age. However, this couldn't be the same thing because his men were gazing uncomfortably at the sky as well, and as the dawn came, the specks disappeared. The eastern sky looked as if it were on fire.

Was this an omen? Could it be some unnatural trick from the monks? Were they still capable of the same miracles from the story of their founding?

No. These were silly doubts. If they were, their compound would still stand. He listened to the thunder of three thousand soldiers marching or riding swiftly behind him, and thought of the other troops they would converge with soon, and the questions faded. A few weak monks would be no challenge. The show of force was merely to impress upon the people of Aposford the futility of rebellious sentiments. That message would quickly travel throughout Pallingham, and no one would dare challenge him again.

The sound of hooves galloping out of cadence with the rest caught his attention, and he turned toward a sight that quelled his doubts completely: Mouna was riding up the ranks toward him. Her stream of black hair whipped in the wind of the wondrously fast horse, tangling with her black robes. Only her pale face was clear in that blur. Evasius enjoyed the fearful stares in the faces of each rank she passed. She pulled up suddenly as she neared, and hailed him.

"Welcome back," he said. He allowed her to ride next to him as she readjusted the shawl over her face. "What do you make of this light in the east?"

"I do not know, my lord. It seems the clouds over our land have dispersed. Perhaps it is the sun."

This new possibility intrigued him. "What might it portend?"

"I do not know, my lord," the witch repeated, bowing her head in deference. "The only methods of divination I have with me are unclear. It could be an omen, but its meaning seems to confuse the bones. If only I had returned under better circumstances, Lord Evasius." It impressed him how quickly she regained her breath to make such a speech after riding so fast.

"How so?" he asked. "Our enemies evaded Fallon—but now when I remove their heads, I will get to see their faces myself."

"I do not know how that is possible," Mouna said demurely. "I saw the monks in Whalesand. From there, they crossed to Ramah, and into the canyons above the cliffs. I doubt they could have flown down from there."

"My other spies reported them leaving Dury, and heading here. Maybe they found the secret passage we've suspected the raiders have."

"Forgive me, Lord Evasius," Mouna said with deadly severity, "but one of us was deceived. They could not have traveled almost three hundred miles faster than I have."

Evasius clenched his teeth. Fallon's death was already assured—if he returned—and now the captain from Dury, along with his messenger, would also be executed. Somewhere, there had to be men he could trust with leadership. If he had to kill all the incompetents to find them, so be it. He was resolved to offer them as sacrifices to his control. With luck, he might find a few worthy replacements on the current march.

The prospect of a new deception from Dury settled another thing in his mind. Aposford would be terrorized today whether the fugitives were there or not. Everyone in Pallingham needed to see he would brook no challenge to his authority. Whether the town survived depended on how quickly they surrendered the Caprics.

He turned to Mouna with a predator's smile. "Then let us continue and find out the truth."

On second thought, perhaps I should let Mouna destroy the town in some inventive way. It seems a fitting reward for their long association with the rebel monks.

Kurian and his friends spent another two hours stumbling down the dark slopes and switchbacks that led to the plains. Finally, approaching a dead end, they found a narrow hole in the floor, through which they saw light. Beside it was a ladder. Kurian stuck his head through to see a cave below, which clearly led back to the outside air. They lowered the ladder, and then climbed down. From the bottom, the hole in the cave ceiling was unremarkable. "Ingenious," Tobin mumbled as he watched Kurian and Rhys shove the ladder back into the upper passage.

The sun was higher in the eastern sky when they pushed through the large shrubs that grew over the cave's mouth. They found themselves in a small clearing of the forest of Dury. The sky had settled into a single rich hue halfway between the dark blue of Tobin's eyes and the sea-grey of Louise's, closer to the plumage of a bluebird. "So, that's what a mountain iris looks like," Kurian said under his breath. He could only guess that it had been two hours since they watched the sunrise, and unless time had changed along with the sky, he thought it was close to eight o' clock.

They squinted and held hands up to block the bright sun that seemed to find every possible gap in the half-bare trees. "It looks like God hung a droplet of molten gold in the sky," said Tobin. Kurian could only nod in agreement, because he thought the beauty of the light was unspeakable. It recast everything in an amber-gold, tinged with that clear blue of the new sky. If this was how things used to be, he couldn't imagine how they ever did anything but stare in wonder at the beauty of the world.

He tore his gaze away and looked at the ground, knowing there were important things to accomplish, but even the forest floor had transformed into something new, a brilliant moving tapestry of dappled lace. Down a very slight slope, through thickening timber, they saw the Cliff Highway a half mile in front of them.

"West or east?" Kurian asked.

"West, most likely," Tobin said. "Gideon was taking us east toward the secret passage."

"We no longer look like Caprics," Kurian said. "Shall we try to buy horses in Dury?"

Rhys agreed. "We look more like mercenaries. This'll be interesting."

"Do we have time to skirt around the forest and come in from the south?" Tobin asked.

Kurian shook his head. "It would be nice to hide our direction, especially since my shield practically announces who sent us." He pointed to the King's symbol on the gleaming metal kite.

"Maybe we can hide our gear in the forest," Rhys suggested.

Kurian was thinking this over when two figures stepped out from the tree line and beckoned to them. The larger figure was unmistakably Gideon, the enormous woodsman who had helped them escape from Dury the first time. It was a relief to see him alive, and to know they would be under his protection again. The other was Louise. Something caught in his throat at the sight of her.

"I don't think we have to worry about any of those problems," he said to his friends.

Rhys ran to meet his new hero. Kurian wanted to run and lift Louise in a sweeping embrace, but she looked upon him with a cool stoicism.

"Hail, King Kurian," Gideon said when they were close enough to speak quietly. He knelt, which did little to make him less imposing, for even kneeling his head came nearly to Kurian's shoulders. Louise knelt beside him, and then they both held out their weapons in salute. "As you follow the King above, so I will follow you," Gideon finished before Kurian could object.

He didn't know how to react to this. It was not the reunion he hoped for, and even though he had accepted the King's calling to take on the authority to rule, he had not considered how it would change his relationships. What did they want him to do?

In a moment, almost as if someone had nudged him and whispered the answer, he remembered the story of the King's great ancestor. He had not desired rule, but he accepted the calling placed upon him. At least as far as Kurian had read, that king did not grasp for power even when it was rightfully his, but had patiently waited until his authority had ripened. It seemed to be an appropriate response now.

"Thank you, but I'm not king yet...not for some time, I think."

"You are king if he called you king," Gideon said. He pointed up toward the cliffs with one thick finger.

"Still, I would prefer just Kurian for now." He paused, feeling the blush on his cheeks. "Your sword is still very welcome in the fight we have coming. You have been the King's servant for longer than we have, so we could also use your guidance." He looked at Louise as well. "Both of you."

Louise rose first. "I really hoped you would come around," she said.

There was something different in her that he couldn't define. She seemed more at ease suddenly. And she looked at him with a queer smile that he could not interpret.

"How did you get down here?" Tobin asked her. "I thought you were taking those who couldn't fight to safety."

"I did," she said. "Then I was told to get down here as fast as I could. I didn't think it would take you so long to follow." There was her teasing. Maybe he only imagined a difference.

"We have horses," Gideon said, getting to business. He led them into the trees a short distance, where five of his large horses were tethered. "But before we go, we brought food in case you were hungry." He pulled bread and cheese out of his satchel, along with some cured ham, and they enjoyed an impromptu feast. The boys ate as if they had not had a meal for days. In truth, Kurian did not know when he last ate. In the caves, he had not been hungry, but while descending the cliffs, he began to feel weak and his stomach growled. The hasty meal was filling, and restored his energy.

"We cannot afford to waste any more time," he said, rising from the forest floor. "The King only said he had arranged a meeting with Evasius, but he did not say when. We have to ride as quickly as possible."

Gideon gave him a knowing smile. "Most of you make a light load, so my beauties should be strong enough to carry you faster and further than common beasts. But my message might have ruffled Evasius' feathers, so I wouldn't plod along at my normal pace." He had the adventurous glint in his eyes that Kurian remembered. If it weren't for their sparkle, they would almost be lost in all the hair. He winked, one eye disappearing like a bird hiding in a bush, then added, "I think he's arranged things so you will arrive right on time."

Noeman desired sleep. Two long nights of fire, blood and battle in a month were too many for a man his age. He was grateful for whatever miraculous thing it was that broke the assault—Xander had told him it was the King's doing——but the work had continued until dawn as they wrestled to detain the attackers who went into a mindless rage, and comfort those who were injured. Most of that time, he had been in the house of healing, where he felt like a novice again, compared to the mastery of Charissa. Her deftness at bandaging wounds and her knowledge in herbal remedies were impressive. Her skill humbled him, but her sense of humor made it bearable—even enjoyable—to be her assistant. Surprisingly, he found working with a woman preferable, in some ways, to working with his brothers.

He stepped out of the healing house for the first time that morning and was dumbfounded at the transformation before him. The whole world was bright in a way he had never seen. Immediately, he thought of the stories and paintings from the time of Fin. *My imagination was too feeble to conjure this*, he told himself.

Still, his body demanded rest, and weariness tugged at his grit-filled eyes. He stepped to the spring beside the house, where water trickled out of the sheer wall into a delicately carved fountain bowl, and then spilled into a small pool on the ground. He splashed his face and it was cold and refreshing, but little match for the sleepless night. Then he took a sip and the liquid cooled him all the way down to his belly. Suddenly, he felt rejuvenated, as if he had enjoyed the best sleep of his life. No, he felt stronger, surer of himself. The aches and pains that haunted him for a decade seemed to vanish. He felt young again.

"Good, isn't it?" said Xander from beside the house.

"It's life-giving!" he replied.

"Just wait," Xander said. He rapped on the small fountain and the gentle flow became a gushing jet of water. The pool it fed, bloated from the seasonal rains, had already spilled over its edge and a small rivulet ran down through the camp. Now it became a steady stream. That was when Noeman noticed the old, shallow riverbed crossing straight through the square between the three largest buildings. The stream filled the center of the riverbed, then gathered beneath a cleft in the encircling canyon walls where blue sky showed over the cliff's edge. A crowd was gathering to either side of the growing reservoir.

"It can't be," Noeman said. He suddenly felt a very unfamiliar emotion; he was giddy.

Xander nodded with the excited look of a young boy sharing a secret. "I'd stand back, if I were you."

The ground began to tremble.

"Which way?" Kurian said to Gideon when they were all mounted.

"The quickest way is to take the road back toward Dury and then turn to follow the Apos before we reach the city," Gideon said.

They rode at a brisk pace until they neared the riverbed, then slowed to a walk, dismounted and left the road. Gideon led them to a hiding space within the trees where they could see the city's eastern gate. They saw no guards near the closed doors.

"Looks like they locked the city down," Rhys said.

"Scared of the sun," Gideon said, shaking his head. "Superstitious clods!"

Behind him, Kurian heard Tobin grunt, before a harried, "No, no, no!" He looked to see him struggling to hold back the big horse, which was heading straight for the forest edge. The other horses also started pulling on their leads, and only Gideon was able to restrain his mount. Eventually he released it anyway. The animals all pushed through the undergrowth toward the riverbed and the cliffs.

"Don't go after them," Gideon grunted. "Wait and see if the guards respond."

Tobin let go and fell backward. Then they all watched as the horses trotted to the cliffs. The stone looked wet, and a large puddle stood at the foot of the cliff face. The horses drank greedily, until the puddle was only a muddy patch in the soft loam of the riverbed. There was no alarm from the city. When the horses returned to the trees, they carried a sweet smell about them, like the earthy scent that came with the first rains of autumn, but mingled with the aroma of spring blossoms in the orchard. The water was more proof of everything the King had told him, and he silently rejoiced.

"This is good news," Gideon said.

"Don't tell me the river is going to start again, too," Tobin said. One corner of his mouth began twitching. Kurian, Gideon, and Louise looked at each other and nodded together.

Tobin let himself grin. "If everything from Fin is coming back, then what are we waiting for?" he shouted.

He rushed into the open and lifted himself into the saddle. In a moment, the others did the same and they headed south at a brisk canter. Tobin's enthusiasm encouraged Kurian's growing confidence. Then, they crossed the southern corner of the city and his heart sank when they heard shouts from the walls behind them.

The southern gate was open, and a contingent of soldiers ran for their own mounts, waiting nearby. Kurian heard the whisper of arrows flying dangerously close.

"Run!" shouted Gideon. The horse raced to a gallop before Kurian could give a command.

In what felt like moments, he saw the edge of the forest and the open plains. Wind and hoof beats thundered in his ears, but behind them, he heard the thudding of many more hooves tearing at the ground. Glancing back, he saw a pack of riders a half mile behind. He was tempted to stop because he was so tired of pursuit. It was time to stand and fight, as his friends had stood at the gates of the King's camp. The horse started to slow, as if in response to his thoughts, and the others pulled ahead of him. The rumbling of the horses grew louder in his ears until it engulfed all other sound, even though his horse continued to slow on its own. Ahead of him, Tobin, then Louise and the others slackened their pace as well.

The booming noise began to sound nothing like hoof beats at all. It turned into a dull, chaotic rumble that came from all around him. Then he noticed that the ground itself shook, and the horse struggled to keep its footing.

He pulled on the reins and came to a rough stop, then turned in the saddle, barely holding his balance. Tremors convulsed through the ground, and the trees of the forest swayed like tall grass in a breeze. The pursuing horses stumbled and reared. Some fell, or threw their riders. The cliffs towering above the forest seemed to be the only solid thing within sight because of their massive size. He looked to their heights just in time to see a torrent of water shoot from a cleft in the top. There was so much water that he thought it would drown the city of Dury. The cataract fell to earth with a boom that overwhelmed the earthquake, leaving only the rushing sound of the oncoming flood.

A wash of mist spattered his face in the same moment that he saw a wave charging from the forest. It ploughed through the riverbed in a wall half as high as the trees. He watched in horror as it swallowed fifteen soldiers and their horses, and then his own horse was scrambling to reach the riverbank. They crested the bank just before the seething river devoured them. Spray and foam thrown from the tempestuous wave soaked him as it roared past. There was no sign of the soldiers it had washed away.

The ground shuddered once more as the flood passed south, and finally, everything was calm. The swift water at his feet was the only moving thing. The same nauseous shock that came after the fight in the apple grove swept over him. He was lucky to be alive. For a moment, he sat in the saddle, immobile. Frozen in the tug-of-war between awe and terror. He was about to dismount and gather his wits when the horse nickered and took off at a fresh gallop, chasing his friends and the vanguard of the river.

As the horse drove forward with reckless speed, one final thought came to him as if spoken from someone else: *this is what the King meant when he said help would come.*

Awakening Aposford

Gideon's enormous horses were impossibly fast. They galloped along without tiring, almost without seeming to touch the ground. The heavy hoof beats Kurian was expecting became only a light patter, barely audible above the sound of the wind in his ears. And the sound of that gale came in great rhythmic gusts like the beat of enormous wings. With each flurry, the horses skimmed over the earth as if they floated on invisible pinions.

The flood of the river surged ahead, faster than any horse could possibly run for so long, and yet they kept pace with it, following less than a mile behind. The ruins of Fin appeared on the horizon and before Kurian realized what they were, he was within the city, and then it was behind him. Then the wonders truly began.

The river passed the outlying farms of the old city, which had lain fallow for so long that the grass of the plain had reclaimed them from the feral crops. As glittering waters poured by, Kurian saw the grass darken to a deeper green. Then the fields came to life with tender new shoots that reached above the grass. He watched them climb skyward, growing before his eyes, and by the time they flew by in a blur, heads of grain weighed down their stocks and entire fields stood ready for harvest.

It continued mile after mile. The fields sprouted and matured in minutes. Decrepit orchards that had already lost their leaves in the October chill nearly exploded with new foliage, blossomed for an instant, and then drooped lower and lower, their branches laden with fruit.

The long-dry artery of the plain of Apos flowed once again with life-giving water. After long years of restraint, when it was only allowed to sip a few drops of rain, the land drank deeply and was satisfied. With its lifeblood pouring forth again, it shrugged off the death of autumn and the accumulated decay from a century of darkness. In each moment, the world became more fully alive. Birds sang and flitted through the new growth with the same vigor that came after a long winter thaw. The air warmed and became saturated with the perfumes of spring, summer, and harvest all rolling together, bringing with them a bouquet of joyful memories. It was *thaumaturgy* at its best.

With each new green shoot, every fresh sensation of life, Kurian's hope grew until it bloomed into a confident assurance and he felt incapable of doubt. They would face Evasius, and the power his family had seized so long ago would fail. The hope of Fin could be reborn.

Then the people might follow the land's example, finding restoration and life.

Nobody in Aposford saw them riding in from the north. All eyes fixed on the floodhead roaring past. Its height had diminished on the eighty-league journey so that it barely washed over the top of the old stone bridge, but to people who had never seen anything but a dry riverbed, it was an unbelievable sight. It wasn't until the five riders slowed down and their mounts returned to the normal thud of galloping horses that anyone noticed them.

More people than usual milled about the edge of town, looking up into the rich blue sky or staring at the river. From their expressions, Kurian thought they barely believed the vision of armed riders coming down upon them. It was too much for these old, frail, sick people. *Perhaps they think the end has finally come*, he thought. But before he could think too much about their condition, his horse stood among them, and he was shouting through wind-cracked lips. "Where is the mayor?"

The people standing near them either cowered away in fear, or came close to examine these strange, shining riders as if they were ghosts. One old man who he recognized as Mr. Baker stepped close with dazed eyes and gingerly reached out to touch the bridle of his horse.

"Mr. Baker," he said, leaping down from the saddle.

"Are we dead?" said Mr. Baker, looking around, confused. "Is this paradise? It's so beautiful. Look!" He pointed at the river. "The river is back."

"You're not dead, Mr. Baker." *At least not yet*, he thought. Kurian grabbed his shoulders and forced him to look at his face. "It's Kurian Abramson, Mr. Baker. Do you remember me? My father is Jeremiah."

Recognition suddenly dawned on the pale, wrinkled face, and he smiled. "Little Kurian," he said. "My, you've grown. You look like a proper knight in that suit."

"Thank you, Mr. Baker, but I need to find the mayor."

"Oh, there's been no mayor here since you were a boy," said Mr. Baker. "Everybody minds their own business. We're all too old and tired to cause trouble."

"Then, nobody is in charge?"

"Looks like you are," Rhys joked.

Gideon walked his horse into the center of the crowd and blew a long, clear note on an old hunting horn. More people were coming from the center of town to see the spectacle. Soon he had a small, but growing crowd gathered, staring at the three young men in bright armor, and their strangely dissimilar companions. Gideon motioned for Kurian to get on his horse and join him. When they sat side-by-side, he turned to the crowd and began to speak in his cavernous voice, which rose and carried over the entire village.

"Hear me, people of Aposford, and mark the signs of this wondrous day. For the sky veiled to your fathers and grandfathers has been revealed to you. You are the generation blessed to feel the warmth of the sun after a long, cold night. The Apos, for so long a dry bed of death, flows again with life-giving water. Look and see how your orchards and groves thrive out of season. Finally, your own son returns, having been declared the chosen heir to the throne of Fin, and all this land. He comes to free you from the oppression of Lord Evasius, and to return this to a place of peace, prosperity, and goodness. Behold King Kurian!" Gideon held out a hand toward Kurian, and the crowd stared, speechless.

In the silence, a stooped woman with skin like that of a dried-out potato said, "Huh. My grandam always said this would happen. And here's the river and the king on the same day!" She finished with a bemused laugh, and then the entire crowd was in uproar.

Some bowed in fearful submission, as they would to Lord Evasius, or the other royals. Most were trying to shout their own questions above the others. "How do we know he's king?" was the loudest.

Gideon gestured to the river. "Isn't that enough of a sign for you?" he bellowed. His voice overpowered the others and the crowd fell silent again. "If not, then taste of it yourselves. Wade into it and cleanse yourselves of a lifetime of despair. May God strike me if it does not uplift your body and your spirit." This set the crowd into a new commotion.

One or two ventured carefully near the riverbank, while anyone standing near Gideon's horse backed away in fear and suspicion. Kurian glanced at Tobin and Rhys, then let his gaze linger on Louise. They offered only helpless shrugs.

"Friends," Kurian shouted as loudly as he could.

In the quieting crowd, there were several shushes. "The boy-king wants to talk," said a heckler.

"Please, do not bow in fear of me," he said first to those on their knees. "And do not simply accept my friend's word and give me honor that I have not earned. Many of you knew me as a boy, and you saw me sometimes as a novitiate of the Caprics. Now I would like to earn your respect and trust as a leader, and perhaps someday as a king. For now, I have no throne." This got a chuckle from some. "But one with even greater authority has called me to that task. And with every ounce of my life, I would like to see the glory of Fin restored, even surpassed."

Every eye was on him, though some were enthralled while others were suspicious. In the pause, a woman shouted from the riverside. It surprised everyone, and their attention turned to a single figure kneeling on the shallow bank, lifting a handful of water to his lips. The shout had come from a woman standing nearby, holding her hands to her mouth.

"It's the sweetest, freshest water I've ever tasted," called the kneeling man. The crowd murmured. He laughed, and then took another drink. Finally, he jumped knee deep into the river and began splashing about and beckoning for others to join him. The few people who stood near him stepped closer with curious looks. The old woman with the crinkled potato skin hobbled forward on weak legs until she stood deep in the current and could drink without bending. Everyone watched in silence as this matriarch slowly drank her fill.

When she finished, she lifted her head and stood straighter than before, and then turned around. Her hair looked a touch darker, and her skin smoother, to those close enough to notice.

But they all saw that she stood tall and strong, unlike the frail creature they had known for years. She looked at her hands and arms, then giggled. Finally, she strode from the water and began to dance, flinging water all over those who bunched around her. Her laughter continued like music in the air. Those who had been tentative now rushed toward the river.

"You don't have to believe in me," Kurian said. "But believe the one who sent the water. And trust that I truly want to free you from Evasius' tyranny."

"What does that have to do with us?" said the heckler.

"Everything!" Gideon said, "For he comes against you even now. His troops could arrive at any moment." Kurian and his friends stared incredulously at him.

"Right on time, huh?" Louise said dryly. Gideon tried to suppress a smirk, and shrugged.

"Well, it's a good thing we have some time to prepare!" Tobin said, but it was impossible to tell whether he was joining in the joke, or genuinely worried.

More people stepped out of the river, celebrating the healing and rejuvenation they received from the water. Amid their shouts, the rush of the current seemed to beckon to Kurian, offering to soothe his parched tongue. He nudged his horse forward, and slipped from the saddle. His boots pressed firmly into the damp, sandy silt of the bank, and he kneeled down to drink. The water was as pure and cold as the sips he had taken from the fountain in the King's camp. It refreshed him in the same way, and he was certain that it was somehow from the same source. When he rose, the weariness of the long journey— and the long night—fled from his body. He turned back toward the crowd with a fire kindled in his heart, and he knew it showed in his eyes when those who had appeared most suspicious looked on him with burgeoning respect.

"We know Evasius is coming," he said. "We don't know how many soldiers he brings. We must prepare. Any ideas?"

Tobin spoke up immediately, "If everyone in town could fight, we would have maybe five hundred. When they sacked the compound, Evasius brought only a few hundred mounted soldiers. We might outnumber him."

"But look at them," Rhys said. "We can't face trained soldiers in open battle, even if we outnumber them, and especially if they're mounted." Louise and Gideon agreed.

"I'm merely thinking through our numbers," said Tobin, exasperated at the interruption. "And you're right. However, the streets are narrow enough that, if we can draw them in, it forces Evasius into a spot where he can't maneuver." He surveyed the town's exposed mortar and aging thatch. "Maybe we split up. Hide in the buildings, so the town looks deserted, then shoot or drop whatever we can on the passing soldiers. Small groups run up the side alleys to skirmish with the soldiers, and draw his force apart. We set traps and lead them there. We wear them down until they leave."

Gideon and Rhys both nodded. "We will lose many," Gideon said, "but I like this plan. It gives us the advantage of surprise."

"We just have to hope they don't raze the town with all of us hiding inside!" Louise shouted. The crowd jumped at her outburst, and began to mutter nervously again.

Kurian lifted himself into the saddle again. "Tobin," he said, "normally, I would accept your plan as the best chance for success. But I have a feeling that today's battle won't be about numbers and tactics."

"What does that mean?" Tobin asked.

"The King told us that help would come," Kurian said, as much to the crowd as to Tobin, "and look what's happened. I know he sent the water, and look what it's done to everything and everyone it touches. He'll send the help we need to fight Evasius, too. I don't know how I know, but I know it deeply."

Tobin clearly struggled with this answer before asking, "Then what do we do?"

Kurian smiled the way he used to when trying to convince Tobin to bend the rules. It was so transparently manipulative that it still somehow charmed his friend every time. "We have faith," he said, turning the tables.

"Great." Tobin rolled his eyes the way he always had when he gave in. Louise laughed in surprise behind Tobin, and looked like she was about to cry. Yes, she was different. Figuring out how would have to wait.

"If you are fearful, we will not hold that against you," Kurian said to the crowd. "Anybody who wishes to flee may do so without any threat of retribution." Kurian found that the words came easily, as if someone whispered them into his soul and they overflowed through his mouth. A few began trotting back to their houses.

"But if you would fight for your life, and your homes, and your freedom, then stand with us. Who would help us bring down the tyrant Evasius?"

A few brave souls, mostly those who had already been to the river, raised their hands.

"If you fear, or if you doubt, you are free to find your own way, for your fear will only spread, and your doubt will weaken us. However, if there is a seed of trust within you, then go to the river. Drink so that seed may grow, wash so you may be restored. Then join us. We make our stand on the bridge!"

"Finally, an open fight," Rhys said with sudden zeal. "We'll probably all die, but it's worth it to poke a stick in the eye of the man who killed our brothers."

"But first, we get everyone we can into the river," Kurian said. "I don't care if Evasius comes over Capric hill. They are our first priority." He pointed to the crowd. Fewer than a hundred stood around him, but most of those now looked on him with trust and began to make their way to the riverside. Somewhere in the village were four hundred others who either would not— or could not—make it out to witness the sky and the river, or to hear his speech. He instructed Gideon and Rhys to help guide the efforts, and to find those still in the village. He asked Tobin and Louise to go with him. They could leave the riverside for a few moments, since every person coming out from the river was another helper for the relief mission.

"Where are you going?" Gideon asked after dismounting.

"I must see my father."

He raised a hand to knock on the door of his childhood home, and remembered that this had been where he stood when Evasius first attacked the compound and uprooted his life. What he had not thought then in his juvenile frustration was that his father might not live here, might even have died. He would not have known, since the Order felt no compulsion to inform the brothers of family deaths. They were supposed to have severed those ties when they took their oath.

He recognized now that his situation had been unique among the brothers. No others had family living close enough that they might bump into them regularly. He had last spoken to his father when he was twelve, after five years of confinement in the compound. He'd last seen his father from a distance in town over three years later. He remembered seeing the familiar leather bag, bulging at odd angles, hanging at his father's side. The wooden mallet still poking out from the top. His young heart leaped when he saw that bag and recognized the figure holding it. But his father had not seen him that day. And he had not seen his father again.

A terrible thought crossed his mind: *perhaps the Order didn't like me seeing him, and told him to leave me alone to focus on my training.* He could imagine the dean convincing his father to disappear from his sight. For his own good, of course. What did it do to him to agree to that?

That was the thought that made him pause with his hand poised to knock. Then he forgot about formalities and lifted the catch on the door. Tobin and Louise entered silently behind him.

Inside, the light was dim, and a musty odor filled the room. Clearly, someone still lived there, because a fire burned in the hearth. But the room was disheveled, and it did not look like food had been prepared in the kitchen for some time. The only neat and tidy place was the corner where his father's tools and workbench stood in perfect order. A small pile of unfinished shoes sat on the floor, and above them hung the leather satchel, now a little more worn than in his memory.

He called and heard movement upstairs. He took the stairs to the small bedrooms above, and found his father lying in bed. He had never been a particularly large man, but he had always been strong and healthy. Now he was gaunt, and his face looked waxy and pale in the strong light coming through the windows. Kurian kneeled at the bedside, and when recognition dawned in his father's eyes, they welled with tears, and a smile twitched at his mouth.

"My boy," said his father in a cracked voice. "They told me you died."

"I've come home, Papa."

"How?"

"It's a long story, one I hope we'll have time for later."

His father reached out and felt his armor. "New uniform?" he asked, puzzled. "Where are your robes?"

"The Order is no more," Kurian had to fight back his own tears. "Only Dean Goodman survived. My two friends and I were sent to negotiate with Lord Evasius, so we also escaped. But now we have found a new mission."

"You look like a Lord yourself in that armor," his father said, and let his head fall back with a satisfied smile. "I knew you would be something great one day."

The questions in his mind lost the anger behind them when he saw his father's pride, but he still needed to ask them. "I don't understand," he said gently. "You must have seen that the Caprics weren't like all your stories anymore. How could leaving me with them lead to something great if they were only a shadow of their past?"

"Because I knew you, son." His father coughed, adding to the blood stains on his pillow. Kurian looked back at Tobin and Louise with concern, but he knew they were not healers like the King. "It didn't matter if their glory was gone. God put greatness in you. I knew you could become a man like the ones in their stories, even if they were not. But a cobbler could not teach you how to fight or to think. I could not teach you about the bravery and sacrifice that makes a man heroic."

"But you did, Papa," Kurian said. "Your stories kept me in the Order even when I wanted to run away. They made me so determined to protect their treasure that when it disappeared, I would do anything to find it. I almost lost myself—I think I passed through death before I did find it."

"Then you've done more than I could have dreamed," his father said.

"Did you know about our family...that we're related to the old kings?"

The old cobbler opened his mouth to speak, but his body convulsed with another coughing fit. He wheezed heavily after it subsided. "Your mother can't stop smiling at you," he managed to say.

His mother had died when he was a child. "Papa, we need to get you down to the river," he said, and tried to lift him into a sitting position.

"No."

"But the river is flowing again. Everyone who goes into it comes out better. They all feel like they're in their prime again."

"See," his father said, smiling. "You're just like the stories I used to tell you. But my time is done. Seeing you like this. It is enough." He grabbed Kurian's hand from his shoulder and held it firmly while resting his head back on the pillow. Slowly, the firmness of his grip diminished. "Go my son," he whispered. "Lead your people." Then he let out a slow, rasping breath, closed his eyes, and his fingers went slack.

Kurian squeezed his hand. "Papa?" He grabbed his shoulders and shook them gently. "Papa, we can heal you at the river."

Tobin stepped forward and laid a hand on his shoulder. "He's gone, Kurian."

"No!" Kurian said through tears. "I'll carry him to the river. It's a day of miracles. He'll come back."

"Kurian," Louise said softly but firmly. "He has done everything he set out to do in this life. I do not believe he would come back even with the river's help. God has called him to rest after finishing his job. Now we must go finish our mission."

Kurian wanted to argue, but suddenly he felt the water he had drank from the river coursing through his entire body, now with warmth, and revitalizing strength. It calmed his grief and returned the hope and confidence that grew in him on the plains. And the whispers in his spirit, which had guided him all day, told him that she was right. His father had seen his victory, and he would not have to suffer the struggle ahead. The river was not for him; and trying it would only cause more pain. But his father had given him a final gift. He knew why his father had left him with the monks. With those words, he understood that anger and grief did not have to chain his heart anymore.

He reached out and placed a hand on his father's forehead, saying a silent prayer. Then he said, "Thank you, Papa," and walked back out into the bright sunshine.

Out of Time

Kurian noticed the constant, strong sound of the river as soon as he stepped out from his father's home. It was a foreign sound to him, and to these people, even if it was merely a long absent friend to the plains. The exotic nature of that sound would have drawn him, even if he weren't going toward it already. But, as they came through the main square, toward the river, the pervasive noise developed a pulse to it that sounded less fluid and natural. More rhythmic and purposeful.

At the river, the crowd had more than doubled in size, and still small groups were breaking off to rush into the heart of the town to find friends and relatives whom they could bring to the healing waters. They made their own raucous noise of celebration with laughter and singing, but behind it was the unbroken rush of the river—and now the rhythmic sound Kurian recognized as separate from the river.

"Do you hear it?" Gideon said, as they approached. He lifted his head high above the crowd, cocking his ear this way and that as if he were hunting in the woods.

Kurian nodded. It was growing louder and more distinct, a steady cadence that could only be one thing.

"They're coming," Gideon said.

Around him, the celebrating crowd settled down and looked to Kurian and his friends for guidance. Most of them had not heard that Evasius was on his way, or had only heard second hand. Now they knew that danger was upon them, and while they showed fear, there was a deeper emotion filling their faces. They did not want to give up this first taste of life.

Kurian looked over the river, past the old decrepit orchards now heavy with fruit, and gazed upon Capric hill for the first time since returning. The compound that stood on the steep mound was a charred scattering of rubble, perfectly visible in the clear air. The wall circling the waist of the hill had fallen over in large sections. The dry-stacked stone buildings had crumbled when the support beams inside turned to cinders and the roofs caved in. Dark ash covered the ground. Topping the hill, the Treasured Oak stood out branchless, like a withered finger turned black with infection. It was now a place of ruin and death, instead of the place of learning and light it once was. It was his brothers' burial mound.

Rounding the south end of this new symbol of death, he saw the first ranks of soldiers marching toward Aposford. Cavalry strode at the front with bright spears held high, as if they would pierce the sun as it dropped into the west. Flying at either side of the columns were standards with the Evasius crest, a red hydra on a sable field. Above each head of the beast was a golden diamond, or lozenge, signifying persuasion.

Riding a short way ahead of the army were two figures, one in shining mail, wearing a bright helmet of gold, the other a smaller figure in black robes. Evasius and one of his witches. Above them, a large flock of crows began to circle, and Kurian shuddered with the memory of the ruins at Fin.

He tore his gaze from the approaching army. "How many have we helped so far?" He asked Rhys and Gideon.

"Maybe two hundred," Rhys said.

"If we're going to make the bridge our defensive position, we ought to move now," Gideon added

"Not yet," Kurian said.

"They're only a mile away!" Rhys objected.

"The people are still our priority," Kurian said forcefully. Then he turned to the crowd and picked out somebody he knew, the tanner who lived near his father. "Mr. Fielding, take thirty men and gather up anything we can use in a blockade, or as shields. Also bring whatever weapons you have." The tanner responded quickly and sent men off in different directions. The rest of the crowd, he sent in groups of three and four to find the rest of those too old or sick, and to bring them to the river.

Finally, he turned back to his friends. "All of you get into the river before the last of the people arrive. Drink, or dunk yourselves. We need restoration, too, after our journey. And looking over there, we need all the help we can get from the King."

He paused in thought for a moment, trying to think of what needed to happen next, and then laughed unexpectedly.

"What's so funny?" Tobin asked.

"Don't you see it?" Kurian said. "We're finally accomplishing what the Order set out to do. All those mercy visits, and not one person was healed. But now, it happens without us really doing anything."

"I suppose you're right," Tobin said, humorlessly. Then he grinned. "Noeman will be sorry he missed it."

Rhys let out a conspiratorial laugh, and pushed Tobin into the water.

The sun burned on Lord Evasius' face. Just another irritation that put him in a foul mood and made him more inclined to let Mouna and his soldiers have their way with Aposford.

Then he saw the charred top of Capric hill, which made him smile. He looked to see the impression it had on Adaminster, and was not disappointed at the awe, tinged with fear on the primping idiot's face. From their direction, the hill and the rampart at its base obscured the view of the town, which he expected would look the same as the hill by morning.

But something else was wrong with the picture besides the bright sun. A thick line of darker color ran across the grass of the plain from north to south where the old riverbed was. He kept seeing flashes of light coming from that line, something like those that erupted from the spears and shields of his soldiers when they caught the sunlight. Whatever it was, this new change took away any joy at seeing the destruction of the monastery.

As they rounded the southern edge of the hill, the changes in the landscape raised an irrational response of fury in his heart. He saw that the riverbed flowed now with quick-running water. The orchards were full of a second, impossibly large harvest. It was not just the quantity—the fruit itself was larger than any he'd ever seen. Normally, he would have rejoiced at the extra resources, the surge in income this would bring, but now it all seemed like a personal affront. The bounty before him was like a challenge to his ability to rule, and the look on Adaminster's face had changed to dumbstruck wonder. He could not abide this.

"Look at the fools," he said, pointing to the tiny human shapes in the distance. As soon as they saw his army, they scurried about like ants in a trampled mound. "They're in a panic," he laughed.

He continued to ride forward until he was a half-mile distant from the river, in the center of the meadows in which the cattle normally grazed. They had fled before the army. Ahead of him was an open area that used to be part of Aposford, but which now held only grass, and a few remaining foundations. The encroaching orchards to the north hedged it in and gave him a near perfect killing field should the village truly attempt resistance.

The army poured out from behind the hill and arrayed themselves in divisions at his back. His first four ranks spread out at an angle that crossed between the hill and the river, nearly filling the space, and forming the long end of a triangle between the river on the east side and the trees on the north. Behind them were sixteen more rows of half that length.

On one side, the river made an excellent protection for his flank, even if it would slow his entry into the town. The hill protected his other flank. But neither would be necessary. The small group of defenders was now attempting to blockade the bridge with refuse. Their efforts were laughable.

"They must be mad," said Adaminster beside him. Mouna tittered on the other side.

"Mad or not, they've sealed their fate," he said. He watched with satisfaction as the blood drained from Adaminster's face.

Kurian and his friends jumped to help Mr. Fielding's small team to crowd the already narrow bridge with debris. They had pulled together an impressive and creative array of shields and barriers in just a few minutes. For shields, they fastened leather straps to small crate lids, and even full-size doors. The makeshift weapons were surprisingly varied; long-hooked blades on poles from the orchards, whips for the cattle grazing nearby, axes, cleavers, and kitchen knives. A few long daggers and aging bows appeared from their hiding places.

Mr. Baker came up the square with a string of twenty horses and mules, most of which looked lame, or too old to ride. "Found these in the stables, young Kurian, if they'll help," he said.

"They will," Kurian said. "Get them into the water, too. A good drink might just revive them."

"If we can sneak them around the back side of the orchard, we might be able to break up his forces there," Gideon said, pointing to the lines by the hill.

"Good idea," Kurian agreed. "Get some volunteers, and make sure everybody on horseback has an appropriate weapon. I don't want to send anybody into harm's way unprepared. Stir up some trouble, but break off before you get bogged down."

"Yes, my King," Gideon saluted.

"And stop calling me that!"

In twenty minutes, the two opposing forces had settled into their respective positions. Kurian and his friends stood on the old stone bridge with nearly three hundred of the people of Aposford, minus the riders who went with Gideon. A few stragglers were still hobbling to the water, and after stepping in, they joined their neighbors on the bridge. They had mounded as much material as they could over the far end, allowing only a narrow lane through which a single horse could pass. Across the field, they saw the six-thousand strong army of Lord Evasius.

"How do you feel about your plan now?" Tobin asked Kurian.

He looked up at the bright sunshine, now descending slowly in the western sky. He guessed that in a couple of hours, the bright setting sun in their faces would make fighting difficult. "It's daunting. But my gut still says to trust the King."

"Fine," his friend said. "Now what do we do?"

"Now we fight!" Rhys said, and raised his fists, trying to excite the nervous farmers and herdsmen. It was mildly successful.

"Not yet," Kurian said.

"Normally there is a form of negotiations before a battle," Tobin instructed them. "I suspect Evasius will want to gloat and threaten us a bit."

"Then let's not disappoint him," Kurian said. He mounted his horse and walked it down the steep arch of the bridge, through the chokepoint in the barricade. His friends followed. He had never prayed so fervently in his mind before, and he felt like he should say something to the people huddled on the bridge before they rode into the field. He turned his horse around and looked over the crowd of men and women with lean, gawky arms holding the tools of their livelihood as weapons.

"Remember what I said before about doubt and fear," he said gently. "If you fear for your life, you may leave now, without reproach. However, I believe that you are all too stout for that. You are the ones who stayed, after all. As the drought and famine claimed the land, others fled. They chased after rumors of abundance and prosperity in other places, but you remained. Perhaps out of stubbornness or fear of change—but you had your chance to renounce those motives today—and you stayed. Whether from love or tenacity, you are the ones loyal enough to Aposford to be here today. As neighbors and friends, you are now its last defenders. Have faith that your actions today are meaningful in a world that eschews loyalty to neighbors and friends. I cannot promise that you will not die today. But if you stand together, your courage will be heralded forever. And your reward will be great in the coming kingdom."

A few heads nodded, but nobody spoke in response.

Kurian turned and trotted ahead of his friends while Evasius, the black-robed woman, and another man approached from the other side of the field.

The surge of confidence which he'd felt since drinking from the river changed within him. Now it felt brash and bold. It wanted to bubble up and pour back out of him. If the dean were here, he suddenly felt capable of confronting him over the years of insult and shame. He thought he might simply assault Evasius if he did not watch himself. In the same thought, he imagined this was what Rhys always felt like. The badger was an appropriate symbol for his shield.

"That's far enough," said the other man with Evasius when they were ten yards away. He was dressed in mail very similar to Evasius' own; the only difference being that it was more highly polished. His helmet was bound with a ribbon that held a piece of silk hanging down over his neck, and a large eagle feather stood out from one side. Down his back was a long cape that covered his horse's haunches as a woman's skirts would have. The crest shown on half a dozen ornaments and baubles told Kurian who he was. His horse was small, and looked fast, though he had covered it with colorful quilted padding as if he were in a parade. Kurian slowed at the command, but continued walking his horse forward.

"I'll say when it's far enough, Duke Adaminster," he said, and continued until his horse was face-to-face with Evasius'. His mount was a full hand taller, and Evasius' horse shuffled back slightly. He flashed a smile that only bared his teeth. "Isn't that better? Now we can speak without shouting."

"How dare you?" cried Adaminster.

Evasius held up a hand to silence him and looked at Kurian, calm, if mildly annoyed. Kurian knew that he had trained to control every expression, and this minor annoyance meant more than he let on. "Young Kurian, what do you think you're doing? Do you wish the death of all these innocent people?"

"I wish nobody's death," Kurian said, "although I will not mourn yours."

"Plucky little monk," Evasius said, and raised an eyebrow. "*You* must have a death wish if you are willing to threaten me."

"No threat, only truth," said Kurian. "Certainly, you don't expect to live forever."

Lord Evasius laughed.

"Laugh if you wish, but I see the fear in you."

"You see nothing!" Evasius took a slow breath, and held a finger to his lips, then whipped it away with cunning shifting into his eyes. "Did you find my treasure, boys?"

"It's not your treasure," Tobin said. His voice was deadlier than Kurian had ever heard.

"I sent you for it. You've returned. That was our agreement. If you have it, then come with me peacefully, and I might consider it a ransom for those innocent people you've turned against me." He gestured toward the bridge.

Tobin pulled the satchel with the treasure into his lap. He had refused to lay it down or store it somewhere in Aposford, and Kurian hoped his gesture would not tell Evasius they held the treasure while they spoke. He pointed to Capric hill, but

Evasius did not look. He merely continued staring into his eyes. Kurian continued to point as he said, "There can be no agreement with you. And now, I have come to tell you that your tyranny in Pallingham is over. Leave peacefully and you may escape justice for your crimes."

"You do threaten me then," Evasius said.

"Only your power."

"You are a fool," Evasius chuckled. "Threaten my power, and you threaten my life. They are one and the same."

"Why are you so fearful of dying at our hands?" Kurian asked dryly. "Do you assume we are as cruel as you? Or is it because you know that is the fate you deserve?" He took a deep breath and spoke with a commanding voice, as close an imitation of the King as he could muster. "I have given you the chance to withdraw and avoid battle. I would challenge you to single combat, but I expect you would only hide your fear behind arrogance and pride because we are so few."

"My army will crush you in a minute. Why risk myself?" Evasius mocked. "I have six thousand, and you have a few hundred. You are a sparrow taunting a hawk. No, even less——you are a gnat drowning in my goblet. It will take only a moment for me to fish you out and flick you away."

"Then prepare yourself for battle," Kurian said, "but remember that this place is known for miracles." He wheeled his horse around to return to the bridge. Rhys chuckled as they rode, and Kurian gave him a wink.

"You should have talked to him that way over dinner," his friend said. "Would've saved us a lot of trouble."

Louise laughed and gave them a look that asked, "*Why must men be this way?*"

"My witch could wipe you out by herself!" Evasius shouted after them, just barely audible over the horses' steps. "You are responsible for this town's destruction!"

"I hope you know what you're doing," Tobin said, and sighed.

CHAPTER THIRTY

The Battle of Aposford

Tobin sat astride his enormous horse on the crest of the bridge, next to Kurian, watching the ranks of archers trotting over the field. The water from the river had definitely swelled inside of him, boosting his spirits, but he had nowhere near the confidence his friend did in their plan. It looked like suicide.

At the same time, he could not ignore the small but resolute place inside of him that wanted to believe because of the miraculous signs they had seen throughout the day. That place had the effect of a tiny, but hefty weight on the scales of doubt that tipped the beam in favor of trusting his friend and believing in the promises of the mysterious King who called them to the Northland Cliffs and gave them this task. He wanted to believe that help would come, to believe that God would bring about miracles like the day that had founded their order so long ago. He simply had a hard time seeing how that was possible against such overwhelming odds.

Rhys, on the other hand, didn't seem to care if they survived. He was looking for a glorious fight so he could prove himself in battle, as if the apple grove or the gates of the King's camp had not been enough. "We'll not get called away from the fight this time," he'd said as they got back to the bridge after the unorthodox negotiations, then shook Tobin's shoulder roughly.

"Kurian, is this the right thing?" he asked as the archers closed into range for an attack.

"It is. Trust me. Trust him." Kurian patted him on the back and smiled.

"I don't see how we can get out of this. We're outnumbered twenty to one." Tobin finally let his concern show to his closest friend. "Where's the help he promised, besides the river?"

"You don't see it?" Kurian asked, then he gave the command, "Shields up!" and the ragtag group of villagers raised their makeshift shields as the archers knocked their arrows. The command to fire drifted weakly across the open field, and Tobin watched in horror as a swarm of arrows took flight. He raised his own shield and closed his eyes as they rained down with metallic clanks and wooden thuds.

When the deadly rain ended, the townspeople lifted their shields with the arrows sticking out of them at all angles. They grinned at each other when they saw nobody had been hurt, and then shouted in defiance at Evasius' army.

The lack of wounded was miraculous considering that they had few true shields, and only three of them wore armor. With the sun behind Kurian, Tobin thought he did see something surrounding his friend. He blinked, and looked again at the people around him, hunkering down for another volley. Each of them was surrounded with a faint aura that he could only see when the light caught it in the right way. He looked at his hands and noticed the same transparent shell less than an inch from his skin. It shimmered a little, and was fluid, like the water from the river. In fact, it appeared as if a second skin or a bubble of the river water covered every part of him. The head and mane of his horse were distorted when he looked through it, but he could not feel the bubble when he touched the muscled neck.

A flicker in the corner of his vision caught his attention, and he raised his shield just as an arrow thudded against it. His glance fell to the woman kneeling beside his horse, where he saw the arrow rebounding from his shield bounce off her back at full speed.

It's just like that first day with Frederick on the hill, the day of the vision. This was thaumaturgy. It was all around him, and he'd seen only half of it until now.

Louise leaned into his field of vision. "It's amazing, Tobin, but that doesn't mean we can let our guard down."

As she spoke, a shout rose from the ranks of archers. Ten riders broke from the orchards on the archers' left flank and bore down almost silently, and with unbelievable speed. Half of them rode on mules or donkeys that looked unridable twenty minutes before. But now they covered the three hundred yards of open space in the blink of an eye. Tobin assumed that he and his friends had flown that fast down the three hundred miles of river that they followed that morning; it was bracing while they rode, but observing it from afar was astounding.

The archers had almost no time to react. Those closest to the trees stood frozen in terror, while those on the far side scattered in a panic. The giant form of Gideon on his enormous warhorse plowed into the lines so hard that men flew through the air like birds scared from cover. He swung his sword in powerful arcs that leveled several men at a time as he passed through the ranks. The villagers swept in behind him in a sharp wedge, further separating the bowmen and causing even more devastation. They made it halfway down the line before Evasius had mobilized his cavalry to counter-attack. He'd been caught completely by surprise, and no doubt, he had never seen such a lightning-fast charge. With a large force of cavalry headed his way, Gideon blew his horn and his small band rode back toward the cover of the trees at the same breakneck speed. They disappeared before the pursuers had reached a full gallop.

On the bridge, the defenders cheered loudly, and then began letting out whoops and shouts when they saw Gideon's second surprise. As Evasius' cavalry chased the ten riders toward the orchard, the other riders from Aposford came around the back of Capric Hill, riding up fast behind the army. They passed by the line of infantry, harassing them with quick swipes of swords and long-handled pruning knives. The infantry at the edge shoved against their comrades to get away, causing chaos in the main ranks. Then the mule riders slammed into the rear of the horsemen chasing Gideon. In a moment, they took out twice their number before the soldiers knew what hit them. They made another pass and twenty more fell. As soon as Evasius' cavalry tried to mount a defense, the riders of Aposford wheeled and retreated behind the hill.

Gideon's attack had divided the squadron of almost four hundred horsemen. The leading troop followed him into the trees, while the second half turned to follow the other group. The archers on the field ran back toward the army with the officers trying to keep them from fleeing altogether.

After a minute, Tobin saw Gideon's entire band of riders dash across the narrow space between the orchard and the river to his right. Gideon's horse leaped the thirty yards of the river's breadth as if it were no wider than a branch that had fallen in its path. Without slowing, the smaller horses and the mules splashed over the surface of the water and reached the other side in two strides.

Tobin's first thought was one of panic. Why were they leading the cavalry behind them? But, then he remembered the impossibility of what he had just seen. The river was shallow enough to ford here on horseback, but it was not so shallow you could take it at a full gallop. Suddenly, he knew with intense certainty that something else would happen to stop the squadron from fording behind Gideon. In that instant, two dozen of them tried to follow Gideon at full speed, assuming the water was only ankle deep. When they hit the deep central current, the horses fell head first into the water, throwing their riders over into midstream.

A conscious officer held up the rest of them and walked his horse into the river, intent on crossing to continue the chase.

Behind him, two hundred of his comrades began entering the water, too. When he had reached halfway, the officer glanced at the bridge, and his eyes rested directly on Tobin. He had a nervous, but cocksure smile on his face, as if this were the most thrilling thing he had ever experienced. He was probably no older than Kurian or Rhys, which meant he was only a few years older than Tobin was. Their eyes locked, and the young man never saw the surge coming downriver like a wave.

It was not raging, as the headwaters had been in the morning. Gently and silently, it simply raised the level of the river until the officer's horse was no longer wading, but swimming. The extra water sped up the current, and suddenly, he and his fellow cavalrymen found themselves drifting irresistibly downstream. The horses reacted before the men did, neighing in fright and trying to swim for shore, but the current was too fast for most of those who had entered the water. It remained high, preventing those still on the banks from entering.

Tobin watched as the officer and his men passed by under the bridge, now so close he could almost touch them, and then they were carried away. The water slurped and gurgled as it tried to squeeze through the narrowing space under the arch, and some of it spilled over the banks at either end of the bridge, lapping at the barricade and threatening to float some of it away.

Gideon rode up to their rear after watching the spectacle. The villagers cheered their own small cavalry. "Excellent work," Kurian called.

Gideon was ecstatic. "I haven't fought like this since my mercenary days, before I met the King. Didn't think I'd get to again."

"Too bad we only get the surprise once," Kurian said. Already, they could see the army strengthening their left flank behind the hill. The other lines, closer to the river, were busy watching the space where the brief action occurred.

Tobin had a thought. "Any chance our few archers could harass their right flank from across the river? Of course, with the way you jumped that river, maybe our cavalry could do it."

"Wind's not right for archers," Gideon said. Then he smiled with a manic glint in his eye. "But we'll have a go." Rhys beamed at his hero, and looked at Kurian, practically begging to join them.

They were about to speed off for another assault when a commotion in Evasius' ranks caught everyone's attention. It was the left flank again, up against the hill. This time, they were prepared for an assault. Officers were yelling commands down the lines, and the infantry braced themselves behind their shields with a unified thud that carried across the field. The archers began firing over the lines, and that was when Tobin saw the handful of figures racing down upon the lines. His heart jumped into his throat. They came from the top of Capric Hill.

The attackers seemed to push their way into the lines almost as easily as Gideon had on horseback. They swung and the army of Pallingham almost melted before them. It was difficult to see details from so far, but Tobin recognized an intense passion in their fighting that raised his own urge to join the battle.

"Who are those fellows?" Gideon asked.

Kurian shrugged his shoulders. "I don't know—but they're helping."

"What's happening, my Lord?" Adaminster asked with a quavering voice when the third flank attack broke upon them, this time from within the ruins of the monastery.

"A trickster's illusions. They're trying to play on the superstitions about this monastery," Evasius said. He grabbed the velvet cape that Adaminster wore and forced him to look in his eyes. "Do not succumb to their ruse, Adaminster, or your men will fail."

How could the man be so ignorant and blind?

"Clearly, they hid some men up there for an ambush to make us think something miraculous has happened: their dead brothers returning for revenge. Ha!"

"But the speed of their...mules, Lord? And the river rising against our men?"

"All tricks. Maybe they know a little magic to dazzle a fool like you, but they don't know what they're up against." Evasius felt his nostrils flare wildly. He wanted nothing more than to strike this dandy with his fancy clothes and decorated stallion. He shrieked at the division commander on the left flank, "Can't you kill five old men?"

"Mouna," he shouted, even though she sat in her saddle at his side, "show them what magic is. I don't care what it costs."

"I will need Duana's help." She signaled, and the circling crows descended in a flurry that condensed into the plump shape of her coven sister.

"We waits for you, Lady Mouna," the witch croaked.

"And it will require a sacrifice," Mouna said to Evasius.

He eyed Adaminster's sweat streaked face for a long moment, then said, "Choose whomever you wish."

"Your largest, strongest warrior would do best, my lord...certainly not him."

The five men continued to weave in and out of the left flank of the army while the people of Aposford cheered.

"We must figure out a way to aid them," Kurian said. "They can't keep this up for long."

His attention fell again toward the center of the lines, where Evasius sat on his horse behind his troops. The black robed woman who had not spoken during their parlay was riding through the lines toward the front, with the squat shape that he recognized—even at this distance—as the witch who had exploded into a flock of crows, right in his face. From the right side of the army strode a man who appeared almost as large as Gideon. He had stripped to the waist, and his enormous frame towered above the two women, after the first dismounted.

Weird screams and chants floated on the wind to them, and then the soldier dropped to his knees before the witches. Both of them placed hands on his head, and then the first one slashed a long, thin blade across his throat with surprising brutality. Louise jumped, and then began praying aloud. He started a silent prayer himself.

"Stand firm," he said to the people on the bridge. "The water in the river is a promise, and you have all been sealed in it. This devilry will not overtake us."

The crow-witch captured the blood pouring from the man's throat in a large bowl, and then the black one flung his body away from her. She leapt on it with the blade and began quickly hacking the limbs off. The fat one splattered the blood over the ground with a rag. Wherever drops landed, small mounds began to form in the grass. With the last of the blood, she smeared the severed limbs of the dead soldier, and then his torso and head.

The skirmishing on the left flank settled down as the strangers retreated behind the hill's ramparts and both sides watched the gruesome ritual unfold.

Gasps and expressions of shock broke from the crowd on the bridge. Tobin even felt one escape unwillingly from his own throat. Across the field, the small mounds grew into hillocks, and merged into one continuous, lumpy swell in the earth.

The witches each took hold of two limbs from the carcass and began beating on the mound, continuing their maddening chants. The torso also grew and morphed into something large and powerful. Legs sprouted from its sides, and when it stood, they saw an enormous bull the color of the soldier's blood. As it tossed its head, it appeared to have two mouths; the first was where it should be, but the second flapped wildly where the witch's blade had sliced through the neck. It stamped madly on its front hooves, and then let out a deafening bellow. The slash in the neck spewed a putrid liquid that steamed and fumed on the grass of the plain.

The two witches ceased their beating when the bull rose, and they tossed the limbs away. With the loud roar of the beast, the squirming mound of earth suddenly burst open and creatures like giant locusts leaped out of the ground like a swarm of angry bees from a crushed hive. The first to break the surface fluttered wings that ran the length of its back, then rose into the air and flew toward the bridge.

One alert archer loosed an arrow as it drew near, but the steel head bounced off the creature. It passed near them with a terrifying hiss, and then returned toward its kin, still crawling from their hole. Its skin was a strong carapace, almost like a thick plate armor made of iron. Several protrusions stood out from its head like a grotesque crown, and it had eyes that were eerily human. The rest of the face was thoroughly monstrous, with sharp, clacking mandibles, and coarse hairs protruding from the cheeks and head.

Hundreds of the creatures poured from the hole and filled the air above the witches. The one in the black robe climbed onto the back of the crimson bull and held out her hands as if to present her work to Evasius.

"They're hideous," cried somebody on the bridge.

Tobin instantly felt the panic in that voice. "What do we do now?" he asked Kurian, trying to hold his own voice steady.

"How do we fight these odds? I want to trust you, but it's hard to see how we fight monsters."

"Don't fear," Kurian said. Tobin could tell it was for everyone, not just him. "The King has already sent help. Haven't you seen it?"

"I've seen an amazing river, and a few strangers on the hill, but the odds are still hopelessly against us," Tobin said, his voice cracking in the stress. "They had us down twenty to one, but I don't know what the odds are against flying demons!"

"No, there is hope," Kurian said, trying to comfort them all. "You saw the protection of the water because you felt it and you believed. Look with those eyes. One of us on this bridge will make a thousand of theirs flee in terror, because there are more with us than with them." Tobin watched his friend ranting and his fear tripled. They were going to die here.

"You said we were outnumbered twenty to one," Kurian went on, "but we have them outnumbered fifty to one."

"What are you talking about, Kurian?" he shouted, and then felt embarrassed for yelling at his best friend who only asked for trust.

Kurian looked hurt, then he bowed his head and sighed. Tobin was about to apologize when Kurian looked skyward and said in a simple, imploring tone, "Open his eyes, so he can see. Let them all see."

Tobin felt warmth behind his eyes and he blinked.

There before the bridge stood ranks of horsemen that had not been there a moment ago. The crowd on the bridge gasped as one, and began muttering in awed whispers. He looked to his left and right. Beside them, standing over the river were more horses, nearly twice the natural size, pulling strange two-wheeled carts in which warriors stood with bows. The vast army stretched into the orchard, and many stood along the slopes and atop Capric Hill. Every one of the horses and warriors blazed and flickered like they were made of flames, and yet they stood firm, guarding the frail people on the bridge. All of Tobin's doubts melted. For a moment, he felt remorse at not trusting Kurian, but that gave way to a conviction that he would always stand at his friend's side, even in the face of doubt.

The horses in Evasius' ranks were skittering back and forth, the riders clearly struggling to keep them from bolting, because of either the monstrous locusts and the bull, or the sudden appearance of the new army with its giants aflame. Tobin thought he even saw the posture of the witch astride the great bull change.

A loud snort blew hot air over his shoulder, and he craned his neck around and was even more surprised. The radiant warriors filled the village, even spilling out onto the plains beyond. He could not count so many in the moment, but it was more than he could ever have imagined. He grinned dumbly at his own blindness. When he turned back, Kurian looked at him with hopeful eyes.

"Now do you see?"

Tobin nodded. It was apology enough.

"I think you might be shy on your odds, Kurian," Rhys said, and prodded Tobin with an elbow.

"It doesn't matter," Tobin said. "They don't stand a chance."

CHAPTER THIRTY-ONE

The Routing of Evasius

The mysterious fighters on the hillside broke the stillness first. As they charged the left flank again, the group on the bridge saw the colorful figure of Adaminster turn his horse and run, his blue velvet cape flapping in the wind like a flag in a storm. Half the cavalry on his side of the battlefield followed him, and chunks of the infantry chased after them in a rout.

The giant locusts began to swarm above that part of the battlefield, driving the five fighters back toward the hill. The bugs landed all around them, and from behind their wings came long tails with many joints. They raised them above their heads and lashed out at the warriors with the sharp tips. The fighters formed into a circle to protect themselves, and the monsters soon surrounded them, with a second ring of infantry completing the trap.

Kurian watched, wondering why the blazing riders atop the hill did not move to protect these few allies. What were they waiting for?

Then it came to him in that deep, quiet whisper that was becoming familiar, which sometimes felt like another voice leading him, and sometimes like his own desire. *They're waiting for you. To be king, you must learn to command.* Beneath him, the horse tensed.

One of the locusts found a gap in the defenses and struck one of the strangers. He wavered but did not fall.

All thoughts of a plan or strategy left Kurian's mind. They weren't necessary with the immense force of burning champions behind him. Immediately, he called out, "We must help them. Go. Go now! Hold nothing back!"

The horse leaped forward, toward the gap in the bridge, and he was the first one onto the field. But before him, the ranks of ethereal combatants raced forward. Behind, the defenders of Aposford ran to catch up. The archers in the strange two-wheeled carts poured over the river and began attacking Evasius' right side, while the golden riders on the hill came down upon the left flank like an avalanche.

A swathe of Evasius' cavalry bolted in all directions. Some directly into the coming onslaught, but most in retreat to the south and west. Evasius' own horse looked like it was barely under his control. With the thunder of the King's army bearing down, the fat witch dissolved into crows again and took flight north. The one in black rode the bull toward the oncoming army with infantry following. She cast dark shadows like billows of smoke before her, which began to obscure the battlefield. But the warriors of light dispersed them with a wave of their swords, which caused a great gust of wind. The witch waved her arms feverishly with no effect on the force bearing down on her, and finally, she turned and fled, riding her beast. It moved with impressive speed, and broke a great, bloody swath through the center of the army, oblivious to the harm it caused to her allies.

Kurian saw all this in a brief moment, and urged the horse on. He felt like it flew across the field faster than ever, but before he closed the gap, the stricken man fell. The locusts jumped onto his body like a hungry pack of dogs. Two of his comrades leaped forward to drive them back, and they also fell, the bugs piling on them in a gruesome frenzy. Then the golden riders cut through the surrounding enemy to the remaining two, and surrounded them in a wall of flaming horses and spears. The infantry attacked, but could not stand their ground, while the locusts buzzed overhead, staying just out of reach.

Finally, he reached the hill, and found he had been screaming for the entire charge. His sword was in his hand, and as he came down on the writhing pile of monsters on top of the fallen men, he swung. A wet crunching broke from the tip of his blade as it sliced into the wings and carapace of the creatures. They let out ear-splitting shrieks, and shuddered on the ground in hideous death throes that left their legs twitching erratically. As he passed, he saw that the bodies of the warriors were only tatters of carcasses. He could not save them. Tobin and Rhys followed close behind and dispatched the remaining bugs in the pile.

"Well met, friends," shouted one of the remaining fighters. He was a tall man, as tall as, but leaner than Gideon. He huffed out the words as if winded from fighting. Beside him, his companion kneeled as if in prayer.

All across the field now, there was skirmishing between the army, bolstered by the locusts, and the blazing warriors of the King. The band of eager townspeople fought in the center of the fray, each one of them supported by the great fighters on either side.

Kurian came around in a wide arc and charged straight toward the ring of infantry from behind the line. He pointed his sword at the enemy, and then waved it to one side. The golden cavalry pushed forward and made a hole, as if he had spoken a command. He rode into their midst, yanking on the reins and came up beside the two fighters with his three friends right behind him. The hole closed, and Kurian dropped down.

Immediately, the larger fighter kneeled as well.

"Well met, indeed, my sovereign. Thank you for aiding us."

"No need for that," Kurian said, panting. "You came to our aid first. I don't know where you came from, but I thank you." The man rose and grasped his hand.

"My king, certainly you know of the assemblage of protectors whose compound this was. I awoke with my compatriots within the hill, and emerged to find this army marching against Viviford. In truth, I believed they had destroyed our compound, but then I saw that the destruction was not so recent. Has so much changed that it has been razed?"

"Much has changed," Kurian said, "for we are among the last of those protectors. Please, tell me your name."

"I am Ward, son of Eric, of Finlay. My friend is Sage, son of Aaron, Bishop of Bennett. We are yours to command." Ward Finlay bowed, and Kurian nearly stumbled back in shock. Tobin let out an emphatic grunt of surprise. It explained their archaic looking armor and weapons, and their sudden appearance atop the hill. Here stood the founders of their order, the two closest advisors of King Frederick, raised from the tomb reserved for all the dual leaders of the compound.

"I am honored to meet such great men," Kurian said. Tobin and Rhys both dropped down and saluted Ward.

"Forgive me, sovereign, but I do not know you."

"We were recently novitiates of the Order. This is Tobin Hart and Rhys Brock. Our other companion is Louise Prescott. I am Kurian Abramson."

"Well met friends," said Ward. His eyes flitted upward in thought. "Abramson. Then you are of the line of the Prince of Besor," he said to Kurian.

"That knowledge was lost to my family. The King merely said I had royal blood."

"By your standard, I had hoped you were him. I long to meet him." A hope so deep it looked painful flashed across his face as he gazed on Kurian's shield. "What of the line of King Frederick?"

"I'm afraid they failed long ago," Tobin said sadly.

"Enough talk for me," Ward said, lifting his sword and resting it on his shoulder. "If you would order it, and if my friend is finished praying, we will deal with this would-be usurper."

Sage Bennett remained on his knees during the entire exchange, but his eyes were shut with such clear straining, and he prayed with such fervor, that nobody thought it right to disturb him. "God moves when he wills," the priest said in a clear voice.

"I'm ready to move when *he* is," Ward said.

A smile played at the corner of Sage's lips. Clearly, this was an old joke between friends. The noise of the battle continued to rage. Even though Evasius' forces fell in great numbers, they continued to fight with the power of an intense hatred.

When the priest finally lifted his head, the hair stood on the back of Kurian's neck. The air suddenly felt charged, and he saw a dense cloud forming over Capric Hill.

"Sovereign?" Ward said expectantly.

"Yes," Kurian sputtered. "Join in the battle, friends."

Ward rushed to the front of the line of golden warriors encircling them and quickly cut down three soldiers. Sage closed his eyes, and gestured to his right. A blast of lightning thundered to the ground outside the circle. Soldiers flew back in all directions. The horses jumped, and Kurian smelled the strangest odor, as if the air burned.

"Forward," he called, as he remounted his horse. The warriors in their ring of protection broke apart and wrapped around the end of Evasius' troops.

They pressed forward, hewing down soldiers left and right. Now, the army of Pallingham was engaged on three sides, nearly surrounded. The King's warriors filled the plain, and still, some waited in reserve in the town. Evasius himself rode back and forth in short bursts, shouting commands and waving his arms frantically. Kurian felt pity for him, and yet he had refused the offer of a peaceful resolution.

Kurian's army continued to press forward on all fronts, compressing their enemies into a tight mass of bodies with no room to maneuver. Bolts of lightning punctuated the struggle with showers of sparks and peals of thunder as Sage Bennett moved forward with his thunderhead. As the wings of his army wrapped further around the jumbled huddle of their enemies, more and more of the soldiers deserted and fled.

Finally, just before the wings closed, Evasius' horse stood in a moment of perfect stillness. Kurian saw his face less than a hundred yards away. It showed only rage and hatred, though Kurian thought he appeared reserved to his fate. Then, he yanked on the reins, turned around, and fled back toward Pallingham castle. The moment their lord and commander abandoned them, the rear half of the army tried to rush through the narrowing gap as well, but only a few hundred escaped.

Those on the front lines gradually began dropping their arms and falling to their knees in submission. Dozens of the locust creatures remained buzzing in the air, and they flew off in every direction when Evasius deserted his army. At first, some of the villagers continued to attack, but Kurian rode quickly to them, shouting to stop.

"No! Anyone who surrenders, lives."

"What about Evasius?" Gideon called above the cries for mercy.

"He's not our concern now. Not today," Kurian replied.

He considered the westering sun as Evasius turned into a distant shadow, and then winked out of sight. Above the battle, the cloud Sage Bennett had summoned dissipated, and the charge left the air. Now, he saw the light was changing again, growing more intense, and lighting the air with the colors of flame, as it had done in the early morning of this long day. He felt tired. Tired and grateful.

Kurian looked around at the battlefield. The bodies of thousands of Evasius' soldiers, and hundreds of the bug carcasses lay on the grass of the plain, staining it red. He could not count them all, but as far as he could tell, only the three resurrected monks had been slain among those who fought with him. Over a thousand of Evasius' soldiers now kneeled on the ground before him.

The guiding voice inside him was silent. He would have to consult his friends, old and new, to discern what to do with them all.

CHAPTER THIRTY-TWO

Viviford

Noeman woke to a sky smeared with hazy oranges and purples unlike any colors he had ever seen. It drew him to the gap in the walls of the camp through which the rushing, roaring river now poured over the edge of the cliffs. Two thousand feet below, it lapped and foamed at the walls of Dury before continuing over the plains to the sea.

To the west, the sun was a burning half-disc of gold on the horizon. The sharp edge of its light had dulled, even as it appeared bloated beyond its noontime size. He was confident that he did not need to pray for its return the following day. But he did ask a blessing for his old students—now his friends—somewhere on the plain. When he did, a sense of peace passed over him, and he trusted they were safe.

"How do you like this new world we have?" asked Xander behind him. He was not sure he would ever learn to like the way his new friend started a conversation, often sneaking up and speaking unannounced, but it no longer set his teeth on edge.

"Isn't it just a return to the way it was intended to be?" Noeman teased.

"Yes and no," Xander said, leaving the air thick with possible implications.

"It's extravagant," Noeman said. "I could spend a lifetime looking at a sunset like this and never stop wondering at it."

Xander nodded silently, looking towards the west.

"Any word from the plains?"

"Not yet," Xander said. He pursed his lips and laid his hands on his walking stick, then rested his chin on top of them. "The King has gone into the wilderness alone. I fear it will be one of his longest journeys, and I won't see him again before I sleep in the ground."

"I hope you are wrong, my friend. Someday I would like to see him face-to-face." Noeman felt like there was nothing else for either of them to say to console each other, so his mind turned to practical matters. "How are the captives?"

"Safe, for now. Most of their minds will heal under our care. Although, this Captain Fallon...I have never seen anyone resist the King so effectively. We must watch him every moment." Xander gestured back toward the camp. "Would you like to take a turn?"

"If you don't mind, I'd prefer to stay in the healing house," Noeman said, and cleared his throat. "There is so much I could still learn from Charissa."

"I'll bet there is," Xander said with a knowing smirk.

Noeman normally would have found the comment offensive, considering that he was a monk. Then he remembered that those vows no longer bound him, and Xander's insinuation made him curious. There was a spark of interest there, and he would be free to discover the potential in the proper time. It was a feeling of freedom he had never known.

"Nobody answered your question last night," Xander said, changing the subject. "They were all preoccupied with the fight, and I believe young Tobin was overwhelmed at the changes he saw in you."

"What question?" Noeman asked.

"About your name," Xander said.

That brought the memory back, but Noeman was silent.

Xander took his eyes off the sunset for the first time and looked him squarely in the face. "Newman is a fine name. In the days to come, I pray more men are made new, and I hope you will have a hand in making them so."

No words of thanks were strong enough to express the gratitude he felt for everything that Xander had taught him in their short friendship. As he struggled to find them, he sensed they were not necessary. Xander already knew his heart. His mentor's wrinkled brown skin blurred into the background of the sandstone walls as the light failed, but he could see the white teeth grinning at him. He turned to look at the final moments of light on this day he would remember forever.

"Let it be," he said, just as the last portion of sun dipped below the horizon.

Before nightfall, and with Sage Bennett's help, Kurian struck a deal with those soldiers who surrendered. If they helped bury the bodies of the other soldiers, and burn the carcasses of the locusts, they would be free to go. Kurian was surprised that both Tobin and Gideon objected because they might return to Lord Evasius, but after witnessing his cruelty and bloodlust, Kurian believed most of them would try to find a quiet place to start a new life.

Dozens of the soldiers tried to pledge their allegiance to Kurian as king. He accepted their pledge, but would not allow them to remain in the town. He was not ready to trust such convenient oaths, which could just as easily be broken. They would have to start afresh as well, ready to fulfill their promises if he ever called upon them.

The people of Aposford wanted to celebrate their victory, and so did he and his friends, but after a day that felt like it had lasted for weeks—they had travelled a distance that would normally have taken that long—they were all too tired but to settle for a hearty, home cooked meal, and then bed. Kurian fell asleep near an open window, gazing at the flowers in the meadows of heaven, twinkling out like his first star, but in innumerable variations. Even the light-infused rain during his illness had not been such a balm to his soul as this peaceful vision of the night sky.

In the morning, he gathered the townspeople in the main square, along with as many of the soldiers as could fit. He stood on an old door laid across the town well to address them.

"Not all of you saw the same events yesterday. But I think we can all agree that the outcome of the battle was miraculous." He expected a cheer, but everyone was silent, waiting for what he would say. "For anyone who desires to end the tyranny of the Evasians, it was a victory worth celebrating. For those loyal to him because of fear and intimidation, perhaps it was a relief. I told you I was sent to oust him from the *de facto* throne his family took for themselves. The one who sent me asked me to restore the throne of Fin, and to build it into something even greater than King Frederick achieved.

"Lord Evasius was defeated yesterday, and he fled, not leading his men in an orderly retreat, but thinking only of saving his own life. We weakened him, but that defeat does not end his power. However great a victory it was, it was only a beginning.

"I intend to see that work through. Any who wishes may join me. But I warn you that it will be a long and difficult road, and I cannot promise that we will always have assistance as we had yesterday. I only promise that I will walk through all those trials with you, as your equal, suffering the same difficulties, and asking no favors as your expectant king. There is no need for decisions or pledges now, because I am certain we will have at least a few days of peace while we finish cleansing this place. A few days in which we can work side by side and you can see my heart."

They looked at him with confusion. They did not know how to respond to such a speech. If they had ever heard one at all, it had been from someone like Evasius or Fallon, who spoke only of the sacrifices necessary from those beneath them. So the crowd was silent for several moments.

On a whim, he placed his fists on his hips and spoke again more forcefully. "Actually, if you do not object, I will indulge in one royal privilege." A few groans came from the soldiers, as if they knew it had been too good to be true. He gestured toward Ward Finlay. "My new friend tells me that long ago this river had a different name. Before it dried up and earned the name of unfaithful Apos by withholding the life-giving water from the land, the people of the plain called it the Vivis. This town, which straddled the river and thrived because of it, was called Viviford. For my first act as unofficial king, I would restore those ancient names in the first city reclaimed for Fin. Do I have your agreement?"

The crowd still stared in bewilderment. A ruler was not supposed to ask for permission to do anything, but many seemed to like the idea. The ancient warriors who founded the order both gave approving nods, and Ward squinted an eye, as if he meant to wink, but found it distasteful for a man of action.

"Let it be!" Tobin shouted from beside them. A few in the crowd voiced agreement, and soon the entire multitude was shouting the phrase.

"Let it be," they shouted, and with each repetition, more voices joined in, until the whole square echoed with it.

Kurian smiled, nodding with the rhythm of their voices, and held up his hands until they settled down. Then he caught Louise's eye, and she, too, smiled broadly at him. That smile roused his tired spirit more than the crowd's approval.

"Very well," he said over the crowd, "It shall be." Then he drew his sword, and held it high. "To Viviford! First city revived among the ten cities of the plain. First glimmer of hope for the renewal of Fin!"

A roar of joyful agreement came from the crowd, washing over him as tangibly and forcefully as the current of the river. He could barely contain the emotions that surged through him as wave after wave poured forth.

The whispering voice finally returned. The same one that had woken him from his poison-fed sleep. The one that lovingly nurtured the tender bud of hope in his heart. It spoke silently in his spirit, but could be loud enough to drown out all other voices. It was almost the voice of his own heart, as he had always known it, but it had mingled together with another voice—one he was beginning to recognize as the resonant utterance of the King prophesying in the cave. It said only three words, but they came in a way that felt as if they could feed his heart through a decade of hopeless struggle:

So it begins.

Author's Note

First, thank you for reading this book. I hope that you enjoyed it, and even more, I hope that it brought a little light into your world. Please take the time to review it on your preferred retailer by going to **books2read.com/TreasureofCapric** because it helps other readers find books they'll enjoy.

I began Kurian's story shortly after moving into a new home and graduating from seminary. I finished the first draft in 2013, shortly before our first child was born. She's five as I write this, and we live in a different home in a different state. The stop and start of trying to publish and continue to write amidst family and work life means that I'm publishing it now, when I'm old enough to have a little bit of hair growing on my ears.

However, in those years, my mind drifted repeatedly back to Pallingham. I thought about conversations different characters would have after the events in book one, and had vague ideas about what would happen to Kurian and his friends through the rest of their adventures.

I knew that I would tell the story of what happened to Cpt. Bacchus after he leapt into the sea toward the sirens, and that story is now complete as the novella *Siren Silence*. You can pick up a free copy by going to **brandonwilborn.com/silence**, or you can be generous to an author and purchase a copy **books2read.com/SirenSilence**. I'm grateful either way.

Book Two of *The King of the Caves* has a rough course plotted, and is working its way onto paper now. I pray that it will be complete before there is hair growing *out* of my ears. Please be patient with me to discover what happens with Kurian and the King. Or if you'd like to nudge me to hurry up, you can email me at brandon@brandonwilborn.com. No spoilers will be provided.

Blessings,
Brandon M Wilborn

Acknowledgements

Somehow, though I doubt few authors have ever completed a marathon, writing a book has been compared to running such a race. As a writer, I might compare it more to short bursts of running alongside whatever story is currently hounding me most. As for the other parts, it's more like a long-distance relay, and such, those people who have a part in the finish require their due of gratitude.

The top-tier thanks for this book must go first to my wife. She endured the race against time to birth this baby before our first child. She has been supportive of this project in every way possible and regales me with regular doses of wisdom and truth.

Secondly, I must thank my editor, Tracy Cartwright. While she edits for a living, she went the extra mile to read the book a second time so as not to miss any details while editing the follow-up novella. Also, I cannot be happier with my cover designer, whom I know only as Darko Tomic. If that's their real name, it's awesome. Third at this level, I must thank Veronika Wunderer, who took my rough sketches of Pallingham and created a beautiful map.

Finally, I offer thanks to my initial readers. Dennis and Nathanael worked with me chapter by chapter in the beginning, and still read the completed manuscript. There were many good conversations and suggestions from them as I pushed through the first draft. It was invaluable to have two more people who I believe experienced Kurian's world with the depth I do. Those who read the full manuscript and helped at launch time include Adriana C., Adrienne S., Alvin and Manda L., Bo-mi W., Brian J., Brian N., Corina D., Eugene N., Gail N., Iesha D., Jana A., Jenny C., Jerusha E., Josh L., Justin C., Kendra L., Kevin N., Kimmie L., Kristi F., Maitha A., Melanie M., Michele W., Neftali T., Peter N., Philip B., Renee B., Ruby M., Sage W., Tammy H., and Tom V. Your support means the world to me. Thank you.

ABOUT THE AUTHOR

Brandon Wilborn is a man with too many interests, and one great love. No, three great loves. Well, five. So far.

But for the purposes here, he has one great love, and that is science fiction and fantasy. (Speculative fiction, if you insist on the singular.) He first fell in love with the fantastical and mythical while playing *The Legend of Zelda* and watching an old cartoon of *The Hobbit* when he was four years old. That eventually led him to dream of writing.

He has now authored *The Treasure of* Capric, his first novel and book one of *The King of the Caves* series, along with a follow-up novella, *Siren Silence: The Fate of Captain Bacchus.*

His love of science fiction and fantasy, along with an education in English and Theological Studies, inspired him to create stories that are full of epic adventure while grappling with deeper questions of life, faith, and our role in the drama of good and evil.

After a wandering youth in a Navy family, growing up primarily in Hawaii, and then wandering a bit more, he has now found a happy home with three of his great loves in Idaho. Find more of his stories and the latest release information for book two of *The King of the Caves* at BrandonWilborn.com